ROSCOE

ALSO BY WILLIAM KENNEDY

The Ink Truck

Billy Phelan's Greatest Game
Ironweed
Very Old Bones
(Collected in The Albany Cycle, Book I)

Quinn's Book
The Flaming Corsage
Legs
(Collected in The Albany Cycle, Book II)

NON FICTION

O Albany!: Improbable City of Political Wizards, Fearless Ethnics, Spectacular Aristocrats, Splendid Nobodies, and Underrated Scoundrels

Riding the Yellow Trolley Car

WITH BRENDAN KENNEDY

Charlie Malarkey and the Belly Button Machine
Charlie Malarkey and the Singing Moose

ROSCOE

William Kennedy

First published in Great Britain by Simon & Schuster UK Ltd, 2002
An imprint of Simon & Schuster UK Ltd
A Viacom company

10 9 8 7 6 5 4 3 2 1

Simon & Schuster UK Ltd
Africa House
64–78 Kingsway
London WC2B 6AH

Simon & Schuster Australia
Sydney

A CIP catalogue record for this book is available from the British Library

ISBN 0–7432–2073–0

Typeset by Palimpsest Book Production Limited,
Polmont, Stirlingshire
Printed and bound in Great Britain by
The Bath Press, Bath

THIS BOOK IS DEDICATED TO MY COHORT
OF EARLY ROSCONIANS:

Harry and Helen Staley, Andy and Betsy Viglucci,
Doris Grumbach, Laurie Bank, Peg Boyers,
Dennis Smith, Brendan Kennedy,
and to my wife, a cohort all by herself,
the endlessly astonishing
Dana

ROSCOE

Roscoe in the Wind

That year an ill wind blew over the city and threatened to destroy flowerpots, family fortunes, reputations, true love, and several types of virtue. Roscoe, moving along the road, felt the wind at his back and heard the windblown voices.

'Do you know where the ill wind comes from, Roscoe?' the voices asked him.

'No,' he said, 'but I'm not sure the wind is really ill. Its illness may be overrated, maybe even fraudulent.'

'Do people think there's such a thing as a good ill wind?' they asked.

'Of course,' he answered. 'And when it comes it billows the sails of our city, it nourishes our babies, comforts our aliens, gives purpose to our dead, tranquilizes our useless, straightens our crooked, and vice versa. The ill wind is a nonesuch and demands close attention.'

'Why should we believe what you say?'

'As I am incapable of truth,' Roscoe said, 'so am I incapable of lying, which is, as all know, the secret of the truly successful politician.'

'Are you a politician, Roscoe?'

'I refuse to answer on grounds that it might degrade or incriminate me.'

The Spheres of War and Peace

Roscoe Owen Conway presided at Albany Democratic Party headquarters, on the eleventh floor of the State Bank building, the main stop for Democrats on the way to heaven. Headquarters occupied three large offices: one where Roscoe, secretary and second in command of the Party, received supplicants and debtors, one where Bart Merrigan and Joey Manucci controlled the flow of visitors and phone calls, and one for the safe which, when put here, was the largest in the city outside of a bank vault. Of late, no money was kept in it, only deceptive Democratic financial data to feed to the Governor's investigators, who had been swooping down on the Party's files since 1942, the year the Governor-elect vowed to destroy Albany Democrats.

Money, instead of going into the great safe, went into Roscoe's top drawer, where he would put it without counting it when a visitor such as Philly Fillipone, who sold produce to the city and county, handed him a packet of cash an inch thick, held by a rubber band.

'Maybe you better count it, make sure there's no mistake,' Philly said.

Roscoe did not acknowledge that Philly had raised the

possibility of shorting the Party, even by accident. He dropped the cash into the open drawer, where Philly could see a pile of twenties. Democratic business was done with twenties. Then Philly asked, 'Any change in how we work this year, Roscoe?'

'No,' Roscoe said, 'same as usual.' And Philly went away.

At his desk by the door Joey Manucci was recording, on the lined pad where he kept track of visitors in their order of arrival, the names of the men who had just walked in, Jimmy Givney and Cutie LaRue. Joey was printing each name, for he could not write script or read it. Bart Merrigan spoke to the two arrivals. Merrigan, who had gone into the army with Roscoe and Patsy McCall in 1917, was built like a bowling pin, an ex-boxer and a man of great energy whom Roscoe trusted with his life. Merrigan leaned into Roscoe's office.

'Patsy called. He'll be in the Ten Eyck lobby in fifteen minutes. Givney from the Twelfth Ward and Cutie LaRue just came in.'

'Have them come back Friday,' Roscoe said. 'Is the war over?'

'Not yet. Cutie says you'll want to see him.'

'How does he know?'

'Cutie knows. And what Cutie don't know he'll find out.'

'Send him in.'

Merrigan told Jimmy Givney to come back Friday and Joey scratched a line through his name, using a ruler for neatness. Merrigan turned up the volume of the desk radio he was monitoring for news of the official Japanese surrender. A large framed photo of the new President hung on the wall behind his desk. On the wall opposite hung George Washington, FDR, who was still draped in black crepe, and Alexander Fitzgibbon, the young Mayor of Albany.

'What can I do for you, Cute?' Roscoe asked.

'Can we close the door?'

'Close it.'

And Cutie did. Then he sat down. George (Cutie) LaRue was an aspiring lawyer who had failed the bar examination fourteen times in eight states before he passed it. He did not practice, but he knew most of the political population of Albany on a first-name basis. He functioned as a legislative lobbyist, and everybody knew him by his large, heavy-lidded, Oriental eyes, though he was French. He had a low forehead and combed his hair straight back. His tic was slicking back the hair over his right ear with the heel of his hand as he exhaled cigarette smoke from his mouth and inhaled it up his nose. Cutie knew your needs and he often lobbied for you, whether you paid him or not. If he delivered, you paid him. If he didn't deliver, he'd try again next session. He held no grudges, for he was ambitious. Cutie once overheard Patsy saying he wanted a book on Ambrose Burnside, a Union general in the Civil War, but it was out of print. Cutie learned that a copy was sitting on a shelf in the library at West Point. He drove to West Point, stole the book, and gave it to Patsy.

'You didn't hear this from me,' Cutie said to Roscoe.

'I don't even know what you look like,' Roscoe said.

'I heard it from Scully's office this afternoon. Straight stuff, Roscoe. I kid you not.'

'Are you just talking, Cute, or are you trying to say something?'

'They want to nail you.'

'This is very big news, Cute. I wish you could stay longer.'

'They have stuff they can use.'

'Like that missing forty thou when they subpoenaed our books? That money is not missing,' Roscoe said.

'They're tapping your lines, reading your mail, watching your wild girlfriend, Trish Cooney.'

'She's easy to watch. Also, she leaves the shades up.'

'They know all your moves with women.'

'They get paid for this?'

'You got a reputation. You know how they like scandal.'

'I wish my life was that interesting. But thanks, Cute. Is that it?'

'They're on you full-time. I heard Scully himself say nailing you was as good as nailing Patsy.'

'I appreciate this news.'

'You know what I'm looking for, Roscoe.'

'Yes, I do. A courtroom you can call home.'

'It's not asking a lot. I'm not talking Supreme Court. Small Claims Court, maybe. Or Traffic Court. I'd make a hell of a judge.'

Roscoe considered that: The Cute Judge. Cute the Judge. Judge Cutie. Cutie Judgie. Jurors in his court would do Cutie Duty.

'A hell of a judge,' Roscoe said. 'It goes without saying.'

Roscoe put on his blue seersucker suitcoat, waved farewell to the boys, took the elevator down, and went out and up State Street hill. The day was August 14, 1945. Roscoe wore a full beard, going gray, but his mustache was mostly black. Trust no man, not even your brother, if his beard is one color, his mustache another. He was fat but looked only burly, thinking about developing an ulcer but seemed fit. He was burning up but looked cool in his seersucker.

He went into the State Street entrance of the Ten Eyck and up the stairs to the lobby, which was also cool and busy with people checking in – three soldiers, two WACs, a sailor and a girl, rooms scarce tonight if the Japs surrendered. He crossed the marble floor of the lobby and sat where he always sat, precisely where Felix Conway, his father, had sat, this corner known then and now as the Conway corner. He signaled silently to Whitey the bellhop to send a waiter with a gin and quinine water, his daily ritual at this hour. He looked across the lobby, trying to see his father. I'm looking for advice, he told the old man.

Roscoe's condition had become so confounding that he had asked Patsy McCall and Elisha Fitzgibbon, his two great friends, with whom he formed the triaxial brain trust of the Albany Democratic Party, to come to the hotel and talk to him, away from all other ears. Roscoe, at this moment staring across time, finds his father sitting in this corner. It is a chilly spring afternoon in 1917, the first Great War is ongoing in Europe, and Roscoe, twenty-seven, will soon be in that war. He's clean-shaven, a lawyer whose chief client is the Fitzgibbon Steel mill, and he also has an eye on politics.

Felix Conway is a man of sixty-five, with a full, gray beard down to his chest, hiding his necktie. He's wearing a waistcoat, suit coat, overcoat, and cap, but also covers himself with a blanket to fend off the deadly springtime drafts in the Ten Eyck Hotel lobby. Felix is a hotel-dweller and will remain one for the rest of his days, which are not many. He had been the thrice-elected, once-ejected Mayor of Albany, and made a sizable fortune brewing ale and lager. He was ousted from City Hall in 1893 after a lawsuit over voting fraud, but his Democrats regained City Hall in the next election and kept it for five years. In those years Felix was the Party's elder statesman, with an office next to the new Mayor, and a luncheon table at the Sadler Room in Keeler's Restaurant, where he held court for Democrats and influence salesmen of all varieties. This lush period for Felix ended in 1899.

In that year the Republicans took City Hall and also found they could afford lunch at Keeler's great restaurant. But Felix could not bear the effluvia they gave off, so he went home for lunch. It took him six months to admit he was not suited to living full-time among his wife, two sons, and three daughters. And when he did admit it, he betook himself to the brand-new Ten Eyck Hotel and told the folks, Goodbye, dear family, I'll be home Saturday afternoons and stay till Sunday tea. We'll have a fine time going to mass, eating the home-cooked meal, won't it be grand? Yes, it will, and then I'll be done with you for a week.

The Republicans of 1917 are secure in their power, and the Democrats no longer even try to win, for it is more profitable to play the loser and take Republican handouts for assuming this pose. Yet Democratic reform elements endure, and there sits Roscoe beside his father, eavesdropping as the old man holds court for a steady, life-giving flow of pols, pals, has-beens, and would-bes. Bellhops daily place 'reserved' signs on the marble tea table, the Empire armchair and sofa, in the Felix Conway corner. At the moment, Felix is in his chair, giving an audience to Eddie McDermott, leader of yet another reform faction that hopes to challenge Packy McCabe's useless but invulnerable Albany Democratic Party organization in the 1917 primary.

Eddie stares into Felix's eye, revealing his plans to reform the Party if he wins the primary, and reform the city if he wins the election. He leans farther and farther forward as he speaks ever-so-softly to Felix, finally rolling off the sofa onto one knee to make his message not only sincere but genuflectional, and he whispers to the Solomon of Albany politics: 'You do want the Democrats to make a comeback and take City Hall again, don't you, sir?'

'Oh, I do, I do,' says Felix. And he truly does.

'I have much to learn, Mr. Conway, but there's one thing I can learn only from you, for nobody else has an answer, and I've asked them all.'

'What might that be, Mr. McDermott?'

'Once we take over the Party, how do we get the money to run it?'

Felix Conway throws his arms wide, kiting his blanket toward the outer lobby, startling Roscoe. He opens both his coats, pulls off his muffler, the better to breathe, and begins to laugh.

'He wants to know how you get the money,' Felix says to Roscoe, and then his laughter roars out of control, he rises from his chair, and shouts out, 'How do you get the money? Oh my Jesus, how do you get the money!'

Then the laughter, paroxysmal now, seals Felix's throat and bloats him with its containment. He floats up from his chair, still with a smile as wide as his head, and he rises like a hot-air balloon, caroming off the balustrade of the Tennessee-marble stairway, and he keeps rising on up to collide with the lobby's French chandelier, where he explodes in a final thunderclap of a laugh, sending crystal shards raining down onto Eddie McDermott, the terrified reformer below.

Felix Declares His Principles to Roscoe

'How do you get the money, boy? If you run 'em for office and they win, you charge 'em a year's wages. Keep taxes low, but if you have to raise 'em, call it something else. The city can't do without vice, so pinch the pimps and milk the madams. Anybody that sells the flesh, tax 'em. If anybody wants city business, thirty percent back to us. Maintain the streets and sewers, but don't overdo it. Well-lit streets discourage sin, but don't overdo it. If they play craps, poker, or blackjack, cut the game. If they play faro or roulette, cut it double. Opium is the opiate of the depraved, but if they want it, see that they get it, and tax those lowlife bastards. If they keep their dance halls open twenty-four hours, tax 'em twice. If they run a gyp joint, tax 'em triple. If they send prisoners to our jail, charge 'em rent, at hotel prices. Keep the cops happy and let 'em have a piece of the pie. A small piece. Never buy anything that you can rent forever. If you pave a street, a three-cent brick should be worth thirty cents to the city. Pave every street with a church on it. Cultivate priests and acquire the bishop. Encourage parents to send their kids to Catholic schools; it lowers the public-school budget. When in doubt, appoint another judge, and pay him enough so's he don't have to shake down the lawyers. Cultivate lawyers. They know how it is done and will do it. Control the district attorney and *never let him go*; for he controls the grand juries. Make friends with millionaires and give 'em what they need. Any traction company is a good traction company, and the same goes for electricity. If you build a viaduct, make the contractor your partner. Whenever you confront a monopoly, acquire it. Open an insurance company and make sure anybody doing city business buys a nice policy. If you don't know diddle about insurance, open a brewery and make 'em buy your beer. Give your friends jobs, but at a price, and make new friends every day. Let the sheriff buy anything he wants for the jail. Never stop a ward leader from stealing; it's what keeps him honest. Keep your plumbers and electricians working, and remember it takes three men to change a wire. Republicans are all right as long as they're on our payroll. A city job should raise a man's dignity but not his wages. Anybody on our payroll pays us dues, three percent of the yearly salary, which is nice. But if they're on that new civil service and won't pay and you can't fire 'em, transfer 'em to the dump. If you find people who like to vote, let 'em. Don't be afraid to spend money for votes on Election Day. It's a godsend to the poor, and good for business; but make it old bills, ones and twos, or they get suspicious. And only give 'em out in the river wards, never uptown. If an uptown voter won't register Democrat, raise his taxes. If he fights the raise, make him hire one of our lawyers to reduce it in court. Once it's lowered, raise it again next year. Knock on every door and find out if they're sick or pregnant or simpleminded, and vote 'em. If they're breathing, take 'em to the polls. If they won't go, threaten 'em. Find out who's dead and who's dying, which is as good as dead, and vote 'em. There's a hell of a lot of dead and they never complain. The opposition might cry fraud but let 'em prove it after the election. People say voting the dead is immoral, but what the hell, if they were alive they'd all be Democrats. Just because they're dead don't mean they're Republicans.'

The 1945 election was twelve weeks away, the Governor's three-year-old investigation was intensifying if you believed Cutie, and who knew what they might come up with? The Republicans, because of the Governor's pressure, were running Jason (Jay) Farley for mayor, an intelligent Irish Catholic businessman who made smart speeches, their strongest candidate in years. And the absence of Alex, the city's soldier-boy Mayor, who was still somewhere in Europe, was a factor to be determined. Patsy had decided that, not only would we win this election, we would also humiliate the Governor for trying to destroy us, and his secret weapon was an old one: a third-party candidate who would dilute the Republican vote, the same ploy Felix Conway had used repeatedly in the 1880s and '90s.

Roscoe, working on his second gin and quinine, sat facing Patsy, who was having his usual: Old Overholt neat. Patsy sat here often, but he was out of place amid the gilded rococo furniture and Oriental rugs of the lobby, and looked as if he'd be more at ease at a clambake. But despite the August heat, there he was under his trademark fedora, sitting where Felix Conway had received visitors a quarter-century ago, looking not at all like a man of power, yet with far greater power than Felix could have imagined having. For Patsy now, as leader of the Albany Democratic Party for twenty-four heady years, was everybody's father, Roscoe included. Patsy, five years Roscoe's senior, was the main man, the man who forked the lightning, the boss.

'What's so urgent?' Patsy asked Roscoe.

'It's not urgent to anybody but me, but it is important. I have to retire.'

Patsy screwed up his face.

'Say it again?'

'I've got to get out. Do something else. Go someplace else. I can't do this any more.'

'Do what?'

'What I do.'

'You do everything.'

'That's part of it.'

'You gettin' bored?'

'No.'

'You need money?'

'I've got more money than I can use.'

'You have another bad love affair?'

'When did I ever have a good one?'

'Then what is it?'

'You know what it's like when you come to the end of something, Pat?'

'Not yet I don't.'

'Of course. You'll go on forever. But it's over for me and I don't know why. It may seem sudden to you, but it's been on the way a long time. There's nothing I can do about it. It's just over.'

'The organization can't get along without you. You're half of everything I do. More than half.'

'Nonsense. You can get twenty guys this afternoon.'

'Counting all my life,' Patsy said, 'I never knew three, let alone twenty, I trusted the way I trust you.'

'That's why I'm giving you plenty of notice. I'll ride out the election, but then I have to quit.'

'It's this goddamned investigation. Did they come up with something on you?'

'Cutie LaRue says they're hot to get me, but we all know that, and that's not it. I'm fifty-five years old and going noplace. But now I've got to go someplace. Anyplace. I need more room in my head.'

'You're leaving Albany?'

'Maybe. If I can convince my head to leave town.'

'You're sick from that ulcer. That's it.'

'My gut hurts, but I've never felt better. Don't look for a reason. There's twenty, fifty. If I could figure it out I'd tell you.'

'We gotta talk about this.'

'We are talking about it.'

'What about the third-party candidate? You got one?'

'I'm working on it.'

'Did you tell Elisha about this plan of yours?'

'He's due here for dinner. I'll tell him then.'

'This is a disaster.'

'No, it isn't.'

'Goddamn it, if I say it's a disaster it's a disaster. This is a goddamn disaster. What the hell's got into you?'

'Time. Time gets into everything. I'm sick of carrying time around on my back like a bundle of rocks.'

'Time? What are you talking about, time? To hell with time.'

'Pat, don't worry. We'll figure it out.'

'Time. Jesus H. Jesus.'

The lives of Roscoe, Patsy McCall, and Elisha Fitzgibbon had been a lock from their shared boyhood on the city streets they would come to own, at the cockpits where their fathers fought chickens, and on the nine hundred acres of Tivoli, the great Fitzgibbon estate in Loudonville created by Elisha's grandfather Lyman Fitzgibbon, who in his long life made several fortunes – in railroads, land speculation, foundries, and steel manufacture. Tivoli was a paradise made for moneyed creatures and small boys. The three walked the virgin woods of oak and maple and birch and hemlock and white pine, they fished the pristine waters of Elisha's tiny Lake Tivoli until they outgrew sunfish and perch and went down to the Hudson River for blues, stripers, shad, and sturgeon. They swam in the Erie Canal and the river, hunted partridge and pheasant on the river flats, wild turkey in the Fitzgibbon woods, and deer up at Tristano, Elisha's family's sumptuous rustic camp in the Adirondacks. The boys brought their river catch and hunters' quarry to Felix Conway's table, for neither Patsy's mother nor Elisha's stepmother would give them houseroom. Roscoe organized all their excursions, fished with the eye of a pelican, and could put a bullet between a snake's fangs at sixty yards. Felix marveled at his son's talent, but it was his own doing, for he'd given Roscoe a .22 rifle as soon as the boy reached the age of good reason.

'Remember,' his mother warned Roscoe at age nine, just after Felix had left her and the children to live at the Ten Eyck, 'never shoot anybody with that gun unless it's a politician.'

But it was the politics of Democracy that cemented the boys' friendship. Their headquarters, even before they'd begun to drink, was the North End saloon run by Patsy's father, Black Jack McCall, the Ninth Ward leader who would become sheriff. The saloon had long been closed, but Patsy reopened it every year to hear the ward leaders predict the vote they would deliver, and then give them their street money to help it happen. The trio's mentor in the liabilities of political honesty was Felix, who helped them plan Patsy's campaign for a city assessorship in 1919, the year he died. Campaign money came from Elisha, who, along with his siblings, inherited the steel fortune accumulated by his grandfather Lyman (who had helped finance Grover Cleveland's first campaign for the presidency). Elisha financed both Patsy's successful run for the assessorship in 1919, and the Democratic takeover of City Hall in the 1921 election. After that, politics was the mother lode for this trio, and money, for most of the decade, was not a problem.

Roscoe and Elisha were in the Ten Eyck dining room, finishing their second bottle of wine with a dinner of shrimp, bluefish, boiled potatoes, and fresh snowflake rolls. Elisha exuded ruddy good health, or was it the flush that comes with a summer evening? He was the picture of composure in his buttoned-down Brooks Brothers shirt, his tie tight on his collar, his double-breasted cream sport jacket impeccably tailored by Joe Amore, his steel-gray hair associated with Men of Distinction in whiskey ads. His age was visible in his receding hairline, but Red the Barber had consoled him that he would not live long enough to be bald. No one looked more stylishly rich than Elisha, the capitalist at his zenith.

The bells of St. Peter's Church began ringing up the street and Roscoe said, 'So it's over.'

'Sounds that way.'

'Alex will be coming home.'

'I hope he's not one of those postwar casualties like that German soldier in *All Quiet on the Western Front*. It's after the Armistice, and he raises his head up out of the trench to look at a butterfly, and a sniper who doesn't know the war is over, or maybe he does, puts one through his brain.'

'Alex is too smart for that,' Roscoe said. 'He'll come home as fit as he went. We'll give him a parade.'

'I don't think he'd march in it.'

'You're probably right. He has that leveling instinct about himself.'

'He'll be leveled in other ways. He won't be as rich as he used to be. None of us will.'

'That's right. The government will cancel your million-dollar contracts.'

'They won't need my steel for their tanks.'

'You may have to make refrigerators.'

'If I do that, my salesmen will have to uncover the difference between refrigerators and tanks.'

'Does that make you sad?'

'It makes me poor.'

'You're not poor, Elisha.'

'No, I still have my shoes.'

'You're a millionaire. You can't kid me.'

'At times I'm a millionaire,' Elisha said. 'But being a millionaire opens you to criticism.'

'Politics also does that.'

'It's a short walk from politics to hell,' Elisha said.

'Ah. It's nice to see that winning the war has lightened your mood.'

'I'm tired of the scandalous liabilities of wealth.'

'Which scandalous liabilities, other than the usual, might those be?'

'Nothing I want to talk about. You'll know soon enough.'

'A mystery. I'll try to understand,' Roscoe said. 'But at no time have I ever been wealthy enough to have such worries, even though I've told people otherwise.'

'I've heard you say that.'

'I'm a fraud,' Roscoe said. 'I've always been a fraud.'

'Nonsense. Nobody ever believes anything you say about yourself.'

'Not even when I'm lying?'

'No, never.'

'What if I said I was quitting the Party?'

Elisha stared at him, inspecting for fraudulence.

'Did you tell Patsy?'

'He wanted to know if I'd told you. Now it's yes on both counts.'

Elisha's smile exuded knowledge of Roscoe's meaning. The man could understand what was unspoken, even unknown. Patsy understood, but could not admit it, for it ran counter to his plans and outside his control. Elisha knew Roscoe's thoughts without having to ask questions. Their friendship had gone through storms of trouble, rich men's poverty, broken love. Especially that, for Roscoe had been in love with Elisha's wife since before the two married. It didn't interfere with the friendship, for Roscoe's love for Veronica was impossible and he knew it and mostly let it alone.

'I wonder what you'll do when you quit,' Elisha said. 'You're not suited for a whole lot of jobs. Will you just loll around spending your money?'

'I haven't carried it that far yet. But I have to change my life, do something that engages my soul before I die.'

'I'm glad to hear you still have a soul.'

'It surfaces every so often,' Roscoe said.

'You don't look like a man with a tortured soul. It's always a surprise how well we dissemble. You're as good as there is at that game, the way you've kept your feeling for Veronica under lock and key – it's admirable.'

'I have no choice. I have no choice in most things. All the repetitions, the goddamn investigations that never end, another election coming, and now Patsy wants a third candidate to dilute the Republican vote. We'll humiliate the Governor. On top of that, Cutie LaRue told me this afternoon George Scully has increased his surveillance on me. They're probably doubling their watch on you, too. You'd make a handsome trophy.'

'Wouldn't I? Do you think I should worry?'

'Are you worrying right now?'

'No. I'm listening to those bells,' Elisha said. 'We should avoid worrying and celebrate peace in the world. They'll call us Jap-lovers if we don't.'

'I loved a Jap once,' Roscoe said. 'She was unusually lovely.'

'I hope that wasn't during the war effort.'

'Much earlier.'

'Then you're safe.'

'We have to battle the plague of jingoism that's about to engulf us. Some modest degree of intoxication seems the obvious strategy.'

'We could drink here,' Elisha said.

'Drinking in a hotel dining room at a time of jubilation,' said Roscoe, 'is not drinking and not serious and not jubilant. We have to mix with the hoi polloi when we drink. We have to bend with the amber waves of grain, roil our juices under spacious skies. We have to join the carnival.'

'EP on the bing,' Elisha said emphatically.

They went downstairs to the Ten Eyck's bar, which was locked and dark. They walked across Chapel Street to Farnham's and found no customers, only Randall, the barman, cleaning his sink.

'We're closed,' he said.

'Closed?'

'The war's over,' Randall said, taking off his apron. 'Alfie says this is no time to drink. Alfie says to me, "Close up, Randall. This is a time for prayer and patriotism."'

'I'll remember Alfie, and I'll remember you too, Randall,' Roscoe said. 'Patriotism is the last refuge of saboteurs.'

'Right you are, Mr. Conway. O'Connor's and Keeler's are also closed.' Randall turned off the bar light. 'I'll be open tomorrow after five.'

On the street they heard bells gonging in several churches, trains whistling down at Union Station, the carillon clanging in the City Hall tower, the air-raid siren wailing for the last time. They saw trolleys at a standstill, traffic grid locked at

State and Pearl, clots of hundreds, soon to be tens of thousands, moving into pandemonium. They walked up State and tried the bar at the DeWitt Clinton Hotel, but saboteurs had locked it.

'The Kenmore won't close,' Roscoe said. 'The bells of Mahoney's cash register are the opposite of patriotic.'

They walked back down State Street, the majestic hill of Albany, this very old city in which they both owned uncommon stock and psychic shares. No merchant, no owner of real estate, no peddler or lawyer or bartender, no bum or pickpocket or bookie or politician in the city, not even a stranger walking the streets for the first time, was aloof from the power of these two men if they chose to exercise it; their power, of course, deriving from Patsy, the man without whom . . . and we all know the rest.

They walked over Lodge Street past St. Mary's Catholic Church, past the five-story Albany County Courthouse, whose ninety-seven janitors were all hired on Roscoe's okay. Cars clattered by dragging tin cans, grown men marched along pounding dishpans, and Roscoe and Elisha followed them down Columbia Street toward Pearl, where youths were throwing firecrackers at the antic crowds jamming the intersection.

They entered the side door of the Kenmore Hotel, eternal center of mirth and jazz and women and ready-to-wear myth. Roscoe regularly left his blues here, an uncounted legion of college girls left their virginity here, Bunny Berigan left his cornet here and Bob Mahoney gave it as a gift to Marcus Gorman, and Jack Diamond left the place an enduringly raffish reputation. In short, life without the Kenmore was not life; and at this moment it was noisy and overcrowded, the back bar three deep with revelers, every table full in the

Rainbo Room nightclub. Roscoe and Elisha shoved their way toward The Tavern, the Kenmore's long barroom, where Bob Mahoney was pouring drink as fast as he could move. Roscoe ordered gin and also asked Mahoney to fill his pocket flask for the long night ahead.

'They been here since noontime waiting for the surrender,' Mahoney said. 'Another two hours like this, I'll be out of beer. I've never seen a drinking day like this ever, and I include Armistice Day, 1918.'

'Nobody drank in Albany on Armistice Day,' Elisha said. 'I was here. We all had pork chops and went to bed.'

'Weren't you in the army?' Mahoney asked.

'I was making too much money. Do you have any ale?'

'I do.'

'Breedy ale don't kitty or cut pips,' Elisha said.

'What? What'd you say?' Mahoney asked.

'He'll have gin with an ale chaser,' Roscoe said. 'Did you call Stanwix about a beer delivery?'

'I called every brewery in four counties. Either they're closed or they won't handle any orders. Imagine no beer with a mob like this in the joint?'

'I'll call and get you a delivery,' Roscoe said.

'You do and you drink free till Christmas.'

'Mahoney, you know how to touch a man's heart.'

Glenn Miller was on the jukebox – At Last, my love has come along – and two dozen soldiers and sailors at the bar were randomly kissing and fondling young and not-so-young women. Civilian males, one flashing his Ruptured Duck, the discharge button that proved he'd also served, stood by for seconds, or thirds. Roscoe recognized a petite woman who worked in his building, who always offered up a dry little smile in the elevator; and here she stood in a prolonged, sloppy kiss, her arms and a provocative stockinged leg wrapped around a sailor.

'This reminds me,' Roscoe said to Elisha. 'Shouldn't you call your wife?'

'Curb your salacious tongue.'

'I mean no insult, old man, but we mustn't be without our women amid all this naked lust. You call Veronica, I'll call Trish, and we'll carry on elsewhere.'

'No need to call Trish,' Elisha said, pointing to a wooden booth by the front door where two soldiers, their caps in a puddle of beer on the table, were muzzling Trish, taking turns kissing her. As Roscoe walked toward her table he saw both soldiers' hands roaming inside her unbuttoned blouse.

'Hello, honey,' Trish said, 'I thought I'd find you here.'

Both soldiers removed their hands from her chest and looked up at Roscoe. One soldier looked sixteen.

'I'll be right with you, Rosky,' Trish said, buttoning up.

'Carry on, soldiers,' Roscoe said. 'They're what you were fighting for,' and he went back to Elisha at the bar.

'Trish is a very patriotic young woman,' Elisha said.

'If sex were bazookas,' Roscoe said, 'she could've taken Saipan all by herself.'

Roscoe saw Trish coming toward him, her walk a concerto of swivels and jiggles that entertained multitudes in the corridors of the Capitol, where she worked for the Democratic leader of the Assembly. She lived in an apartment on Dove Street, and Roscoe paid her rent. With her curly brown bangs still intact despite the muzzling, Trish explained everything to Roscoe.

'Those soldiers were in the Battle of the Bulge,' she said. 'Poor babies. I gave them little pecks and they got very excited. Are you angry at Trishie?'

'Trishie, Trishie, would I get angry if my rabbit carnalized another rabbit? Fornication is God's fault, not yours.'

'I feel the same way,' she said.

'I know you do, sweetness. Now, go be kind to those soldiers.'

'You mean it?'

'Of course. They may have battle wounds.'

'Where will you go?' she asked.

'Where the night wind takes me. Try not to get the clap.'

'Bye, honey,' she said, and kissed him on the cheek.

'Goodbye forever, little ding-ding,' he said, but she didn't hear, was already on her way back to the soldiers.

'You really mean that goodbye forever?' Elisha asked.

'As my sainted father used to say, Irish girls either fuck everybody or nobody. Which category do you think suits Trish?'

Someone turned up the jukebox and a stupefyingly loud Latin tune blasted through The Tavern.

'Let this farce end,' Elisha said. 'The gin isn't worth it.'

'I concur,' Roscoe said, and they downed their drinks and moved toward the door.

'I had a thought about Cutie LaRue,' Elisha said. 'Why not run him as the wild-card candidate?'

'Cutie for mayor?'

'He's such a clown, and he can make a speech. He'd love the attention. People would vote for him just to say they did. And he'd get the liberals and goo-goos who hate us but can't pull that Republican lever.'

'By God, Elisha, that's brilliant. Cutie, the crackpot candidate!'

'Have I helped you stop worrying?'

'No, but now I can smile while I worry.'

A vandal had opened a hydrant on Pearl Street near Sheridan Avenue. A roaming vendor was hawking V-J buttons, flags had blossomed in lighted store windows and dangled everywhere from light poles and roofs, the mob filling every part of the street. As Roscoe and Elisha debated their move, The Tavern's door flew open and a conga line burst into the street, led by a sailor, with Trish holding his hips, one of her soldiers holding hers, and a dozen others snaking along behind them to the Latin music from the bar.

Roscoe and Elisha pushed through the sidewalk mobs, and at State and Pearl they could see a patriotic bonfire blazing down by the Plaza. Roscoe remembered the ambivalent tensions of patriotism invading this block on the April day in 1943 when Alex went to war. Patsy had ordered up a parade with flags, bugles, drums, and an Albany Academy color guard marching the twenty-seven-year-old Mayor into a gilt-edged political future. Alex, off to serve his country as a buck private, marched with a platoon of other young bucks, proles mostly, none out of Albany Academy, Groton, and Yale like him, and none with the boneheaded insistence on rolling dice for his life. Roscoe, titular head of the local Draft Board, could easily have found an ailment to defer Alex, let him continue as Albany's boyish wartime mayor. But Patsy had given Alex the word: 'Son, if you don't serve, you're all done in politics. They'll call you a slacker, and I won't run you for re-election. Go down and join the navy and we'll get you a commission.' But Alex joined the army, asked for the infantry, and got it. And Elisha and Roscoe could not change his mind.

There he came that day, down the middle of State Street, Roscoe and Elisha right here beaming at their boy on his way to becoming food for powder – Elisha, elated by his son's political success, and Roscoe, the exulting mentor: Wasn't it I taught you to hold your whiskey, lad? Wasn't it I instructed you in the survival tactics of the carouse, at which you excelled early? Come back safe and soon, and we'll all rekindle the festive fire.

At Lodge Street they heard the organ music, and Elisha walked toward it through the open doors of St. Peter's. Roscoe arched an eyebrow but followed him into the old French Gothic bluestone church, an Episcopal parish well into its third century. The church was fully lit and half full of silent people staring at the altar, where seven candles burned in each of two silver candelabra, the pair a gift from Elisha's father, Ariel Fitzgibbon. Women were weeping, some in a state of rapture. Elderly couples were holding hands, young people whispering excitedly. A soldier knelt with head down on the back of the pew. A woman in mourning entered and instantly knelt in the middle aisle.

Pews were filling as Roscoe and Elisha stood at the back of the church, Roscoe bemused by Elisha's odd smile. Smiling that Alex would come back alive from Europe? Whatever was inside that stately head, Roscoe could not read it clearly. Elisha was scanning the church as if he were a tourist; but he was surely summoned here by what those familiar bells meant to his encrusted Episcopal soul. One stained-glass window through which the day's waning light was entering had been the gift, in the late 1870s, of Lyman Fitzgibbon. Designed by Burne-Jones, it bore a legend that read, '*Per industria nil sine Numine*' – Nothing through diligence without the Divine Will – which Roscoe translated as, 'Don't make a serious move without the political okay.'

An organist moved through a five-noted chant and then a glissando of the first two bars of 'America,' pausing on a long note, and then he began a second chant. Elisha interrupted the organist, returning to the anthem. 'My country, 'tis of thee,' he sang, with might in his voice, and every head turned to see this intruder continue with 'Sweet land of liberty, / Of thee I sing. . . .' The organist followed Elisha, and the solemnizers of peace joined him, the familiar music and words stirring their souls as the splendid pipes of this chorister from nowhere arced into the vault of the nave; and when the verse ended and the silence longed to explode into applause, Elisha continued with a little-known verse: 'Let music swell the breeze, / And ring from all the trees / Sweet freedom's song. . . .'

People applauded with simple nods and uncontrollably weepy smiles, all of them climbing down from the ramparts, linked by the newness of this peace that also needed leadership, affirming that Elisha had spoken aloud the very prayer they'd all been seeking in silence, the marrow of patriotic holiness achingly evoked by this saloon tenor whom Roscoe had never before known to sing solo in church, or sing so well in any saloon anywhere.

'Bravura performance,' Roscoe said as they went out onto State Street.

'Cheap chauvinism,' said Elisha. 'I couldn't help myself. It was like having holy hiccups.'

'You underrate your achievement. My blood cells turned red, white, and blue.'

'Don't hold it against me. Remember that the kamikazes are still out there, and the war criminals will cut themselves in two rather than face the music.'

'Kamikazes? War criminals?'

'Don't forget I said this.'

* * *

They walked to the Albany Garage, where Roscoe housed his two-door 1941 Plymouth, and they headed for Tivoli to rendezvous with Veronica, an upgrading of life for Roscoe just to see her. But as he drove, distracted, perhaps, by the gin, or by seeing Trish as a soldier-and-sailor sandwich, or relief at being rid of her, or by going public with his plan to quit politics, he began playing eye games with moving vehicles, blanking them out with his right eye, then his left, eliminating them entirely by closing both eyes.

'Why are you closing your eyes while you drive?' Elisha asked.

'I'm playing Albany roulette.'

'Let me out.'

'You'll be home in ten minutes.'

'Playing games with death. You really are in trouble.'

'I'm all right.' But he kept closing one eye, then the other.

'This is a form of suicide,' Elisha said. 'Is that your plan?'

'No. Not my style.'

'It's everybody's style at some point. And if you kill me while you're at it, that's murder.'

'Not at all my style,' Roscoe said.

'Open your eyes and listen to me. I'm the one who's quitting, not you.'

Roscoe braked instantly and swerved to avoid sideswiping an oncoming trolley car, then climbed a curb and struck a small tree. The impact was light, but it drove the steering wheel into the deep folds of Roscoe's abdomen and threw Elisha into the windshield. Blood instantly gushed, and Elisha pressed his pocket handkerchief onto his forehead.

'Let me see that,' Roscoe said, and when he saw the wound he said, 'Stitches.'

He backed the car onto the street and drove to Albany

Hospital. They both could walk to the emergency room, which was accumulating assorted brawling louts and burn victims and skewed drivers like Roscoe, all celebrating peace with blood and fire and pain. As a nurse started to take Elisha off to stanch his bleeding, Roscoe asked, 'What's this quitting stuff?'

'Believe me, it's real,' Elisha said. 'Unless you want to give Patsy a heart attack, don't you run off just yet.'

'What the hell are you talking about?'

'I'm doing a fadeaway,' Elisha said. 'Time's up.'

'Suddenly there's a retirement epidemic,' Roscoe said. 'Do you suppose the Japs put something in our drinking water?'

He felt new pain in his stomach, and his head ached from the resurrection of old doubt. You think you've done something radical and it turns out you've done nothing at all.

Roscoe recognized a nun sitting in the next bay of the emergency room, Arlene Flinn from Arbor Hill, a Sister of the Sacred Heart, hundred and one pounds, tiny, dark-haired, sharp-nosed beauty in adolescence, when Roscoe had a crush on her. Those once-spunky eyes were now reshaped behind spectacles, her hair hidden under her starched wimple.

'Arlene?' he said. 'Is that you?'

'Oh, Roscoe,' she said. 'Roscoe Conway.'

Her tone of voice suggested to Roscoe that she remembered the day he caught her in his arms and kissed her by the holy-water fountain in St. Joseph's Church. Two days later she went off to the nunnery – the beginning of your control over women, Ros.

'Are you ill, Arlene?' he asked her.

'A toothache,' she said. 'The pain is horrible.' She was

humming something that sounded like a Benediction hymn – 'O Salutaris,' was it?

'How's your father?' he asked.

'Oh dear, my father,' Arlene said. 'He died six months ago.'

'I didn't know. I never saw it in the paper.'

'He died in Poughkeepsie. My brother didn't want it publicized.'

'I knew he was down there. I'm sorry, Arlene.'

'He hated all you politicians,' she said. 'Especially Patsy McCall.'

'We offered him anything he wanted when he came out of jail. He wouldn't talk to us.'

'Could you blame him?'

Roscoe chose not to answer. Arlene's father, Artie Flinn, had been the chief plugger for the Albany baseball pool, which Patsy ran. The federal DA indicted Artie when he was caught with plugged pool sheets and heavy money, and he got six years, the scapegoat. Patsy took care of Artie's wife and family while Artie was inside, but Artie came out Patsy's enemy. Also, he went strange, took to jumping off tall buildings into the river, holding the pet pigeon he brought home from jail, and letting the pigeon go before he hit the water. People told him he could fly like his pigeon, but in one jump a piece of sunken metal sliced off part of his left leg. He believed the leg would grow back, and when it didn't, he punched holes in it with an ice pick and had to be put away.

'I see your brother Roy from time to time,' Roscoe said.

'I don't see him,' Arlene said. 'I don't approve of that newspaper he runs. It's scandalous. Roscoe, where's that dentist? I can't stand this pain.'

'Have a swig of this and hold it on the tooth.' He handed her his flask of compassionate gin.

She held the gin, then swallowed it, took a second, squidged her cheek and held it, swallowed it, 'Sweet Mother, Roscoe, this doesn't help a bit,' then a third gin, and he told her to keep the flask as they took him for X-rays of his rib cage.

'When are you going to get this holy woman a dentist?' Roscoe asked the nurse.

'He's on the way,' the nurse said.

Roscoe's X-rays were negative, and a young intern suggested an ice bag for his stomach and gave him a packet of pills for his blood pressure. 'You'll be sore, but nothing's broken and we don't see any bleeding.'

Roscoe saw Veronica standing by a half-open curtain in the bay where Elisha lay on a stretcher. Her long blond hair was wrapped into a quick knot at the back of her head, she wore no makeup and was barelegged in low heels and a candy-striped summer dress. Roscoe thought she looked sublime.

'What's the verdict?' he asked her.

She kissed his cheek. 'They're taking him upstairs for the stitches. How are your bruises?'

Roscoe patted his gut. 'With this padding it takes quite a whack to do me any damage.'

'If Elisha has a concussion,' Veronica said, 'they'll keep him overnight.'

A nurse came to wheel Elisha out.

'Are you all right?' Elisha asked Roscoe.

'Better than you,' Roscoe said. 'Artie Flinn's daughter, Arlene, is here with a toothache. She's a nun.'

'Is that Artie Flinn from the baseball pool?' Veronica asked.

'It is.'

'Artie was not one of our finest hours,' Elisha said. 'What's he doing?'

'He died in Poughkeepsie six months ago,' Roscoe said.

'Tragic,' Elisha said. 'We couldn't protect him. I never knew his daughter.'

'I had a crush on her in school,' Roscoe said. 'My behavior drove her into the nunnery.'

'He's bragging again,' Veronica said.

'I'll catch up with you two after your stitches,' Roscoe said.

In the waiting room Arlene was walking in circles, waving Roscoe's flask, still singing her hymn, very loud: '. . . *Quae coeli pandis ostium; Bella premunt hostilia . . .*' She was off balance from the drink, and a nurse was about to take her in hand when she whirled away and backhanded the nurse's jaw with Roscoe's flask. 'Where are you, Jesus?' she called out. 'I'm in pain. *Quae coeli pandis ostium . . .*'

An intern moved to help the nurse subdue the wild nun, but Roscoe stepped in and said, 'I'll take care of her, Doctor. I'm her cousin, and my brother is a dentist. Tell *your* dentist to go to hell for his next patient.'

'God bless you, Roscoe,' Arlene said. 'The pain is awful and the gin is gone.'

She wobbled and almost fell, Roscoe's first gin-soaked nun. He swept her into his arms, a feather, the pain from his trauma twisting a small knife in his belly as he carried her to the parking lot.

'This is the date we never had, Arlene,' he said. 'I dearly love the way you turned out.'

'Don't you dare be nice to me, Roscoe. I don't want it. I'm going to stay a virgin till I die.' She resumed her hymn – '. . . *Bella premunt hostilia . . .*' – as he drove her uptown in his car with the dented bumper.

'I've never known a woman like you, Arlene.'

'Doesn't surprise me.'

'Let's take a boat to Bermuda.'

'I've still got a toothache.'

Roscoe found Doc Reardon, who did free dental work for select Democrats, and he promptly eliminated her pain and fixed the blessed tooth. Arlene then promised Roscoe and the doc a place among the lesser angels.

'God bless you, too, Arlene,' Roscoe said. 'God bless all nuns and all women.' Then he thought of Trish and added, 'Most women.'

He drove Arlene back to the Academy of the Sacred Heart at Kenwood, hoping her time with him would incite a convent-wide scandal, then went back to the hospital to check on Elisha. But he'd been sent home, no concussion after all. It was ten-thirty, too late to visit, a missed opportunity to be with Veronica. Roscoe went back to his car in the emergency-room parking lot. Where to go now? He watched ambulances and cars come and go with the dying and the wounded from the peaceful home front. He dwelled on Artie Flinn, casualty of the political wars, a man who'd been making a fortune but ran out of luck. What other disasters will unfold for Roscoe on this night of radical developments? He could go to Trish's apartment and retrieve his clothes out of her closet. She might be there with four sailors. Go home and get some sleep, Ros. But who can sleep on V-J night? Go find a woman, then. Shouldn't be difficult tonight. But if you don't score, don't even think of buying one, they're watching you. You should have kidnapped Arlene, your prototype of ideal beauty. You could've talked about the good old days of young sin. They don't make sin like they used to. Also, your stomach is rumbling. You never finished your dinner. Forget women and celebrate the Jap surrender with a steak. Or three hamburgers. Or a hot beef sandwich at the Morris Lunch, two hot beefs with double home fries and a wedge of apple pie with a custard-pie chaser. He drove to the Miss Albany Diner on Central Avenue, open all night, found it dark. A sign in the window reported, 'No Food.' The Boulevard Cafeteria, never closes, was open but no steaks, no roast beef, no ham, no hamburgers, no eggs. All they had was bread, coffee, and no cream. The whole town ate out tonight. Roscoe had two orders of buttered toast, a plate of pickle slices, black coffee, and went back to his car. The streets were busy but no more traffic jams. The frenzy wanes. Who'll be at the bar in the Elks Club? Who cares? Roscoe did not want to talk about war or peace or politics, not even the Cutie Diversion. What *do* you want, Ros? How about Hattie? Yes, a very good idea. Hattie Wilson, his perennial love. He did love her, always would. He wouldn't lay a hand on her. That's not what Roscoe is looking for right now. What's more, isn't Hattie married to O.B., Roscoe's brother? Yes, she is. Roscoe wants only straight talk, smart talk, maybe a little sweet talk with Hattie, who is wise, who is a comfort. Six husbands and still nubile. Get your mind off nubility, for chrissake. He drove to Lancaster Street east of Dove Street and parked across from Hattie's house. All four floors were dark. She could be awake in the back of the house, probably asleep. Roscoe did not want to get her out of bed to carry on a conversation – about what? Why are you waking me up in the middle of the night, Rosky? I wish I knew, old Hat. Never mind waking up. Some other time, Hat. Roscoe drove back to the hotel and told the doorman to send his car back to the garage. He decided to go upstairs, order room service, and go to bed, but the saboteurs had preceded him. No more room service tonight. So Roscoe settled into his suite on the tenth floor, ordered ice for his ice bag from the bellman, ate a Hershey bar out of the drawer, poured himself a double gin, hold the quinine, swallowed his blood-pressure pills with the gin, toasted peace in the world and freedom from politics, then went to bed hungry.

A Flagrant Departure

V-J Day-plus-one was a holiday for much of the city, a day of prayer, thanksgiving, and patriotism, the main speech of the day given on the Capitol steps by Marcus Gorman, the noted criminal lawyer who had become Albany's Demosthenes. Bart Merrigan, in his role as Albany's commander of the American Legion, was master of ceremonies and introduced Marcus, who thanked God in his mercy for restoring justice and honor to the world, two commodities Marcus had spent his career subverting. Roscoe sent Joey Manucci up to Patsy's summer house on the mountain with news of Cutie LaRue as a possible candidate. Patsy loved the idea and sent word back to Roscoe to hire Eddie Brodie as Cutie's speechwriter, the man who would help Cutie lose. Brodie, an ex-newspaperman, had helped Jimmy McCoy lose in 1937 by coining his campaign remark: 'I never met a woman I liked as much as my dog.'

At late morning Veronica called Roscoe to say Elisha woke with a headache but was feeling better, and talking about going to the office in the afternoon. Roscoe spent half the day in bed with his ice bag, ate supper alone in the hotel dining room, then went back to bed. A phone call woke him and he sat up in the darkness to answer it: 4 A.M. on the luminous face of his alarm clock. He heard Gladys Meehan say, 'It's Elisha, Roscoe.' He switched on the bed-table light, and there was Elisha on the wall in that famous photo with Roscoe and Patsy, election night, 1921, when those three young rebels, their smiles exuding power and joy at taking City Hall back from the Republicans, were about to found the new city of war and love.

'What about Elisha?'

'Everything,' Gladys said. 'Come immediately. The mill.'

Roscoe had the bellman call up his car and he drove to Fitzgibbon Steel, a small city of twenty-nine buildings – rolling mills, forges, furnaces, shearing shops, machine shops, and a maze of Delaware and Hudson Railroad tracks running through it all. It covered twenty-eight acres between Broadway and the river in the northeast corner of the city, and had employed fifteen hundred men and a hundred women in the peak war years.

Roscoe parked by the mill's office in the machine-shop building and went in past the night guard, up to the third floor, the stairs aggravating his pain. He found Gladys in a leather chair staring at Elisha, whose horn-rim glasses were on his desk, a flesh-colored bandage on his forehead where it had hit the windshield. The sleeves of his tailor-made blue shirt were rolled to the elbow, his dark-blue tie loose at the open collar, his gray suit-coat on the back of his chair, hands folded in his lap, chin on his chest, wearing his favorite cordovan wingtips, and facing the fireplace full of ashes. His face was pale blue, and strands of his hair, gray as the chromium steel he manufactured, hung in his eyes, which Gladys had closed.

Elisha at fifty-four.

As Roscoe stared at him, Elisha stood up, walked to the bathroom, and began shaving with his electric razor. Roscoe followed him.

'Who gave you the okay to die?' Roscoe asked.

'You know what they say,' Elisha said. 'Never meet the enemy on his own ground.'

'Which enemy?'

'If you don't have a solution, you transform the problem.'

'What problem?'

'The same old EP on the bing and the kitty bosso . . .'

Then Elisha, in the midst of his peerless babble, fell over backward, dead again.

'I've been here all night,' Gladys said to Roscoe. 'He came in at seven o'clock last night and called me at the house and asked me to come back.'

'With that head injury, I'm surprised Veronica let him go out.'

'He convinced her he was all right.'

'When did he die?'

'I don't know. I slept, I woke up and saw him, and I called you. We worked hours in the file room pulling out old letters. I got filthy moving those boxes. He knew the exact years. He'd read one file and ask for another. Then he'd burn some in the fireplace. He said to give you this.' She handed Roscoe a notarized letter from Elisha naming Roscoe executor of his estate. 'He told me, "The enemy is closing in," and I asked him, "Who?" and he said, "Roscoe will figure it out." What enemy, Roscoe?'

'We have many,' Roscoe said, pocketing the letter. 'What did he burn?'

'Real-estate files, contracts, deeds, canceled checks, letters, insurance papers, bank statements out of the safe.'

'Write down any specifics you remember. Why did you stay so late?'

'After he burned the papers I started to leave, but he said, "Can you stay tonight? I need your company." It's the first time he ever admitted he needed me. Twenty-five years, every day all day, sometimes weekends, trusting me to do what needed doing.'

Gladys stared at Elisha in his death chair, put her hand on his forehead, and stroked the hair off his face. He opened his eyes and winked at her.

'Mac was coming over to the house on his dinner break,' she said, 'but I called and told him I was working late. Then Elisha poured us some whiskey from a Christmas bottle he had on the closet shelf. I never drink whiskey.'

The whiskey and two empty glasses were on Elisha's desk.

'Where did you sleep?'

'On the sofa. He stayed in the chair, thank you.'

'How did he do it?'

'What? You think he did it?'

'So do you, don't you? Why did you call me instead of the ambulance?'

'Who else would I call?'

'How about Veronica?'

'She wouldn't know what to do, how to protect him. She'd end up calling you anyway.'

'You find any bottles or pills?'

'I didn't look.'

They looked in the desk, in the safe, in Elisha's coat, in the cardigans hanging in the closet, in the medicine cabinet, in all his pockets, but found no pills, only a wallet. Roscoe counted its cash: 'Four hundred and seventy-seven,' he said, and put the money back in the wallet and pocketed it.

Roscoe examined the photos on the desk: Elisha and Veronica sailing with their boy Gilby; Alex in battle jacket, steel helmet, and boots, jabbing his rifle-with-bayonet at the camera. On the wall, Elisha was being sworn in as lieutenant governor, and Roscoe remembered his line after taking the oath: 'This is a great job for a man with misguided ambition.' There was Elisha at a 1929 political dinner with Governor FDR, and again in 1943 with President FDR as he made Elisha a dollar-a-year man for donating his expertise in steel production to the wartime government, the check for one dollar framed with the photo.

In a corner of the office stood another fragment of history, a silvery-gray 1860 Fitzgibbon woodstove, chrome-trimmed, three mica windows, sculpted feet, a work of foundry art made by Lyman Fitzgibbon, who established the foundry when the world was new and turned out three hundred stoves a day, ninety thousand a year, until the industry went west to the ore sources. The foundry tripled the fortune Lyman had already made through land speculation and railroads, the same fortune Ariel, Elisha's father, would fribble away, and that Elisha, when he was barely out of college, young magus of the new day, would replenish. With the help of a Yale classmate's father's two patents, for making rail joints and springs for railroad cars, he stabilized the firm. He then oversaw the introduction of the first electric furnaces for making alloy steels, and the very early pouring of stainless steel in the U.S., both ventures coming just after the first war. How did he know so much about steel? He began at the blacksmith level, rolled up his sleeves with every worker who could teach him anything; did the same at the research level of the industry and became an intuitive wonder.

It was going for five, and the first shift of the shops came in at six-fifteen. Roscoe swept the ashes out of the fireplace and flushed them down the toilet, Gladys vacuumed the fireplace and rug and dusted the room, and Roscoe called his brother at Hattie's house.

'Who's calling at this hour?' Hattie asked.

'It's Roscoe, Hat. Put O.B. on.'

'Yeah,' said the half-asleep O.B.

'Need you at the mill,' Roscoe said. 'There's been a bad accident and I need you. Immediately.'

'What accident?'

'For chrissake, just get here.' And Roscoe hung up.

Gladys handed him her list of files Elisha had burned, then collapsed back into her chair. Roscoe started to pour two short whiskeys but decided that maybe this whiskey was poisoned. He let it sit and found an unopened bottle on Elisha's closet shelf and poured the drinks. He and Gladys sipped the whiskey while they waited for O.B.'s official police inquiry to begin, an inquiry that would willfully discover death from natural causes and little else. If anyone discovered anything true about this death it would be Roscoe.

'Whiskey twice in the middle of the night,' Gladys said. 'What's the world coming to?'

'Less and less.'

Roscoe opened the drapes on the interior picture window that offered a view of the great machines in the shop below: lathes, drills, punches, boring mills, monster planers, and the great cranes that loomed over all three bays of the shop. Elisha had built this window for the vision it gave of the world he'd salvaged out of the ashes of his father's folly, a world he'd known so intimately for thirty-four years and which, until this morning, depended on him for its perpetuation, just as the Party had depended on him. Roscoe watched the sun entering the machine shop's windows, watched it rise on Fitzgibbon Steel's thirty-six smokestacks and shape them into long black fingers pointing upward into this shabby new day.

'Could you have predicted this?' Roscoe asked Gladys.

'Never.'

'What was the situation here at the mill this week?'

'His brother, Gordon, really thought he was taking charge. He and his sisters have been scheming to take control, because Elisha's been in Washington so long and profits are down. They blame him, but anybody with half a brain knows it's because the war was ending. They had awful fights.' Gordon was the senior vice-president of the City Exchange Bank.

'Elisha wouldn't kill himself for that,' Roscoe said.

'Riddles,' Gladys said. 'This place'll go straight to hell without him, and Alex won't have anything to do with it. It'll be a battle royal between Veronica and the family lawyers. And I'll be out on the street.'

'Whoever runs it, they'll need you.'

Roscoe felt an odd intimacy with Gladys. For as long as they'd known each other they'd each spoken only to the other's public self. Gladys sipped her whiskey, gave a shudder, and set the glass on the desk.

'You know what he did last night, Roscoe? He kissed me.'

'He do that often?'

'Once a year, maybe, on the cheek. Last night on the mouth, sweetly. He always kept tabs on my skirt. Somebody sent him pictures of naked women about fifteen years ago, and of course I always opened his mail. "You in the market for this stuff?" I asked him. He held one photo up. "That's what I figure you look like," he said. "It's close," I said, "but you'll never know." "I know," he said, "a bitter denial."'

But 'bitter' wasn't the word. Roscoe understood how Elisha could have worked up a quiet, arm's-length love for Gladys, a woman of durable good looks that fluctuated with perms and marcels not always in her own best interest; sturdy, busty, feminine, always wore pumps, and everyone, not only Elisha, monitored her legs. She'd gone the novena route for years and tried to keep the commandments. But going with Mac the cop must have led to repetitive spiels in the Saturday-night confessional: Bless me, Father, for I have sinned; I did it again with that same fella. She dressed modestly in fashions that didn't change much, and Elisha once said her smile could warm the north wind. She'd never married, and Mac wasn't a prospect. Mac's wife had left town years ago, but he wouldn't divorce her. Also, that subterranean love Gladys and Elisha shared, a silent love presumably without consequence, had probably spoiled her for others.

'That kiss,' Roscoe said, 'that was the extent of it?'

'No. He also said, "If I ever told you what I felt, you'd put your hat on and tell me to go to hell. But you know it anyway." And I did know. I always knew. I'm so glad I was here, Roscoe. I fell asleep after the whiskey, but I remember asking was he going away anyplace, and he said, "If I leave you'll know it."'

'Do you want to go home and sleep?' Roscoe asked.

'The last time I fell asleep Elisha died. Besides, I should call the undertaker.'

'That's Veronica's job.'

'I always make his travel arrangements. Aren't you going to call Veronica?'

'I'll go get her when O.B. gets here.'

'You can start over with her now,' Gladys said.

'Start over.'

'She'll expect it. So will everybody else.'

'What does that mean?'

'Really, Roscoe, do you know how transparent you are sometimes?'

Roscoe heard car doors closing. Oswald Brian Conway, his younger brother and Albany's chief of police, unshaven and in his baggy gray sharkskin, stepped off the elevator with two of his Night Squad boys behind him, Bo Linder and Joe Spivak. Roscoe asked the detectives to wait outside and let no one in. O.B. went directly to Elisha and stared at him.

'What happened to him?'

'He decided his life was over.'

'I don't get it,' O.B. said.

'Nobody does,' Roscoe said. 'Who's the coroner on duty?'

'Nolan. I didn't call him yet.'

'Don't. We'll do this alone for now. It goes down as a natural death.'

'Are we sure it's a suicide and not a murder?'

'Gladys was here all night, working with him.'

'How are you, Gladys?' O.B. said. 'You didn't murder him, did you?'

'Not even in my dreams. Is Mac coming?' Mac was O.B.'s partner.

'He must be in bed,' O.B. said. 'He went off duty at four-thirty. Does Patsy know?'

'No,' said Roscoe. 'I can't use the phone for this. Send one of your boys up to tell him. But don't mention suicide. And don't, for God's sake, let anybody leak it to the press. I don't want Veronica hearing it on the radio.'

'When are you getting her?'

'Now. You want a lift home, Gladys?'

'I suppose so,' Gladys said.

'You go get Veronica,' O.B. said. 'That's priority. I'll see Gladys gets home. This thing stinks out loud.'

'It'll get louder,' Roscoe said. He picked up his suit coat and went out.

Roscoe and Veronica

Everybody knew he was insane about her when they were young. Insane. Pressing, pressing, pressing her to marry him. But Elisha dazzled her with his razzmatazz and the family fortune he had regenerated. And Veronica, with sweet pets and kisses, told Roscoe one of her lovely lies: 'My darling Ros, you love me so much you'll absolutely die if I marry you, but Eli will die if I don't marry him.' Roscoe remembered trying to decide which train he should walk in front of; but he got over that and tried not to blame Veronica for defecting. She was no golddigger, just a moderately rich girl who suffered from money. And Elisha had much more money than she. Also, Elisha was a winner and a great guy, and who the hell was Roscoe, anyway? A young punk lawyer with a talent for fun. Roscoe brooded and did the next best thing to marrying Veronica: he married her sister, Pamela, a liaison that carried on interminably for four days, then turned into several previously unknown forms of unkindness.

Roscoe stopped at the Morris Diner in North Albany to get just-baked French crullers and coffee for Veronica. She loved those crullers (so did Roscoe), and with the coffee and sugar they'd give her a rush so she wouldn't nauseate in front of dead Elisha. He then drove up the hill to Van Rensselaer Boulevard, where the great estate of Tivoli – Veronica suddenly its sovereign – had stood since Lyman built it, a landscape of dream for Albanians of the last century. The estate's mansion was sited on the plateau that ran along the crest of the river valley, giving a vista of the serene and turbulent Hudson, the green heights of Rensselaer, and the Berkshire Hills beyond. But vista was secondary to the builder, who wanted solitude, isolation above the crowd, a desire that belonged to yesterday. Now Roscoe moved along the boulevard past a row of new and boxy little houses owned by Italian grocers and German plumbers, past Wolfert's Roost Country Club, founded by newsmen and politicians, then drove through the open wrought-iron gates and up the long, winding driveway to Tivoli, his second home.

'Why are you here at this hour?' Veronica asked him over coffee in her breakfast room. 'The last time you brought breakfast you and Elisha were going fishing.'

The sight of her in a Chinese dressing gown, her golden hair loose and only slightly mussed from sleep, quickened Roscoe's heart, but he told it to behave itself.

'I need your help,' he said. 'Eat a cruller.'

'You need my help?' She bit into a cruller.

'Elisha.'

'He didn't come home last night,' she said. 'He stayed at the office.'

'I know that.'

'Were you with him?'

'I was.'

'Is he in trouble?'

'No.'

'Is it the head injury? He was fine when he called.'

'He's in the office. In his chair. Now, don't hold me to this, Vee, but I think he killed himself.'

She squeezed her bitten cruller between fingers and palm, rolling it into a wad of dough as she looked at Roscoe.

'No,' she said, and shook her head, 'he wouldn't do that.'

'Maybe he didn't do it. I could be wrong.'

'You're certain he's dead.'

'I'm certain.' And he put Elisha's wallet on the table.

'That bastard. That *bastard*!'

'Atta girl. You tell him.'

She dropped the wadded cruller and it rolled across the table to Roscoe. She picked up the wallet and put it against her face.

'He wasn't ready to die,' she said, and the tears were coming now. Roscoe couldn't look at them.

'Go get dressed, Vee. I'll take you down to the mill.'

When she was dressed and they were in the car she asked Roscoe, 'Why do you say suicide?'

'He burned papers and files he didn't want anybody to see. It was a methodical ending.'

'How did he do it?'

'I don't know. Not with a gun.'

'Why didn't he come home and do it?'

'Maybe he didn't want to make a mess for you. Maybe he didn't want anybody saving him. Or maybe the idea of death arrived in such a perfect state that he had to act instantly, a fatal muse descending, and there was only submission, no alternative.'

'Something's very wrong with me. I never saw it coming.'

'None of us did,' Roscoe said.

'It's me he left. He was through with me.'

'Nonsense. Who'd ever leave you?'

'He ran away from something, or somebody. Who else is there to run away from?'

'There was no cowardice in him,' Roscoe said. 'He'd face anything.'

'You're so loyal. To both of us.'

'I'm not loyal,' Roscoe said. 'I'm a traitor.'

'Of course you are. God should give the world more traitors like you.'

When he drove into the office parking lot at the mill, Roscoe saw men already at work in the traffic manager's office, so, rather than subject Veronica to their scrutiny, he parked at the side entrance. They went briskly in past the security cubicle, where Roscoe saw Frank Maynard and two of his guards whispering – The word is out – and up the back stairs to Elisha's office. Joe Spivak sat by the door, guarding the integrity of the death room. Nothing had been taken away or added, but as Roscoe entered, the room became an antechamber where he sensed he had to begin. Begin what? Not courting the widow. He might get to that. Might. This was something else, and he knew it wouldn't easily be defined. He also knew he now could not quit the Party; and he knew Elisha had known that would happen.

Veronica walked to the dead Elisha and looked down at him, shaking her head no, no, no. 'Oh Lord, Roscoe, it's true.' And she crumpled in front of Elisha.

Roscoe gestured to Joe Spivak to get out, then lifted Veronica into the large leather chair where Gladys had also sat to stare at her dead love. 'Slow, now, Vee. Take it slow.'

'He doesn't even look a little bit sick,' Veronica said, her eyes wet again.

'Maybe he wasn't sick.'

'He had to be.'

She stood up and walked to Elisha, hiked her skirt and straddled his lap, ran her hands through his hair.

'Were you sick, Elisha? How could you be that sick without my knowing it? You're already a chunk of rubber.' She gave him a weeping kiss. 'What went so wrong you had to quit everything in such a hurry? You couldn't wait to see your son come home from winning the war? Whatever it was we could've fixed it.' She lifted his left hand and studied it, then took his diamond ring and gold watch from the dead finger and wrist. Lacking pockets, she put them inside her brassiere. She stared at Elisha, then kissed him and sat back. 'Look at you. Look what you've done to yourself. Bastard.' She slapped his face.

'Veronica,' Roscoe said. 'Get a grip.'

He helped her stand and she tried to stop weeping.

'I thought I knew him. He's a dead stranger.'

'Staying alive isn't anybody's obligation,' Roscoe said. 'I'm betting he had a reason.'

Veronica let Roscoe put his arms around her while she wept – spasmic, throaty crying. Roscoe held grief in his arms and knew he could die of happiness, a traitor, embracing his best friend's wife. Yes, it's true, Elisha, old pal. You're dead and we're not. Then Veronica stabbed him in the heart with her breast, a wound that meant nothing to her. Sweet Roscoe, comfort me, let me fail in your arms, hold me close, feel how soft I am. But this is all you get, and don't think this counts. You're a wonderful fellow, Roscoe. Don't crowd me.

'It's okay, Vee,' he said to her. 'Let it out.'

'Oh, Roscoe, Roscoe,' she said. 'What is going on here?'

'A temporary mystery. We'll figure it out.'

'I loved him so.'

'Sure you did.'

She raised her head off his shoulder, trying to stop crying, and he saw she was abashed by their embrace. What a surprise. She smiled and stepped back from him, walked to the desk, and picked up the photo of Elisha, Roscoe, and herself in the winner's circle with Pleasure Power the day he won the Travers at Saratoga.

'I want to take this home,' she said.

'I'll get an envelope.'

She picked up the photo of Alex in his army uniform. 'We have to tell Alex,' she said.

'We'll call the army, have them cable him. I'll do that.'

Roscoe would do it all. And Alex would come home safely from the war to find that his father, not he, was the post-armistice casualty. Roscoe slid the Saratoga picture into a large envelope and sealed its clasp. He walked Veronica down the stairs and toward the line of men arriving for work in the machine shop. They had all heard about Elisha, and Roscoe answered their condolences with nods and salutes as he and Veronica passed them.

Sorry, Missus Fitz.

The sunlight was making intensely black shadows of the men as they stood in line to punch the time clock in the mill. They all spoke their regrets.

Sorry, sorry, Missus Fitz. Sorry, sorry. Really sorry.

'Good morning, men, and thank you,' Veronica said in a sharp, recovering voice, raising her head to meet their eyes. 'Good morning, yes, good morning, men, and thank you. Thank you so much. Such a beautiful day to die.'

Roscoe and the Flying Heads

Roscoe moved silently into the theater with the crowd, the seats filling quickly. When the curtain rose, ten men and ten women were in two lines on stage, all in white tie and tails, tap-dancing and singing, with brio, 'Somebody Else Is Taking My Place.' As the performers danced, the heads of one man and one woman flew off and sailed across the stage to land atop the headless torsos of another man, another woman, whose heads were flying to the dancing torsos of yet another man, another woman, and so it went until all twenty singing heads were flying to and fro across the stage, perfectly synchronized in the labyrinthine choreography of their arcs.

Roscoe, sitting in the balcony, saw Elisha pushed onto the stage from the wings, obviously confused to find himself in the midst of this performance. But as the singing heads criss-crossed in air, Elisha seemed to realize this was a command performance for him, and he moved his own head from side to side in rhythm with the music and the dancing torsos.

'Yes, I do understand the question that's being asked,' Elisha said aloud. 'It's the music of the spheres.'

The audience applauded his remark and Roscoe ran down from the balcony to ask Elisha: What question is being asked? Why the spheres? But the theater was now dark, and the audience, dancers, and Elisha were gone.

Love, Scandal, and Horses

When you are three, as in that 1921 photo on the wall of Roscoe's hotel room, and one of the three is subtracted, the sum is less than you'd expect; for the mathematics of the spirit are complex. Now, at Elisha's wake, they were two, Roscoe and Patsy, both feeling like leftovers after the banquet. Patsy, in politics since he was old enough to deface Republican ballots, was at his first wake since his brother Matt died (Patsy did not like the dead), looking bumptious, the only way he knew how to look, even in his new blue suit. Roscoe had combed and gracefully parted his beard, draped his corpulence stylishly in a white Palm Beach suit, and stood somberly dapper by the bier with white shoes, black pocket handkerchief, black tie.

The wake sprawled over the vast, pampered lawn of Tivoli, with its upper and lower mansions, its sculpted gardens, surrounding woods. Servants' quarters stood behind the upper mansion, and beyond that the barns, stables, and racetrack that Lyman had built in the 1870s for his trotters, and which Ariel, and later Elisha, modified for their Thoroughbreds. It was a day full of sun and small breezes, and under a broad white canopy, Roscoe, Patsy, and O.B., a late arrival, stood watch alongside Elisha, the enigma in the open coffin, who looked great dead, in his gray linen suit and white tie, his head wound cosmetically banished.

'What do you know that I don't?' Patsy asked when Roscoe arrived at his side.

'Alex is on the way home. He was already a day out on the troopship when he got the news. Bart or Joey will pick him up when he docks.'

'I'm talking about Eli's autopsy.'

'Mac's bringing that over.'

'He's on the way,' O.B. said, looking authoritative in his police chief's uniform, buttons polished and gleaming in the sunlight. 'We did two autopsies, one real, one fake.'

'But we don't know why he did it,' said Patsy.

'We will,' Roscoe said. 'He can't just kill himself like this and get away with it.'

'He took a hell of a lot with him,' Patsy said. 'We'll need six guys to take his place.'

'Six is nowhere near enough,' Roscoe said.

Elisha's coffin lay on a pedestal beneath the canopy, halfway between the gatehouse and Veronica's swimming pool. Shiny green smilax leaves covered the bottom half of the coffin, which was ringed with orchids from the Fitzgibbon hothouses. On the lawn's very long slope perhaps a thousand floral arrangements, far more than anyone could ever recall seeing in one place, lay as a crescent-shaped blanket of regret that Elisha had gone away.

He had five official mourners: Veronica, and their twelve-year-old adopted son, Gilby, who looked sticklike and bored in black linen suit and black tie, his hair brushed flat, his acne getting serious; Elisha's two sisters, Emily and Antonia, and his brother, Gordon, the banker, who were already crowding

Veronica for control of the mill. Roscoe, Patsy, and O.B. stood as unofficial mourners at the head of the coffin, close to Veronica but away from contact with the endless line of wakegoers.

And here they came, into their third hour: wealthy lawyers, doctors, bankers, and businessmen, the financial peerage with whom Elisha had lunched almost daily at the Fort Orange Club; also the blue-book women, lady golfers, legislative wives, garden-club matrons whom he courted socially and won politically; several Catholic priests and rabbis, and all the Episcopal clerics in town; countless steelworkers and secretaries from the Fitzgibbon mill; and all three rings and sideshow of the Democratic circus: pomaded ward leaders, aldermen and committeemen, underpaid undersheriffs, jailers, lawyers and clerks, bloated contractors, philanthropic slumlords, nervous bookmakers unaccustomed to sunlight.

Happy McGraw, no known occupation, ever, edged out of line to shake hands with the rumpled boss who ran the town: Hello, Patsy, how's yourself, what a loss, Pat, you and Eli were friends a long time, he was such a good fellow, keep well, Pat, you're looking grand, can you spare five? And Patsy: Not here, Hap, button your pants before they fall off and see me Sunday after mass, not saying which mass or which church, he'll find me. Ah, God love ya, Pat, Hap said, fading away with a smile.

Ex-Governor Herbert Lehman, who fought Elisha for the gubernatorial nomination in '32, held Veronica's hand, and Walter Foley, ex-editor of the *Times-Union,* the first paper to support Patsy's run for assessor in 1919, kissed her on the cheek, as did Marcus Gorman. Patsy's brother was in line, Benjamin (Bindy) McCall, who'd gained a hundred and fifty pounds in the six years since the Thorpe brothers hired Lorenzo Scarpelli to kill him; and, behind Bindy, Joe Colfels, who, because he went to school with Elisha, was now a Supreme Court judge; and Moishe (Mush) Trainor, who made seven million running beer with Patsy in Prohibition and blew it gambling; and Deputy Mayor Karl Weingarten, who took over as mayor when Alex joined the army. They'd all come for a last look at the dead leader who had helped create their politics, their livelihood, their city, came also to prove publicly their personal loyalty to the leaders who weren't dead, Roscoe and Patsy.

The harmony of the Episcopal boys' choir signaled the advent of the ceremonial moment, and the end of personal contact with the mourners, though two hundred were still in line. Seventy incumbent state senators and assemblymen walked toward the coffin, paying collegial homage to the erstwhile Lieutenant Governor, who had presided over the New York State Senate during the 1933–34 sessions.

Roscoe moved to Veronica's side before the legislators reached the canopy. He could not resist the urge to touch her, for she was solemnly but irresistibly seductive in her elegant black chiffon mourning gown and strand of pearls, a gift from Elisha. Her eyes, without tears, were brilliant with rapt obligation to public grief.

'How are you holding up?' He touched her shoulder.

'I'm a zombie,' she said.

Most beautiful zombie Roscoe ever saw. 'How are you doing, Gilby?' Gilby was staring at Elisha in his coffin.

'He didn't say goodbye, Roscoe.'

'That's true. He went very suddenly. But we're saying goodbye now.'

'Everybody should say goodbye to him.'

'You're right. And everybody *is* here.'

'Not everybody,' Gilby said, and he looked at his mother.

'Who's missing?' Roscoe asked. But Gilby was running across the lawn toward the stables.

'You gave him permission to get the dogs,' Veronica said. 'He wanted them here but I said no. We put them in the tack room.'

Roscoe saw Gilby open the stable door as the dean of the Episcopal Cathedral began reading the funeral service, the lesson from St. John: 'Jesus saith, let not your heart be troubled,' which is easy to say. And then followed a hymn of comfort, 'The Strife Is O'er; the Battle Done,' a wrong message, for the battle hadn't even begun. How can you do battle if you don't know the point of the war, or who the enemy is?

Roscoe broke away from the hymn singing when he saw Mac crossing the lawn, and went to meet him. They went to the far end of the east portico, where no one could eavesdrop. Mac, full name Jeremiah McEvoy, wearing a blue-and-white seersucker suit, blue tie, and coconut straw hat with a blue-and-white band, ficey little well-dressed cop, handed Roscoe two autopsy reports, one for publication on Elisha, dead of coronary occlusion; and one on Abner Sprule, an alias the Party used instead of John Doe when it suited them. Chloral hydrate killed Sprule, enough to put away two people.

'Is there a body that goes with the Sprule autopsy?' Roscoe asked.

'We got a wino out of the river we can use.'

Elisha had obviously gambled that Roscoe, Patsy, and O.B. would find a way to cover up his death. They'd done it for others. Yet it was sloppy; and Roscoe concluded Elisha ran out of time for punctiliousness, sudden death his only pressing issue.

'A whole lot of chloral hydrate,' Roscoe said.

'You're gonna do it, do it so it gets done,' Mac said.

'You know that, all right.' And Roscoe remembered when Mac, tipped by an informer, went to Union Station to meet a gunman coming to town on a train to either collect a gambling debt from Roscoe or shoot him in the knee. Mac disarmed the visitor, put him in the back of his detective car and shoved a pistol under his rump, explaining that Albany was a city of law and order, shot him through both buttocks, and drove him to see Dr. Johnny (The Butcher) Merola, the designated abortionist for and inspector general of Albany's prostitutes, to have his wounds treated. Johnny doped up the visitor, and Mac and his partner put him in a Pullman compartment on the train back to Buffalo so he could suffer in private when he woke up. Roscoe, knees still intact, thanks you, Mac.

Roscoe read in the Sprule medical report that Elisha's heart was twice its normal size. He could've dropped dead anytime. Both autopsies were done by Neil Deasey, coroner's physician, who found whatever Patsy told him to find in any given corpse. So now Veronica and the Party would not be publicly embarrassed, and Elisha's insurance not jeopardized. As to the real cause of death, that was the Party's business. Was Elisha's enlarged heart a true fact or a Neil Deasey fact? Could Elisha have known this about his heart? He could. Blighted kamikaze. Roscoe put the autopsies in his inside coat pocket.

'Mac,' Roscoe said, 'you know when every pimp and felon sneezes in this town. You ever hear any threat to Elisha?'

'I hear the troopers are ready to move against the organization, but no word on what or who. Maybe close down our gambling, don't know. You wanna shut down the city before they do?'

'That'd be a first,' Roscoe said. 'Maybe close the horse rooms.'

'Is that a yes? I'll start making the rounds.'

'Let me talk to Patsy.'

'Right. You take Gladys home the other night?'

'Why do you ask?'

'She said you did.'

'Don't you believe her?'

'I like to make sure she gets home safe,' Mac said.

Roscoe saw O.B. coming at quick time across the lawn to the portico.

'Patsy wants the autopsies,' O.B. said to Mac.

'I've got them,' Roscoe said. 'I'll see he gets them.'

'This thing is almost over,' O.B. said. 'I'm not going to the cemetery. I'll ride back with you, Mac.'

'Mac says word's around about a crackdown, maybe on gambling. You hear that?' Roscoe asked O.B.

'Twice a week, every week.'

'We should take it seriously. Patsy'll probably want to close the horse rooms. Let 'em do phone business.'

'You don't think the troopers'll tap the phones?'

'The bookies take that risk, not us.'

'They're gonna scream,' O.B. said.

'You ever know a bookie didn't scream?' Roscoe asked.

O.B. and Mac went down the steps and toward Mac's car, and Roscoe crossed the lawn to hear the boys' choir singing 'Nearer My God to Thee.' He saw Gladys sitting at the end of a row with, guess who, Trish, also Minnie Hausen, who handled legislative patronage for Patsy, and Hattie Wilson, dear old Hat. Roscoe stood in Gladys's sight line until she eyed him, then he went to her, took her aside.

'Did you tell Mac I took you home from the mill?'

'No.'

'Why would he say you did?'

'I said you offered to. He keeps tabs on me.'

'Not on my account.'

'It's everybody.'

Roscoe stood with Patsy for the rest of the hymn singing, wondering whether Gladys or Mac was lying, and why. At hymn's end the Episcopal dean opened his prayer book, and Roscoe heard the snort of a horse. He turned to see Gilby riding out from the stable, a collie and a German shepherd at the heels of Jazz Baby, the eleven-year-old Thoroughbred gelding that had held such promise for Elisha as a racehorse until he turned into a bleeder, going too fast too young, and Elisha brought him back, but as a riding horse, and gave him to Gilby for his tenth birthday. Gilby, his black coat and tie both gone, his sleeves rolled, at home in the saddle, rode Jazz Baby slowly toward the wake and stopped at the outer edge of the crowd.

'My father didn't say goodbye to Jazz Baby,' Gilby said. He ducked his head, moved the horse forward under the canopy. The mourners stepped back to make room.

'Bizarre,' said Gordon Fitzgibbon.

'Not at all,' said Roscoe, and he walked ahead of the horse, slowly, as Gilby positioned Jazz Baby's head facing Elisha in the coffin.

Veronica was smiling for the first time in three days, and Roscoe, a sap for animals, was near tears. Gilby held the horse for a long look, then said, 'Okay, Baby.' He threaded the horse between coffin and mourners and, on the lawn, broke into a canter toward the woods.

Elisha smiled up at Roscoe. 'EP thinks that boy is ready ratoo,' he said. 'Right on the bibbity bing.'

The Gossip Begins

Six days after the funeral Roscoe walked up the wide, curving path to the Tivoli swimming pool where Veronica said she'd be if he came over before noon. The walkway was sculpted with gray stone that Duke Willard had carted down from the Helderbergs in his wagons when Ariel leveled part of the south meadow to build tennis courts for his wife, Millicent, the mother of Elisha. Roscoe and Elisha played on the courts as boys, but after Ariel caught Millicent naked with her tennis teacher and divorced her, she ceased being mentioned in the family, and tennis as a pastime went to hell. Elisha, in turn, excavated the courts out of existence, building in their place the swimming pool Veronica wanted. Roscoe remembered two suckling pigs rotating on the spit, and the famous oyster roast catered by Jack Rosenstein for Veronica's pool opening, where Elisha announced that roast oysters were the next-best thing to money.

Roscoe did not think so highly of money, the principal difference, after not having Veronica as a wife, between himself and Elisha. Roscoe made money from the Stanwix brewery he inherited, also from politics; but money was never a reason for him to get out of bed. As to Veronica, a reason for any man to get *into* bed, there she was, sitting by her pool, all alone with the new totality of her fortune, sleek in her rattan lawn chair, long legs elevated, feet in open-toed straw sandals, only her tanned arms and legs getting the noonday sun. Her straw picture hat shaded her face and neck, and her white sundress shielded the rest, except where it dipped at her breasts and fell away at one thigh. Remember her in that white tank suit at the pool opening? It can still bring Roscoe low, thinking how close he came to having this woman for his own. Now he has another chance; also another chance to be brought low. Elisha stood beside her that day at the pool opening, wearing his dinner jacket over bathing trunks, proclaiming her the Empress of Water. Look at her now, even in grief exuding the poise of a queen, while Roscoe, the serf, trembles with subjection. It's good he no longer needs her.

Veronica smiled as Roscoe sat in the lawn chair facing her, that smile bidding him welcome, her head tipped at the angle of affection which he read as being for him alone. But think, Roscoe: isn't that how she welcomes the world?

'You found me,' she said.

'Remind me, did I lose you? Lately?'

'You're always in my life.'

'How's your condition?'

'Perfectly dreadful and getting worse. A communiqué from my sister.'

She handed Roscoe a fold of papers that lay on a table beside her: a writ of habeas corpus from State Supreme Court, through the law firm of Voss, Gorman, and Kiley. Roscoe read: 'People ex Relator Pamela Morgan Yusupov, plaintiff, against Veronica Morgan Fitzgibbon, defendant . . . We command you that you have the body of Gilbert David Rivera Yusupov, by you imprisoned and detained, as it is said, together with time and cause of such imprisonment and detention . . . before Supreme Court at a Special Term in the County Court House in Albany,' etc. And from Pamela's petition: '. . . your petitioner, as mother of Gilbert David

Rivera Yusupov, an infant of the age of twelve years, makes application on behalf of said infant for a writ of habeas corpus. Petitioner further shows she is the mother of said infant, having given birth to him on July 12, 1933, that his father is the late Danilo Yusupov. . . .'

'Is this the first she admitted she's Gilby's mother?'

'As far as I know. She called Elisha months ago and said she wanted Gilby back. He told her that was absurd; nobody was taking Gilby. He thought it was a desperation scheme to get money and that we wouldn't hear any more.'

'He never mentioned this to me. Was she his enemy closing in?'

'Perhaps she was. Will you handle the case, Roscoe?'

'Me? I'm rusty on trial work, Vee.' He slapped the legal papers with the back of his hand. 'She's got Marcus Gorman, best criminal lawyer in town. They were made for each other.'

'Will you *please* take the case?'

'What does Gilby know about this?'

'He doesn't even know Pamela's his mother.'

'Oh boy. Who knows?'

'You, me, and Elisha. It was always our best-kept secret. Now everybody will know. Will you, *will* you take the case?'

'Get a solid trial lawyer, Vee. Get Frank Noonan.'

'Gilby loves you and I don't care how rusty you are. You're smarter than twenty lawyers.'

'If I was smart I'd have taken the case already.'

Veronica leaned forward, her face inches from Roscoe.

'You took it when I handed you the papers. You play dumb when you think it's the smart thing to do.'

'Are you trying to make me feel dumber than I am?'

'No, but see how smart you are to think so?'

* * *

Veronica, Pamela, and their late brother, Lawrence, were children of Julia Sullivan, a poor Irish Catholic girl from Arbor Hill, and David Morgan, son and heir of a German immigrant peddler who built a fortune making scouring powder.

Pamela Marion Morgan, the second child of Julia and David, gave birth in 1933 to a son in a lying-in clinic in the elite Condado section of San Juan, Puerto Rico, near the beachfront house she won in a divorce settlement from her second husband, a Puerto Rican sugar baron. She lived the last five months of her pregnancy there with Esmerelda Rivera, a Puerto Rican cook and maid of temperate personality who, by the end of the fifth month, had been transformed into a quivering but well-paid wreck by the rages of Doña Pamela. Obsessively secret about her pregnancy, Pamela went out rarely, and wore a black wig when she did. She received few visitors, among them her wealthy fiancé, Danilo Yusupov, an exiled Russian prince who, like Pamela, was thrice-wed; both he and she famous for being married splashily and often. Pamela's festive blond hair and Yusupov's mustache were recurring images in New York society pages.

Veronica, Elisha, and Roscoe also visited Pamela, the first time to have her sign the agreement Roscoe had drawn up, and to arrange its filing with San Juan's birth registry. It legitimized Veronica and Elisha's custody of this child of anonymous mother, without Pamela's yielding her right to repossess the child. Veronica went to Puerto Rico a second time, with Roscoe but without Elisha, whose duties as Lieutenant Governor kept him in Albany, to register the child's birth and bring him home. The boy was given the first name of Gilbert for John Gilbert, the silent-film star with whom Pamela claimed to have exchanged passions after he broke up with Garbo; middle name of David, in memory of his grandfather; and fraudulent surname of Rivera, expropriated from Pamela's maid.

When Pamela told Veronica she was having the child – 'I don't want it but won't abort it, do you want to raise it?' – Veronica read this as Pamela's sympathy for Veronica's loss of her five-year-old daughter, Rosemary, in 1928, and for Veronica's ongoing inability to conceive another child. Then, in the beach house after the birth, Veronica watched Pamela, propped in bed on pillows, eyes exhausted, her dark-yellow hair a bag of strings, her face flushed and blotched, throwing peeled hard-boiled eggs at the overweight poodle she saw by appointment. The poodle caught the eggs on the fly or chased them like tennis balls and swallowed them without a chew. Pamela smiled with her bee-stung lips, painted for her visitors, and said with great verve to Veronica and Roscoe, 'Thank God, thank God I'm no longer a mother,' and threw the poodle another egg. Veronica, ecstatic with the infant in her arms, understood then that motherhood would be a splotch on Pamela's social canvas and, should the splotch become an out-of-wedlock scandal, her marriage to the royal Yusupov would not happen. Also, Prince Yusupov, with two children from other marriages, had only contempt for this bastard son, and wanted no more children. Veronica clutched Gilby closer as she realized this. Then she and Roscoe spirited him out of Pamela's life and onto Elisha's private plane back to Albany.

'First they take my beautiful daughter, then my husband, now they want my son,' Veronica said to Roscoe at poolside.

'The law may say he's Pamela's son.'

'She gave him up. We have it in writing.'

'It wasn't a legal adoption, Vee. All you have in writing is permission to raise Gilby. She could always change her mind. Mothers have clout.'

'After twelve years? I'm his only mother.'

'That's what the court hearing will be about.'

'No, the hearing will be about money, what Pamela's always about. The Prince just died and Pamela wants custody as the widowed mother so she can claim support for the child Yusupov fathered.'

'Did Elisha know this?'

'He thought she'd sue us if she got frantic. Gilby also has a trust fund with a hundred thousand in it, and Elisha made it Pamela-proof. But if she gets wind of it she'll try to tap into that too.'

'Does she ever see Gilby?'

'She sent him a train set last Christmas. "From your loving Aunt Pammy." He outgrew trains three years ago.'

'Do you see her?'

'Not in years. You know how close we were as children, but when boys came along I was the enemy. She bedded every man she fancied. She was always after Elisha.'

'Did she nail him?'

'Don't *you* know?'

'Me?' said Roscoe. 'How would I know?'

'Even if you knew you'd never say,' Veronica said. 'This is so unbelievably awful. Elisha not dead two weeks and she tries to steal my boy.'

'She thinks you're vulnerable.'

'God, Roscoe, I can't abide any more of this.' Veronica took off her hat, tossed her hair, and smiled. 'So. So. How are you and Trish-trash doing?'

'I thought I got rid of her, but she came flying back like a boomerang.'

'She seemed very civilized at the wake.'

'A polite pause between psychotic eruptions.'

'Why do you bother with her?'

'Do I have to explain that?'

'You shouldn't be so needy.'

'You don't know about need, Veronica . . .'

'Oh, don't I?'

'. . . or the charm of trash.'

'Elisha was amused by trash.'

'Really? I never noticed that in him.'

'Of course you didn't, you two trash collectors.'

'Did you swim yet this morning?' he asked.

'Not yet. Do you want to swim? You have trunks in the pool house.'

'Do *you* want to swim? That's the question.'

'We're in this deep water together now, aren't we?'

She stood and took off her sundress. Contoured sublimely by her clinging tank suit, solid black for mourning under water, she walked to the pool's edge and dove in, Olympically. Roscoe watched her swim, then walked to the pool house, shed his clothing, and pulled on his bathing trunks, the snake's new skin. Slithy Roscoe: protector of widow and child, surrogate husband without privilege, barrister and sleuth for hire, quester for buried love and answers to vexing secrets, what a useful tub-of-guts you've become. He blinked as he stepped into the sunlight, exposing his Homeric girth to her inspection.

'Are you prepared to gaze upon this pale orb of corpulence?' he asked.

'You seem to be getting thin,' she said, treading water.

'Your lies are like candied kumquats,' he said. 'But neither largeness nor love can be hid.' He bounced twice on the diving board, then cut the water with a graceful arc, pleased with his boldness, and saying in midair, 'We must all to the wars – again,' and with pain stabbing him in some unidentified internal organ, he sank beneath a great wave of his own making.

A Fitzgibbon kitchen maid brought to poolside the iced tea and crustless ham and chicken sandwiches Veronica had requested. On the tray with the food was the *Albany Sentinel*, which had arrived by courier with a cover note from Gladys Meehan: 'Dear Veronica, This came into the office this morning with the other newspapers, and I thought you should see it as soon as possible. If there's *anything* I can do, please call.'

Roscoe unfolded the paper, which was open to the page with the 'Ghost Rider,' a gossip column, and he and Veronica read together the item Gladys had outlined in red pencil:

> **COURTROOM DRAMA!** The Mayor's kid brother, Gilby Fitzgibbon, may only be his cousin! Mayor's mother, Veronica Fitzgibbon, is being sued by her socialite sister, Pamela Morgan Yusupov, for custody of Gilby, who, she sez, is her boy. Coming atop of sudden death of hubby Elisha Fitzgibbon, this is doubly troubly for Mrs. Fitz. . . . Fitzgibbon death also a big loss for local Dems. . . . Remember Mayor Goddard dying strangely in Havana in 1928? . . . Speaking of grave matters, Ghost Rider hears a recent sudden death from natural causes looks like suicide!

'How did they get that?' Veronica asked.

'Her lawyer had to file the petition with the county clerk,

and some reporter found it, or was tipped off. Nasty but legal.'

'You think they're talking about Elisha's suicide?'

'I think I'll visit the *Sentinel* and inquire.'

He wrapped two chicken sandwiches in a napkin and ate them on the drive to the *Sentinel*. The gossip boiled his juices, and by the time he reached Newspaper Row at Green and Beaver Streets he was shaping the curses he'd heap upon Roy Flinn, the publisher. The Flinns were cascading back into Roscoe's life: first Arlene, then dead Artie, now Roy.

Roscoe climbed the stairs to the loft where the weekly *Sentinel* had been founded by Warren Skaggs, a printer, in 1909, and thrived in the era of Republican control of the city. Skaggs did city printing business for the Republicans and also started printing, then backing, the Albany baseball pool in 1920 as a neighborhood venture with a fifteen-dollar weekly prize. Popularity grew, prizes swelled to nine hundred dollars, then three thousand, and the pool's take kept escalating.

Players, for a dollar a play, chose six numbers (from one to sixteen), one for each day of play: Monday to Saturday. As the week began, the pool published a key that matched a number with each of the sixteen big-league baseball teams. Pool players whose numbers matched the six teams that accumulated the greatest number of runs during the week won the prize. The game appealed not only to baseball fans but to every sucker who believed in the easy dollar, and Albany was blessed with many.

Patsy paid serious attention to the pool for the first time at Willie Altopeda's funeral in 1924, when he saw Warren Skaggs, a Republican, driving a four-thousand-dollar

Cadillac. 'I knew the bum when he couldn't afford a wheelbarrow,' Patsy said.

Artie Flinn, a quick-witted gambler from Arbor Hill who'd grown up with Patsy, enlightened him on how profitable Skaggs's baseball pool was. Patsy then invited Skaggs and his partners to share pool profits with him fifty-fifty. Skaggs gnashed his teeth and said no. Patsy threatened to have the police close the pool and put Skaggs and company in jail, but said he'd accept a lesser cut if Artie Flinn became a pool associate.

Patsy, the pool's new panjandrum, expanded its territory and sales force, and by 1926, when he took it away from Skaggs entirely, pool plays were selling all over New England and New Jersey, and grossing four million for the year, not enough. The next summer Artie and Patsy implemented a plan to plug the pool – put thousands of dummy plays into competition with the public play. Artie oversaw the plugging, hiring young women at twenty-five dollars a week to write books full of plug plays, more than a hundred books a week, each book with twenty plays. Artie, his cohort of pluggers, and twenty accountants manipulated and published thousands of plays and combinations, okaying payoffs for enough legitimate winners to keep word-of-mouth at a frenzied pitch.

In May 1927, the pool announced its first prize of twenty-two thousand dollars had been won by 'Mutt,' second prize of sixteen thousand by 'Joan,' and third prize of eleven thousand shared by 'John Doe,' 'Beautiful,' and 'Marie,' all anonymous, and there were forty ties for the low prize of five thousand dollars. None of this bothered the public. Callers clogged newspaper switchboards for baseball results. Broadway, across from Union Station at four-thirty on

Saturday afternoons, was impassable to traffic as Sport Schindler posted, in front of his speakeasy, inning-by-inning scores of major-league games crucial to pool prizes. By the end of the 1928 baseball season the pool's gross for the year was five million; by 1929, seven million.

Warren Skaggs, a grumpy loser, kept his *Sentinel* running as a pesky hornet trying once a week to sting Democrats. That his paper survived at all was because of its racy coverage of divorces and scandals. Cautious readers carried it home under their coats. In 1929, it printed two dozen torchy love letters, all forgeries, from a 1908 Love Nest Scandal involving an Albany playwright and an actress, and when the playwright won a libel settlement against Skaggs, Patsy used this outrage as a reason to pressure advertisers to withdraw their ads. Skaggs had to close the paper.

In September 1930, a federal prosecutor moved against the pool for violation of the interstate-lottery law, indicting Artie and two dozen others, including Warren Skaggs, who testified with great relish about Patsy's takeover and Artie's plug system, and also brought Elisha's name into it. Patsy was subpoenaed to appear before Artie's grand jury but vanished and lived as a fugitive for three weeks before he figured out what to say. He surrendered to his attorney, Roscoe Conway, and came to federal court to testify.

Q: Are you in business in Albany?
A: I have no business in Albany.
Q: Are you in business anywhere else?
A: No, sir.
Q: How do you make a living.
A: I am vague on that.
Q: How did you formerly make a living?

A: I ran my father's saloon until the Volstead Act closed it.
Q: You haven't worked since 1920? How do you live?
A: I do a little betting on horses and prizefights.
Q: On baseball pools?
A: I refuse to answer because it might degrade or incriminate me.
Q: You make a living on betting?
A: That and what I owe.
Q: How can you make a living on what you owe?
A: A good many people do that.
Q: Have you ever heard of the Albany baseball pool?
A: I am vague on that.
Q: Do you know a man named Warren Skaggs?
A: I am vague on that.
Q: Did you know anyone named Skaggs connected to a baseball pool?
A: I am vague on that.

The judge found him guilty of contempt and sentenced him to six months in a federal jail in Manhattan. No other charges were brought, for only Skaggs's word linked Patsy to the pool. Artie, some of whose accountants and young-lady pluggers testified against him to avoid jail, was convicted and sentenced to six years, the start of his enmity toward Patsy over the imbalance of justice. Warren Skaggs was fined five thousand dollars and given a year's suspended sentence.

Skaggs felt less than welcome in Albany after his testimony against Artie and Patsy, so he sold his printing plant, plus the rights to his defunct *Sentinel,* for a pittance to the only buyer who dared be interested, Artie's son, Roy, who had been a *Sentinel* scandal editor before Patsy took over the pool.

Was Roscoe disturbed by the plugging? It did seem less than sporting. But can one sensibly retreat to the moral high ground when major money is on the table? Roscoe's cut made him flush enough to dabble in racehorses with Elisha and Veronica, but his cut was minuscule compared with Patsy's, which was bundled and banked out of state in Wilkes-Barre under various names, and held in readiness for the next Democratic crisis. What did Patsy do for himself with his new millions? He left larger tips at Keeler's and the Elks Club bar, let ward leaders steal more than last year, bet heavier on chickens, and bought a new Panama hat.

Roy Flinn continued the Skaggs printing business and in 1943 asked Roscoe if the organization would let him resurrect the long-dead *Sentinel* as a patriotic sheet covering local people in military service, plus local gossip in and out of the courts, but absolutely no political content. Roscoe and Roy had been classmates at Christian Brothers Academy, an Albany military high school, and because of that connection, and still smarting with guilt over Artie, Roscoe persuaded Patsy to give Roy the okay. Roy ran the paper with two reporters and a photographer, and also wrote the anonymous 'Ghost Rider' himself.

Roscoe halted at the door to the *Sentinel* and took six deep breaths, his usual tactical pause to retreat from rage. First find out what Roy knows, for he does tell secrets.

Roy Flinn's Secret

In their senior year of high school, Roy came to Roscoe's house to tell him that he had a chancre, a gift from the eighteen-year-old girl he'd been boffing, with modifiers, four times a week, and who told him one night, Roy, gimme it for real, and who turned up at the side door of Roy's house on Christmas Day with a predictable second gift, asking for help getting rid of it.

Roy came to Roscoe because Roscoe knew people, and Roscoe talked to Patsy, who recommended an Arbor Hill doctor who said, sure, thirty bucks up front, which Roy and the girl did not have. So she got some how-to-do-it advice elsewhere, waited until her parents left town, then went at it in the cellar with assorted implements and a piece of wire, sitting on a spread of newspapers. After a while she strapped herself to keep the blood from staining the world and called in sick at Marie's Millinery on North Pearl Street, where she sold ladies' hats.

When she could function she went to Roy's and brought him home, opened the door of her furnace, and showed him how she had burned the bloody papers but not the baby. 'He don't burn,' she said. Roy took out the fetus, stoked the fire with wood, and heaped on the coal, terrified that the girl's father might walk in and murder him on the spot. He wrapped the unburned baby in a blanket of newspaper and put it on the flaming coals with a shovel. Soon there was a strong odor in the cellar, said Roy. He kept feeding the fire, and after a few hours there was nothing at all among the coals. Roy still had his chancre, however. And arsenic, mercury, bismuth, and shame were his treatment for years afterward.

He never married, was rejected by the army in the Great War, and turned into a peephole columnist, voyeur at the sex games his trauma had kept him from playing. You are one sad bastard, and it could happen to anybody, Roy, but that's no excuse. Roscoe whistled his way into the news office at the front of the print shop.

'Roy Flinn, where the hell are you?' Roscoe called out jovially as he entered. He saluted two reporters typing at their desks and saw Roy emerge from the back room with a handful of galleys. Tieless, in shirtsleeves, fingers stained with printer's ink, Roy Flinn was an angular, bony figure, his hair plastered down with Vaseline, a twisted and bitter freak of fate.

'Roscoe, you rascal,' said Roy, 'what brings you here? You have some news for me?'

'News? What would you do with news, Roy? You know less about news than my sister, who thinks Wilson is still President. You find your news scrawled on public-toilet walls. Even your saintly sister, Arlene, is repelled by your sheet. News, Roy? I'm stunned you can even use the word in a sentence.'

'Roscoe, old mushmouth, I've heard your song before. Why are you here?'

'Why do geese run funny, Roy? I'm here because your scurrilous scribbles summoned me.'

'The item on the Fitzgibbon custody suit?'

'That suit is public record. I'm talking about your innuendo on Goddard, and that Elisha committed suicide.'

'I didn't say that.'

'Roy, I am fluent in the English language, and you are fluent in the language of pollywogs.'

Roscoe pulled the *Sentinel* out of his pocket and read from the 'Ghost Rider' item: '"Remember Mayor Goddard dying strangely in Havana in 1928? . . . Speaking of grave matters, Ghost Rider hears a recent death from natural causes looks like suicide!" Dying strangely, grave matters, and suicide. I consider that innuendo, Roy.'

'Goddard's death was never explained and you know it.'

'He died of an infection.'

'After he fell out of a car.'

'He was drunk,' Roscoe said. 'Drunks fall out of cars. Drunks fall out of bed.'

'A lot of people thought it was strange.'

'I find it strange that you bring it up in context with Elisha and then add that insidious suicide item.'

'That item has nothing to do with Elisha.'

'Who, then?'

'I can't reveal that.'

Roscoe grabbed a handful of Roy's shirtfront, shoved him against a wall. 'Are you invoking constitutional privilege here, Roy? Or claiming protection under the sacrosanctity of journalistic ethics? What are you talking about?'

'I can't say.'

Roscoe slid Roy up the wall with one hand and held him there, the move pulling out Roy's shirttail and tightening his collar into a noose.

'You're a lying stringbean traitor. You were told no politics.'

'Let go of me, Roscoe,' Roy said, a windpipe croak.

'Why did you print that, Roy? Tell me why.'

'You people are in trouble,' Roy said.

Roscoe slid Roy down the wall and released his shirt. 'Trouble?'

'You'll probably beat it like you always do,' Roy said, righting his collar, 'but you're in for a dogfight.'

'With what dogs?'

'The Governor's people know Elisha owned a block of whorehouses. That's just the beginning.'

Roscoe's right elbow suddenly bent upward, and his fist,

from a position of rest, whomped Roy's face with three rapid snaps of the full forearm, Roy's head hitting the wall and rebounding into each new whomp.

'There, Roy,' Roscoe said as Roy stumbled sideways to lean on a desk, 'there you have your headlines. Lawyer punches out editor for maligning his friend. Genuine news.'

As he left, Roscoe saluted the two reporters, who were out of their chairs, trying to decide how to rescue Roy. 'See you later, fellas,' he said, reveling in the vision of Roy's blood and licking his own bleeding Purple Heart, his big knuckle stabbed by Roy's hostile fangs. He remembered his father's commandment on justice – Never let an enemy go unpunished – and he thought, I did all right, Pa, didn't I?

Roscoe drove twenty-five minutes to Patsy's summer place to give him the news. It was situated on a Helderberg mountainside that gave a one-hundred-and-eighty-degree vista of Patsy's Garden of Eden, the city and county of Albany. Patsy's father had built a cedar-shingled summer bungalow on the land when he was sheriff. When the old man died, Patsy winterized the place, added a second story, built outbuildings to breed fighting chickens and a pit where they could fight. In the years after the Party took City Hall, the house became the summer hub of political action. Principal Albany Democrats made regular pilgrimages here to listen to Patsy the oracle tell them what they should think tomorrow.

Wally Mitchell, an ex-heavyweight who knocked down Jim Jeffries and was now Patsy's driver and bodyguard, unlocked the chain across the driveway and waved Roscoe in. Such security had been the norm since a homegrown gang of bootleggers tried to shoot Bindy and later kidnapped his son,

Charlie Boy McCall. Roscoe saw Bindy's custom-made, bulletproof black Packard, and he parked alongside it. He stepped out into the sunshine of a clear August afternoon and could see everything, from the beginning of the patchwork fruited plain at the base of the mountains, all the way in to the tower of Albany's splendid City Hall and the Al Smith State Office Building, Albany's modest skyscraper. He saw the shadow of a cloud moving fast across the plain below, but in the clear, blue-white sky he could find no cloud. He saw Patsy and Bindy near the chicken coops and went to them.

'How fare the chickens of this world?' Roscoe asked.

'Chickens is chickens,' Patsy said. 'Fight 'em and eat 'em.'

'The received wisdom of history,' Roscoe said. 'Don't you fellows have a main coming up?'

'Tomorrow night, up in Fogarty's,' Bindy said.

'Been weedin' out my sick ones,' Patsy said, a chicken under his arm. 'One of my tough guys's got the megrims, feedin' it too much. And this guy got the chicken pox fightin' his friends. His head's pecked all to hell.'

The McCall brothers had raised chickens since early adolescence in North Albany. Later, when they moved to Arbor Hill, Patsy kept his coops in a stable next to his house on Colonie Street, but as the chickens grew in number he was deemed a neighborhood nuisance and told to get rid of them. A politically connected neighbor let him put his coops on the Albany County Courthouse roof, the beginning of Patsy's life above the law.

Patsy put his poxy chicken back on the walk and led the way to the kitchen. Wally Mitchell was lifting a blue roasting pan out of the oven, two cooked chickens in it. He put forks under the chickens and moved them onto a white stoneware platter. The house smelled like Sunday.

'Cook those yourself, Wally?' Roscoe asked. Wally's left ear, from heavy use by others, looked like a partly eaten chicken wing.

'I don't cook,' Wally said. 'I do the heavy liftin'.'

Rose Carbone, Patsy's full-time housekeeper ever since Patsy's wife, Flora, died, stood at the sink washing a pot.

'Did you make the gravy?' Patsy asked Rose.

'I did not and I would not and you know it,' she said.

'Good,' said Patsy.

Rose went out of the kitchen and Patsy said, 'She's all right but she can't make gravy.' He took a tin of flour from the pantry and put the roasting pan with its drippings on the gas stove and lit the burner. He mixed the flour with some water, poured it into the pan as the drippings began to boil, added salt, pepper, a splash of Kitchen Bouquet, and water from a kettle, then stirred the mix with a wooden spoon. Roscoe knew better than to try for Patsy's attention when he was cooking, so he sat at the kitchen table to watch a ritual that dated to their adolescent fishing trips, when Patsy cooked in self-defense against Roscoe's and Elisha's life-threatening concoctions; and again in the army in 1918, when shrapnel knocked Patsy off his horse; and after his leg healed they made him a cook's helper. Patsy poured the thickened brown gravy into a bowl and set it beside the chickens.

Bindy came out of the bathroom into the kitchen. 'You see that stuff in the *Sentinel*?' he asked Roscoe.

'I have some serious news on that,' Roscoe said.

Patsy nodded and put down his spoon and the three men walked through Patsy's workout room toward the parlor. Patsy punched the hanging bag and bent it in half. He sat in his parlor rocker, feet crossed on the floor, a book, *Hard Times*, open on his reading table, and under it the *Sentinel*.

His brown fedora sat on a straight chair by the door under the holy-water font, which was a Christmas gift from Father Tooher, pastor of St. Joseph's.

Roscoe sat in an armchair facing Patsy and Bindy, who weighed three pounds less than a horse and made Roscoe feel thin. Bindy sat on half the sofa, eating peanuts from a silver dish.

'I just punched out Roy Flinn,' Roscoe said.

'Nice,' Patsy said.

'That little pimple,' Bindy said.

'Veronica's a nervous wreck. I only went down to yell at Roy, but then he said Elisha owned a block of whorehouses. So I hit him.'

'Good,' Patsy said.

'He said we're in for a dogfight with the Governor. What do you make of that, Bindy?' Control of brothels and gambling had been Bindy's responsibility since the 1921 takeover.

'Dogfight?' Bindy said. 'I'll tell him about dogfight. I'll break both his legs. Put the Night Squad on him, Pat. Break both his legs.'

'You hear anything about raiding the whores?' Roscoe asked.

'They been snooping around Division Street,' Bindy said, 'but it don't feel like a raid.'

'Shouldn't we close the whores down to be safe?'

'How will anybody get laid?' Bindy asked.

'Tell the boys to have a go at their wives,' Roscoe said.

'We'll see a lot of rape.'

'This isn't forever,' Roscoe said. 'Just till we see the whites of their eyes.'

'If this goes public I'll catch hell from the Bishop,' Patsy said. 'Wouldn't hurt to give the girls a vacation.'

'How could Roy say that about Elisha?' Roscoe wondered.

'We had a big buy-up in '33,' Patsy said.

'I remember that,' Roscoe said, 'but not Elisha.'

'You were in Kentucky, screwing around with racehorses,' Patsy said.

'It happened fast,' Bindy said. 'Income from the madams fell two thousand in two weeks, two owners died, one left town, and three houses went dark. I told Patsy we oughta own them places, so we bought 'em. And kept buyin'.'

'Elisha bought them?' Roscoe asked.

'He organized the investors,' Patsy said.

Bankers panting to do business with the city could prove their sincerity by investing in whorehouse real estate, and lawyers could do the same by representing the whores when they were periodically arrested to put their pictures in the files, and to justify the Vice Squad's existence. Within two months the neighborhood of the whores was stabilized through dummy corporations, and whoredom also had new friends at court.

'Roy said Elisha owned the houses,' Roscoe said.

'He never owned 'em,' Patsy said.

'I wonder if his name is on any deeds.'

'He used front people.'

'But can they prove he was behind it?'

'I don't know how,' Patsy said. 'And who's gonna indict a dead man? They want us up against the wall for Alex's re-election. What I don't get is where Roy Flinn borrowed the balls to take us on.'

'Maybe he wants to get back at us for what happened to Artie.'

'Artie?' said Patsy. 'That's fifteen years ago.'

'Artie died six months ago in Poughkeepsie,' Roscoe said.

'Maybe it affected Roy. He didn't even want a death notice in the papers.'

'Where's his leverage?' Patsy asked.

'He's cozy with the Governor's gang, so maybe he feels protected,' Roscoe said. 'Also, his paper's heavy with ads from outside Albany – summer hotels, nightclubs, restaurants, dude ranches that don't worry about pressure from us.'

'Send a fire inspector down to that firetrap of his,' Bindy said. 'Make him spend thirty grand to bring it up to code. He'll come around.'

'Bad scene,' Roscoe said. 'Harassing the press, and the patriotic press at that. There are other ways.'

'Name a few,' Patsy said.

'Take over his block. You did it with the whorehouses.'

'The whole block?'

'It's a small block. Condemn one side to widen it for improved traffic flow, put in new sewer pipes. Pay Roy a quarter of what his building's worth, settle sweet with the – what? – three, four other landlords? Then we own the block. When Roy is gone and we've got the property, cancel the project.'

'Condemn the block,' Patsy said. 'Goddamn it, Roscoe, you are one twisted, beautiful sonofabitch.'

'That's what my mother always said.'

'You want some chicken?'

'Of course I want some chicken.'

'The gravy's good.'

'Life without gravy is not life,' Roscoe said.

As they went back to the kitchen for lunch, O.B. called to report that Roy Flinn and his lawyer were filing a third-degree assault charge against Roscoe. Roy's eyebrow and lip were badly split and his nose was broken.

'Have Rosy open court at two o'clock for the arraignment,' Roscoe told O.B. 'Tell him to set my bail at four hundred to make Roy feel good.'

'You'll be here, like an upstanding citizen,' O.B. said.

'Of course I'll be there. Two o'clock. On the dot.'

Patsy looked at his watch. 'Two o'clock's too early,' he said. 'You gotta eat your chicken.'

'Make that three o'clock,' Roscoe told O.B.

In Police Court, Roscoe could hear Roy Flinn's nose throbbing under its bandage as they stood before the bench to hear Rosy Rosenberg, whom Roscoe and Patsy had put on that bench, read the law relating to assault, and then set bail at four hundred dollars, 'in default of which you will be remanded to Albany County jail.' Roscoe smiled at Rosy, waved at Roy, and paid the four.

Horse Talk

They were in the east parlor of Tivoli when Gilby read the item about Pamela in the *Sentinel* and asked Veronica, 'Is it true she's my mother?'

Veronica told him, 'I'm your mother. She gave you up before you were born.'

'Now she wants me back.'

'She can't have you, and she won't get you.'

'Who's my father?'

'He's dead,' Veronica said. 'You didn't know him.'

'I don't know anything,' Gilby said, and he went out onto the porch.

'Where are you going? Listen to me!' But he kept walking. She caught up with him. 'Did I ever tell you what your

Grandma Julia used to say? "Patience and perseverance took the snail to Jerusalem."'

Gilby shrugged.

'When she was a girl,' Veronica said, 'she'd throw a penny off the bridge into Washington Park Lake and say, "I'm going to have a big, big house and a butler named Johnny," and she did.'

Gilby stared at her.

'She only went to third grade in school, but she owned the world. I'm talking about overcoming problems. Do you see that? It's like breeding a champion Thoroughbred. Your father and I always wanted that for you. You have money and brains and love, and you can't give that newspaper story any importance. What does the stupid *Sentinel* know about champions?'

Gilby went onto the back deck, vaulted the railing with one arm, and ran down the drive toward the stables.

'Gilby!' Veronica yelled. 'Listen to me! I want to tell you about this.' But he would not look back. She went down the steps of the deck and ran after him as fast as her high heels would allow. When she reached the second stable, he was saddling Jazz Baby. Ticky Blake, who for twenty-two years had trained Fitzgibbon horses, stopped brushing Mr. Bantry, Veronica's bay, and listened.

'Gilby, your life won't change,' Veronica said. 'I won't let it. I'm a strong person. Do you believe I'm strong? Well, I am, and we have powerful friends in all the courts, and I have more money than your aunt does to fight this, and I've won every fight I ever had with her.'

Gilby, in his white sneakers, stepped up into the saddle.

'Gilby,' Veronica said, 'talk to me.'

The boy nudged Jazz Baby onto the road and into open

pasture, toward the trail through the western woods.

'Saddle Mr. Bantry for me, Ticky,' she said, and she ran to the house and up to her bedroom and pulled herself out of her dress and slip and shoes. She stepped into her riding britches and boots, then shoved her arms into a pullover shirt, and double-timed down the stairs with her hair flying, a *laissez-faire* beauty when she wanted to be. She mounted Mr. Bantry and rode at a gallop into the woods after the boy, praying to her trinity of Gods – Jewish, Anglican, Catholic – that she would not lose Gilby, because she absolutely could not lose another thing, *not one*. Yet she seemed to be galloping toward more loss and new shame, the press again prying just as it had when Elisha was named a profiteer in the crazy baseball pool and he fled with her to Europe from a scandal that never really amounted to much, so supported was he by clergy and politicians of every stripe. Elisha, grand husband, you're gone, and you left Veronica in wicked confusion: grief still green but waning; men hovering at the wake, eyes probing her widowed beauty for just one wrinkle of welcome. But Veronica rejected every eye, wants no affection while she still cries in the half-empty bed. She's fighting the fears her loneliness generates, but they are smothering her.

She rode the trail to where it came out of the woods at Lake Tivoli. Maybe Gilby would go to the fishing shack to be there with his memories of Elisha. She should have told Gilby the history of his birth, as Elisha wanted, but she'd waited for him to come of age, so he could handle such disturbing rejection. They told him only that he was adopted, his parents' names unknown to them.

She saw the shack and dock and lake, which Gilby had not yet outgrown but would now think of as no longer his. It is yours, Gilby, and I'll see you keep it. She wanted to find him on the dock but he wasn't in sight. She turned onto another trail, seeing him ahead of her, then not. She stopped and listened for him, heard the rustling breath of the forest, the breath of her horse, but no sound of her boy. She had lost him. No, she would never lose him. He was gone. No, not gone. Gone. Never.

She came slowly back to the stables. Ticky was feeding the horses alfalfa and bran, and the shredded beet pulp. She stabled Mr. Bantry and looked toward the woods for Gilby. She saw Roscoe coming out of the house, and the sight of him was tonic. Things would change now.

Then here came Gilby, riding across the west pasture. He swung himself out of the saddle, and she was again struck by his resemblance to Elisha: lean and lanky and growing taller, and that same resolute jaw. His straight black hair blown wild, and those black eyes. Yusupov also had dark features. But from Gilby's boyhood, Veronica suspected Elisha, not Yusupov, was his father. She hinted this once to Roscoe, who explained that children grow up to look like the people they live with, and so do bulldogs.

'So you come back,' Ticky said as Gilby walked Jazz Baby to the hose bib outside the stable. 'You gonna stay awhile?'

Gilby did not answer.

'Aren't you going to talk to us?' Veronica asked.

Gilby did not answer, or look at her.

'What ails you, boy, you don't talk to your mama?' Ticky said. 'Where you get off on that?'

Gilby looped Jazz Baby's reins over the rail fence and took off his saddle. He filled a bucket with water from the hose, and washed the horse with a sponge.

'Lookit this boy don't talk to his mama. What kind of boy is that?'

'I don't have anything to say,' Gilby said softly.

'You got a whole lot to say you ain't sayin'.'

Gilby washed Jazz Baby's nose and whispered to the horse.

'Boy talks to his horse but don't talk to his mama.'

'It's all right, Ticky,' Veronica said, 'he'll talk when he's ready.'

'I did that with *my* mama,' Ticky said, 'my papa'd say, You don't wanna talk to peoples you get outa this house go live with that horse.'

'I can do that,' Gilby said.

'He can do that,' Ticky said. 'He can live with Jazz Baby, and Jazz Baby gonna cook breakfast for him. Jazz Baby gonna buy his shirts. Hey, Roscoe, you know this boy here don't talk to his mama, he gonna live with his horse.'

Roscoe nodded to Ticky, touched Veronica hello on the shoulder.

'You believe in horses, is that it?' Roscoe said to Gilby.

Gilby dropped the sponge into the bucket, took the scraper off its nail, and scraped water off Jazz Baby's flanks, shoulders, and haunches.

'Do you know how stupid horses are?' Roscoe said.

'They're not stupid,' Gilby said, scraping the haunches.

'Stupider than crabmeat,' Roscoe said.

'Horses are smart,' Gilby said, scraping faster.

'Gimme that scraper,' Ticky said. 'You gonna skin that horse.'

'Don't tell me how smart horses are,' Roscoe said. 'They tell too many lies.'

'Horses don't lie,' Gilby said.

'Are you serious? There's a broken horse for every light

on Broadway. You ever try to hide a tennis ball in a horse's ear? You can't do it. On the other hand, I never met a horse I didn't like.'

'Me either,' said Gilby with a tight-lipped smile.

'Why do you want to live with your horse?'

'Nobody tells me anything.'

'You mean that stuff in the *Sentinel* about the lawsuit?'

Gilby nodded.

'That's how you learn. You read the papers. You know you'll need a lawyer to fight this thing in court. You have any lawyer friends?'

'No.'

'Sure you do. Me.'

'Are you a lawyer?'

'I'm *your* lawyer. Your mother hired me.'

'When?'

'This morning.'

'She didn't tell me that.'

'We don't tell you everything all at once. We parcel it out. We ever tell you about Einstein's theory that light curves with gravity? We ever tell you how John Calvin tried to cancel Sunday baseball?'

'Nobody even told me where I was born.'

'San Juan, Puerto Rico. I was there.'

'You were? Where's Puerto Rico?'

'Down there in the middle of it all. It was a very hot day. Bright and sunny, the trade winds blowing in off the Atlantic, palm trees, sandy beach, whitecaps on the ocean. You were very good-looking when you were born. You looked like a pineapple. We brought you back here in your father's airplane right after you left the clinic with whatsername.'

'Aunt Pamela?'

'That's the one,' Roscoe said.

'Why does she want me? She doesn't even like me.'

'I don't know anybody she *does* like. She wants money and needs you to get at it, even though she couldn't wait to get rid of you. But your parents loved you and wanted you even before you were born.'

'What's my real name?'

'Gilbert David Fitzgibbon, as always. A stately name.'

'What's stately?'

'Dignified, magnificent. Don't let anybody change it.'

'Me and Alex have the same name, but he's not my brother.'

'He'll always be your brother.'

'He's my cousin.'

'Then he's your brother-cousin. Do you love him?'

'I guess so.'

'No guesses. Do you love him, yes or no?'

'Yes. But my father's not my father.'

'No, of course not.'

Roscoe took off his hat and coat, handed them to Veronica, and rolled up his shirtsleeves. He tipped over a bale of hay and stood on it, took Jazz Baby's reins, threw his right leg up, and mounted the horse.

'You gonna ride him?' Gilby asked.

'I might.'

'I didn't know you could ride. You don't have a saddle.'

'I used to ride bareback in rodeos. I was in ten or fifteen rodeos, one after the other.'

'You were never in the rodeo.'

'Well, you're right, But your father and I rode bareback plenty down in Texas. They all ride bareback down there.'

'My father didn't ride.'

'He gave you a pony, didn't he?'

'Yes.'

'And when you outgrew it he gave you a horse.'

'Yes.'

'But he wasn't much of a father, because he never rode a horse, right? And he never took you fishing, never took you to New York to see the lights of Times Square, never introduced you to Jack Dempsey, never gave you a bicycle or started a bank account so you'd have your own money, never sent you to one of the greatest schools in town, never taught you how to throw a baseball and a horseshoe, never took you down to Hyde Park so you could shake hands with the President, never let you sleep with him and your mother when burglars were coming up through the steam pipes, never took you to Laurel-and-Hardy movies and bought you White Tower hamburgers, but, hey, we all know he whipped you with his riding whip so you'd bleed all over the bed. We also know he woke up every day of your life and talked to you about something important. I know, because I was in on a whole lot of those breakfast conversations. Can you possibly imagine how much your father shaped who you are? And you say he's not your father? Baloney gravy, kid. Who else would've done those things for you?'

Gilby looked at his mother and at Ticky, who kept nodding his head. Gilby wanted to say his father shouldn't have tricked him, but the image arrived of Elisha pitching a horseshoe. Before Gilby could answer him, Roscoe moved Jazz Baby forward and, when he was in open pasture, rode him at a canter, then into a gallop, across the whole pasture to the woods, and then galloped back to the stable and slid gracefully off the horse's back, doubling over in pain.

'What happened?' Veronica said in panic, and she took Roscoe's arm. 'Are you hurt?'

'Just the usual bareback shock waves,' Roscoe said. 'It happens to everybody.' He slowly straightened himself. 'Ticky,' he said, sitting on the bale of hay, 'tell Gilby what your father told you about horses.'

'Oh, my father,' Ticky said. 'Peoples used to say about my father, "Oh, he's a good man with a horse," and I'd say, "Pa, what you doin' with that horse? Is that the way you do it?" And he'd say, "Shut up, boy. You wanna learn, go out on your own," and he wouldn't teach me. I worked for other horsemens and they'd teach me. But I didn't have no father about knowin' horses.'

'Me either,' said Roscoe, who was trying to sit in a way that controlled his pain. 'Now, you take *my* father. He created a big family and then he left us to live in a hotel. When he lived home he never let me into his bedroom, and if he caught me there he'd lock me in the attic. So I'd stay in my room, reading atlases, memorizing poems and songs and countries and cities, and my brain got so crowded there was no room for the baseball scores. But I liked it so much they took me to the doctor, who talked to me for a week and then said nothing was wrong with my head and all I needed was to go up and see those ghosts again, the ones your father and I saw when we were kids up at Tristano – two old men who came out in the middle of the night and sat by the fireplace in the Trophy House and drank brandy and talked and looked out at the moon until the sun came up on the lake, and then they got up and went away.'

Gilby stared at Roscoe and said, 'You saw ghosts?'

'Absolutely.'

'You talked to them?'

'We could hear them whispering. They'd say to one another, "Wisha-wisha-wisha-wisha-wisha."'

'What's that mean?'

'It's ghost talk.'

'My father never told me about that.'

'He was saving it till you were old enough to appreciate ghosts.'

'I'm old enough.'

'Then I'll tell you what. I'm of the opinion that your father could very well be up there at Tristano with those ghosts. It's the sort of place fathers go when they die, especially a father like yours, who liked to talk and fish and was very fond of ghosts. We'll both go up there one of these days and wait till the ghosts come out, and then we'll sit and watch them and listen to what they say. And when the sun comes up and the ghosts go to bed, we might even do some fishing. Sound all right?'

'All right,' Gilby said. 'All right.'

Ticky was nodding, and as Roscoe stood up, in obvious pain, Veronica handed the witch doctor his hat and coat. She felt blackly excited by his presence, a new thing that hinted there would come a day when her marriage to Elisha would be over. She couldn't tell Roscoe about this feeling, because she didn't understand it herself. It was new and unwelcome and she felt guilty for having it. Roscoe had made Gilby's smile steadfast, but the boy wasn't out of danger just because his mood had changed. It was possible to lose him, as she'd lost her sweet baby Rosemary.

She put her arm around Gilby and squeezed him as they walked toward the house. Roscoe walked very slowly behind her, his coat slung over his shoulder, his hat on the back of his head, always close in her life, always a puzzle, so gifted, so audacious, so shy. Sometimes she decided Roscoe was spiritually illegal, a bootlegger of the soul, a mythic creature made of words and wit and wild deeds and boundless memory. She looked at him and saw a man of immense spirit, a man for loss, just as she was a woman for loss. She reached back and took his hand.

When they were in the main parlor of the house and Gilby had gone upstairs, she took both Roscoe's hands in hers and, standing in the burnished light of this rare Tivoli afternoon, she raised her face to his and kissed him on the mouth in a way she had kissed no other man since the Elisha of a sensual yesterday. Roscoe, suddenly transformed into six feet two and a half inches of tapioca pudding, tried to firm himself; and he grew bold.

'Will you spend one day alone with me?' he asked.

'A day alone? Where?'

'Tristano. I'm asking for a day, not a night.'

'It takes half a day just to get there.'

'We can leave early, come home late. A long day. Or we can stay over if you want to, but that's not what I'm asking.'

'We wouldn't be alone. There are caretakers at Tristano.'

'We'll blindfold them. Are you creating impediments to avoid an answer?'

'I have an answer.'

'What is it?'

'Perhaps.'

'You crush me,' Roscoe said, 'under the burden of hope. I pray I can survive it.'

As he walked to his car, Roscoe saw a crow, blacker and larger than crows he had known, and female, which he deduced after she landed on an upper branch of an oak tree and was immediately set upon by another large, black crow, which mounted her; and they lay sideways on the branch and copulated. Roscoe stopped the car to watch and became convinced the female crow was smiling. Roscoe might have taken this to be a good omen, but it was too proximate to his kiss, the crows were black as sin, and they were crows enthralled by passion. They were the crows of fornication.

What did you expect, Roscoe, the bluebirds of happiness?

Roscoe in a Courtly Mode

On the road, Roscoe met the women who died of love, some naked, some garbed as when love took them, a legion stretching to the horizon.

'Roscoe, Roscoe,' one warned as they passed, 'love is a form of war.'

'I always knew that,' he said.

'Keep yourself chaste for your beloved,' said a woman dressed as a bride, 'and if you want love, avoid lies and avarice.'

'I have no beloved, lies are my business, and without avarice we'd have chaos in City Hall,' Roscoe told her.

'Do not lust for every woman,' said a naked siren, still voluptuous in death, 'for that turns a man into a shameless dog. Seek love where nubile women are found: the horse races, the theater, the law courts.'

'I've looked in all those places, but I've yet to find one for me. You have a nubile look about you. What are *you* doing tonight?'

'Nice try,' said the dead siren. 'Just keep remembering that the pursuit of love makes an ugly man handsome, a fat man thin, that love transforms shame into glory, and falsity into truth. And if you fail with love, your only consolation is food and drink.'

Then she passed on, and Roscoe was enveloped by hunger, thirst, desire, and gloom.

Women He Has Known

Picture Roscoe: he is wearing his blue-and-white-vertical-striped pajamas; his stomach pain from the accident seems worse, though he is trying to ignore it, trying to sleep in the double bed of his suite in the Ten Eyck. He is a hotel-dweller and probably will remain so for the rest of his days. He has no yen to live the landed life of Patsy of the mountain, or Elisha of the manor, though Veronica could talk him into the manor if she played her cards right. He is by nature a guest, not a host, though he usually picks up the check. He has never craved the permanence so many others desire, but he does seem permanent here, at least in open-ended continuity; for in these rooms his father lived the last years of his life: in this very same bedroom, bath, and sitting room, though the rug is new.

His father's influence is everywhere in Roscoe, even in those names of his: Rosky, Ros, Rah-Rah (what Gilby used to call him), diminutives of Roscius, from Quintus Roscius, the Roman comic actor and friend of Cicero, 'so you wouldn't be typed as an Irishman,' Felix told him. Roscoe is a lawyer because Felix read law in Peter Coogan's office but never finished law school. He's in politics because it was in his bones; and Felix, before he died in 1919, counseled Patsy, Elisha, and Roscoe regularly on how to invent themselves as the saviors of Albany Democracy. It's true Roscoe has gone beyond his father by becoming a lawyer, but, no, he'll never match his father's political fame, indeed has never held a public office.

Roscoe, unable to sleep any more this morning, rises from his bed and stands amid his possessions, almost all he has in the world – an overflowing bookcase, overflowing desk, overflowing closet, overflowing bar, plus the evidence that he exists amid a population outside his mind: photos on the walls of himself with Al Smith, FDR, Jimmy Walker, Harry Truman, Bing Crosby, Connie Boswell, Jock Whitney, Earl Sande, Sophie Tucker, Patsy, Elisha, and Veronica; above the mantel the cockfighting painting Patsy gave him after Flora wouldn't let it hang in his own house; over the sofa, a Falstaff poster heralding a London production of *Henry IV, Part One,* a gift from Elisha.

Roscoe's pain, he discovers as he moves, is worsening. It comes but no longer goes, and he realizes that, once freed of today's obligations, he must attend to it. It is a nonspecific malaise in stomach and chest that he's had since his blunt trauma in the car accident. It occupies the same area as his wound by gunshot during the Great War, and because of this Roscoe believes the pain is self-generated: You are doing this to yourself, you idiot.

In the past when he's said this, the pain has diminished, then vanished; but not now. He speculates that this pain may be rising from powerful forces of fraudulence far beneath the shallow hysteria that usually creates Roscoe's phantom pain, then banishes it when it's recognized. This could be a new element in his soul that is resistant to unconscious reason. An alternative explanation is that the pain is genuine, and so weird that it may be fatal.

Fatal.

The endgame of the immense life that lives in Roscoe's brain? What will the unfinished world do without him? He asked himself this in 1918, when his first blunt trauma was imposed upon him – The one that should have killed you, Ros. Now you've got another chance to do yourself.

How Roscoe's *First* Wound Came to Pass

Roscoe and Patsy join all-volunteer 102nd Engineer Train, 27th Division, of New York National Guard, at Albany in the summer of 1917, mustered into federal service, leave Albany for Manhattan, Spartanburg, Newport News for training through April 1918, board one of six transports in convoy with ten destroyers, cruiser, sub chaser, shot at by German subs, one sub blown out of the water, staging camp at Noyalles-sur-Mer, then Agenville and Candas, where Jerry's bombs kill seventeen horses of the Engineer Train, Roscoe and Patsy together on the same wagon in the Train, but not hurt, four horses at each end of their new wagon, four men in the middle, each man controlling two horses, Roscoe in the saddle on left horse of lead team as they move, Patsy riding with rear team, moving from nightfall to daybreak on bombed-out roads, through towns in ruins, Saint-Argues, Saint-Omer, German planes always overhead as they near front with ammo and rations, to Cassel, heading for Belgium, Engineers gassed by a long wave, don't lose that gas mask, no civilians in ruined towns, rain is constant, feet and clothes never dry, water flowing into tents, mud the mattress whose ooze you settle into, Jerry overhead, then with

Patsy in a French church for high mass said by Father Skelley from Cohoes, chaplain for the 27th, Train bringing tools and trench irons to infantry to shore up trench walls, plus equipment to Engineers repairing roads so the heavy artillery can pass, battlefield laid out in lines of trenches, front-line trenches, then the approach trenches, and reserve trenches in rear, infantry in each trench, first line pushes forward to the objective, second follows to mop up wounded or straggling Germans and bring back our own wounded, the boys are driving Jerry backward and he's moving fast, so Train returns to reload and heads up to the line again, hip boots issued, Train shelled by pilot who personally tosses bombs from his cockpit, Roscoe and Patsy meet John McIntyre from Albany, halfback with Patsy on the Arbor Hill Spartans, who's retrieving dead and wounded, dangerous duty, for the corpses may be booby-trapped, back again to load up ammo, trench irons, rations, barbed wire, sand bags, gravel for trench work, all trenches infested but don't try to get rid of cooties with creosote, then a break and there's a big crowd at mass and we move up again, fearing gas more than anything, animal loss heavy, road so badly bombed it's not a road, sudden shell burst and Patsy's leg is hit with shrapnel, he's carried to the rear, barrage from 1 to 4 A.M. and it's as bright as under the electric lights at State and Pearl Streets, everybody waiting for an attack by the Huns, too quiet, we ride all night in cold rain, no food and almost no sleep, our troops massing on front line, 106th Regiment of our 27th doing the main push, so we're in for overtime, Train is up the line as far as possible and it's a slaughterhouse, except in a slaughterhouse they kill the cows and here some boys are only half killed, fields covered with so many English, German, Yank dead you walk on them, drive your wagon over their faces, we're

50 percent dead but others are worse off, and a shell blasts all four of our horses and wagon, Dumas knocked senseless, Weeper Walters blown off his horse and the wagon runs over his arm and hand, horse returns with dead Dumas lying across his back, Sammy Jones's horse cut in two by a shell, another horse dosed badly with gas, everybody got a whiff, Sammy puked in his gas mask and took it off, God knows what'll become of him, everybody's half blind and you don't move because that spreads the gas in your lungs, only two on the wagon now, Roscoe and Mike Ahearn from Worcester, roads are mined and we're moving ammo, taking it as far forward as wagons can go, no way to turn back in this rain, this mud, so Roscoe and Mike dig a hole three feet deep beside roofless barn walls, sink four posts with corrugated iron as a roof, a large can for a stove, keep those shoes on or the rats will steal them, enemy planes upstairs so the 106th isn't budging yet, but the word is that a great drive by Yanks, French, English, and Aussies is about to begin, and here comes the British artillery with its rolling barrage to soften up Jerry, our shells carrying shrapnel, smoke, mustard gas, the first time we've used the gas, and then the 106th moves out, heading toward the outworks of the Hindenburg Line, which the Germans think is unbreakable, and maybe it is, one Yank unit moves beyond the point it was supposed to hold and those Yanks are bottled up by a Hun machine-gun nest and waiting, Aussie regiment coming up to help them, and Roscoe thinks of his pals blown apart, shot, gassed, dead of fright or exhausted hearts, and he lies down in the mud and closes his eyes so he can stay awake and, by a mundane miracle, sleeps, or seems to, until a shell explodes the barn wall and Mike Ahearn wakes screaming for his mother, he and Roscoe overrun by a colony of black rats from the blasted barn floor,

half a dozen rats crawling on Roscoe, one sucking blood from his neck, and he screams, rolls over, and shakes himself and the rats fall away but not the one on his neck, a goddamn snapping-turtle rat, and Roscoe reels, never having known terror like this, not even from the mustard gas, pure rat terror, and he tries to smack the rat with his rifle but still it clutches his shoulder and his neck, a goddamn warrior rat, don't shoot it, Roscoe, or you'll shoot yourself, and Roscoe stands and whirls in a circular frenzy, drops his rifle, squeezes the rat to death, but not before he's bitten on both hands, and then he runs, done with this war, runs toward the rear, bleeding at the neck, poisoned with rat plague and surely dying, he'll run to Albany to get well, fuck all rats, double-fuck this army and this war, and he runs, oh how he runs, but without his rat and without his rifle, Roscoe lost in the night, and he turns back toward the barn-that-was – is this the way back? – but all is blackness until a star shell lights up the field and he sees he's in no man's land, running toward the German barbed wire, and he'll get there if he keeps going, and he leaps into a shell hole, drawing fire from a machine gun, probably that goddamn nest everybody wants, and in another star shell's light he heaves a grenade toward the gun and it blasts back at him, no cigar, Ros, but an Aussie one-pounder finds the nest and that's that for those Hun sonsabitches, and Roscoe is up again and running low toward his own line, yes, go back and get that rifle, he's got the direction right this time and the boys see him coming, but what they really see is crazy Jerry coming after them single-handed – Hey, hey! it's not Jerry, for God's sake, don't shoot, it's only The Roscoe! – but Roscoe in the dark is Jerry on the attack and they shoot Roscoe and he falls at his own line, speaks, and is recognized, and they pull him bleeding into the trench and ask him, Roscoe, what the hell you doin' out there, tryin' to get 'em all by yourself? What guts this guy's got, drawin' their fire like that, sorry we shot you, buddy, Roscoe bleeding under his tunic and he feels a nonspecific pain in chest and stomach – ratness and a bullet transformed into the malaise of the heroic deserter.

It was 8:04 A.M. and Joey Manucci would be making Roscoe's coffee at Headquarters. But Roscoe was not up for coffee, or even for walking across the street this morning, and so he told Joey by phone to get the car and pick him up at the hotel. Roscoe brewed a Bromo-Seltzer for his stomach, ate the two Hershey almond bars he'd bought last night, all the breakfast he could handle, and took the elevator down to the street.

The heat was already unbearable, a day to sleep in some lakeside shade or loll about in a tub of ice. Roscoe, tie open, cord sport coat on his arm, asked doorman Wally Condon for his report on the state of Albany this morning ('Going to hell, Roscoe, be there by noon'), then he went out and stood at State and Chapel Streets to wait for Joey and to watch the city opening its doors: jewelers, cafeteria workers, newsboys, cigar dealers lowering awnings, sweeping sidewalks, washing windows, stacking papers, all dressing their corner of the universe for another day of significant puttering. Lights were on in Malley's, across the street, begun by the Malley brothers as a saloon, then a speakeasy, now grown into a major restaurant. Here came Jake Berman, up from the South End on his way to his Sheridan Avenue walkup, where, with staunch backbone, he defends, for pennies, every socialist caught in the hostile legal system, admirable penury. And Morgan Hillis going into the State Bank, a man born with an outdoor privy, now a vice-president handling Democratic accounts in the modest millions.

And Glenda Barry, Mush Trainor's girlfriend, manicurist at the Ten Eyck barbershop, who, when she cuts your cuticles, wears a white, freshly starched, skintight, wraparound smock, removable for special occasions. And, ah me, coming down State Street with that aggressive stride of his, Marcus Gorman, Pamela's barrister, clear the way for Mighty Marcus, who won Jack (Legs) Diamond two acquittals and never got a nickel for it. Stiffed by the stiff. But you coasted miles on those acquittals, old man.

'Morning, counselor,' Roscoe said to Marcus.

'Roscoe. I understand I'll see you later this morning.'

'You will indeed.'

'Wellllllll, *bonne chance,* my boy.'

Boy? Two years younger than your own creaking bones, you arrogant Republican bastard. And we almost made you a congressman; but proximity to Jack Diamond killed that. And so Gorman the Grand rose another way: becoming Albany's Demosthenes, Albany's own Great Mouthpiece for a continuing line of criminals after Diamond: Dutch Schultz, Vincent Coll, Pittsburgh Phil Straus, Pamela Yusupov.

Watching the stirrings of these myriad creatures of significance in the city – even the robotic repetitions of Ikey Finkel, the fifty-year-old newsboy, hawking his papers, 'Mawnin' pape, mawnin' pape' – shot Roscoe through with depression. He would, in an hour, make his way to headquarters for another day of Party rituals that would perpetuate the bleeding of his soul.

Joey stopped the car at the corner, and Roscoe, with difficulty, climbed in beside him. Joey, six six and two fifty, barely fit behind the wheel. Roscoe was wide but not so tall. Ordinary automobiles were not made for their like, especially for Joey, a *genuine* giant, the kind of giant you wish you were,

Ros, an authentic military hero for pushing forward alone after the rest of his squad had been killed, seeing four Nazis putting a machine gun into place, killing them all with his pistol, then holding the position until reinforcements arrived and forty more Nazis were captured, all of which won Joey the Congressional Medal of Honor. Now Patsy's running him for the State Senate. What will Joey do with a stack of legislative bills when he can't even understand the Ten Eyck lunch menu and Roscoe has to read it to him? You think people want an illiterate senator? And Patsy: You think anybody'll vote against the Medal of Honor?

Medals? Roscoe has medals. The same Senate seat Joey will soon occupy was Roscoe's for the asking in the early years, after the Democrats took City Hall; and it would have moved him one step closer to matching his father's political achievements. For a few minutes, back then, Roscoe felt safe as a hero, for not even Patsy knew that after Ros rejoined the Engineer Train he worked in company headquarters and wrote, in the dead captain's name, and forged, in the dead captain's hand, the citation lauding Roscoe Conway's bravery in drawing enemy fire, a prize-winning work of fiction that earned Roscoe the Distinguished Service Cross. Fraudulent? Perhaps. But he *was* in the heavy action, he *was* under direct fire at the German line, and *his own buddies* shot and damn near killed him. Must we quibble about motives? When is a hero not a hero? If a hero falls alone in a trench does he make a heroic sound? Take a guess.

Patsy was convinced the DSC would easily win Roscoe the Senate seat, but Ros said, Thanks, Pat, but I would prefer not to. For by then the malaise had set in, and Roscoe was just another time bomb waiting to explode with shameful publicity for everybody. The Party didn't need that.

'You sick?' Joey asked.

'Do I look sick?'

'I would never say so, and don't hold me to it, but you look like a dying dog.'

'I am sick but not that sick. Stop talking about it and let's go to Hattie's.'

And Joey drove to Lancaster Street, to the modest brownstone from which Hattie Wilson managed her real-estate empire: forty-six three- and four-story rooming houses, four hundred and forty tenants whose rents Hattie collected personally, except for the eight buildings that functioned as brothels, and for those rentals Hattie received monthly cash payments in person from Mame Ray, Bindy McCall's woman, and the supervising madam of all eight thriving whorehouses. Dark history had been made by some of Hattie's tenants: Mrs. Falcone, who brought home two drifters to stab her husband fifty-seven times and who then moved from Hattie's basement to Death Row in Sing Sing; history made also by visitors to Jack Diamond, who was in bed in a Hattie house on Dove Street – Hattie herself was actually in the basement to stoke the furnace that very early December morning – when the boys went upstairs and put Jack into deep cool.

Roscoe's mission this morning was to talk to Mame Ray, but he couldn't use the phone and, with the spies watching him, he couldn't pull up to her whorehouse in daylight, especially before breakfast. Hattie's place was safe, and Hattie was a storehouse of gossip herself, for her tenants were a cross-section of The Gut, Albany's night city: bartenders and waitresses, burglars on relief, family outcasts and runaways, semiaffluent winos who could still pay rent, motherless queens, hula dancers, B-girls and strippers, horseplayers doing their best to die broke, dishwashers aspiring to be short-order cooks, good-time girls learning what it takes to go pro, and all the flakes, flacks, and flukes who got around to putting their heads on their greasy pillows just as the sun was also rising on the rooftops of The Gut. A famous question in the neighborhood was: Are you married or do you pay rent to Hattie Wilson?

The word on the street was that Hattie hoarded cash in her walls, but the last burglar who checked that one out turned up mostly dead in a ditch, courtesy of the Night Squad, which protected Hattie and her empire not only because she was O.B.'s wife, but because she was a prime snitch for the cops and a treasure to the Party for two decades, a compelling force in getting four hundred and forty people to the polls on Election Day – no relief checks, no mail, no heat or water in the joint until you vote the right way, the Democratic way, and we do know how you vote.

Joey parked and Roscoe went up Hattie's stoop slowly.

'You even walk sick,' Joey said, and he hit the doorbell.

'Just shut up and open the door,' Roscoe said.

They went into the hallway and Roscoe knocked at Hattie's inner door.

'Open up,' he said. 'It's a raid.'

'At this hour it couldn't be social,' Hattie said from the other side of the door, and then she opened it to Roscoe and Joey, with Bridget, her Irish setter, at her heel. Hattie was fifty-one, wearing a flowered housedress, her hair both prematurely white and unchangingly bobbed since the mid-1920s, smoking a Camel, as usual, moving into a bit of broadness at the hips but still with that hourglass waist, and, to Roscoe, even at raw morning, a woman worth looking at, as she had been since he first intersected with her at Patsy's victory party in 1919. He would have married her if he wasn't so down on marriage and she wasn't already married; and she was always married, except for brief pauses between the 'I do's: the perpetual bride, outthinking or outliving her husbands, or leaving them behind and finding another, always eager for that ring, because it meant a focus on the hearth and not just the bed. It also meant she had not another breadwinner, for she'd already won all the bread she'd ever need, but another cohabiting love slave, a focus on one man, even though she always had her eye on half a dozen, couldn't help it, the poor thing, always such a magnet for men, such a triumph when they won her, had her, not knowing that it was she who had them, that they could never win her if she hadn't first singled them out of the crowd, faithful to each in her own way, never trespassing on the previous or the current one, no matter how many mounted up on her scorecard; and Roscoe always in on her action, whatever, whomever she did.

'You're right again, old Hat,' Roscoe said, and Hattie stepped aside to let him and Joey into her parlor, whose furnishings, like much in her life, like Roscoe, were secondhand and at least a generation out of fashion.

'Turn on your fans,' Roscoe said. 'A day like this, even dogs leave town and head for water. Why aren't you out at the lake, Bridget?' And the dog licked his hand. Hattie was as intense about dogs as about husbands, and visited some of her neighbors only to talk to their dogs. Roscoe draped his suit coat over a chair back and sat on the sofa facing one of Hattie's electric fans, waiting for air.

'You don't look like yourself, Rosky,' Hattie said, and she switched on both her fans.

'I told him he looked sickly,' Joey said.

'You got any iced tea?' Roscoe asked.

'In the kitchen. You go make it, Joey,' Hattie said, and Joey left the room. 'What's wrong with you, Rosky? Your color is off. And you're puffing.'

'The hell with that. You hear about anybody making a move on the whorehouses?'

'Anybody who?'

'The troopers, the Governor.'

'I thought you got the Governor off your backs last year.'

'He won't quit. Election's coming.'

'All I hear is that business is great since V-J Day. Now that the war's over, people can think about something else.'

'They didn't think about it during the war?'

'Don't get on me. You want me to call a doctor?'

'No doctors. I've got too much to do.'

'Somebody else to punch out? You're in the papers again.'

'Some people need punching out for their own good.'

'You never change, Rosky.'

'I change like an emanation of nature, my dear. I change like an oak tree developing acorns. I change like churned milk, I change like a turnip growing ever larger, ever rounder, and palatable only when seriously boiled.'

'You still look like the boy I got to know in Malley's back room.'

'That billygoat. You knew so many like him. You ever keep count?'

'I can't count that high, love.'

'If we'd gotten married, I'd be dead and gone like your first five husbands. You're a lethal woman, Hattie.'

'Floyd is still alive, out west. He sends me postcards. And O.B. is holding his own.'

'O.B. is alive because he sees you in moderation. Smart man, O.B. Floyd I never understood.'

'Floyd made me laugh, read me poems, played the harp. I bought him a lovely big one and he played it every night.'

'But you never screwed him.'

'I never had to.'

'Not his preference.'

'I couldn't take him serious after I caught him parading around in my stockings and garters. He took a drawerful when he left. The harp too.'

'Your figure still makes me giddy. I'm feeling the need to take it in hand again.'

'In your condition it might do you in.'

'What better way to go? Better than Elisha. Are you ready if I come by some night?'

'If you promise not to die on me, I'll love you like a husband.'

'Good. Now I need a favor.'

'Of course you do.'

'Call Mame and ask her to come over. So many politicians move through her place, and she does loosen their tongues. Don't mention me on the phone.'

'You're worried about this.'

'I'm paid for what I know about this town, and what I don't know will eat my gizzard.'

Hattie went to her telephone table and called Mame, out of Roscoe's earshot. Joey came in from the kitchen with a pitcher of tea, three glasses, a cut lemon, ice cubes, and the sugar bowl. No spoons, but otherwise a wonderful achievement. Roscoe would not ask anything more of him today.

Mame Ray was forty, child of a whore, raised in a whorehouse, a practitioner at puberty, a madam at twenty-five, who brought to whoring an attitude which her man, Bindy McCall, articulated to Roscoe early on in his relationship to her: 'She's a degenerate broad, but all broad.'

Roscoe could agree, having known Mame on and off for three months before Bindy took her over, a wild trimester of melodramatic sex that curdled when Mame invited paying spectators to watch them through peepholes. Roscoe now avoided Mame unless he had a reason to see her. He considered her a narcissistic cauldron of spite, a felonious virago if crossed; but an acute manager of business and people, effective scavenger in grocery marts and ten-cent stores for poor but shapely salesgirls ready to be rented, a wizard concerning the textures of desire, and at turning even casual customers into slaves of their own sexuality. In her early twenties she was a roving freelancer, and then princess of whichever house she settled into – in New York, Hudson, and finally Albany in 1930, when Roscoe found her. Bindy, after he took her over, saw to it that she spent less time on her back, more time counting revenue from the eight houses he gave her to supervise, all eight in Hattie's buildings.

Mame's main brothel, Hattie's only building outside the rooming-house district, was an old Prohibition roadhouse in the city's West End, known first as the Come On Inn, now called the Notchery, and it was all gold. Its first two floors were luxuriously furnished for a whorehouse, and Mame lived amid high-fashion décor on the third floor. It was also the collection depot for payoffs to Bindy from all city brothels, and these sums he passed on to Roscoe three times a week at Party headquarters after he took his cut, which Patsy suspected was getting larger lately, a point of contention between the brothers.

When Hattie saw Mame step out of the taxicab, she opened the inner door for her and went back to her chair. Roscoe, sipping his second glass of iced tea, watched Joey playing solitaire on the coffee table. Joey was cheating, yet losing. What kind of a senator is this? Mame flounced through the open door, her hair a new shade of auburn since Roscoe last saw her, her seductive amplitude unchanged, and wearing a tan linen skirt and white blouse. Mame's face was not her fortune: her nose was a bump, her eyes too small, her cheekbones lost in the puff of her cheeks, but her mouth and its savvy smile offered serious intimacy.

'My God, Hattie,' she said, leaving the door ajar, 'it's hotter here than outside. Pour me one of those teas, Roscoe.'

'Glad to see you, too, Mame,' Roscoe said.

Hattie closed the door, then poured an iced tea for Mame, who sat on the other end of the sofa from Joey.

'Hiya, Mame,' Joey said.

'How's it hangin', Joe?'

'Down to my knees.'

'Send my regards,' Mame said.

'Never mind the shoptalk,' Roscoe said. 'We hear the Governor may make a surprise raid on some of the girls.'

'How could that happen?' Mame asked. 'We pay off everybody, including one of the Governor's lawyers, and a couple of the very best state legislators.'

'You hear any rumors?'

'Pina said the troopers were talking to South End pimps, and she mentioned they're interested in Division Street.'

'Tell me something I don't know.'

'They're also talking to the Dutchman, and Pina says they know a beat cop taking payoffs, eight dollars a week.'

'Eight dollars. A fantastic specific, but not quite grounds for a raid. Who told Pina that?'

'I didn't take it serious,' Mame said.

'Who could it have been? When was it?'

'Last night. Could've been anybody.'

'You and Pina worked last night?'

'We never close.'

'Everybody else closed,' Roscoe said.

'So I heard.'

'Patsy sent the word out yesterday to shut down.'

'Patsy, Patsy, Patsy. Fuck Patsy. We're using the peephole. Only people we know get in.'

'Did you say fuck Patsy?' Hattie asked her.

'I did. He came to our place years ago, then all of a sudden he stays home and says his Rosary. What I think is his dick fell off. I hope it did.'

'Oh, Mame, Mame,' Hattie said. 'You've gone bedbugs.'

'What you're saying is Bindy *won't* close? All eight places are running?'

'Just the Notchery,' Mame said. 'You know how much money we're losing with seven places dark? How are people supposed to live?'

'You know the money it'd take to get you and your girls out of jail? Lawyers, bail, greasing judges we don't own, appeals if anybody's convicted? This is happening at the state level, sweetheart, and the election is coming.'

'We've had raids before,' Mame said. 'Nothing changes and then we go back to work. God, Hattie, I can't stand this heat.' Mame opened her front buttons and slipped off her blouse. She wore a corselette that put much of her chest on exhibit.

'Lookin' good, Mame,' Joey said.

'I don't overeat,' Mame said.

'Wanna go in the bedroom?'

'Thanks, Joe, but I never fuck before lunch.'

'So,' said Roscoe, 'you're saying Bindy's now in business for himself?'

'Wasn't he always?' Mame said.

'I'll think about that,' Roscoe said. 'In the meantime, madam, I suggest you guard your peephole very vigorously.'

Roscoe walked slowly down the hallway toward Supreme Court at one minute to ten, Veronica and Gilby beside him. Photographers from the local papers were ahead of them, shooting, walking backward as they reloaded their Speed Graphics. You're on tomorrow's front page, Ros. Suck in your gut.

As they entered the courtroom, Roscoe moved Gilby a step ahead, then he and Veronica walked down the aisle together, maybe his only chance to do this. Pamela and Marcus Gorman had not arrived, but the courtroom was half filled, mostly with women who had come to see the socially notorious Pamela. The *Times-Union* this morning carried a capsule history of her marriages and scandals, her liaisons with millionaires, royal exiles, and Caribbean gigolos, and it highlighted the night she spent in jail for smashing a woman's face with a champagne glass, thirty-two stitches, because the woman had insulted President Roosevelt. Give the devil her due. She's still a Democrat.

'She's not here yet,' Roscoe said to Veronica. 'Have you figured out what you'll say to her?'

'That I'll cut out her heart and throw it to my dogs the way she bounced hard-boiled eggs to her poodle.'

'Splendid,' Roscoe said.

He settled his clients at the defense table and checked on the press: Frank Merola, who covered courts for the *Times-Union,* a friendly face, another way of saying he was on the

Party's payroll and would not be hostile to a Roscoe client, especially Elisha's widow; Bill Cooley of the *Knickerbocker News,* who was also on the payroll but whose story might be less friendly, for one of his editors was born and would die a Republican; and also Vic Fenster from the goddamn *Sentinel.*

Roscoe heard Pamela before he saw her, her volume announcing the grand dame's arrival. She wore a lavender picture hat, more suitable for the racetrack than the courtroom, a matching lavender dress, and red shoes. Her nylon stockings had a rare sheen, unlike any Roscoe had seen when he shopped with Trish, these surely from the *haute-couture* black market.

'I feel so secure with you on the case,' Pamela was saying as she entered, smiling up at Marcus Gorman, who was beamish beside her. They came toward the bench, Marcus nodding a restrained collegial greeting to Roscoe. Pamela paused to stare at Gilby, who sat at the defense table beside Veronica. She walked to him.

'Oh, Gilby, sweet boy, how handsome you look.' She grasped his hand and squeezed it.

'Leave him alone,' Veronica said. Pamela ignored her and went to the table where Marcus was waiting. A court bailiff entered the judge's chambers, and then George Quinn, the court crier, announced that court was in session, the honorable Francis Finn presiding, all rise. Finn was a young question mark, for, although he owed his presence on the bench to Patsy's endorsement, it was Marcus who had used his influence to get him into Albany Law School right out of high school, without an intervening college education.

'I've read your petition, Mr. Gorman, and your response, Mr. Conway,' Judge Finn said, 'and it seems to me there are issues of fact to be determined here. Do you agree?' He looked to Marcus, a formal figure in dark-blue suit and subdued red tie, who stood and spoke with unusual restraint – flamboyance, not understatement, was Marcus's trademark.

'No, Your Honor,' Marcus said, 'for we are dealing here with the biological right of a mother, under law, to possess her own child. There was no legal adoption of this boy by Veronica Fitzgibbon, only a temporary custody arrangement agreed to by a deeply troubled mother whose circumstances would not allow her to raise the child as she wanted him raised. But she has triumphed over adversity and now reclaims her right to cherish her own flesh and blood, to give him the upbringing he deserves from his true mother. And we ask that immediate custody of her only son be granted to her – today.' And he sat down.

'What do you say to this, counsel?' the judge asked Roscoe.

And Roscoe stood and recounted the Gilby prenatal adoption plan, noted the absence of contact between biological mother and child for three years after the birth, and only eight mother–son meetings during the next nine years.

'And so Pamela Yusupov,' said Roscoe, 'who gave her child away with a great expression of relief *before he was born*, has seen the boy only ten times in his entire life, including the day of his birth and this sighting today. Yet she wants to take him from the mother who, while cradling him as her own when he was only hours out of the womb, heard Pamela Yusupov say, "Thank God, thank God I'm no longer a mother." Now this unnatural mother seeks to wrench that child out of the only mother's arms he's ever known. The boy does not want to leave, and it would be tragic to place him, against his will, in custody of this stranger. What's more, this stranger's sole purpose here is to obtain money from the estate of her late ex-husband, who disowned her five years ago, who was father to this boy but never saw him – not once – in his entire life. Should the profoundest of human bonds, between mother and son, ever be measured by the financial gain it will bring? Your respondents ask that this mischievous suit be dismissed.'

Judge Finn shook his head and said, 'Let's not waste the court's time here, Mr. Gorman, Mr. Conway. The way to resolve this is through sworn testimony, and we must hear from the infant.'

'Then we request that testimony be taken in chambers,' said Roscoe, 'to make the environment less frightening for the boy.'

'We will reconvene here, in my chambers, two weeks from today,' the judge said.

To Roscoe, Veronica had been a savvy childhood goddess, creature of heavenly body to which he had modest privilege; but then she became, oh yes, high priestess of betrayal and venal dreams, human after all. Pamela was Veronica manquée, savvy and single-minded, the vulvaceous creature of devilish body and venturesome sin. Roscoe loved the blood that flowed in the young sisters' bodies, loved their vitality and, of course, their beauty. That both were beautiful no one disagreed. When Veronica was nineteen and about to marry Elisha, she was photographed in a white parlor of her home, wearing a white, off-the-shoulder evening dress with no trace of vulgarity in her bare shoulders, standing in a smoky light that obscured her right hand and gave her an aura of ethereality. The photo was everybody's favorite when it appeared in magazines and rotogravures, and so Pamela, at nineteen and about to marry Roscoe, had an identical photo taken to prove Veronica's image was not a singular phenomenon, and proved the reverse. Pamela's photo accented her shoulder bones and her curiously inelegant posture, and Roscoe concluded that, though she tried to stand upright for the portrait, her crooked soul betrayed her. Now, twenty-nine years later, here she was in court, still getting even for genetic inequities.

When he married Pamela, Roscoe had a modest income from his father's Stanwix brewery, an enterprise that dated to 1886, when Felix bought it from John Malley, who gave up making beer in order to sell it retail in what his sons would develop into the city's largest saloon. Two years later, Felix was elected Albany's first mayor of Irish extraction, and the day after his election he led a parade of twelve Stanwix wagons, each drawn by a double team through the entire city, to let it be known that good things would happen to saloonkeepers who served Stanwix beer and Shamrock ale, the Democratic Party's new official beverages. The brews remained such even after Felix was removed from office for fraud, for he continued as a figure of power in the Party, and the brewery made him a fortune. It also kept his wife, Blanche's regal standing in the First Irish Families, that elite social unit with which Felix would have nothing to do, for, as all know, elevated social status turns the Irish into Republicans.

When the Democrats lost City Hall in 1899, Stanwix beer had a sheer falling off. But its quality kept it popular and, by 1914 its profits gave Roscoe enough income to travel comfortably in the Fitzgibbon social circle, which included the Morgan sisters. And it was these sisters, not money, or politics, that focused Roscoe's mind. He had proposed to Veronica Morgan when he finished Albany Law School, but she married Elisha and his fortune.

Then came Pamela.

Roscoe studied Pamela the plaintiff, who remained photogenic for the newspapers, her essential blond hair durably bottled in bond. But her smile had changed: two of her incisors gone crooked. And that tantalizing body he had pressed against so often, on sleigh rides, at dances, even when pursuing Veronica, had developed into one of Pamela's worst fears: the thickening middle. Together at Veronica's wedding reception at the Albany Country Club, Roscoe and Pamela had watched thick-middled Honey Mills, fiftyish, hair like straw dyed black, talking with three men sitting on chairs across from her, and offering them all a prolonged revelation of her thigh. Pamela said an ugly, shapeless woman doing such a needy thing was pathetic, but then she and Roscoe went off to the shadowy cloakroom, where Pammy kissed him and gave him exploration rights. Divested of one sister, Roscoe took the other. He courted Pamela, went with her Downtown, even to Fifth Avenue on the New York train, shopping for hats, coats, dresses. He kept her company when she was blue, took her to Dr. Warner's office when she had the stomach pains, sometimes associated with her monthlies, took her to dinner at Keeler's, to dances at the Yacht Club and the Hampton Roof Garden, and went with her on vacation to Tristano, the great Adirondack camp Lyman had started building in 1873. It was both Ariel's and Elisha's favored retreat. Elisha always invited Roscoe, and Roscoe always went, for Veronica would be there.

But Pamela became his primary interest during this visit to Tristano, where social fantasia pervaded the air like the scent of pine trees. Accessible from the railhead at North Creek only by horse-drawn carriage and then by steamer across the lake, Tristano was isolated amid the loons and raccoons, the foxes, eagles, and great horned owls, and surrounded by alders, spruces, cedars, white pine, and hemlocks. Its twenty-four buildings along the shoreline seemed on first approach to be the edge of a small city that extended infinitely backward into the estate's two thousand wooded acres. And indeed it bustled like a city when family friends and servants put it to full use. Life amid this animated isolation, this log-cabin luxury of the uncommonly rich, offered the visitor a transformation of expectation. What happened here seemed a charade played out among real people by unreal rules with improbable consequences – Roscoe, for instance, alone on the floor with Pamela on two raccoon coats at four in the morning, proposing marriage, being accepted, then bringing her back here as a bride.

Their honeymoon was romantic solitude in front of open fireplaces, long walks in the pineydown woods, cool swims in the lake's morning stillness, and pointed talk, never about tomorrow, but about how they would spend the abundance that was today. Looking at Pamela in the courtroom, Roscoe remembers that vivid yellow hair when the yellowness was real, can see her in a shimmering blue summer evening gown, then slipping effortlessly out of it, remembers how she walked or provocatively sat, and how much he loved her. But he now knows this love was independent of Pamela, a consequence of his own unruly capacity for love.

After Veronica married Elisha, Roscoe could no longer love her as before; and so loved Pamela instead, and she loved him, and they married, made love, and made love again, half a dozen times the first day. In between they ate what the Tristano servants cooked for them: fresh fish from the lake, a pheasant shot by Kendrick, Ariel's resident woodsman. They drank lightly to keep love at a sharp edge, took the boat out on the lake to find a place where there was no sound. Their lives became elemental, centering on the forest, the water, the bed, and the belief that life was purposeful, even though its only discernible purpose was love, effortless love that Roscoe could give and receive at will. And he loved it, loved Pamela, loved that he loved her, loved women, loved love.

When they woke into the third day of the honeymoon, Pamela was revisited by her old pain. She ate sparsely and said she would not give in to it. They fished off the dock by the Trophy House, and Roscoe was reeling in a small trout when they saw the steamer coming across the lake. He threw the trout back and stowed the fishing rods in the house, and they walked to the pier to meet the invaders. Ariel was first off the steamer.

'Ah, my little ones,' he said to Roscoe and Pamela, 'I didn't expect to find anyone waiting for us.'

'We're three days into our honeymoon,' Roscoe said.

'What a pity to disturb you.'

'But we're disturbing you in your own house, Ariel,' Roscoe said. 'Elisha did know we were coming. I'm surprised he didn't tell you.'

'Elisha and I aren't talking,' Ariel said.

Ariel on the pier was a handsome, salient figure in blue blazer and white slacks, pencil-line mustache, a preposterously large ruby on his left ring finger, and a full head of pure white hair. He did not look his sixty-eight years, and he exuded a sense of mature dignity that was wholly unearned. Ever since Elisha relieved him of power at the steel mill, he had been in perpetual motion between Albany, Manhattan, Miami, Saratoga, and the pleasure domes of

Europe, never alone, devoting all his days to the hedonistic carnival his life, in late years, had become. Now, as his servants unloaded everyone's luggage, Ariel introduced Roscoe and Pamela to his traveling companions as they came down the ramp: Lamar Kensington, the insurance executive who backed the Broadway musical with him, *Encore, Maestro*, a hit that renewed Ariel's exchequer after he left the mill; three Broadway dancers, Billie, Lillie, and Dolly, from another Ariel-Lamar show that had just flopped; two judges from downstate whom Ariel introduced only as Jerry and Ted; Ariel's chauffeur, Griggs; his personal chef, Philippe; and, last off the boat, his physician, Roy Warner, and Warner's bosomy wife, Estelle. Ariel saw or talked with Warner every day of his life to combat the shifting pains, maladies, and other multifarious disguises that death assumed in its never-ending pursuit of Ariel's ailing soul and body.

'Oh, Dr. Warner,' Pamela said when she saw him, 'thank heaven you're here. You don't know the pain I've been in.'

'She's been suffering since yesterday,' Roscoe said to Warner.

Dr. Warner, an affable, jowly man in his forties, with large ears and a perfect bedside smile, shook hands with Pamela. 'Your stomach acting up again?' he asked.

'It gets better, then it comes back.'

'Do you have the pills I gave you?'

'Gone. But I haven't needed them for weeks.'

'I'll get you some when we settle in and I find my bags.'

'You'll join us for lunch, and late dinner,' Ariel said. 'We have a continuing feast, you know.'

'Of course,' said Roscoe, who was already making plans to leave.

* * *

Half an hour later, Roscoe had escorted Pamela to the Warners' cottage and was walking with Ariel, both of them coatless under the ardent July sun. They were nearing the Swiss cottage, the most elegant of the secondary buildings, built to match the main lodge, with twisted cedar and shaggy spruce. On the sloping lawn in front of it, Billie, Lillie, and Dolly were sunbathing on the grass, all supine and naked under small lap-towels.

'Excessively lush, the scenery at Tristano,' Ariel said, and he waved to the women. They all waved back and Billie removed her towel.

'And it changes radically from minute to minute,' Roscoe said.

'You hardly need anything along these lines at the moment, Roscoe, but you should know that these young women are very friendly.'

'But I have a very friendly bride.'

'You also have a reputation for diversity, and it's a comfort to have excess on hand for emergencies.'

'I can't imagine one arising,' Roscoe said. 'Which of those excessive creatures belongs to you?'

'Oh, that's not how it's done. We have no ownership here.'

'Sweet land of liberty. *E pluribus unum*?'

'There you have it.'

Ariel's sexual excesses distanced many, but they amused Roscoe. Since childhood he had developed a friendship with Ariel that was familial. It had been painful to watch him squander his money and weaken the steel mill as he became a full-time satyr. But the dream assumes curious shapes.

'I suppose you miss the mill,' Roscoe said.

'Not at all,' said Ariel. 'I gave it all I had. Now I'm doing the same for myself.'

'I grieve over the trouble between you and Elisha,' Roscoe said. 'The war between fathers and sons is unwinnable and usually a self-mutilating pursuit. And Tivoli isn't the same without you around.'

'Ah, you grew up well, Roscoe, and you have the gift of talk. I thought you'd rise in political office like your father.'

'I wasn't cut out for public life.'

'We never know what we're cut out for. Who could have predicted I'd swap my stable of horses for a stable of women?'

'Some might consider that an improvement.'

'As do I, on those days when I don't think I'm dying.'

'Psychic sex as an antidote to psychic illness. Are you dying now?'

'Not at the moment. But the day is young.'

'We won't clutter your demise,' Roscoe said. 'We'll get out of your way by morning.'

'Don't be in a hurry. There's always room for two more at Tristano. Too many is just enough. And the time allotted for frolic runs out, Roscoe. Take my word.'

Estelle Warner was alone on the porch of the main lodge, drinking what looked like gin, when Ariel and Roscoe settled into green rocking chairs. Lee, an Oriental servant, appeared at their elbows as they arrived, asking whether he might bring drinks. Whiskey and whiskey, the two men said, and Lee vanished into the lodge.

'Did you have a nice walk, Ari?' Estelle asked.

'We did. The girls are taking the sun.'

'I thought of doing that myself,' Estelle said, 'but it's a bit too high in the sky for me. I'll get the freckles in odd places.'

'Nothing wrong with freckles in odd places,' Ariel said.

'You like the odd places,' Estelle said.

Estelle smiled at Roscoe, revealing a set of teeth so egregiously false they neutralized all meaning in her smile. Her manner, like her bosom, was ebullient.

'Are you waiting for the doctor?' Roscoe asked her.

'He's having a session with his patient.'

'Pamela, you mean.'

'Oh yes, Pamela. They do drag it out.'

'I know,' Roscoe said. 'I've taken her to his office.'

'She takes you with her, does she? He's had her in hand since she was fifteen. He's brought her along.'

'Oh yes? How do you mean that?'

'He's taught her how it's done. Roy does love the little chickadees.'

'Estelle, Roscoe and Pamela are married.'

'Married, are you? How cozy! You and I should have a matching consultation. We could have it right now, right here on facing chairs. The servants would never intrude, and Ari could cheer us on. You know, I'd wager that Roy is readjusting her pelvis even as we speak.'

'They're on their *honeymoon,* Estelle.'

'Honeymoon! Oh, that is *very* spicy, and the doctor having a house call from the bride.'

Roscoe remembered Pamela's face that day when she walked up the steps of the porch with Dr. Warner. It was a half-smile, a mask of relief at the presumable banishing of pain, the restoration of light to her dark condition, but also, in her cheeks and lips, the flush of gratification that Roscoe knew well. The force of the doctor's jaw, his parsimonious grin, expressed quiet triumph.

'Walk me back to the room, Roscoe,' Pamela said. 'I still feel lightheaded. I need to lie down.'

As they left the porch, Roscoe decided that none of what

Estelle had suggested was true, that it was Tristano imposing its aura of fantasia. In their room Pamela opened her body to Roscoe with such fervid immediacy that he understood, even if he could not confirm, that it was not Tristano's fantasia but the experience of receiving a second lover within a quarter-hour of the first that was driving Pamela's ecstasy; that this arose not from either act of love but from their whorish succession. Roscoe then realized this had been the pattern of their love since he first came to know it, that hers was no more related to him than his was to her, that they were both artful stylists enacting a loveless ritual that had no meaning beyond the orgasmic. Meaning would destroy the ecstasy. Roscoe now thought of it as loathsome pleasure, consummated by mutual traitors. Life without betrayal is not life.

He finished her off, then left her to sleep away her loathing. He walked out the back door of the main lodge and into the woods, took a circuitous path to the boathouse, and when he looked back at the city of Tristano he could not see any aura of fantasia, nor could he believe there ever was such a thing. Your only fantasia, Roscoe, is your gullibility.

He untethered the outboard motorboat and rode it almost across the lake, where it sputtered and stopped, out of gas. He dropped anchor, dove into the water, swam the last hundred yards to the steamer dock, then walked to the railroad station at North Creek. With damp money he bought a ticket back to Albany, where ecstasy was the impossible love of Veronica, plus two dozen oysters at Keeler's.

'You were always a malicious bitch,' Veronica was saying to Pamela in the courtroom, 'but this is an evil act.'

'I only want what is mine,' Pamela said.

'Gilby is not yours and never was.' Veronica turned to see

if the boy was still at the table, and lowered her voice. 'Do you even know who his father is?'

'Oh, I do indeed.'

'Your dead Russian never accepted him.'

'What is your point, Veronica? Do you have secret information about his father? By all means, let me in on it.' Pamela was smiling.

'You won't get this boy.'

'We'll see, won't we?'

'Veronica,' said Roscoe, 'there's nothing to be gained by this. She'll do what she'll do, and we'll overthrow it.'

'Still slobbering after her,' Pamela said, 'like the fat little Roscoe you always were. And still so insufferably smart. But you know better than anyone what you'll never have and never be. I love how that must torture you.'

'My torture ends, Pamela,' Roscoe said, 'when you leave the room.'

Gilby stood up from his chair and Pamela walked to him.

'We *will* be together, my darling one,' she said for all to hear, and she embraced him. 'I love you and I'll take care of you forever.'

'I don't even like you,' Gilby said.

Pamela stood away from him.

'You will,' she said, 'you'll love your mother. Remember that I love you.'

'You're not my mother,' Gilby said.

'Cut your losses,' Roscoe said to Pamela. 'Go home and put a dagger in what's left of your heart.'

In Pamela's face Roscoe saw raw malice, malignant need. Elisha was right: she was desperate, would do anything to attain her goal. But despite this lawsuit, her goal wasn't necessarily Gilby's custody. She confirmed that when she whispered to Veronica, 'It's a wise child that knows its father.'

Roscoe sat alone in Keeler's Sadler Room, beneath a W. Dendy Sadler print of twelve happy and fat old monks being served a sumptuous supper by six sullen and thin young monks. When he ate, Roscoe identified with the fat monks. On the room's walls were dozens of other Sadler prints of eighteenth-century English men, and now and then women, always celebrating or ritualizing, or pensive or bereaved, amid food and drink. Roscoe dipped an oyster cracker into his cocktail sauce, well into his second splendid bottle of Cheval Blanc, and five oysters into his second dozen of bluepoints. Would he go for a third dozen? He would consider it, for this might be his last meal in the civilized world. Now he stopped dwelling on oysters to consider the news just given to him by O.B., who was sitting across the table with Mac, the odor of witch hazel, O.B.'s aftershave lotion, mixing with the aroma of cocktail sauce, not a happy fusion. The news also was not happy: the Dutchman, proper name Vernon Van Epps, a pimp with a nightclub, had been found murdered in his flat upstairs over his Hudson Avenue club, the Double Dutch.

'Two dozen stab wounds, back and chest,' O.B. said.

'I'm cheering,' Mac said.

'Don't cheer too loud,' O.B. said.

'He was a worthless bag of chicken guts,' Mac said. 'They should bury him in pig shit.'

'You didn't care for him,' Roscoe said.

'He was a no-good fat fuck,' Mac said.

'Keep this up,' O.B. said, 'they'll lock *you* up for it.'

'What'd he do to you, Mac?'

'He took Mac's girlfriend off the street and put her to work in his bar,' O.B. said. 'Then she wasn't Mac's girl any more.'

'Are you talking about Pina?' Roscoe asked. 'Giuseppina?'

'Pina,' Mac said.

'She's a working girl,' Roscoe said. 'She's been on the street ever since I know her.'

'Right,' Mac said, 'but she came home to me.'

'Touching,' said O.B. 'The Dutchman was informing for the Governor's people. He probably told them about the Division Street payoffs. The troopers found him dead.'

'Who said he was informing?'

'A plainclothes trooper, Dory Dixon. He's an inspector and was making it his investigation. Our beat cop, Eddie Miller, saw trooper cars and called the desk. I went down and they got guards at the Dutchman's door. "Wait a minute," I say, "this is still Albany. Who the hell are you to set up guards without us?" Dixon says somebody killed their informant. "Maybe so," I say, "but they killed him in my town, and this is my investigation from this minute on, and my coroner is in charge, and the coroner, as you goddamn well know, can arrest *you* if he's in the right mood, so get your troops the fuck out of here and if you're nice I'll let you sit in on the autopsy." He was boiling, but he pulled off his guards. I called Nolan and he came down and took the body over to Keegan's.'

'They probably think we did it,' Roscoe said.

'Wouldn't surprise me,' said O.B.

'We didn't, did we?'

'Not that I know of,' said O.B.

'You tell Patsy?'

'I couldn't find him. That's why I came here.'

'He's up in Troy for a chicken fight. He and Bindy are going at it.'

'You want me to go up and tell him?'

'I'll go,' Roscoe said. 'I was going to sign myself into the hospital after my oysters.'

'Them goddamn things'd put anybody in the hospital. What do you mean, hospital?'

'The pains from the accident. They don't go away.'

'You go to the hospital, then. You go, and let me find Patsy.'

'No, I want to see him and Bindy both on this.'

'You got a ride to Troy? You want a car?'

'Bart's coming here to take me to the hospital.'

'Where's Manucci?'

'He went to New York to get Alex. You have a clue who did this?'

'Anybody can stab a pimp,' O.B. said.

'Pimps need to be stabbed,' Mac said.

'Whoever it was knew him pretty well. He was in bed, naked.'

'You find the weapon?'

'We found a lot of clean knives,' O.B. said. 'No money in his wallet. The whole place ransacked. He must've had five thousand dirty pictures.'

'Robbed and stabbed,' Mac said, 'and he dies naked, broke, full of holes, and covered with blood. I like it.'

The Game Game

Patsy and Bindy McCall were born into short-heel cockfighting, 'short-heel' referring to the modest inch-and-a-quarter length of the needle-pointed spurs, or gaffs, their birds wore to fight. The boys' grandfather, Butter McCall, had owned the Bull's Head tavern on the Troy Road, where chickens and bareknucklers battled from mid-century; and their father, Jack McCall, grew up serious about chickens. Then, in 1882, Butter sold the tavern to Bucky O'Brien, who kept on with the 'knucklers but didn't like chickens. Elisha's grandfather Lyman also bred birds and fought them at the Bull's Head, which was where the first interlocking of the McCall and Fitzgibbon families took place, the alliance that would control city politics far into the next century.

Jack McCall, after his father sold the Bull's Head, fought his chickens at Iron Joe Farrell's cockpit in the North End. Patsy and Bindy learned the game there and matured into dedicated breeders, eclipsing their father's local fame. Roscoe entered this world through Felix Conway's tie to Iron Joe, which was strictly political. The only animals that won Felix's attention were the horses that pulled his beer wagons; and he liked his chickens roasted. Roscoe, passing time at Iron Joe's, developed friendships with Patsy, Bindy, and also Elisha, who fought a few birds as a boy but faded away from the fighting to become, like Roscoe, a spectator at the McCall brothers' rivalry, and at their battles with other chickens of the world.

At their peak, Patsy and Bindy probably owned eight hundred birds. Patsy's Albany and Half Albany strains developed into some of the great fighters of the Northeast in the late 1920s and 1930s; and Patsy claimed his fighters were the best in the world. Some agreed he had a claim. Bindy's strain was subordinate until the late 1930s, when he crossbred his Whitehackles and Spangled Blues with Spanish cocks from Cádiz and Jerez, birds he bought and flew up from Puerto Rico. He then began beating the best, including Patsy's, which intensified the chicken wars on into the present moment.

To Roscoe, spectating at cockfights was a lifelong education in tension, cowardice, unpredictable reversals, and courage. The birds, bred for battle, fought for neither God nor glory, neither to eat nor for love. They fought to conquer the other, to impose death before it was imposed. Just like politics, Roscoe decided, but without the blood. Well, sometimes there's blood.

One idea defined the purpose of this sport: to have, to understand, and to witness gameness, and to profit from it psychically or financially, or both. Roscoe had watched Patsy test a Blueface stag for gameness out at his country place, setting six birds to fight the Blue, who battled for five, or ten, or maybe twenty minutes against each one of the six in sequence, without a rest. They tore him, pecked holes in his head, disabled one wing, blinded both his eyes, riddled him with their spurs till he was all but bloodless, yet he kept fighting, hurt all six, and died only when he could no longer kick, or stand. He gave one final peck at enemy number six just before his body finally failed his spirit. Patsy bred his Albanys from this brave stag's relatives and created a line of suicidally aggressive winners, one of them the granddaddy of the Ruby, Patsy's bird in the next fight.

But winners did not win by suicidal aggression alone. As usual, winning could also be begat by imaginative fraud. 'Forty-five years of teaching by crooks,' Patsy once said to Roscoe, 'means you always have to come up with an ace.' How did the crooks do it, and how did Patsy show his ace? Let Roscoe count the ways. The instant a crooked handler (the other fellow's or yours) touches a chicken, he can secretly break his thigh with a thumb, or incite pain by pressure on his kidneys or his vent, or rub his eyes to blind him. Or, if your bird is hung up with the other bird's spur in his chest, when the handler separates them he can wrench the spur so your bird's flesh is torn open and he'll bleed to death fighting.

Your handler can do the same to your own chicken, if you prefer to bet against yourself. You can also train your bird to lose: practice him with muffs so he becomes a coward, take away his protein or his water, give him a candle to study all night before a fight to paralyze his pupil, give him diarrhea with Epsom salts, drug him with cocaine, tie his spurs so they're too tight, or too loose and fall off, or so their angle will make him miss his target; and if an eye is gone, pit him on his blind side so he can't see the enemy. Or, conversely, put curare on your bird's spurs to paralyze the enemy; put grease, or drops from a heated lemon skin, on his head to make it slippery, so the enemy's bite won't hold; put cocaine or Xylocaine on his feathers so when the enemy bites his mouth goes to sleep and precision is skewed; put grease or flour or stove black on your best fighter's head to make him look sick and people will give you the long odds; feed one of your cowards tomato juice to give him a suntan, the color of winners, but bet him to lose. If you have patience, create a bleeder out of one of your best fighters: slowly feed him an anticoagulant – coumadin, say – until a tap on his hip or thigh raises a hematoma; and then you're ready. Collude with another owner and both birds will wear spurs one-sixteenth of an inch shorter than regulation, so your bleeder won't be able to hit, fatally, the carotid artery of his enemy, but when he himself is hit he will bleed. His neck will swell with blood and he'll be cyanotic, presumed dead. The savvy handler will quickly massage the blood out of his neck in the ring and revive him before he goes into irreversible shock, then will do it again at the first-aid bench, and the bird will recover, but now be known as a loser. Take him off the coumadin and fight him again, with long odds against him now as the loser; but this time he'll be wearing proper-length spurs to kill, he will have fought and lived, and he will think with the serrated edge of a survivor. When he makes his kill, collect your winnings.

The chicken war between the McCall brothers was taking place at Fogarty's, in South Troy, which was, in the opinion of cockers east and west, north and south, the most famous cockpit in the Northeast, maybe in all of America. Tommy Fogarty, a grocer, butcher, and hotel owner who became superintendent of the Public Market under Troy Democrats, grew up at cockfights, illegal then and now. But, since he opened his pit in 1917, he'd never been raided. He functioned in the Irish neighborhood that bordered Troy's nineteenth-century riverfront iron foundries. By the mid-1920s, cockfighters high and low, lumber handlers, lawyers, ironworkers, bankers, bricklayers, politicians, judges were streaming into South Troy with money and chickens, for this had become headquarters: more big-money mains fought here than in all other pits in the U.S. and Canada put together, so they said. Under Fogarty's twelve 100-watt pit lights, there strutted, bled, and died the gamest chickens mankind could breed: forty-four one-thousand-dollar mains, some drawing crowds of a thousand, almost one main a week in 1928 alone, the pit's peak year. Even now, in 1945, a waning year for the sport, seventeen mains had been held, and it was only August. Tom Fogarty's reputation for fairness, and his intolerance for cheaters, made his pit a place where cockers challenged the best, and where they expected and got a fair deal.

Patsy, who met Tommy Fogarty when they were boys, had fought chickens in the Fogarty pit since it opened. If Patsy had a friend closer than Roscoe or Elisha, it was Tommy. The most honest man alive, his knowledge of chickens uncanny, Patsy said – he can feel a young chicken and tell how firm his flesh is, how strong his thighs and his beak, how muscular his breast will be, how much of a truly coiled spring he will or won't become when he's ready to fight. All his life Patsy never found a handler that smart. Maybe five times a week he and Tommy talked on the phone about breeding, feeding, and fighting chickens – cockadoodledoo, Patsy called it.

Bart Merrigan let Roscoe out of the car near Fogarty's door, and went to park in an abandoned foundry lot, a hundred cars here already. A pair of Troy detectives sat in their sedan, guarding Fogarty's peace. Roscoe, using the cane Bart had bought him, walked slowly into what was once Fogarty's four-story hotel, now only a place where favored chicken-fighters could stay, and then into the barroom, Kayo Kindlon behind the small bar reading *The Sporting News*, nobody drinking, the fights are on. Roscoe went through the back hall and into a separate wooden structure with exposed, unpainted beams, and a circular dirt pit twelve feet in diameter, with a padded canvas wall three feet high encircling it. Maybe five hundred men and three dozen women sat on wooden bleachers watching the fight in progress, the crowd bigger than usual, for it wasn't every night you saw the McCall brothers, their bankrolls, and their fierce breeds of chickens, fighting each other.

Roscoe saw the blur of two birds in the air, one falling, bleeding from the head, and landing on its back, a wing twisted outward. Patsy and Bindy were faced off across the pit, Bindy smiling. Roscoe sat down beside Tommy Fogarty and shook his hand.

'Seven to six, Patsy,' Tommy said, 'but Patsy's chicken is on his back.'

'What's the bet?'

'I'm holding forty thousand, and the betting's heavy.'

'They're fairly serious.'

'There's sparks tonight. They're not talking.'

'It's been going that way,' Roscoe said.

Cy Kelly, Patsy's white-haired handler, who worked mornings as Judge Rosy Rosenberg's clerk in Albany Police Court, stepped into the pit and folded the fallen bird's wing under his side, then put the bird on his stomach. But clearly he could not stand. Even so, Bindy's bird kept his distance from Patsy's downed bird, whose head followed his enemy's every move. Then Bindy's bird feinted, and Patsy's thrust his bleeding head at the comer with fierce strength, a game but fatal move. Bindy's bird, with wicked speed and unexpected strength, caught that extended neck in a bill-hold and worked it, worked it, finally snapped it. Then he stepped on the corpse and crowed victory. Some of the crowd roared.

Seven to seven.

Roscoe edged his way to the first row of the bleachers, where Patsy was sitting between his driver, Wally Mitchell, and Johnny Mack, who ran the White House on Steuben Street, Albany's oldest gambling parlor. Johnny, Patsy's personal bookie, was paying off bets against Patsy's dead chicken.

'How's life, John?' Roscoe asked.

'Life looks dead, Roscoe, but there's always another chicken.'

Some of the crowd moved to the bar for a ten-minute drink, and Cy Kelley carried the dead bird to a corner where the corpses were stacked.

'I hear you're winning,' Roscoe said, sitting behind Patsy.

'Not with that one. What's with the cane?'

'Protection against women who find me irresistible. Anybody tell you yet that somebody murdered the Dutchman?'

Patsy shook his head and waited.

'Stabbed two dozen times. He was informing for the troopers.'

'Informing on what?'

'Whores, pimps, that's all he knew. I wonder what Bindy thinks of it.'

'Ask him. I won't talk to the stupid bastard. He kept the Notchery open last night. I had O.B. put a prowl car out in front. That'll stop his traffic.'

'My guess,' Roscoe said, 'is they'll link us to the Dutchman, even if they know better. Coming after that Roy Flinn business, it can't be coincidence.'

'Sounds like a passion killing, hitting him that many times.' Cy Kelly was coming toward them with chicken in arms. 'Here comes the Ruby,' Patsy said. 'I gotta pay attention.'

'I won't see you later,' Roscoe said. 'I'm checking into Albany Hospital with these pains of mine.'

'You need any help?'

'Bart's driving me up.'

'Have him keep me posted.'

The crowd drifted back in from the bar, and Roscoe went to where Bindy was sitting with his driver-bodyguard, Poop Powell, and his handler, a man Roscoe didn't know. The handler was holding the next battler, a speckled bird with a black breast and dark-brown wings, one of Bindy's Swigglers. It was Bindy's pride in this new breed that had led him to challenge Patsy, their first main in a year.

'Bindy, old man,' Roscoe said, 'you're doing okay. I saw that last one.'

'We're moving,' said Bindy. 'What's on your mind, Roscoe?'

'The Dutchman. He was stabbed dead last night. And a trooper told O.B. he was one of their informers. After that business with Roy Flinn, I doubt this death is a coincidence.'

Bindy just looked at the bird his handler held. It was serene and only half visible in the handler's arms. Bird, you don't look like you might be about to die. I'll bet the Dutchman didn't either. And certainly not Elisha.

'You ever figure the Dutchman as an informer?' Roscoe asked.

'He'd rat on his mother for a free beer,' Bindy said.

'You have anybody in mind we oughta talk to?'

'I'll think about it.'

'He hang around the Notchery?'

'He came looking for Pina when she went to work for Mame.'

'Maybe Pina has an idea,' Roscoe said.

'She was all done with him. Leave her out of it. Sit down and watch the chickens. You want some candy?'

He offered Roscoe the half-empty two-pound box of Martha Washington chocolate creams he'd been eating, a remarkable gesture. On a trip to Saratoga with Roscoe, Bindy had eaten an entire box in twenty minutes; and when Roscoe asked for a piece, Bindy told him, 'Get your own candy.'

'I'm on a diet,' Roscoe said to the new candy. 'Who's your handler?'

'Emil,' Bindy said. 'Say hello to Roscoe, Emil.'

'Hey, Emil,' Roscoe said.

Emil looked up and said 'Uhnnn,' and turned his attention back to the chicken in his arms.

'Emil's worked with chickens in New Orleans, San Francisco, all over.'

'This bird got a name?' Roscoe asked.

'This is the Swiggler,' Bindy said. 'You ever been swiggled?'

'Not by a chicken,' Roscoe said.

Bart came over to Roscoe. 'How you feeling? You want to leave?'

'I feel terrible,' Roscoe said, 'but I can't leave now.'

'I'll be at the bar,' said Bart, who loathed chickens, even in sandwiches.

Roscoe moved away from Bindy to a center position between the brothers, taking no sides. Jack Gray, Tommy Fogarty's matchmaker and referee, gave the birds their second weighing-in of the night on the corner scale, the Ruby three pounds nine ounces, the Swiggler three eight and a half, a near-perfect match, and Jack pronounced them ready to fight. Emil took the Swiggler off the scale; Cy Kelly lifted the Ruby into his arms and then both men circled the pit to give the spectators a close look at the combatants. The birds, spurs on, rested easefully in arms, healthy, the color of winners. The betting was six to five on the Ruby, who was a veteran of one fight, which he'd won in the first twenty seconds. The Swiggler was also a one-time winner who had taken some cuts, but danced the better dance.

'Five hundred on the Ruby,' Johnny Mack said.

'You're on,' Bindy said, and the betting dialogue began, the crowd's overture of grunts and gestures, fingers raised and fingers back, money, money, and more where that came from, an escalating hum, the electric music of rising expectations.

'I like the speckled, fifty dollars,' a woman said, and Roscoe saw Bridie Martin, who cleaned houses for a living, a durable gambler.

'You got it,' a man said, 'but if I win we go for a drink.'

'I'm not fond of knickknacks,' Bridie told her suitor.

'You're on anyway,' the suitor said.

'Bill your cocks, boys,' said Jack Gray, the third man in the pit. Emil and Cy stood behind their chalk lines, four feet apart, facing each other, each bird held with both hands. They moved the birds' beaks till one pecked the other, hackles rising, pecked again; and then both handlers crouched behind their lines. Jack said 'Ready,' and the birds' feet touched the dirt, they stood; Jack said 'Pit 'em,' and each bird, set free, went at the other's head, chest, throat, flew up and kicked, up and kicked; and with each kick by those flying needles the bettors roared, they know punishment when they see it, kick, kick, and kicks too fast to see, whap, whap and the Ruby is seriously punched, flies backward, falling, but up again and at that sonofabitch, they're in a smash-up now, rolling, stabbing each other, then hung, spurs in each other's chest, thigh, anyplace, and Cy and Emil approach the bundle, disengage the spurs – Easy, boys, don't hurt anybody.

'Pit,' said Jack Gray, and the handlers took the birds to their lines while Jack counted to twenty.

Bindy said, 'Way to go, Swiggler.' And that bird of yours really is a bit of all right, Bin. Patsy, you're not happy, but what the hell, it's chickens. You only think you know them.

'I got a hundred to eighty on the Swiggler,' somebody said.

'On,' said Johnny Mack.

'. . . nineteen, twenty,' said Jack, and the electric hum rises again as the birds resume the dance, the Ruby with wings wide to hit the Swiggler from the top down, but where the hell did that Swiggler go? There he is, up, up, and slashing with both feet at the Ruby one's head and chest, but the Swig feels steel himself – through the throat, is it? And he's on his side, the Ruby's beak holding his neck, Break it, Ruby, bust him in two, but the Swiggler rises from below and whack, whack, you bitin' bastard, and they stick each other and fall over, the Swig bleeding from the throat, and it rattles, but lookit that Ruby fella, gushing it from his chest, pooling.

'Pit.'

'Five hundred to two fifty on the Swig,' a bettor offered.

'On,' said Johnny Mack.

So it's two to one against, Patsy. Your boy is game, but what about the fabled strength and cunning of those Albanys?

'Give him hell, big fella,' Patsy said.

'. . . eighteen, nineteen, twenty.'

The birds rise, flying up to heaven, high as Jack Gray's belly, a pair of wild fliers pecking, pecking, popping their wings, born to fly but not far and not high, those bloody heels shuffling now on the way down, faster than angels dance, feathers cut and fluttering, a wing broken – the Swig's or the Ruby's? The Ruby's – but, hey, that won't stop that Ruby fella; wing or no wing, he's kicking, on his back and he's gotcha, Swig, got your eye. Oh, how we all hum as the one-eyed Swiggler moves and kicks, but oh so slowly, where'd he go, that Ruby sucker? He flies at the Ruby, sinks a needle into his heart, yes? No. But it's close and it's hung, one more time.

'Pit.'

Pull that needle from the flesh, Cy. How's your Ruby lad doing? Not well. But we won't count him out.

'Two fifty to fifty,' said a sport.

'On,' said Johnny Mack.

'... fifteen, sixteen ...'

Patsy cleans his glasses at five to one, and Roscoe knows the gesture means Patsy is worried. Roscoe is worried by the pain in his own chest, maybe what Ruby feels with those holes around his heart. Roscoe has stayed longer than he planned (he does that), but who could leave now? He holds the wooden post by his seat. Don't fall over, Ros, and, no, you're not identifying with wounded Ruby. None of that maleficent animal death symbolism, you did that with rats. No more martyrdom to your own ineptitude. But to tell the truth, Ros, if you had any sense you'd be in the hospital.

'... nineteen, twenty.'

The noise of this crowd will destroy Roscoe's hearing. This is a fight and a half, a sweet-Jesus-lookit-that kind of fight, them are dead-game chickens, I'm givin' ten to one on the Swiggerooney – gutsy bastard, that bird – and, hey, Bindy's offering *fifteen* to one now; come on, little chicken.

The pain is gouging Roscoe's heart, and he again wonders if he's doing it to himself: all this tension with pimps, cops, lawsuits, whores, votes, birds. Same old story, Ros. You can't get away from yourself. If he could, if he could even stand up, he'd blow this joint, but he can't take his eye off the Swiggler, who faces off Ruby boy, both chickens too tired to fly to heaven, so whack that chest, Ruby, knock out his other eye, kill that fucker. But good old Ruby can't quite. He's got the Swiggler's neck, going for the break, 'Break it, break it,' and they're moving, the Ruby's wing dragging, blood flying. Whose? Who knows? The Swig has a spur in Ruby's chest, Ruby's kicking, and they roll, then the Swig's spur is out but Ruby's second wing is dead and he's on his side looking mortal, so up goes Swig, his very last flight tonight, up and then down onto fallen Ruby, and the hum is a roar as the spurs go in, one a heart shot? Did he hit it? Doesn't matter. He whaps into the Ruby head, straight into the old medulla oblongata, and Ruby is stilled, but on and on the Swiggler stabs.

That's quite enough now, Swig. Your work is done.

Let's hear it for the Swig.

And he does crow, for now he knows, and he stands and preens with his own steady blood-flow, where'd you learn to fight like that, young fella? He crows victory. Ruby is dead, long live swingin' Swig.

And Roscoe saw it all, even Patsy's head shaking out the loss, and Emil picking up the Swig, who's still crowing the news in Emil's arms. Cy Kelly picks up dead Ruby – give *him* to the Little Sisters of the Poor. Johnny Mack pays Patsy's debts, and the winners smile as the losers lean back. Bridie Martin collects her fifty, and Tommy Fogarty hands the forty thousand to Bindy, who is halfway out the door as soon as he takes it. Roscoe should follow suit, but Bart is asking, 'What's wrong, Roscoe?'

Roscoe doesn't reply. All he knows is that people are leaving and taking their noise with them. It's quiet, which is nice, and the chickens have gone away. And you know what else, Ros? All of a sudden, so has the light.

Roscoe and the Fum

Roscoe, carrying his valise along the road, came upon an aged billygoat who resembled Elisha. 'You may be a goat,' Roscoe said, 'but your death doesn't make sense.'

'Try looking at Pamela's grab for Gilby as a paternity suit,' the goat said.

'Ah! So you did fall into Pamela's clutch.'

'You think so? What's her leverage in threatening a dead goat?' And the goat sniffed at Roscoe's valise. 'What's in this?'

'It could be money, it could be rocks,' Roscoe said. 'My question is, Why do I have all this pain?'

'Pain,' said the goat, 'is the only music you ever dance to.'

'I'm tired of it,' Roscoe said. 'I must upgrade life.'

'Upgrade life again?' The goat smiled. 'Have you heard of the fum?'

'The fum? I have not.'

'The fum,' said the goat, 'is a musical instrument that predates the Aeolian pipes. You string clavichord wire across the asshole of a dead cat, and you play it by picking its strings with your teeth. And, Roscoe, I believe if you thought it would improve your condition you'd start practicing the fum.'

'I'm in no position to argue. Care for a treat?' Roscoe put a Hershey bar in the mouth of the goat, who ate the wrapper, spat out the chocolate.

'Cakey action don't kibble at the Café Newfay,' the goat said.

Heartache

The needle went into Roscoe slowly, the surgeon aspirating the syringe as he pushed through skin and flesh toward the pericardium, the sac enclosing Roscoe's heart.

The cardiac monitor and a tank of carbon dioxide for resuscitation sat beside Roscoe, who was strapped to a stretcher in a sitting position. His heart readings as the result of his tamponade were dangerous: paradoxical pulse, high venous pressure, low arterial pressure, muffled heart sounds. The surgeon, fearing cardiac arrest, had reacted with salvational speed after Patsy and Bart Merrigan carried Roscoe into the emergency room. Now the surgeon aimed his needle at Roscoe's sternal notch, its route anesthetized by 1-percent-plain Xylocaine, and as it entered, with difficulty, the leathery, membranous pericardium, six centimeters into the corpus, the pain intensified sharply in Roscoe's chest and he cried out.

'Good,' said the surgeon. 'We hit it.' And he withdrew the needle a few millimeters, until Roscoe's cries eased. He then aspirated the syringe, drawing out blood from the pericardium. 'There it is,' he said.

When Roscoe was X-rayed after the accident, no damage was detected to the sternum or ribs, and after his collapse at

Fogarty's, the X-ray showed no change in cardiac size or shape; nor was congestive heart failure a likely diagnosis. The surgeon chose pericardiocentesis, or the needle, and as he was aspirating Roscoe's blood into his syringe he was saying that the cause might be an aneurysm from the trauma of the accident, that it could have bled, healed, and, dramatically, bled again, and only if they opened him up, a perilous move, could they confirm that diagnosis.

Roscoe, though sedated, processed this surgical patter with some disquiet. Nothing gets Roscoe's attention quite like the prospect of his own funeral, especially when he is conjuring the Golden Annals of the Party he is planning to dictate one of these days – Elisha's story, Patsy's, Veronica's, Hattie's, all of us, how we did what we did, what became of us, and what it meant, including our fraudulence, a golden tool, for none of these lives could have been lived without it, something Roscoe discovered in the Christian Brothers grammar school, when he too-precociously perfected a test, then wrote a brilliant essay, and was accused of cheating, though Brother William, known as Knocko, could not say how he cheated. All he could say was that Roscoe, this inattentive boyo who wanted to be in the woods with birds and game more than in the schoolroom, could not possibly have written this. Knocko, so known for his whacks with the ruler and his use of knuckles on skulls, and who never encouraged his students to be smarter than himself, arranged to prove Roscoe a fraud with a second test. Roscoe, who could have repeated his perfection, or nearly so, chose to write inept answers on the second test, sufficient to pass but not excel (Magellan sailed around the world, from Ireland), and Knocko, plus Roscoe's parents, who were summoned to discuss the crisis, beamed at his achievement. The boy is normal – wholesomely mediocre. We won't prosecute him for sinful superiority. It happens to many a lad. He'll do fine.

So Roscoe as a fraud was a great success. You certainly know how to rise in the world, Ros. A year later, he confessed everything to his father, and Felix was so proud of his boy that he bought him a rifle.

This event would, of course, go into Roscoe's Annals, which had one fiat: leave nothing out, including old Mr. Considine, the custodian at School Five, where Roscoe went before his father put him in the Christian Brothers grammar school to teach him discipline. Mr. Considine tended the boiler, swept the halls, and opened the doors for the pupils at morning. His white mustache looked like a paintbrush, and he wore a long coat and a hat that had been in style in Civil War days, a relic, as Mr. Considine was a relic, a man whose life depended on politics, and who, soon after the Republicans took the city in 1899, was gone. Mr. C, we missed your kindly patience with unruly boys, missed your vast bundle of keys, your painful walk, your missing index finger, your nose like an eagle's beak. For Roscoe, Mr. C personified all men dependent on the prevailing political wind, and when the wind changed, here came idleness, and the shame of sitting on the stoop, hoping for the dole. This vulnerability Roscoe etched into memory, a principle upon which he, Eli, and Patsy founded the Party. If you're vulnerable to caprice, we can help you. But if you're not with us, you're vulnerable to our caprice.

By late afternoon after his pericardiocentesis, with fifty milliliters of fluid withdrawn from the sac and an indwelling catheter in him for further drainage, Roscoe's pain and general malaise diminished dramatically, and he received his first visitor: Alex, in his army uniform, a thin private first class.

'Alex, my boy,' Roscoe said, 'you're back, but, God, you're skinny.'

'I suppose I am, Roscoe, but the same can't be said of yourself.'

'At it already. No respect for your elders.'

'Haven't I come to see you? Before my wife and mother? I wanted to have a chat before you died of bloat.'

'Ah, you have a charitable heart.'

'Are you all right or not? As I get it, you were watching a chicken fight and fainted at the sight of blood.'

'A perfect analysis. Too much death in my life. Parallel mortality. So they stabbed me in the heart to ease my pain.' He raised his shirt to show Alex the catheter. 'This tube is in here so they can stab me again.'

'Have them put a faucet on it and drain the fat.'

'A compassionate suggestion.'

Alex was six four, usually the tallest man in the room, his hairline not what it was when he left. He had his father's Roman nose and that loose way of moving his lanky body, plus that widely known ladykiller smile that was all his own. He wore a row of military ribbons on his shirt: the Good Conduct Medal, marksmanship medals, European-theater ribbon with three battle stars, presidential unit citation to his battalion for valor in the Battle of the Bulge, the Combat Infantryman's Badge, and the Purple Heart.

'We never knew you were wounded,' Roscoe said.

'Very minor. They now give Purple Hearts for hangnails.'

'Tell me your war stories,' Roscoe said. 'Cheer me up.'

'I did nothing. I went nowhere.'

'That's why they gave you all those medals.'

'These aren't medals, they're souvenirs.'

'When were you wounded?'

'Late afternoon.'

'Where did they get you?'

'On a green hill partly covered with snow.'

'Did you get to keep the bullet?'

'I wasn't shot. I was raked by the teeth of a flying dog.'

'Fascinating. When I get out of this bed we'll have a party with Patsy and all your friends. Like the old days. People will want to hear your flying-dog story, and we're long overdue for an all-nighter.'

'No, no all-nighters.'

'Don't tell me you've given up drink.'

'Not at all.'

'But you've given up questing in saloons for the Holy Ghost.'

'I believe so.'

'The army ruined you.'

'The real question is, what ruined *you,* my corpulent friend?'

'Ah, me. I wasn't aware I was ruined yet. Getting there, of course.'

'You've arrived, old fellow. Here you are on your back, your system breaking down from wretched excess. You're a capital ruin, Roscoe. We should register you as a historic landmark, in need of shoring up.'

'Your tongue was viperized by the army. But I forgive your calumnies. All we want to do is re-elect you.'

'I'm for that. Let's launch the campaign instead of a party. What are you cooking up for me?'

'You'll have a press conference at City Hall in your uniform and praise everybody for how they carried on in your absence. You'll tell them how we're going to pave the streets and improve the water supply. You'll praise Karl's job as acting mayor in handling our coal crisis. You'll dedicate the Honor Roll in the Ninth Ward, in memory of all the boys from the North End who served. Pop O'Rourke's been after me for months to have you lay the wreath.'

'Pop is still alive?'

'He wouldn't declare the Honor Roll finished until you came home.'

'What about my opposition, Jason Farley?'

'You don't mention him. Let him get his own publicity. Now that we know you've been wounded we'll drop a hint and let the press quiz you. You'll be modest, won't talk about it.'

'It's not worth talking about.'

'Fine. The mystery will intensify your myth.'

'Is that it?'

'No, there's Cutie LaRue. Remember Cutie? He doesn't know it yet, but we plan to run him against you on an independent line, maybe the Flatulence ticket. Patsy wants a third candidate.'

'Why?'

'Dilute the opposition. The usual reason.'

'Isn't that what I'm supposed to do? Who needs a third party any more?'

'You've been away, boy. The Governor's attacks on us got a lot of ink in the papers.'

'Turn me loose, I'll get a lot of ink.'

'You will, but this is Patsy's plan. He wants to humiliate the Governor with numbers. Troopers will be at every polling place, looking for violations. We've filed suit to stop them on grounds of voter intimidation, but if we don't prevail they'll cut into our control of the vote.'

'But Cutie LaRue – he's a bad joke.'

'Yes. Patsy's bad joke.' Roscoe's voice stiffened. 'Don't you laugh at Patsy's jokes any more?'

'Since you put it that way.'

'That's still the way it's put in this town, Alex. Don't stay away so long next time.'

Alex looked at his shoes and did not speak.

'Tell me about my father,' he said. 'Joey only said it was sudden.'

'That's the truth. He was more ill than anyone knew. His heart was twice its normal size. He told me he was retiring, but I couldn't imagine it was for health reasons. He looked fine. He was in other trouble, but didn't explain.'

'What trouble?'

Roscoe shut his eyes and rubbed both eyelids with thumb and forefinger, hiding. No way out of saying what has to be said. Say it, Roscoe.

'Listen, Alex. You have to know. Your father ended his own life. He took a huge dose of chloral hydrate.'

These facts did not register on Alex's face. Behind a grim stare he seemed to be trying to process their logic.

'Why did he do it?' Roscoe said. 'That's the obvious question you're asking. It seems like an act without purpose, but that wasn't your father's style. If there's a key to this, we'll find it. Your own loss, your mother's loss, it's very great. And I can't remember when I've known such diminishment.'

'Was he depressed?'

'Not to the naked eye. We celebrated V-J night together and he was fine. We had a little car accident and he got a bump on his head, not serious.'

'You must have a theory.'

'He burned some papers but we don't know why. It could be linked to the Governor's investigation of the organization.

Also, your Aunt Pamela is in the mix. She's suing your mother for custody of Gilby. She went public for the first time that she's his mother, and we're already in court. Your father talked with her weeks ago about it. He saw it as a money scheme, but I don't know how this affected his behavior.'

'Why in the hell is Pamela doing this?' Alex asked, his lips tight and white. 'What's wrong with her?'

'I'll take a week off sometime and explain it to you.'

'But Gilby was adopted.'

'Yes, and from her, anonymously. I drew up the agreement, which wasn't quite an adoption. Your mother and I went to San Juan to pick up Gilby and bring him home.'

'Such villainy. Goddamn her.'

'We can hope for that too,' Roscoe said. 'You should talk to Gilby about the lawsuit. He told me you weren't his brother any more. It was a bad moment, but I think he's over it.'

'What do you mean about Pamela looking for money?'

'She may really be blackmailing the family,' Roscoe said. 'I don't like to bring this up, but she may threaten to say that Elisha was Gilby's father. Did that ever occur to you?'

Alex threw back his head and wheezed, 'Jesus, what next?'

'Did it?'

'Never.'

'It occurred to your mother, and me. But I don't believe it.'

'Good. Neither do I.'

'That won't stop Pamela from threatening to go public with it.'

'The bitch. The lousy bitch.' The look of white fury was on him. Roscoe could not remember ever seeing it in his face before. A nurse came into the room to take Roscoe's vital signs and Alex stood up. He untucked his overseas cap from under his belt and put it on.

'Welcome home, soldier,' Roscoe said.

'I may stay in the army,' Alex said.

After Alex a parade of visitors came to Roscoe's room. Hattie brought him half a dozen sugar buns, buttered. Trish came and showed him her new brassiere, and offered to move into his hotel suite to take care of him. Roscoe said, Thank you, Trishie, that's very sweet, but I'd rather be cared for by wolves. Joey Manucci came back after taking Alex home and brought Roscoe the New York tabloids, four Hershey bars, and the news that Bart was keeping Patsy current on the action at headquarters and would stop by later.

Roscoe also received a telegram from his maiden sister, Cress, who still lived alone in the Conway family brownstone on Ten Broeck Street. 'Dear Roscoe,' she wrote, 'I hear you are ill with chicken pox. Does your doctor know you had that in childhood? You can't get it twice. You probably have something else. Do not let those doctors fool you.'

And then, at last, Veronica came, in a pink summer frock, pink shoes, pink necklace, matching bracelet, and bearing a vase full of partly pink orchids from the Tivoli hothouse. She kissed Roscoe on the cheek, raising his blood pressure, then sat in a chair facing him and crossed her beautiful legs.

'What did they do to you?' she asked him. 'Nobody can get it straight.'

'They put a needle into the sac around my heart to draw out blood, and they may do it again. If that doesn't work they'll cut open my thorax and sew up the wound in my heart. If that doesn't work I told them to cut my throat. I'm out of pain and, seeing you, I'm brimming with pleasure. But just trying to sit up in bed is like running two miles.'

'When will they let you leave?'

'When I feel better.'

'Who'll take care of you? Who'll feed you?'

'I'll hire a nurse. And use room service.'

'That won't do. You'll come to Tivoli. The servants and I will take care of you until you're well.'

'Tivoli,' Roscoe said.

'Don't argue with me,' Veronica said.

'Who's arguing?' said Roscoe.

When Roscoe's pain was all but gone, and the catheter removed, the doctor said he could go home, but in a wheelchair, for he would be slow to regain his strength. Bart Merrigan drove him to the Ten Eyck to help him pack for his stay at Tivoli.

'How do you feel today?' Bart asked him.

'Better.'

'Is your heart all right now?'

'Fantastic. What's your point?'

'Nobody wants to upset you, Roscoe, especially me.'

'You're upsetting me with questions. What the hell is on your mind?'

'Patsy's in a black mood. Bindy's handler switched birds in that final match. Bindy had two Swigglers, marked like twins, both the same weight, so this had been planned for a while. One twin fought only once, but the other had been in five fights, and he's the one did in Patsy's chicken. Ruby was overmatched. Tommy Fogarty thought something was wrong during the fight, but he didn't figure it out till after he'd paid Bindy Patsy's forty grand. He and Jack Gray searched Emil's truck and found the twin chicken in a sack. He also checked out Emil in New Orleans. He'd pulled the switch down there two or three times before they ran him out of town.'

'What's Bindy say about this?'

'Nobody's seen him. O.B. says he's hiding.'

'The man is nuts. You do a thing like that, you can't hide from Patsy. Forty grand plus all those side bets. Christ. Now we've got a goddamn blood feud to deal with.'

Veronica ordered Roscoe's lunch from Keeler's and had it delivered to Tivoli in a taxi: strawberries in cantaloupe, a dozen oysters on ice, lobster salad, *petits pois*, glazed carrots, potatoes *au gratin,* and the choice of blueberry pie or Keeler's famous ladyfingers. She had the servants open a bottle of Sauternes for the oysters and Pouilly-Fuissé for the lobster, and had everything served in the former conservatory, with its hanging geraniums, Wandering Jews, potted banana trees, and electrified hurricane lamps.

He had never sat here with her before, and it seemed calculated to create intimacy. She wore a golden chiffon scarf as a choker, and her hair was pulled back behind her ears. He fixated on her beautiful left ear, which he wanted to nibble.

'Do you like your lunch?' she asked.

'This is a room of enchantment. I like much more than my lunch.'

'Don't like too much more.'

'The more you like, the happier you are. Is it wrong to try to be happy?'

'Don't try to be too happy,' she said.

'Elisha would want us to be happy. He knew how to be happy.'

'No, he didn't. He killed himself.'

'He did that for other people,' Roscoe said.

'Which other people?'

'You. And the boys.'

'How can you say that?'

'I'm eliminating possibilities.'

'Killing himself for me. You're crazy, Roscoe.'

'He also may have done it because he owed me.'

'What did he owe you?'

'You. He took you away from me. Maybe he's trying to give you back. I'm not sure it's working, but so far, so good. You're saving my life, and we're together in this beautiful place.'

'I don't think it's wise to talk about this. Elisha would want us to be wise.'

'You think that's all he'd want us to be?'

As he watched her across the table he thought: This is the most sublime woman ever put on this earth; perhaps I exaggerate. But all Roscoe wanted from the world right now was to look at her, talk to her, love her, have lunch with her, right here, forever. Was that asking so much? Also, once in a while, he'd like to kiss her, fuck her, forever, here, anyplace, on the table, once in a while. Was that asking so much?

The Soldier Boys Campaign

Roscoe in his wheelchair looked like a wounded old soldier, which he was, as he stared out from under the umbrella he held to fend off the foglike drizzle. Beside him stood Veronica, with Gilby holding an umbrella over her. Gilby had decided that even if Alex was only his brother-cousin he was more brother than cousin.

'He looks wonderful,' Veronica said to Roscoe. 'I see so much Elisha in him. His gauntness makes him more of a man. Don't you think, Roscoe?'

'He's very like his father was at that age.'

'We'll leave after his speech,' she said. 'Gilby has to be at the dentist.'

'I'll see you for dinner,' Roscoe said. 'It's years since I've gotten emotional about dinner.'

The block had been closed to traffic, and on the lawn in front of School Twenty, with the army, navy, and Marine color guard behind him, the soldier-boy Mayor was on the platform dedicating the communion of names of sailors, soldiers, and Marines who spent their young years fighting Japs, Nazis, and Italian Fascists, as a crowd of four hundred in the middle of the street listened. The names on the Roll were a stark listing of alphabetical love, a scroll of blessedness. Several names were separated out, writ larger. The Mayor pointed to one.

'Charley Becker, a Marine private from Walter Street – I used to play tennis with him,' the Mayor said, 'and I could never return his serve. He was cut down in the first wave at Saipan. Bobby (Shadow) Valentino, an army corporal from Mohawk Street who could outrun my dog, was killed in the battle for Salerno. Captain Ray Ergott from Bonheim Street, a bomber pilot who played real good banjo, was shot down by Nazi anti-aircraft fire over Berlin. I saw other men, some of my great pals, killed on the battlefields of France. I won't forget them. Neither will you, my friends, and neither will this city. Their names here will be revered as long as we . . .'

He stopped speaking. He took off his overseas cap and looked up at the sky and let the rain hit his face.

'I hate talking about this,' he said. 'I hate it that they're dead. We live on and we leave them behind. How *can* we remember them? They fade. I already forget the name of the soldier who was shot a few yards away from me. I'm not sure I ever knew his name. Maybe it was Dave. He fell and the rest of us kept running until a shell hit Dave directly and the blast knocked me over. I was stunned, not hurt, but Dave's blood was on my field jacket, my hands, my rifle. And that blood was all that was left of him. We couldn't even find his dogtags. He died and I didn't and I don't know why I didn't, but I know I consecrate his blood here today, and the blood of Charley Becker and Shadow Valentino and Ray Ergott. And I'm going to try to keep that blood of their short lives flowing in my memory until I'm not here any more. That's not very much to do for those fellows, and it sure won't help them. But that's all I can do. That's all anybody can do. Now I'll stop talking. I'm sick of words.'

Nobody moved, nobody applauded. It'd be like applauding a funeral mass. Alex stood the laurel wreath on its end on the Honor Roll's pedestal. Then he put his cap on and saluted as the bugler played taps and the newspaper photographers took pictures. People waited in the rain to welcome Alex home, shake his hand, women he knew kissing his cheek, tears in their eyes, what a wonderful speech, don't you look grand, we were worried about you. Veronica was right. In his voice, his inflection, Roscoe heard the echo of Elisha's clear intelligence, but laced with the ease of a workingman's speech pattern. Alex had been exposed to plainspoken language all his life by his father and Patsy and Roscoe, who took him to Party meetings, and ball games, and cockfights, and saloons, but the boy's elite education had fortified his resistance to anything of a common order, and he spoke publicly with the unbendable rhetoric of a patrician. Today he spoke as a peer of those working-class dead men he'd known, no longer just Patsy's boyish Mayor but now his own man, a personage: a rich man's son with a common man's heart. Goddamn it, Alex, that is an unbeatable combination. You can be Mayor forever.

The crowd broke up and Roscoe spotted Townsend Blair, bent over and staring at the ground, looking for money, people said, but that wasn't it. He carried a burden. He'd been the Democratic candidate for mayor in 1919, our breakout year. He raised his head and looked at Alex, then turned to face Roscoe. Their eyes met and Roscoe nodded, but Blair's face was a frown, and then he walked off with his bent back, the old anger still there.

Pop O'Rourke, diabetic, florid, and spiffy as always, whispered to Roscoe, 'How do you like this turnout, Roscoe? And on a dreadfully stormy day like this. I'm exceptionally happy how we got our people out.'

'The Mayor must be happy, too, Pop,' Roscoe said, smiling at the loyalty of it all. 'I see Townsend came out for the ceremony.'

'A rarity, indeed,' said Pop. 'I never see him. Poor fellow, he still talks about it, collars people at the ballpark and says, "You know what happened to me in 1919? You know what they did to me?"'

'He still does that?'

'He does.'

Win Clark stood in the rain behind Pop, waiting to greet Roscoe, thank him again for his job as sidewalk inspector: tell us which flagstones need fixing, Win, and stay off the sauce, the ruin of Win, who drank the inheritance from his wife's death. Only the sidewalk job put him back on his feet. But why shouldn't we help a loyal committeeman, a stalwart for twenty years till he tipped over sucking the bottle. Win would want to tell Roscoe his bladder joke.

'Hiya, Roscoe,' he said. 'What's this with the wheelchair?'

'The old bladder's acting up, Win.'

'I had a bladder stone once. You know how I got rid of it?'

'Tell me.'

'Like everything else, I pissed it away.'

'Stay dry, Win.'

Roscoe waved to Father Fearey, the assistant pastor at Sacred Heart and everybody's favorite priest after Bing Crosby. Wally Kilmartin, the current Ninth Ward alderman, gave Roscoe the high sign, ready for a chat, but Dinny Rhatigan beat him to the wheelchair. Dinny was pushing eighty-five, and had been in on the election of Patsy in 1919. Patsy made him leader of the Ninth Ward when we took City Hall.

'You ailin', Roscoe?' Dinny asked.

'I'm resting up for the football season,' Roscoe said.

'I hear Patsy got chickenswoggled.'

'Where'd you hear that?'

'He called me.'

'Well, if he says so.'

'My God, is he pissed at Bindy.'

'So I understand.'

'I wouldn't want to be Bindy.'

'Bindy won't want to be Bindy if Patsy catches up with him.'

'The Mayor survived the war well.'

'He did.'

'It reminds me of 1919, Roscoe, after the war, and so many were against us.'

'It does exactly, Dinny. It does exactly.'

'But we'll do fine this year.'

'I think we will, Din.'

'How long are they keeping you in that chair?'

'Till I get out of it.'

'I remember Felix in a chair like that. At the Phoenix Club.'

'I remember it too,' Roscoe said.

'It was 1919,' Dinny said. 'That same year.'

'That very same year,' said Roscoe. 'A musical year.'

'Musical?' Dinny said.

'I always remember it that way,' Roscoe said.

Opus One: Overture, 1919

The Phoenix Club, a one-story brick building with a step-gabled roof, Dutch-style, was a leftover from the days when the North End was part of the demesne of the patroons of the Van Rensselaer family, a tract forty-eight miles long and twenty-four miles wide, seven hundred thousand acres on both sides of the river, with sixty to eighty thousand tenant farmers living on it under feudal conditions. The building had been an office of the patroon's manor, but in the late nineteenth century it became the Phoenix, the *sanctum sanctorum* of North Albany Democracy. Dinny Rhatigan, who owned the ice house on Erie Street, and thirty or so other men – Black Jack McCall the saloonkeeper-sheriff; Judge Brady, a hero when he ruled against that damned cleric who tried to stop Sunday baseball; Jack Maloney, the paving contractor, whose son Bunter held the city speed record for laying red bricks, 5,545 in forty-five minutes; Iron Joe Farrell, who ran The Wheelbarrow, the little Main Street saloon with the cockpit out back where Patsy sometimes fought his chickens;

Emmett Daugherty, the old Fenian and labor radical; Pat McDonald, leader of the Eighth Ward, who rode his bicycle with the North Albany Wheelmen – these good fellows, and more, were keepers of the covenant in the old club: two rooms, two card tables, a pool table, six spittoons, and two heavily curtained windows nobody could see into or out of. In the great blizzard of '88, six of them were playing cards when it started to snow. They raised the curtains to watch it fall, saw it get so deep that they decided not to go out. It snowed four days, and those snowbound fellas would've starved to death if their wives hadn't come down with baskets of food.

It was a hot July day when Roscoe brought Felix to the Phoenix. Felix was sixty-seven and in the wheelchair with troubled lungs, wrapped in his blanket and trying to forestall pneumonia, the ailment that he feared would kill him and which, in three months, would. He had been coming to the club after the eleven o'clock mass every Sunday during all the twenty years the Republicans ran the town. It was a political haven, for, with Phoenix dominance, the ward had gone two-to-one Democrat, even in Republican landslides. For this reason also, Patsy had come along today with Roscoe and Felix to announce his candidacy for city assessor.

Felix instantly responded to Patsy's plan: 'Yessir, that assessor's a good choice, it's their Achilles' heel. Same as it was ours thirty years ago.'

Assessment was a perpetual issue: high tax assessments on the property of political enemies, low assessments for loyalists and friendly corporations. Everybody did it if they were in, nobody liked it if they were out.

'What makes you think you can win?' Dinny asked Patsy.

'I'm up against Straney,' Patsy said, 'and he wasn't in the

war. I'll campaign in uniform, and I got a team ready to work with me, knockin' on front doors till we drop. Elisha Fitzgibbon's financing me, and Roscoe'll manage me. They're both smarter than me, so we can't lose on brains.'

'Don't matter how many brains you got,' Dinny said. 'The Barnes organization can steal more votes than you can count.'

'I know that,' Patsy said. 'Why the hell do you think I'm here?'

And in the laughter and then the silence that followed that brash remark, Roscoe saw that Patsy had transformed himself in the eyes of these veterans: had become not the fresh, ambitious pup he might seem at first, but a young fellow with a savvy that came from early exposure to politics at Black Jack's knee, and then as bartender at Jack's saloon, where politics was as important as the ale. Patsy talked the lingo and was ready for anything, even speaking the unspoken. He had a sharp, squinty eye, and an aggressive chin, ready for an argument. People knew him as fullback for the Arbor Hill Spartans, the team nobody could beat. He tilted his chair back until it leaned against the wall, his legs dangling in his high shoes.

'The Ninth Ward always goes two to one,' Patsy said. 'Am I right?'

'Usually,' said Dinny.

'Can it go three to one? Four to one?'

Heads shook. Four to one? The fellow is crazy.

'It's been done,' Patsy said. 'Right, Felix?'

'That was when we had total control. Now it's not so easy.'

'Can that control be organized. Can we buy it?'

'We can price it out,' Dinny said, 'if we know the money is there.'

'It's there,' said Patsy. 'This is the year to move. We can

win. McCabe is running Townsend Blair for mayor, and he's definitely got a shot.' Packy McCabe was the longtime ineffectual boss of Albany Democrats.

'Who said they're running Blair?' Felix asked.

'McCabe. I told him we had a candidate for mayor, and he laughed and said it was taken, that Blair had it. "Captain Blair of the 51st Pioneers," he says. "All right, Packy," I say to him, "then how about Roscoe Conway for district attorney?" He says that's taken too.'

'You never told me this,' Roscoe said.

'You don't wanna run, but you could win. You got that medal. So I say to Packy, "Are you tellin' me there's no room on the ticket for anybody from the Eighth, Ninth, and Twelfth Wards? Are you sayin' we're outsiders, the lot of us, the gang of us that won the war?" And Packy says, "No, no, my boy, not at all." "All right," I say, "then I'll run for assessor." He says, "Let me think about that," and I say, "Don't think too long or you're gonna lose us. We're big and gettin' bigger, and it's a new day. We got the vets and their families, and I got a whole lot of friends who won't go your way if I don't, and we're ready to primary if we're not on your ticket." "Let me think about that," he says again, and I say, "Okay, I'll see you in church." That was yesterday, and I saw him at St. Joseph's an hour ago, and he says he'll back me for assessor.'

'By the great goddamn, that's splendid, Patsy,' Felix said. 'You've assaulted the barricades single-handed.' And the Phoenixers nodded and grunted their approval of this fighting spirit suddenly made visible in their clubhouse.

'Make no mistake,' Felix said. 'Townsend Blair's a hell of a candidate. And James Watt is not the most popular mayor this town ever had. He can be beat this year. Blair will get the soldier vote.'

'He will and so will I,' said Patsy, 'and I'll get coattails from those that know him but don't know me. You trust Blair, Dinny?'

'He's smart, and he's honest,' Dinny said.

'That's always a problem,' Felix said.

'The real problem,' Patsy said, 'is he's a captain. If he's elected he'll think he's in charge.'

The Phoenix Club members heard this wisdom and looked at the precocious Patsy as if he'd just been born out of the ashes of one of their old cigars. They then took the entire discussion under advisement and went home for their first Sunday dinner under the new political order they did not quite realize had just come into existence.

The First Movement

Captain Townsend Blair of the 51st Pioneers Regiment stepped out as grand marshal of the election-eve parade, two hundred of his fellow Pioneers and five thousand others behind him, plus thirty thousand watching from the stoops and sidewalks, recognizing him from photos in the newspapers, and in the paid ads always in his uniform, garrison cap, and captain's bars. He wasn't a half-bad speaker, had a pleasant look, and money: his family foundry had been Lyman Fitzgibbon's chief competitor in the stove era. Also, he was a Protestant, and that, plus wealth, was deemed essential in a mayor – for you know what happens when they elect a Catholic. Remember Felix Conway? Kicked him out for vote fraud. Who'd ever kick out a Protestant?

Blair also had the backing of Arthur T. Grogan, which was confounding as well as bad fiscal news for Patsy. Arthur Goddamn Grogan, Patsy called him. Grogan had begun his career as a teenage oyster-shucker at the Delavan House in Albany, graduated to bartender, bought a large shipment of tea on speculation from a traveling tea broker, and quadrupled his investment. He compounded that money as a politically connected contractor, first paving streets, then building sewers and bridges, then owning a gas company, trolley lines, electric-power companies, eventually building subways in Brooklyn, Queens, and Chicago, and it's all done through politics, boys. That's how he became the richest man in town, whenever he was in town, a Knight of Malta Catholic who had backed Felix Conway for mayor in 1890 and 1892.

Grogan preferred incumbents, liked money, not struggle, and when the Republicans came in here in '99 he stayed with them for twenty years. But he kept his eye on electables, and this year of potential change gave a quiet but sizable sop to Packy McCabe on behalf of Townsend Blair, who had won the support of both labor and half the Fort Orange Club, the social sanctuary of Grogan's financial peers. This year of 1919 just might be yet another season for Democrats, like 1918, when we elected Al Smith Governor. Now Prohibition's coming, and people don't want it. They're going to blame somebody, and the Republicans are in charge here. This town is changing. If Blair wins this year, and he can, Packy McCabe will be on horseback with an elected mayor and also with Grogan, his absurdly rich benefactor. And they'll all settle down together for God knows how long in City Hall, which Patsy has his own eye on; and so Patsy has a special problem with this.

Grogan was a problem of a different order for Roscoe and Elisha. They lived with the memory of his visit with David Morgan, Veronica's father, who in 1914 had bought the mansion of a deceased dry-goods merchant on State Street, in an elite block facing Washington Park. Morgan bought the house when it came on the market, and moved his family out of the three-story South End brownstone they had outgrown. Roscoe was courting Veronica that year, and she told him the story of Arthur Grogan's visit to the mansion. Grogan had pulled up in his Buick touring car and sent his chauffeur to bring David Morgan out to speak with him.

'My father knew him, of course,' Veronica said. 'Everybody knew him.'

Grogan lived a block down State Street from the Morgans' new house, in the city's largest and most luxurious townhouse. David Morgan stood alongside the auto and Grogan said to him, 'You know who lives in that house next door to you?'

'No,' David Morgan said.

'The Bishop's family,'' said Grogan. 'The family of the Catholic Bishop.'

'I look forward to meeting them,' Morgan said.

'You can't live here,' Grogan said. 'You can't live next to the Bishop's family. You're a Jew.'

'Does the Bishop know you're speaking on his behalf?'

'Don't get a fresh Jew mouth on you,' Grogan said. 'Just get off this street. You don't belong here. Go live where Jews live.'

'We live everywhere.'

'No, you don't.'

The next day, Grogan moved stealthily to buy up stock in David Morgan's scouring-powder company with the aim of taking control. Elisha learned of the scheme from his broker and, moving more quickly through Morgan family access to records of the diverse holdings, he bought the stock in Veronica's name, then gave it all to her father as a loan.

Grogan's threat evaporated, and David Morgan was ever grateful, his daughter even more so: to the point of ending her courtship by Roscoe and marrying Elisha. A spoiler at many levels, Mr. Grogan.

The Morgans remained in their State Street mansion, and David Morgan gained a nodding acquaintance with the Bishop's family next door.

It smelled like victory to Roscoe, even a large plurality. They marched past cheering crowds, past dozens of bonfires that illuminated the night, along with the fires in all their bellies, and they moved through the length of Downtown, from Arbor Hill toward the Farmers' Market on Grand Street, to the tunes of the fife-and-drum corps of Christian Brothers Academy, Roscoe's *alma mater*. And they chanted:

Who ate the beans? Blair.
Who brought home the bacon? Blair.
Who took us over the top? Blair.
Who gets the soldier vote? Blair.

Elisha did not walk in the parade, but he helped pay for some of it. His steel mill had made a few million on war contracts, and out of guilt and friendship, and because he loved politics more than steel, he spent prodigally on Patsy's campaign rallies, on election cards, on banners spanning half a dozen streets, plus ready cash for workers who wore out their shoes working the wards for Patsy. There'd be street money tomorrow to reward male voters for their vote, and silk stockings to reward the women. Bountiful newspaper ads, paid for by Elisha, had appeared with Patsy's picture in uniform above his letter to the Women's City Club promising assessment reform and agreeing with everything Captain Blair ever said.

Roscoe marched alongside Patsy, half a step behind, leading the third division, a thousand in line behind them – Patsy's own booster club, North Enders, Arbor Hillers, soldier pals – and the chant went up for *'Patsy, Patsy, Patsy.'* Hell, even women were coming out, and, for the first time in history, they would work alongside vets and goo-goos as poll-watchers to guard against peeping at ballots, mirrors on the ceiling, bullies in the Donnybrook wards who block the door and either drive you away or force you to fight your way to the ballot box. We'll have none of that in this year of our heroes, Captain Blair and Corporal Patsy.

Roscoe, walking at the head of this loyalist throng, felt the vibration of the marchers and spectators, their great numbers, the rumbling of their planetary music. Looking back at them as the parade stretched halfway up North Pearl Street, he wanted to dance that dance of love – show me that you love me – vote for me. Ah, the power of numbers. The power of all things and all people moving in their rightful place on the planet. You can hear the close harmony of their motion, the heavenly music of the spheres.

'What do you think, Roscoe,' Patsy said as they stepped along, 'are we going to win?'

'I've got a bet on it,' said Roscoe.

'You could be the new district attorney. Why the hell didn't you run?'

'Public office isn't what I'm after.'

'It's not public office, it's politics.'

'I don't want to go like Felix.'

'He had a good run of it. He built some schools, he made his fortune.'

'He never got over the disgrace. I can't live that way.'

'What the hell do you mean? You don't want to stay with us?'

'I'm with you. I'll just stay out of the limelight.'

'The only way around McCabe is to get elected.'

'I know, and you'll do that,' Roscoe said.

'I might. We did the work. I think they're with me.'

Patsy kept waving, calling dozens by name, passing out smiles. Men stepped out to shake his hand, women to kiss his cheek. *'Patsy, Patsy, Patsy,'* came the chant. We'd heard the same at football games when Patsy ran and passed but mostly bulled through center, the dominant strategy that kept the Spartans undefeated for eight years. Patsy, bored with winning, quit the team and it disbanded. Roscoe saw that same athletic energy in the man now as he marched, shaping the military-hero image he would abandon as soon as the parade ended, a public man with less love for the limelight than Roscoe, yet driving himself into it and beyond to beat those sonsabitches. Why?

At the Farmers' Market, Townsend Blair made his final campaign speech to what was supposed to be a block party. But rain clouds opened and he only managed to say, 'Our plurality over Mayor Watt will exceed our wildest predictions. Our information now makes it a sure three thousand.' As he said this, someone hit him with a potato and his fedora fell off. His optimism drowned in laughter and a cloudburst as the crowd ran for shelter without the villain's being caught. The next day, in the *Albany Argus,* Willie Ryan, the fruit-and-vegetable dealer, took an ad to say, 'I didn't know who threw the potato but I know where he bought it.'

The Second Movement

The *Argus* reported on election morning that Republicans were spreading the word not to vote for Abner Straney, the incumbent assessor. Voters were confused as to why his own Party would cut Straney, and so was Straney. Republican bosses said it wasn't true they were cutting him.

Roscoe and Patsy were not confused. As Blair's popularity soared and Republicans foresaw the loss of City Hall for the first time in twenty years, Patsy had an idea: Tell Billy Barnes, the Republican boss, if he cuts Straney, we'll cut Blair in the three wards where our troops are in place. We can probably guarantee a cut of eight hundred in just the Ninth Ward.

Roscoe took the plan to lunch with Edgar Wills, Billy Barnes's lawyer, and after lunch the word came back: Done. The Straney rumor was on the street in every ward as soon as the polls opened, and the cut-Blair advisory ran wild among Democrats in select wards.

The Third Movement

Just as the polls were closing on election evening, in the front of Joey Corelli's barbershop on Broadway, which was the polling place of the third district of the Ninth Ward, Fortune Micelli turned up with twelve Italian veterans who wanted to vote. They all roomed in the ward, in Micelli's rooming house on Broadway, which had six cots and sixty-two registered voters. The vets had U.S. Army honorable discharges in hand, but no naturalization papers, and spoke little English. Micelli, a high-school classmate of Roscoe's, demanded that these war heroes, who had risked their lives for America, be allowed to vote, but Republicans argued it was illegal; and bilingual shouting and pushing turned into a rolling battle of ethnic pride, patriotism, and bigotry. Roscoe interpreted their constitutional rights for the pushing and screaming Italians, but he agreed with the Republicans that they couldn't vote and had to move their chaos out of the polling place and into the street, that the voting day was now at an end. And while workers of both parties and the volunteer poll-watchers formed a human blockade to prevent the Italians from assaulting the polls, the barbershop door was locked. Inside, Eddie Pfister, a plumbing-supply salesman who worked the voting table for the Republicans, and Bart Merrigan, his Democratic counterpart, alone at the table, unlocked the ballot box and quickly separated out all ballots marked for Straney. They drew an 'x' next to Patsy's name on each ballot, thus invalidating it with a second vote, then put all ballots back in the box and locked it.

Patsy carried the ward, 1,196 to 458, and defeated Straney city-wide for the assessorship by 145 votes. Straney demanded a police probe of Ninth Ward vote tampering, but it was denied.

Townsend Blair carried ten of the city's nineteen wards but lost the Ninth Ward to Mayor Watt by 850 votes, and lost the election by 1,200 votes. Three days after the election, Blair, meeting with newspapermen immediately following the recount that he and Straney had demanded, spoke aloud for the first time the loser's lament he would repeat for the rest of his life: 'They counted me out. They counted me out.'

Getting Wet

On the night of the recount, Patsy's victory party in the Malley brothers' Beaver Street saloon, the largest in town, was a mob scene, easily three hundred on hand to celebrate the election. All saloons in the state, Malley's included, had closed October 28, after the Senate passed the Volstead Act over President Wilson's veto, but this was a private party and no one would be dry tonight, everything free, the Stanwix kegs, courtesy of Roscoe, stacked in the Malleys' back room, the last beer made before the brewery went dark. Giving beer away was as illegal as selling it, but Roscoe had Bart check with the federal enforcers, and they would not be enforcing tonight. Too soon.

Roscoe saw Patsy, surrounded by neighbors, ward pols, and women who touched him when they smiled up into his face. 'Oh, Patsy, they can't stop you now,' this from Mabel Maloy, an Arbor Hill beauty who'd worked as a poll-watcher for him. Flora Pender beside her, a neighbor who'd had Patsy's attention for years, plus three women Roscoe didn't recognize, all found the new city assessor irresistible.

Roscoe intruded to ask Patsy, 'How do you like your party?'

'Better than gettin' hit with a potato.'

'Do you want to make a victory speech?'

'Didn't you hear about the politician who made a speech and lost the election?'

'You won the election.'

'That's because I didn't make a speech.'

Roscoe saw Elisha in the crowd with Veronica, a permanent, walking glory, and he lost her and still can't shed the pain after five years. He waved to Elisha, nodded hello to

Veronica, and turned away. Craig Leland and Frank Rice were edging toward Patsy, a pair of young bankers who'd backed Townsend Blair and longed to break Barnes's City Hall tie to old-line banks, and could Patsy be the way? He could, which gave this night an importance beyond the winning of a simple assessorship. People were starting to believe this was the hole in the dike and next would come the flood. Corbett Atterby, a young lawyer with a moneyed pedigree who'd soured on the Barnes machine and came to work for Patsy, stood at the hero's elbow, exploring one of Patsy's spillovers: an open-minded blonde who worked as a secretary in the law office of Patsy's brother Matt, the reclusive lawyer whose firm would become the leading law group in the city in five years; and Matt was here with Liza, his beautiful wife nobody liked. Tim Wiley, whose Molders Union backed Patsy, was here, and there was Louie Glatz, assistant brewmaster at Stanwix, who took over after Felix's longtime brewmaster, Franz Prediger, saw Prohibition coming and found work in Argentina.

Roscoe searched faces, found uncountable strangers. Who brought them? Who cares? Join the Party, folks, the new Party. He saw Hattie Wilson and went toward her. She had organized this celebration, cooked the corned beef, chicken, ham, the works, raised the victory banner over the bar – PATSY DID IT! – brought in dishes and silver – she also did picnics and clambakes – the most organized woman in town, and a tantalizing eyeful to Roscoe's eye: that full bosom, covered to the neck tonight, with matching hips and slender waist, proportions definitely not made in heaven. You couldn't call her pretty – her face was too full of experience for such a delicate term – but its soft, full, not fleshy contours held a promise of pleasure, a wish for it, or was Roscoe imagining this? He would find out one of these days. Her first husband had died in the Argonne, and now she was seeing Louie Glatz, who, Roscoe decided, was wrong for her. Roscoe asked her, 'Did you cook enough to feed this mob?'

'Even you won't be able to eat all the leftovers,' she said.

'You look too good to be a cook,' he said.

'I do other things too.'

'Those are things I'd like to see.'

'I'll bet you would.'

'How much'll you bet? I want to see the color of your money.'

'You'll have to make an appointment.'

'All right. Tonight. Here.'

'Here where?'

'I'll figure it out,' Roscoe said.

'Here?'

'Here.'

She cocked an eye at him and moved away toward the food. Was that a yes? He threaded through the crowd toward Bindy and a stranger who, if he was Moishe (Mush) Trainor from New Jersey, was about to bring money back into Roscoe's life. With the brewery closed, Roscoe's income had vanished overnight. He could carry on as counsel for Elisha's steel mill, but it bored the bejesus out of him, just as the mill often bored Elisha's bejesus, both of them preferring the new vice of political excitement, the rush of blood during the campaign, the vital hangover from all that creative fraudulence, and the anticipation of power according to Patsy McCall, who would insist Packy McCabe put Elisha and Roscoe on the Party committee that would control the next election. Here we come, Packy, and we can see daylight. Also, as a politician, Roscoe gets to use his wits, of which he has several. And although all know how smart Patsy is, he can't run this rump faction alone. He has the desire, the talent for making friends, and profound savvy about the human proclivity for deceit, but he needs an active lawyer as much as he needs money, to create a political future out of nothing but will power.

Money: it suddenly seemed available to Roscoe, if the scheme conjured by Bindy, with Patsy and Mush Trainor as his partners, worked out. Roscoe's dead brewery, his peculiar bequest from Felix, had new reason to exist, perhaps even thrive in these dry times. Felix had moved back home from the Ten Eyck when his pneumonia worsened and he was unable to take care of himself, came back after almost twenty years to his old brass bed in the Ten Broeck Street brownstone, and Blanche welcomed him as if he'd only been gone for the weekend. Why did she do this?

'It was peaceful when he was gone,' she said, 'no spittoons or politicians. He was no use around the house and he'd never go anywhere with me. But he did come to visit. He'd give us anything we asked, and never ask a thing from us, just to live alone in that drafty hotel. Then, one day, he says to me, "Could I come home to die, Blanche?" And wouldn't I be a fine one to say he couldn't?'

Blanche and the Conway girls – Cress, Marianne, and Libby – monitored his breathing to see if he was still here or gone up, and O.B., Dr. Lynch, and Roscoe kept him company part of the day. But he lingered, refusing to die until he was sure Patsy had been elected and Blair hadn't. Roscoe gave him the news as soon as he heard it, and explained the Blair and Straney cuts.

'You fixed both sides?' Felix asked.

'We did,' Roscoe said.

'How delicious. I'm proud of you. And proud of Patsy.'

'We had a good teacher.'

'Next stop City Hall.'

'That could be.'

'Do that for your father,' Felix said, beaming at having given this boy the proper upbringing, and also at the prospect of a vicarious, posthumous return to the Mayor's office, the only form of redemption left to him. He'd raised this boy right. He stopped talking and smiled up at Father Loonan from St. Joseph's, who had come to forgive Felix his political sins. The priest began with redemption through Jesus, but Felix raised a hand to protest.

'Jesus was a nice fellow, Father,' Felix said, 'but he was a con man.'

The priest nodded and forgave him his blasphemy, and Felix said, 'Remember Satan offering him that deal? "Fall down and worship me and I'll give you the kingdoms of the world"? The poor devil never had a chance, Father. The fix was in upstairs. Jesus conned hell out of him, just like his father and that apple. You think he didn't know what Adam would do once he got a look at that apple? Of course he did. A con from the get-go, Father, a con from the get-go.'

Father Loonan was forgiving this further blasphemy when Felix said, 'I'm nothing, Father, and never was, and the same goes for this splendid son of mine, and for you too. None of us is worth an old man's piddle and we never could be, because the whole world is fixed against us, Father. The whole damn world is fixed.'

As the priest forgave his insults and profanity, Felix closed his eyes and lapsed into sleep. When he awoke he said nothing more of equivalent eloquence, and then he died, leaving the bulk of his estate, nearly a million, to his wife and daughters. To O.B. and Roscoe he left the Stanwix Brewery, controlling interest to Roscoe, plus a few hundred thousand for the boys to split, which would keep them respectable but hardly affluent, his reasoning being that women had it hard and men should make their own way; and Roscoe and O.B. surely could find some use for the brewery, even if beer was illegal. Be willful, boys, was his verbal bequest, which was why Roscoe was moving toward Bindy and Mush Trainor, entrepreneurs of the new age descending, in which the illusion of beer would replace beer, the illusion of gin would replace gin, and the illusion of jurisprudence and justice would transform the populace into hoodlums, chronic lawbreakers, professional hypocrites, defiant drunks, and political wizards, the grand exalted whizzer being Patsy. Roscoe had already had an opportunity to sell his brewery for a very decent price to the new consortium – Patsy, Bindy, Mush, and God knows who else – and let them do what they would with it. What they wanted to do was make near beer, 0.5 percent alcohol, and people would drink it and think they were getting drunk. The consortium would soon make it easier for them to think that by infusing alcohol into the beer, then selling it for twice, maybe triple, what a half of beer had sold for last week. Take it or leave it, folks. Roscoe considered this offer and decided for sentimental reasons that he would not sell his father's brewery but would himself become keeper of the golden vats – vats that brought wondrous ease to all those defiant drinkers, and serious profit to their owner.

He touched Bindy's arm and Bindy said, 'All right, Roscoe. Mush, I told you about.'

'Hello, Mush. Do people really call you Mush?'

'Don't you like it?'

'It's fine with me. I never heard the name.'

'Some heard it,' Mush said.

Mush was slight of build, a bit of a dude, with pocket handkerchief, silk vest, and gold watch and chain. He had a scratchy voice and a face scarred by an old pox, his small blue eyes his chief agent of analysis. As Roscoe talked, Mush seemed to listen less than he scrutinized Roscoe's face for strength, weakness, venality, stupidity.

'You decide what you wanna do with the brewery?' Bindy asked.

'I'll hold on to it.'

'We can raise the offer.'

'Not for sale, Bin. If it runs, I run it.'

'You ready to do business?' Mush asked.

'You're handling the beer for Bindy,' Roscoe said.

'That's my job.'

'You'll pick it up, find the customers, deliver it.'

'I'll do that. You ready to do business?'

'I am.'

'I'd like to see the place.'

'I don't go to the brewery,' Roscoe said.

'Why not?'

'I only went there to see my father. He never wanted me selling beer. Then he gave me the brewery.'

'How do you run it?'

'With a bookkeeper, and Louie Glatz the brewmaster. My brother, O.B., will be around when you need somebody, and we'll rehire whatever crew we need to keep your trucks rolling. How much beer will you need?'

'How much can you make?'

'That much, eh?'

'People want beer.'

'It won't be beer. It'll be oh-point-five.'

'That's right.'

'Any stronger, they'll padlock the place and me with it.'

'How does it taste?'

'The best in town. But when we run it over the heat to get the alcohol out, I don't know.'

'Nobody'll complain. We'll fix it so it does what it's supposed to do.'

'What do you know about beer, Mush?'

'Nothin'. I just move it.'

'How long you been moving it?'

'Two weeks.'

'An old hand.'

'I moved other stuff.'

Mush was known as a swagman, a dealer in stolen jewelry – his gold watch and chain were probably hot – and as a domestic smuggler of heroin wrapped in cigars and sealed inside Christmas candles. By repute he now had close ties to a Jersey brewery that had been preparing to go clandestine ever since Prohibition became a sure thing, which was why Bindy brought him to Albany, a major market for which the McCall brothers were anxious to compete. Six months earlier Patsy had bought an empty soap factory that covered half a city block in the North End to garage his trucks for hauling the beer, and to sell car and truck tires as a front. Bindy had set up stills in half a dozen city neighborhoods for making home brew, and was building a major still on Westerlo Island in the river. These would only begin to cover the demand.

'You plan to bring in the real goods, I hear,' Roscoe said to Mush.

'Right. As soon as we control some roads and trains. Where's this brewmaster guy? Can he show me the layout?'

'I'll have him do that.'

Roscoe found Louie Glatz, a dull, good-looking, yellow-haired German of thirty who was the third-generational brewer in the Glatz family. Roscoe brought him over to meet Mush, and Louie took the new partners to the brewery. Would this partnership last? Probably not for long. But in the short run, Stanwix's income could skyrocket. We might even go round the clock making the stuff, and nothing illegal about it except the distributors. But what those fellows do is not my province, says the Ros. Let them spike the beer if they want the risk. Roscoe does not want a Felix reprise: cast out in disgrace. Roscoe is an honest man. Every man has his fault and his is honesty. But isn't it true there's no such thing as an honest man? Anyone who says that is himself a knave. Yes, of course. Honesty is the best policy for people striving to be poor, and an honest man's word is as good as his bail bondsman. But as a practical matter, if a man insists on dealing *only* with honest men he'll have to stop dealing. Roscoe knows how honest men think and it is terrifying. Wouldn't showing yourself as partially honest be the smarter way to wealth, even though shameless dishonesty would quicken profits? Yes. And a man ought not be simply good, but good for something, and so Roscoe will try to succeed by making it a practice to be honest whenever it seems feasible.

Roscoe made rounds of the celebrants and drank a little Stanwix with many: Neil Tilton and Rob Cooper, a pair of young Fort Orange Club lawyers who were close to Elisha, and Will Smith and Mike Reagan, who were jubilant over their re-election as alderman and supervisor of the stalwart Ninth Ward, and Cody Gilpin, the midget emcee for Malleys' entertainers, when the saloon was running. Cody was on the small stage at the end of the bar playing very well a string of slow, sad tunes on his baby piano, 'You Made Me Love You, (I didn't want to do it),' 'Come to Me, My Melancholy Baby,' and so on.

'Can't you play something lively, Cody?' Roscoe said. 'This is a celebration, not a wake.'

Cody banged a double-handed discord and got up from his stool. 'Nuts to music,' he said, and he climbed up the barstool and sat cross-legged on top of the bar. He was in shirtsleeves, with his trademark derby.

'I didn't mean to hurt your feelings,' Roscoe said.

Bart Merrigan moved in. 'What happened to the music?'

'Gimme a beer, Sammy,' Cody said, and when Sam Malley, the co-owner of the saloon, poured him a very short beer, Cody told Roscoe and Bart about his wife, Absinthe, also a midget. 'She ran off this morning with a little dink of a dancer to go back into vaudeville.' Absinthe and Cody had been part of a song-and-dance troupe playing Albany's Empire Theater when they decided to settle here. Their jobs now gone with the new dry law, Absinthe wanted no more of Albany. But Cody liked the town.

'No saloons to work in,' Cody said. 'You think Patsy'll get me a job?'

'What kind of job?' Roscoe asked.

'Anything small.' Cody quaffed his baby beer, asked for another. 'That little bitch,' he said, 'she was my queen. I loved her like a slave.'

Little jilted guy, where would he find another Absinthe's size in Albany? Roscoe, fearful of laughing or weeping, left Bart to cope with Cody. His eye found Hattie and he went to her.

'I'm here for my appointment,' he said.

'We don't have an appointment.'

'I'm making one now.'

'For when?'

'Two minutes from now.'

'Where?'

'In the back room.'

'What do we do at this appointment?'

'You could show me the color of your money.'

'You sent Louie away.'

'Wasn't that clever?'

'The back room's not a good place for an appointment.'

'Is there anybody back there?'

'No.'

'Then it's a fine place. Come and see me.'

And Roscoe went to the back room, which was stacked with beer kegs and several crates of whiskey. The Malleys also kept mops, brooms, the ice chest, an old woodstove, and trash barrels for the empties back here. Roscoe lit a wall sconce and drew the shade on the single window, then stood behind the kegs waiting, thrilled to his bones by what might be about to happen. But it seemed too easy. She would not come. Why should she yield to such a direct request? He had not uttered one courting line, not one word of affection, nothing but eyes and innuendo. She won't come. But she didn't say she wouldn't. Roscoe had imagined this encounter before he went to war, then came home to find her a widow, and everything seemed possible. She's a woman of substance. She knows who she is. She won't come if she doesn't feel anything for you, Ros. If she comes, that alone is a triumph, unless she comes in to say, Never do this to me again, who do you think I am? But Roscoe had seen reciprocation in her eye, hadn't he? The back room of a saloon full of people, there must be a better place. Yes, but not now.

Hattie entered the room with a key in hand. She locked the door and came directly to Roscoe, and, without a word, he embraced and kissed her. They lingered over it, brand-new sweetness, and his possession of her face, the amplitude of her body, his hand on the small of her back moving downward and not repulsed, it was all so fine. She fits you, Ros, and he stopped kissing her so she could look at his face, see what she was doing to him.

'The color of your money,' he said.

'I don't know how you talked me into this. We wouldn't be here if Patsy hadn't won the election.' And she unbuttoned one of four buttons on her shirtwaist.

'Then this must be political, like everything else in life,' said Roscoe, undoing a second button.

She undid the rest and opened the shirtwaist, revealing the lace shoulder straps and lace bodice of her white chemise, the splendid depth of her cleavage, and the northern hemisphere of her sumptuous breasts. Here were the partial but exquisite spoils of political war.

'Do you like the color of my money?'

'Beyond words.' And he kissed her in the latitude of Mexico. She raised his head and rebuttoned the shirtwaist.

'So soon?' he asked.

'It's a beginning. Now you know what I look like. Why do you want to start with me, Roscoe?'

'I wanted to start before I went in the army. You know that.'

'You never said so.'

'I don't always act in my own best interests. You're a full woman, Hattie. You thrill my heart.'

'I have a feeling for you, Roscoe. You're honest, outside politics. A man should have that.'

'I won't contradict you.'

'And I like the way you kiss me. You have a knack. That's a sign a man has paid attention.' And she kissed him again, but would not linger.

'When do I see you?' he asked as she broke the embrace.

'I'll try to think about that,' she said.

'Do you suppose we'll get past the chemise next time?'

'It's been known to happen.' And she unlocked the door and went back to the party.

What did it mean? A certain measure of adventure, and Hattie did find value in him. Something rare seemed to be happening to Roscoe. His life was moving in an upward spiral: political victory, a new Democracy in the offing, restoration of his income, and now the blossoming of something like love. It was too soon to love Hattie, wasn't it? But this certainly was something akin, and it was coming to him despite his fears, his fraudulence, his profound flaws. He was part of something that wouldn't be the same without him, whatever it was: Triumvirate? Group? Party? Fusion of patrician and hoi polloi? All were in forward motion with the promise of fruition, a new brotherhood out of the old fatherhood, all, as Roscoe now saw it, an oblique creation of the dead Felix, who said Roscoe was a splendid son, not worth an old man's piddle; and, in this spirit, Felix was everywhere here tonight, pushing Roscoe into an alliance with bootleggers, making him privy to the twisted glories of politics, and, through political consequence, forcing him to seduce a lovely woman away from his own brewmaster, leaving Roscoe awash in guilt, which he doesn't accept. Life made me do it, he concluded. I'm innocent. I would never do such things on my own. It's a trick. It's a trap to make me powerful, rich, and happy. I don't trust it.

Et Cetera

On Election Day, 1921, precisely two years after Patsy's party, the McCall Democrats elected a new mayor of Albany, Henry J. Goddard, an Episcopal banker (Albany City Savings, founded by Lyman Fitzgibbon) who had gone to Albany Academy with Elisha. Patsy's legend was by this time growing wild in the streets, but he had refused re-election as assessor and retired from public office forever to tend to patronage and, with Bindy, the care and feeding of the city's drinkers and gamblers. Mush Trainor had proved himself a valuable personal connection for Bindy, who, having drunkenly shot out the lights of a ceiling fixture in a 55th Street speakeasy in Manhattan, a fixture that demanded to be shot out, and having then been blackjacked and trussed with clothesline by bouncers prior to being dumped in an alley who knows how dead, said to his trussers, 'Mush Trainor's my partner,' and off came the clothesline, out came a fresh bottle and glass, and the apology: 'You shoulda said so.' And Bindy thereafter smiled inwardly whenever Mush's name surfaced. A dozen or more people had died in Albany from drinking poison wine and beer, and a pair of Italian immigrant undertakers were convicted of mixing embalming fluid with dago red. Home brew laced with wood alcohol had killed or maimed the innards of numerous indiscreet drinkers, and from this had come the drinker's test: Pour a little on the sidewalk and light it. If it gives a blue flame, drink it. If it's yellow, sell it and run. Stanwix continued to produce near beer, and Mush kept pressing Roscoe to up the alcohol content – not a whole lot, Ros. But Ros said no, and the argument continued. Federal agents found barrels of Stanwix stored in cellars and back rooms of thirty presumably defunct Albany saloons, but because the beer was 0.5 percent alcohol, no one was prosecuted.

Cody Gilpin, drinking with Bart Merrigan at the dead end of Patsy's party, fell off the bar in a stupor and didn't move. Sam Malley said to Bart, 'You don't leave him here,' and so Bart stood Cody up and walked the wobbly midget to State and Pearl Streets, where they boarded the West Albany trolley for Central and Lexington Avenues, Cody's stop. But Cody was comatose at Lexington, and Bart the Samaritan sat him on his shoulder when they reached the Watervliet Avenue stop and carried him to his own home, where Bart lived with his mother and maiden aunt, deposited him on the parlor couch, covered him with a blanket, and went to bed. Bart awoke to his mother's scream and rose from bed to find her hysterical at having found, on her way to the seven o'clock mass, which she had not missed in twenty years, a naked midget asleep on her sofa, snoring, with his little hand clutching his erected little member. Bart, furious with Cody, bundled his clothing and pushed him, and it, out the front door onto the stoop ('What'd I do wrong?' Cody was asking) and was shutting the front door when Roy Osterhout, the beat policeman, seeing the midget emerge onto the stoop naked followed by flying clothing, stopped dead at the vision, trying to understand it, then said to Bart, 'You put that whatever it is back in the house, or wherever the hell else it came from.'

Bart then monitored Cody as he dressed in the parlor, walked him to Central Avenue, put him on the West Albany trolley going east toward Lexington, and thought that that was that for Cody Gilpin forever. But Roscoe, responding to

Cody's request for a small job, talked Patsy, later in the week, into hiring Cody to train his young chickens.

Patsy would, before long, marry Flora Pender, and not Mabel Maloy as he thought he would, in the same way Roscoe married Pamela and not Veronica, and Hattie married Louie and not Roscoe. Roscoe confirmed a rendezvous with Hattie at the Malleys', her choice of location, on the morning after Patsy's victory party, when she was tidying up the saloon. Together they re-entered the back room, where she had spread a quilt on the floor, and there the chemise barrier fell away. Hattie and Roscoe would continue the affair for twenty-five years, during which Hattie and Louie would marry, cohabit, and separate; she would thereafter marry her third – Jabez Vogel, an engineer on the Delaware and Hudson – also her fourth – Benny (the) Behr, a veterinarian who brought her puppies to play with – and Floyd, the fifth, all without ever defaulting on her ripening love for Roscoe, who loved her in return. Roscoe watched her build her rooming-house empire, which he would find ways to merge with the work of the McCall political machine, in which he had become a key player. Neither he nor Hattie made demands of the other, only affirming from time to time that their love still waxed strong, and that neither of them cared to do without it.

First it was 1921, then 1923, and so on, a serious decade for the development of power, money, eminence, the high life, major trouble, and love, just the beginning.

Roscoe and the Pope

As he walked along the river road, Roscoe saw the Pope riding the Papal bicycle up from the quay, and he said, 'Hello, Pope, where are you headed?' The Pope explained that Patsy had invited him to judge a fox-trot contest at the Armory, a fund-raiser for the Little Sisters of the Poor.

'I was rereading Habakkuk, Your Holiness,' Roscoe said, 'and I wonder, as Habakkuk did, how can God remain silent while the wicked prosper?'

'Remember, my son, that God reassured Habakkuk that the divine way will prevail over wickedness. But it takes a while.'

'How can he let the arrogant and the rapacious survive, while the innocent suffer?' Roscoe asked.

'God did say he would subdue the drought god Mot and the sea god Yam,' said the Pope.

'Mot and Yam, it's a beginning,' Roscoe said. 'But what about the damn Governor?'

'Woe to him,' said the Pope, 'who builds a town with blood, and founds a city on iniquity.'

'Are you talking about any town I know?' Roscoe asked.

But the Pope was already cycling on to the dance.

Negotiable Love

There is nothing like the back room of a dimly lit bar on a summer afternoon when the heat is smothering the city's life; and so Roscoe has come to a half-walled private corner in Mike Quinlan's dark dungeon of drink to triumph over this unseasonable heat, a ninety-eight-degree day when summer should be spent. A cold beer in a short glass, and then another, cures the heat in Roscoe's heart, and the sweat of the glass cools the palm of his hand. Slowly the sweet placenta overgrows his brain, and the afternoon moves weightlessly along, as he waits for whatever comes next in his scheme to unleash the new Roscoe.

He has lost fifteen pounds since they stuck the needle in him, has recovered provisionally, is not out of the woods, but out of the wheelchair, and has sought retreat in Quinlan's (proper name the Capitol Grill), across State Street from the Capitol, a spa for lawmakers, politicians, and newsmen, where Roscoe has been palming beer glasses since Mike Quinlan opened the place two days before repeal. It is where political winners host banquets in the large back room, and it's a consolation pit for losers: piano music nightly (Al Smith often sang with this piano). Its walls are dense with photos of major, minor, and less-than-minor pols – FDR, Wendell Willkie, Jim Farley, Thomas E. Dewey, Patsy, Elisha, and Roscoe, among many – also with cartoon images of governors, senators, presidents in Napoleonic hats, dunce caps, admiral's uniforms, Santa Claus suits, Roman togas, and underwear, riding donkeys, elephants, and dead horses, commanding sinking ships. Wherever you look you see images of yesterday's politics fading away.

But the place has also given Roscoe pleasure, song, blue romance, and, in off hours, peace and solitude, which is what he is now seeking: an hour alone before Mac arrives with his difficult news. Mac had called headquarters asking Roscoe to meet him, a first for this exemplar of self-reliance, and when Roscoe asked, 'What's the problem?' Mac answered, 'Chickens,' and Roscoe understood that the Patsy-Bindy feud was heating up.

What the hell ails Bindy? Why would he con Patsy after all these years? Well, there's the usual rub of money, never enough, plus the brothel shutdown reminding him again he's only a second banana in this town, which Mame often tells him. Patsy gives the orders, Patsy controls the wealth, Patsy has the famous chickens; and so Bindy needs to win. But he usually does: eight winners in eight races at his favorite trotting track last July, when Roscoe went with him; nine winners with his own trotters at nine different tracks the same season. He can't gamble in Albany, because everybody knows he can't lose – *his* dice, *his* cards, *his* dealers, *his* joints, *his* town – and players drop out when he drops in. Even when the game is straight, Bindy wins. So he leaves town to gamble, goes maybe to Troy, to Fogarty's.

'Bindy always does exactly what he wants to do,' Patsy once said. Well, yes, but how could he think he could con not only Patsy but also the unconnable Tommy Fogarty? It seems to be in the man's nature to believe the con will prevail, for he learned it early. Hawking newspapers at age ten, he also worked as lookout (for strolling cops) for young Midge Kresser as Midge worked his three-card monte game in front of the Broadway hotels. Bindy grew up among grifters and gamblers who liked sure things – Mush, for one, who taught him that stuffing a sponge up the nostril of a racehorse enhances its ability to lose. He and Mush subsidized card thieves who worked the trains and the night boats. He won twenty thousand at a crap game one night in Saratoga and was then arrested for using slugs to make calls on a public phone.

Yet Bindy is no miser, just a man who delights in deceit. He was always cheerful, a right guy, yes, generous, paid his debts, good company in joints like this, bought drinks for the crowd, gave losers taxi money home, always good for a touch, if you paid it back. Roscoe drank many a night with Bindy, always liked him, still does. But then he turned sour, grew fatter after the Thorpe gang broke in on Mush, still Bindy's partner, and burned his testicles with a candle to get the combination to his safe, which Mush yielded in exchange for medium-rare testes.

The Thorpes also brought in Lorenzo Scarpelli from Newark to kill Bindy over beer, for he and Mush (Patsy the true power, but always in the background) managed its total flow into Albany, and the Thorpes could not enter the market. Scarpelli fired three shots at Bindy on his front porch, all near misses. Bindy leaped into the bushes, betrayed by his spaniel, which wagged its tail at the bush. Scarpelli shot the bush and missed again, Bindy returned fire with the pistol he kept in his milk-bottle box, and Scarpelli sped away.

Starved for action, Scarpelli crossed the river to Rensselaer, held up a bank, killed a guard, and was sentenced to the chair. Mush, Bindy, and Roscoe, all close to the warden at Sing Sing (who came to Albany to straighten himself out with gin after every execution), drove down to watch the Scarp sizzle.

The afternoon was so quiet that Roscoe could hear Georgie Moisedes open the tap and let the beer, still Stanwix, flow into one glass, then another. Cutie LaRue and Eddie Brodie had been sitting at the bar when Roscoe came in, and now he heard them talking.

'Let's go tell Roscoe the campaign plan,' Cutie said.

'You don't want to be seen talking to Roscoe,' Brodie said. 'You're supposed to be the enemy.'

'Yeah, don't bother Roscoe back there,' Georgie said. 'He wants company he'll come out here.'

'He wants to be alone,' Cutie said.

'He's figuring it out,' Georgie said.

'Figuring what out?'

'Whatever it takes.'

Smart. Georgie is smart; but not entirely; finally got enough money to open his own poolroom and card game, then bet it with Mush against Billy Phelan in a nine-ball match. When Billy won, Georgie handed Mush the door key, and went back to drawing beer for pols like Roscoe, whose glass is empty. Ros got up and walked to the bar, stood next to Cutie. Is this a free country? Cutie can't talk to me? What will they accuse us of, conspiracy to confuse the election process? Cutie can't win, can't begin to win, so why is he running? Must be a Democratic trick – I saw him talking to Roscoe. Republicans already saying such things.

'Mr. Brodie, Mr. LaRue,' Roscoe said, pushing his glass toward Georgie with another in his eye.

'Glad to see you out and about, Roscoe,' Brodie said. 'You had a siege of it.'

'A martyr to the caprice of automobile travel,' Roscoe said.

Edward Brodie began his newspaper work as a reporter on the *Sentinel,* and later, after Patsy had forced the paper to close, moved to the *Times-Union* and enshrined himself on Patsy's high altar by rebutting a federal report that Albany, an incorrigible city of speakeasies, was also one of the most openly sinful cities in the nation, abounding in bawdy houses and streetwalkers. Brodie conducted a survey of civic and city agencies, plus man-in-the-street interviews for his article, and found that in ten years no one had complained of any vice. One arrest had been made for procuring in 1928, along with four transient women convicted of prostitution, jailed, then exiled forever from the city by police. Men on the street told Brodie: 'Albany is a clean town . . . Albany is nowhere near as bad as they say.' Three weeks after his story appeared, Brodie was appointed Albany's commissioner of charities and communication, writing speeches for every politician Patsy allowed to make one. Roscoe called him the Oracle.

'Cutie, I heard you say you wanted to talk to me,' Roscoe said.

'Since you're the opposition in this election, Roscoe,' Cutie said, 'I wanted to warn you we're organizing heavy attacks. I plan to campaign as Uncle Sam, in a suit of stars and stripes, a beard, and a tall hat, and I will put you and Mayor Fitzgibbon on notice that I mean what I say about good government.'

'Will Uncle Sam make speeches?' Roscoe asked Brodie.

'He will,' said Brodie. 'He will insist on lowering the price of meat, for, as you know, Uncle Sam was a butcher in the War of 1812. He will stump for the right of soldiers to get out of the army now that the war is over, and he will demand more shade trees be planted downtown. Uncle Sam will also sing "God Bless America" at the close of every rally.'

'Sounds like this'll be our toughest fight ever,' Roscoe said.

'Watch out for me, Roscoe,' said Cutie.

Mac came through the open door in hat and shirtsleeves and nodded at Roscoe as he approached. He only looked at Georgie, Brodie, and Cutie, then back to Roscoe.

'Beer, Mac?' Georgie asked, pushing Roscoe's beer across the bar.

'Vichy water,' Mac said. He didn't drink any more, except a little port now and then with Gladys.

Georgie poured Mac's Saratoga Vichy on ice. As Roscoe paid for a round, picked up his beer, and started back to his corner, a sparrow flew through the door and panicked, soaring the length of the bar and back, corner to corner, lost, trapped.

'Jesus, Mary, and Joseph,' said a lone middle-aged woman at the end of the bar, a martini in front of her. Roscoe knew her, but not by name: a reporter who covered the Capitol for downstate newspapers. She rummaged in her purse, pulled out a rosary, and waved it at the sparrow, which was still soaring frantically from wall to wall. 'It's bad luck when a bird flies inside the house,' she said, and raised her arm higher to swing the rosary like a lariat.

'He's just getting out of the sun,' Brodie said. 'Buy him a beer, Georgie.'

'You're right that birds are bad luck inside a house,' Roscoe said, 'but never in a saloon.' He watched the crazed bird, which hovered, then changed direction, in quick and aimless flight. Georgie flapped a bar towel at the bird, intensifying its panic.

'Don't hurt it,' the woman said. 'That's worse.'

'Just waving it toward the door, dear,' Georgie said. 'First time we ever had a bird in here.'

'Who you kidding?' Roscoe said. 'This place caters to cuckoos.'

Back and forth went the bird.

'Now, everybody calm down,' Roscoe said. 'Sit perfectly still and just shut up. Don't make him more nervous than he already is. Quiet.'

No one moved or spoke. They all watched the bird fly back and forth, back and forth. As the bar fell unnaturally silent and still, the bird perched on a hanging light fixture. It twitched its wings, looked up, down, sideways. Then, with coordinates under control, it zoomed straight down from the fixture and out through the open door. The woman kissed her rosary and put it back in her purse.

'Thank you, sir,' she said to Roscoe. 'You understand birds.'

'I know what it's like when you're in the wrong place,' Roscoe said.

'So,' Roscoe said to Mac, 'tell me about the chicken war.' They were alone in Roscoe's corner.

In a whisper Mac answered: 'Patsy wants to bust the Notchery, with Bindy in it. He wants Bindy in jail.'

'He can't want that. That's insane. Where did you get this?'

'O.B. got it from Patsy last night and gave it to me this morning. It's my baby.'

Roscoe had talked with Patsy and O.B. both at morning and Bindy was never mentioned. So, Roscoe, Patsy doesn't trust you on this. He's afraid you'll find a way to stop the raid before it happens; and O.B. joins him in a second brotherly conspiracy.

'You're organizing the bust? O.B.'s not going in with you?'

'He'll be on the outside, but that's fine,' Mac said. 'I wanted a second opinion before I made the move. You're the only second opinion in town.'

'How do you even know Bindy'll be at the Notchery?'

'We saw him go in this morning and he didn't come out.'

'You still have that prowl car out front?'

'Gone. Let him think we left. But we're watching from two houses.'

'Don't you think he knows that?'

'He might.'

'You move in with your troops, knock down the door, back up the wagons, and haul off Bindy, Mame, the lot.'

'Right.'

'Who's in there?'

'Pina, anywhere from three to eight girls, the maids, and Mame's bouncer and bartender. Plus Bindy, and maybe some customers.'

'You get to bust Pina.'

'Would you believe.'

'But you can't do it. That's why you're here.'

'I can do it,' Mac said. 'Mac does what he's told. But Patsy and Bindy been going at each other like this for as long as I know them. They fight and then patch it up. If that happens after I bust Bindy, where the hell am I?'

'Very astute, Mac. When is this happening?'

'Tonight.'

'What if Bindy's not there when you break down the door?'

'I don't know. Buy Mame a new door?'

'Can you imagine how happy the Governor will be over this? And what it'll do to Alex's campaign?'

'I'm only a lieutenant, Roscoe. I got an order I gotta go with. Unless you know how to stop it.'

'I'll go up there with you now. We'll have a cup of tea with Bindy, talk things out. How's that sound?'

'Cup of tea.'

'Bindy likes his cup of tea. Four and a half teaspoons of sugar.'

'Something you oughta know, Roscoe,' Mac said, and he leaned closer, spoke in the softest possible whisper. 'Pina did the Dutchman. Her prints were all over his room. O.B. and Patsy know this, but nobody else.'

'Nobody except you, now me, the fingerprint boys, Pina herself, who told Mame, who told Bindy, and by this time every whore in town knows.'

'The troopers don't know about the prints. The FBI don't.'

'Let's hope that's true,' Roscoe said, standing up, once again readying his backbone for a move into the hideous maw of subsequence. Dutiful Ros, should be elsewhere, he's still here. And the blue devils are running loose.

Mac, Who Was Once a Child

In 1914, Jeremiah McEvoy's father left his wife with five kids in their rotten house in Sheridan Hollow. Mac was eight and went to work at Bensinger's Steam Laundry. Heat, stink, lifting, hauling, fourteen hours, buck fifty a week. He came thirty minutes late one day, they docked him fifty cents. Mac broke two plate-glass windows, spread ashes on two rooms of clean laundry. Mrs. Bensinger shoved two dollars at him, saying, 'Leave us alone.' Mac danced on the street for nickels and pennies, got a fiver from Jimmy Walker, the assemblyman, which gave him lifelong affection for politicians. When he was ten, the city took all five McEvoy kids from Mac's mother, too sick. She moved in with her sister, who had a house. Mac, too old for the orphan asylum, went on the job auction block. This farmer looked at his teeth, no rot there, made him walk and pick up a chair, told him, 'Get in the wagon,' and they rode eight miles to one hundred and eighty chickens.

Mac ate rotten smoked ham every day, hates ham, collected eggs, fed chickens, cleaned coops, hates chickens, walked horses to the pond, got squeezed between them, doesn't like horses either. The farmer cursed Mac for mistakes, knocked him down with the flat of a pitchfork, he'll kill me, Mac decided. At dawn he turned the horses loose, threw the sleeping farmer's only shoes into the pond, left on the run, got a ride to Albany with a housepainter who hired him to do first coats, but the weather changed, no painting. His aunt also told him the bank was kicking her and Mama out of the house, three months' rent overdue, so Mac went to Albany City Savings Bank and asked for President Henry J. Goddard, who was eating a banana.

'You want a banana, young fella?' President Goddard asked.

'My mother is losing her house and I have to help her.'

'How can you help?' the president asked.

'I'm a housepainter,' he said. 'I clean and paint houses.'

'A regular contractor.'

'I can fix houses for the bank,' Mac said.

'This is a great, great country,' President Goddard said. 'Put the boy to work.'

A bank guy took Mac to one of the bank's worst houses,

three floors, five apartments. 'Forty dollars when they're all cleaned, painted, and papered,' said the bank guy. 'Here's ten on account.'

Cleaning, painting was easy, but the wallpaper was peeling, filthy, Mac ripped it down. How do you put it up? Woman across the street saw Mac going in with armloads of wallpaper, watched him dump the same paper in the trash, something wrong. Woman, Hattie, asked Mac what happened. Mac said he'd put fifteen double rolls on five ceilings but it fell off. Hattie said she'd fix that and showed him the secret: a broom that swept the paper tight and straight. Mac got the knack, collected his thirty dollars, and bought his mother a hundred roses and a toy diamond ring.

Mac moved into Hattie's house, went to school, got work delivering oysters anyplace for Bill Keeler's restaurant, including whorehouses. One of the Poole sisters let him in one night, took the oysters, put them in dirty dishwater. She left Mac in the kitchen, didn't pay him, went into the parlor, and fell over. Mac looked in and saw the four Poole sisters, good-looking whores, all whacked on the pipe, money on the table. Mac pocketed the money and grew out of oyster transport, but not before he got to know whores, and liked a few.

He stayed on with Hattie, quit school after eighth grade, and grew up with chalky teeth and the wrong jobs, housepainter, would-be carpenter. Then, one day, Hattie told him to go see O. B. Conway, the police detective who was king of the night, and Mac became a cop.

Mac Rising

In 1928, after he disarmed, with a garden rake, a one-eyed Polish psychotic wielding a shotgun, an act of indisputable initiative, dexterity, and courage, O.B. persuaded the chief: Take Mac out of uniform, make him a detective.

In 1929, after Pauly Biggers killed two people and took a fourteen-year-old girl hostage and said he'd kill her, too, if they didn't let him drive to Canada, Mac, unarmed, talked an hour and ten minutes to Pauly, making the Canadian escape arrangements. When Mac and Pauly finally agreed and shook hands on it, Mac shot Pauly between the eyes with a .22 pistol device he had rigged into the left armpit of his coat, in emulation of Albany's Silent Gunman of 1916. O.B. got Mac a ten-dollar raise.

In 1930, Mac and O.B. found four members of the Polka Dot Gang, who all wore polka-dot ties on the job, raiding a boxcar loaded with alcohol destined for Al Brisbane's two downtown drugstores. Mac shot two of the three, but O.B. got hit in the leg and went down in the open. Mac stood up and covered him, two guns blazing, pulled him out of danger, shot a third Dotter (the fourth got away), but took a bullet in the side, and everybody went to the hospital. Mac was wearing a silk shirt, and when they pulled the shirt out of his wound, out popped the bullet, no surgery needed. Mac realized bullets don't go through silk, and after that O.B. also wore silk shirts. O.B. threw a party for Mac, thanks for saving my life, and bought him a new .38 police special with a pearl handle.

Mac and O.B., close as brothers, roamed the city, and Mac met Patsy, who was Jesus, also Moses. O.B. had organized the truck convoys that brought Patsy and Bindy's beer into town early in Prohibition and was so savvy and ruthless Patsy made him deputy chief of the Night Squad, with orders to keep out hotshot hoodlums and freelancers with beer to sell. Nobody but the organization sells beer in Albany. Let no hoodlum set up shop in our town. Mac and O.B. shot up several trucks of Italian bootleggers who ignored the rules, also several Italians. Patsy thought the world of Mac and his shooting, but O.B. was Patsy's man, and in 1930 Patsy made him supreme boss of the Night Squad.

Mac and Pina: A Love Mess

Mac met a cute singer at the Kenmore and they married and lasted long enough to have twins. One morning Mac's wife, in her small black hat and fur jacket, stood in the doorway saying, 'If you want me, come after me.' Mac said, 'You're back in two days or don't bother,' and watched her high heels, her black stocking seams, and the sweet swagger of her ass as she walked to the taxi. The end. Mac bought a two-family house on Walter Street, moved his sister in downstairs, no rent if you raise the twins, Sis. Mac lived upstairs and saw the twins sometimes. One night at Joey Polito's Spaghetti House (opens 3 A.M., two broads always, no spaghetti), Mac saw Giuseppina serving drinks, just off the boat.

'You like?' Joey asked Mac. 'I dress her up for you.'

Joey sent Pina into the ladies' room with a suitcase and she came out, *Madonna santa*, too much for this joint. You shoulda seen her. Mac got her a waitress job in a real restaurant with good tips, and then it was Mac and Pina. One customer, a car dealer, gave her a Pontiac. She had no license, but she drove to Atlantic City for a garment makers' convention, came back, and threw eleven hundred in tens, twenties, and fifties on her bed for Mac to see. Some tips. He could have cried over how great she looked, that long black hair, those perfect calves, those fantastic tits, how she rose so high in the world working for tips, which is what she called it. Do what you know how, was Mac's credo. Mac and Pina, for months and months. Mac and Pina, this could last.

O.B. got to like Pina's looks. One morning, after work, when Mac was going to Pina's place, he saw O.B. come out and get into his car. Some say O.B. should not have done this, and Mac is a member of that club. Pina said O.B. paid for what he got, just another Giovanni. Mac made an effort to believe her. Pina could've given Mac the clap, the crabs, and the syph, he wouldn't mind as long as she was there after work. But then she stayed out. Where? Mac tried patience, but had none. The way his wife left him, bingo, he left Pina, who moved out of her place and in with the Dutchman, upstairs over the Double Dutch nightclub, where the Dutchman had B-girls of his own but none like Pina. Pina liked the Dutchman's big apartment, nice plants, thick rugs, picture window looking at the river, watch the boats go by. Dutchman played Italian music for Pina, Mac never thought of that. Dutchman gave her a diamond big as the end of a cigarette, Mac couldn't afford that. Dutchman bent her in two, tied her up, gagged her, Mac didn't go for that stuff, didn't know Pina did, a girl's gotta have her fun. Pina would still screw Mac silly if he came around, but Mac gave up Pina. Everything except thinking about her.

Mac and Jack

Roscoe stuffed himself into the front seat of Mac's car for the ride to the Notchery, imagining what was happening inside Mac's head, same old thing, revving himself up with the necessary iron to face the unknown worst the world offered him day after day. But today had substantially more gravity, as Mac prepared to lead the invading army into a war between the McCall men maddened by the will to excess, power gone berserk, not a first for either brother. When these fellows are wrong they are wrong *fortissimo*.

Today was also different for Roscoe, the outsider about to become the intermediary; and nobody but Mac knew that yet. There was an antecedent for such a condition: late fall 1931, Jack (Legs) Diamond, still recovering from being shot in the arm, lung, and liver seven months earlier, on bail waiting for his second trial in Troy for kidnapping and torturing a trucker, here he was suddenly in the Elks Club, pulling up a chair to sit down for a little pinochle with Roscoe, Marcus Gorman, and Leo Finn, one of the Party's aging bagmen, an ex-schoolteacher and still a bit of a *literatus*, who knew his Yeats and Keats and could call up fragments on cue, which amused Jack.

'So – how are all your bullet holes doing, Jack?' Roscoe asked.

'You don't have to answer that,' said Marcus, whose fame was in a crescendo from representing Jack in court.

'They're coming along,' Jack said.

'You don't seem to mind being shot,' Roscoe said, 'you handle it so well and so often.'

'Being shot's not so bad,' Jack said. 'The problem is getting even.'

'My buddies gut-shot me in the war,' Roscoe said.

'Accidentally on purpose?' Jack asked.

'Exactly.'

'Amazing,' said Leo. 'Just what Willie wrote.'

'Willie?' said Jack. 'Is that one of your old poets?'

'The same . . . "A heavily built Falstaffian man / Comes cracking jokes of civil war / As though to die by gunshot were / The finest play under the sun."'

'Civil war,' Jack said. 'I know about that. It was my buddies who shot me in the back with two shotguns.'

'Your war never ends, does it?' Roscoe said.

'No, but I'm too young to retire,' Jack said, and Roscoe dealt the cards.

Jack was thirty-four and had been an outsize presence in Albany all that summer, turning up at the Elks, at the best restaurants, a regular at the Kenmore's Rainbo Room, headlines in the papers every day about his upcoming trial and his crushed mountain empire. Since the late 1920s Jack, the best-known gangster in the East, had been the Emperor of Applejack in the Catskills, doing business in eighteen counties, running beer out of the Kingston brewery he took over after Charlie Northrup disappeared, highjacking fellow bootleggers, his specialty. He'd terrorized most Catskill roadhouses and hotels into handling his goods, converted law enforcement to his persuasion – the sheriff of Greene County gave pistol permits to his whole gang, made Jack a deputy with a badge. But then Jack kidnapped and tortured Clem Streeter (burned his feet, hung him from a tree) for refusing to say where he was hauling twenty-four barrels of hard cider, the raw element of applejack. And when Clem told his story next day, well, that did it. We can stand anything but torture, said Governor Roosevelt. And in the spring of 1931, he sent state troopers and his attorney general down to rupture Jack's empire up the middle and sideways.

Marcus won Jack a change of venue from Catskill to Troy, and Jack then transferred his wife, girlfriend, and select henchmen into a six-room suite on the second floor of the Kenmore. In July, the jury at Jack's first Troy trial acquitted him of assaulting the trucker, and Jack the celebrity soared socially over Albany rooftops, ubiquitous in the town's speakeasies, awaiting the second trial – another acquittal? His ultimate plan: go into business upstate, away from the Catskills, new gang, new territory, new connections.

Long story short: Jack, after the Elks Club pinochle game, offered Roscoe a business proposition – cheap beer, no matter what price he had to undercut, cheaper by a dollar a barrel than the Waxey Gordon beer Mush and Bindy were bringing into Albany. Save your money! Buy from Jack! Where was Jack getting his beer now that the troopers had closed his brewery?

'There's beer everywhere,' said Jack, who had links to breweries in Fort Edward, Troy, Yonkers, Manhattan, Coney Island. But Jack's beer came with Jack's baggage. Albany Detective Sergeant Freddie Robin had been slouching on a sofa in the Kenmore lobby, assigned to watch Jack's pals troop in and out for business and sociality: the Thorpe brothers, homegrown thugs who, a year hence, would bring in Lorenzo Scarpelli to kill Bindy and Mush; also Honey Curry and Hubert Maloy, who would evolve into kidnappers themselves in 1938, holding Bindy's son, Charlie Boy, for ransom; plus Vincent Coll, Fats McCarthy, and Dutch Schultz, a trio of swaggering notables who had left corpses all over Manhattan in the beer wars. Newsmen had kept score on who was ahead in the corpse count, and Jack won. Did Albany need beer that came in coffins?

'Jack, your proposition sounds tempting,' Roscoe said, 'but Waxey's beer is well liked. I can't imagine the boys switching.'

'Can you check it out with Patsy and Bindy?' Jack wondered.

'I'll pass the question along,' said Roscoe.

When he told Patsy about the offer, Patsy said, 'That fella's going to be a serious nuisance if they don't put him in jail.'

Roscoe *at that moment* became the outsider in future Jack talk: Patsy trusting him like nobody else, but keeping him apart from certain cosmic decisions. You run the Party, Roscoe, I'll run the nighttown – as if they could be separated. But Patsy believed in separate realms of power, pitted even his closest allies against one another when it suited him. Like pitting chickens. Competitive truculence. See who survives.

And so monitoring Jack fell to O.B. and Mac. They followed him when he left the Kenmore and moved into the Wellington Hotel, next to the Elks Club. They pressured the Wellington to put him out, and followed him to the Pine Hills where he stayed with the bootlegger Nick Farr. With the Thorpe brothers, Farr was helping set up Jack's embryonic upstate beer network. Farr's neighbors hadn't known what he did for a living, but they recognized Jack from the newspapers and alerted the police. O.B. and Mac told Jack he was upsetting the citizenry and was no longer welcome in Albany. Get lost, Jack.

Jack sent his wife, Alice, to her apartment on 72nd Street in Manhattan, then moved in with his girlfriend, Marion (Kiki) Roberts, upstairs over Sylvester Hausen's card game on Nineteenth Street in Watervliet. He switched between there and a house in North Troy until the second week of December, when the trial was about to begin. He also called Bindy and said he'd dropped the idea of bringing in beer, but how about permission to go into the insurance business in Albany? Insurance meant collecting premiums that insured the buyer against Jack Diamond's resentment of people who wouldn't buy his insurance. Bindy, like Roscoe, passed Jack's request on to Patsy.

Jack then rented rooms for himself and Alice; his brother

Eddie's widow, Kitty; and her seven-year-old son, Johnny, named for Jack, who were all humanizing presences at Jack's trials. A fella with a family like that, he's gotta have some good in him. The rooms were ten dollars a week each in one of Hattie's houses, 67 Dove Street, rented under the names of Mr. and Mrs. Kelly.

Jack was back in Albany.

His residential slide from Kenmore luxury to a ten-dollar rooming house was strictly financial. Heavy expenses for hotels and high life, hospitals and lawyers, payoffs to politicians, keeping his women happy, were taxing. He had booze of every kind stashed in a dozen drops upstate but, being under surveillance, he couldn't get to it to peddle it – a prisoner of his own glittering infamy. The stash, much of it originally stolen by Jack, was eventually rounded up by troopers and valued at ten million, its street price. But it wasn't worth forty cents to Jack at the moment. He was broke.

On the afternoon of December 17, Jack, with Marcus Gorman's assistance, was acquitted of the Clem Streeter kidnapping. He celebrated with a party at Packy Delaney's Parody Club in Albany; fifty people – Alice, Marcus, the night crowd of gamblers, pimps, grifters, a few newspapermen, a priest, an ex-railroad cop named Milligan – came to his party. Assorted Albany detectives also came: Freddie Robin, Tuohey and Spivak from the Gambling Squad, taking notes, and O.B. and Mac, who had been at the trial and now, from their car, watched the celebrants enter and leave, all night long. About one o'clock, Jack left them all and went up to Ten Broeck Street to see Kiki in the new apartment he'd rented for her. They drank and whatnotted while his cab driver, Frankie Teller, and his lookout, Morty Besch, waited three hours for him. After four o'clock, Frankie dropped Morty downtown and drove Jack to Dove Street, then helped him climb the stoop and the inside stairs to his room. Alone, Jack undressed and fell into a drunken sleep in his underwear.

At 4:30 A.M., a dark-red Packard sedan that had been idling with its lights out a block to the north, moved up to the curbstone in front of 67 Dove. O.B. and Mac got out and went up the stoop, into the house, past the potted plant in the hall, and up to the second-floor-front room where Jack lay sprawled in sleep. Mac and O.B. shone their flashlights in Jack's face and pointed their .38s at his head.

Roscoe and Jack

From the *Times-Union* and *Knickerbocker Press,* both delivered to his room at the Ten Eyck, Roscoe learned of Jack Diamond's murder at 4:30 A.M., police not called until 6:55 A.M. The police Teletype was silent all morning: no messages sent to State Police or any other police agency to announce the killing, or to ask for help in finding the killers. The State Police had to confirm Diamond's death by calling the newspapers, which wrote that it was a gangland slaying, and probably we'll never know the truth. So many out there who wanted vengeance on the man. Whoever did it, give him a medal, one cop said.

Yet hadn't Jack neutralized or eliminated those old enmities? He behaved as if he had, running free like a public man, playing pinochle, drinking, dancing, partying with friends, talking of a Florida vacation, spending those late hours with his light o' love, Kiki – not an unusual way for a liberated man to celebrate. Jack wasn't living in some psychic cave of fear. He went to his bed ready to wake into a new day of freedom from justice. But he went to his bed alone, in Albany. Mistakes. You usually ride them out, and Jack the nimble, Jack the quick, had ridden many. But now he's Jack the dead, and a mystery is here. Why did he go it alone?

Roscoe dwelled on that silent police Teletype. Why ask for help in solving a murder when you know who did it? Jack back in Albany: didn't he believe O.B. about leaving town? Here's the new message: 'Welcome back, Jack. Patsy sends his best.' Roscoe would hear the story more than once from O.B., never from silent Mac. Unsolved murder. Everybody knew the rumor, but who dared say it out loud?

Roscoe saw himself as an accessory in bringing Jack's life to a close. So many people discover ways to destroy themselves – Elisha, maybe Pina, and Jack – and sometimes we help them along. Roscoe had liked Jack, an excessive fellow, deadly, yet a charmer. But Jack had become careless, a thief all his life, a creature of fraud and deceit, walking around for years with an open wound of the soul (many have it), plus all those body wounds, and then behaving as if he was just another legitimate citizen with nothing to fear, a man who could do what he couldn't, be what he wasn't. That's the way to bet, of course, and who knows better than Roscoe? Go for the impossible. But now Jack knows: sometimes the impossible is impossible.

Prelude to a Whore

Mac pulled the car into the driveway of the Notchery, blocking access to the side door of the old three-story roadhouse that once was the Come On Inn. The place was an antique with a swayback roof, cedar-shingle siding, and the promise of ribald, unsanctioned pleasure. Olive Eyes

Wheeler, Mame's beefy new bouncer, came out immediately and waved Mac away. Mac turned off the motor, and as Roscoe got out of the car he felt chest pain. Another needle in the heart to look forward to? He and Mac went up the stairs from the parking lot, and Roscoe saw Mame inside the doorway. Mac wore his suit coat to cover his pistol.

'You can't leave that car in front of the stairs,' Olive Eyes said.

'Yes, I can,' Mac said, and he showed his shield.

'We're looking for Bindy,' Roscoe said.

'Don't know anybody by that name,' the bouncer said.

'Very good, Olive. You should look for work in the movies. Tell Mame Roscoe is here to see Mr. McCall.'

Roscoe could hear violin music, classical, maybe Bach? Who could tell in this heat? He walked through the doorway and Mac followed. Mame had vanished. Olive Eyes bolted the door, still fitted with the steel kick-plate that had slowed down several break-ins by dry agents during Prohibition. The old walnut bar was still in place, and bartender Renny Kilmer, who'd had the yearning but not the brass to be a pimp and made a career compromise by working as Mame's bartender, was sitting behind the bar reading the year's hot novel *Forever Amber*.

The inn's modest dance hall had been expanded to create the main parlor, where a three-piece band entertained Fridays and Saturdays, solo upright piano every night but Sunday, when the Notchery closed to honor the Sabbath. The area bordering the dance floor was covered by a maroon-and-purple Oriental rug that was impractical for spilling beer and throwing up on, but Mame had chosen it for its elite tones. One of her regulars, an architect, had redesigned the place in exchange for several months of free visitations, and had bought artwork for the walls, female nudes by Degas, Goya, Renoir, Botticelli. You could order a whore on the half-shell for an extra five.

The violin music upstairs continued – very fine stuff, Roscoe decided. Why am I listening to fine stuff in a whorehouse? It wasn't the radio – they don't allow one – and it wouldn't be on the juke box. Another mystery.

Two women in transparent white panties, negligees, and white high-heeled slippers were sitting in the cones of two electric fans near the jukebox. A dozen arm- and armless chairs and two sofas, where the whores waited for, or sat on, customers, were spaced along the walls. One of Mame's regulars, whom Roscoe knew only as Oke, a retired insurance salesman, was dancing to the violin music (a Bach partita, yes) with the whore Roscoe knew as the Blue Pigeon. The Pigeon could drink a fifth of whiskey in an evening and stay aloft. Her negligee was off both shoulders to ensure contact of her very contactable breasts with the naked chest of Oke, whose blue shirt was open from throat to belt. The two whores in armchairs stood up for the arrival of Roscoe and Mac, and slinked toward them.

'Pina around?' Mac asked.

The whores looked at each other, shrugged, how would we know?

'Upstairs with the fiddle player,' Oke said, breaking his stride with the Pigeon and coming over to visit. The whores zapped Oke with their eyes, couldn't believe how stupid. Oke didn't notice. Oke wore dentures, and the joints of his palsied hands were swollen with arthritis. His face had the deep-smiling fissures of a man who didn't brood.

'What fiddle player is that?' Mac asked.

'Don't know his name,' said Oke, 'but can't you hear him? Is that great fiddle? Forty years in whorehouses, I never heard anything like it.'

'What is he, a snake charmer?' Mac asked. 'Plays for customers who can't get it up?'

'If he can do that I'll give him a job for life,' Oke said. 'I couldn't come if you called me.'

'I know how to fiddle if you're interested,' the whore Trixie said to Roscoe. Trixie was a candidate for the beef trust if she didn't watch her diet.

'Some other time, sweetheart,' Roscoe said. 'You know where Mame went?'

'Are you a cop?' Trixie asked. And Roscoe smiled.

'Mame,' said Oke, 'has the most powerful pussy in the North Atlantic states. You couldn't get into it with a crowbar if she didn't want you to. Then she says okay and takes you in and you can't get out. She's got pussy muscles doctors don't know about.'

'You're good friends with Mame,' Roscoe said.

'I been coming here for years, here and Lily Clark's joint. Tell the family I'm going fishing, then stash the fishing rods in a locker at the train station and come here for the weekend. One whore, Rosie, the way she liked me you'd think I was the greatest screw in town. "Marry me, Oke," she says. "We'll have fun and then you can divorce me." She was a hot one.'

'You see Pina down here today?' Mac asked Oke.

'Pina,' said Oke. 'Now, there's a broad. I'd give my left ball for one night with her, a lotta good it'd do me. I couldn't come if you called me.'

'You're here just to dance, is that it?' Roscoe asked

'If that's all there is it ain't bad,' Oke said.

'How much a dance?'

'Twelve bucks for all afternoon, with anybody who's free, once a week.'

'Like paying dues at the Elks Club,' Roscoe said.

Oke lifted the Pigeon's negligee to her shoulders. 'You don't get these at the Elks Club,' he said.

'Anybody want a drink?' Renny Kilmer asked.

'Ginger ale, lots of ice,' said Roscoe.

'Two,' said Mac, and the slender whore whose name Roscoe didn't know brought their drinks.

'How long has that fiddle been going?' Mac asked.

'About an hour,' said Oke. 'He stops playing and gets a little action.'

Mame came down the back staircase and across the parlor to Roscoe, Madam of the Afternoon, red hair in a businesslike upsweep, professional body camouflaged by a floral tent-like frock. Her whores went back to their chairs and Oke followed them.

'We can go up,' Mame said to Roscoe. 'But only you.' She gestured at Mac. 'Why is he here?'

'He's my driver for the day.'

'I don't believe you.'

'That's smart. I don't believe anything I say either. But that's my story, Mame, and you're stuck with it.'

Roscoe quaffed his ginger ale and went over to Mac. 'I'll be right back. Wait here.'

'I don't wanna wait,' Mac said.

'Don't get excited till I tell you.'

'I'll go up and get Pina.'

'Not yet, for chrissake. *Not yet.*'

Mac sulked and sipped his ginger ale. The violin music stopped, and Mac stared bullets through the ceiling. Mac never liked the violin, although hillbilly fiddlers weren't bad. Last week he saw a report on a stolen violin worth a lot of money. Mac liked the piano. Trixie pushed a button on the jukebox and 'Paper Doll' played: the Mills Brothers lamenting about playing the doll game. Mac has played that game.

Bindy was naked to the waist, three electric fans blowing directly on him, two pitchers on an end table beside his chair, one with iced tea, one with ice cubes, plus a pile of small towels next to the pitchers. He was toweling his chest, his arms, and his high forehead, a sweating Buddha in the love shrine. Behind him sat his large safe, covered by a velvet tapestry, which was Mame's way of preventing it from offending the plush décor established by her decorators: George III armchairs, pink linen drapes on the windows, marble horse figurines on the marble coffee table, a baby-grand piano given to Mame by an ardent customer, a portrait of Mame as a young beauty – in sum, the escalation of Mame's sense of herself as mistress of a world different in kind from her hot-mattress domain downstairs.

Bindy gave Roscoe a serious handshake with the old Bindy smile, always so likable; but does today's smile mean he thinks he's a winner?

'What's on your mind, Roscoe? You got trouble I can help you with?'

'We all got trouble, Bin. I'm trying to solve it.'

Roscoe, awash in the sweat of his own brow, sat facing his host, who turned a fan in his direction. The last time Roscoe saw him, Bindy offered candy; now air currents. In thrall to generosity.

'Iced tea?' Bindy asked. He poured the tea into a tall glass and added ice.

'That bet you won up at Fogarty's,' Roscoe said, taking the tea, 'Patsy wants to get even.'

'He should get better chickens.'

'He's not happy about the switch.'

'Wasn't any switch.'

'Haven't you heard, Bin? Fogarty found the Swiggler was twins, and the wrong twin won. The way out is give Patsy back his forty thousand.'

'Is that all?'

'No. Pay him another forty. The wrong bird's a foul, which doesn't cost anything if they don't catch you. But they caught you. Pay the man, Bin, the trouble'll fade.'

Bindy's naked flesh rollicked with heavings and ripplings as he laughed. 'That's good, Roscoe. Very funny.'

'Not funny. Patsy is ready to close this place and bust everybody in it, including you.'

'He wouldn't do that.'

'That's what he said about you switching chickens. But he put the order out last night. I kid you not. And if I can't stop it, everybody loses except the Governor. We could blow the election.'

'Patsy raids us, he goes down with us,' Bindy said. 'I could put him in Sing Sing. And I'll fight the Governor, too. We got sound movies of one of his top guys in fishnet stockings in bed with three broads.'

'Won't that be great? First Pina and the Dutchman, now orgy movies.'

'What *about* Pina and the Dutchman?' Mame asked. She had been hovering nervously.

'They know she did it, Mame. Her prints were all over his place.'

'She used to live there,' Mame said.

'Prints with his blood.'

And Roscoe listened to their silence. 'Maybe you should get Pina a lawyer.'

'We should get her out of town,' Mame said.

'She wouldn't get off the block. This place is under surveillance.'

'It was self-defense,' Mame said. 'That Dutch bastard tied her up and tortured her.'

'The word's around she likes tie-ups.'

'Who cares what she likes? He hurt her bad.'

'You're saying O.B. is ready to raid us?' Bindy asked, the news finally penetrating.

'Patsy might charge you with harboring a murderer. He can get nasty when he puts his mind to it.'

Roscoe watched Bindy think. Having organized that harebrained chicken-switch, here he goes again, considering the defiance that will destroy what he's spent a lifetime creating, his empire of negotiable love, plus splitting the Party all to hell in an election year, and maybe crash-landing himself in jail. Money in the safe, surrounded by love-seekers, and all he wants to do is beat his brother, another impossible bet. Is everybody nuts?

Olive Eyes came into Mame's parlor, knocking as he entered, and said, 'That cop is gonna shoot the guy with Pina,' and Mame moved on a run down the stairs, Olive Eyes after her, and Roscoe following. And there, indeed, in the parlor was Mac, .38 in hand, Pina in her negligee next to him, pistol not quite pointed at the young man holding a violin by its neck.

'No doubt about it,' Mac was saying, 'this is the stolen fiddle. Worth thirty thousand, they say.'

'It's not stolen. I've owned it seven years,' the young man

said, handsome kid, the look of a gigolo. 'I bought it for two hundred dollars.'

'I think you're a thief,' Mac said.

Pina looked convinced that Mac might do something with that .38. The barman and Oke were in a corner with the whores, behaving like wallpaper.

'Put the gun away, please,' Mame said. 'We don't need this.'

'I'm arresting a thief,' Mac said. 'Are you protecting a thief?'

'I'm no thief,' the young man said.

'He stole this violin in Chicago,' Mac said. 'Took it off a musician about to give a concert.'

'I never been in Chicago,' the young man said.

'He called the musician and said he found it in a taxi and he could have it back for ten thousand dollars,' Mac said. 'That's not a thief? That's extortion set to music.'

'I didn't do any of that. That's crazy.'

'Can you prove you own the violin?' Roscoe asked.

'I bought it, ten bucks a week, at the Modern Music Shop Downtown. They know me.'

'We can check this out, Mac,' Roscoe said.

'He's a nice-a boy,' Pina said. 'Never no trouble.'

'We'll check it out,' Mac said, and he holstered his pistol. 'I want to talk to you,' he said to Pina, and he took her arm and sat with her on an empty sofa. He stroked her hair, kissed her, like old times, then talked to her. Giving her the news?

'They shouldn't let him near a gun,' Mame said to Roscoe.

'Sometimes he's right about these things,' Roscoe said.

Olive Eyes looked twitchy, ready to do something to restore peace to the Notchery, but what? Shoot a cop? Renny Kilmer went back to his bar.

'Anybody want a drink?' Renny asked, but got no takers.

Oke stood up from his seat among the whores, buttoning his shirt and tucking it into his trousers. 'Too much stuff goin' on here,' he said. 'Guess I'll move along.'

'See you next week, Oke,' Mame said.

'That guy gonna be here?' Oke asked.

'No, he's just here today,' Mame said.

'This kind of stuff ruins the atmosphere,' Oke said.

The violinist stood up and asked Roscoe, 'Is he really arresting me?'

'I don't think so,' Roscoe said. 'Leave the violin. Pick it up tomorrow.'

'Thanks, mister, thanks,' the young man said, and as he and Oke walked toward the door, Roscoe heard Bindy's heavy step coming down the stairs, also heard the sound of gunshots, and the front door being smashed open, and he thought, Goddamn, O.B., why are you doing this now? We're nowhere near ready.

But it wasn't O.B. It was half a dozen state troopers, and more on the street, a dozen cars with thirty troopers surrounding the Notchery and every street bordering it, the Governor coming to visit. Roscoe noted that Bindy had put on a shirt for the occasion.

The troopers moved through the building, confiscating papers and taking note of Bindy's safe, which he would not open for them. They arrested Mame for running a disorderly house, her four whores for whoring, and Renny Kilmer and Olive Eyes for abetting prostitution.

Dory Dixon, the State Police inspector whom O.B. had ejected from the Dutchman's murder scene, said he was padlocking the Notchery, and holding Mac, Bindy, Roscoe, Oke, and the violinist, for consorting with whores. The women and the two johns were escorted to police vans waiting in the parking lot. Two Polish women who did cleaning and laundry for Mame were let go.

'Sorry to interrupt your afternoon fun, Roscoe,' Dixon said.

'If you're really arresting us,' Roscoe said, 'my fun has just begun.'

'Tell me you weren't here to see the girls,' Dixon said. 'Tell me I didn't see McEvoy in a corner with a naked whore.'

'The lieutenant had a tip that a stolen, priceless violin was here. I refer you to the instrument on top of the piano.'

The inspector went to the piano and picked up the violin.

'This is priceless?' he said.

'I couldn't say,' said Roscoe. 'I'm no expert on the Stradivarius. Are you?'

'No.'

'We'll have an expert appraise it,' Roscoe said.

'You came along to help the lieutenant carry the violin?'

'I was conferring with Mr. McCall about my client in a homicide case.'

Bindy had collapsed onto a sofa in glum silence when the raiders entered, but this remark won his attention.

'Quite a busy afternoon,' Dixon said. 'A priceless violin recovered, and a homicide. What homicide?'

'I can't tell you that.'

'It's a unique defense, Roscoe. I'll give you that.'

'Where are you taking us?'

'Justice Dillenback in Colonie.'

'And we travel in your vans?'

'I think you can get there in your own vehicle,' Dixon said.

'My clients as well? Mr. McCall and Lieutenant McEvoy?'

'Agreed. We'll follow along in case of any confusion.'

'Fine. And take care of the cow, Inspector.'

'Cow? What cow?'

'The cow that's going to follow you around after you leave here.'

Roscoe, Bindy, and Mac went in Mac's car to a pay phone, where Roscoe called O.B. with the bad news: as chief of a raiding party, you've been one-upped.

'What the hell are you doing out there?' O.B. asked.

'Saving the world,' Roscoe said.

'Mac is with you? On whose orders?'

'Mine. And because he and I both have more brains than you.'

'You don't know what I'm dealing with.'

'Hey, O.B., an avalanche is coming. Get Patsy and meet us at Black Jack's grill. Patsy without fail, you hear?'

Roscoe called Freddie Gold, the Party's bondsman, and told him where to post bail for anybody who needed it, and to bring a car for the working girls.

In Justice of the Peace Elgar Dillenback's court in Colonie, a Republican stronghold, the Governor's investigators could feel secure in filing their charges, comparable security not always likely in a court presided over by one of Patsy's judges. The press had been notified, and photographers awaited the arrival of Mame, her ladies, and her courtiers. Pina, the beauty in the bunch, won star attention, but Mac, Bindy, and Roscoe were the catch of the day. Another front-page coup for Roscoe. How does he do it?

Before Justice Dillenback, a bland little man with hair dyed the color of stove black, everybody pleaded not guilty, Oke weeping as he did so, his way of life, and maybe his family, exploded. 'I only went there to dance,' Oke said. 'I don't consort with whores. I couldn't come if you called me.'

All charges were misdemeanors and bail was obligatory, five hundred each. Sin is an act, vice is a habit, whoring is dicey.

'You are charged with consorting with prostitutes; how do you plead?' the justice asked Roscoe.

'Less guilty than yourself, with all due respect, Your Honor, for you weren't there and, really, neither was I. Not guilty.'

'Curb your remarks, Mr. Conway.'

'Curbed, Your Honor.'

'Bail is set at five hundred dollars.'

The justice called Bindy, another not-guilty five hundred, and then Mac, for whom Roscoe had another defense: 'A policeman investigating a theft is himself arrested. This should not be, Your Honor.'

'Perhaps not, but that's how it is. Five hundred.'

Bindy pulled from his pants pocket a double-fold of cash three inches thick and held by a rubber band. He peeled two one-thousand-dollar bills off the fold, more of the same underneath, paid bail to the court clerk for Roscoe, Mac, and himself, and waited for change.

'Is that your cash from the safe?' Roscoe asked him.

'Pocket money,' Bindy said.

'Any left in the safe?'

'Nothing.'

Roscoe focused on Pina across the courtroom: disheveled beauty in a clinging blue dress and high heels, hair in need of sprucing for the next photo shoot. The bondsman was posting everybody's bail, and Pina was about to leave with the other whores. Roscoe nudged Mac.

'Tell Pina she'll ride with us,' Roscoe said.

Roscoe and Bindy moved toward the door, and Mac brought Pina. Dory Dixon was talking to a reporter from the *Sentinel.*

'Your cow will be along any minute, Inspector,' Roscoe told Dixon.

In the car, Roscoe asked Pina, who sat in the back seat with Bindy, if she knew why she was here.

'Mac tells me,' she said.

'What did he tell you?'

'That I go to jail.'

'Are you ready for that?'

'I no want go to jail.'

'But you killed the Dutchman.'

'Sometimes.'

'Once is enough.'

'He's-a no good.'

'True. And we'll try to help you.'

'Why you help me?'

'Because he was no good.'

'Okey dokey. What I do?'

'You tell us what happened.'

'When?'

'When you killed him.'

'I'm-a no guilty.'

'Good. Now tell us what he did to you.'

Pina's Story

Pina liked it when the Dutchman tied her up and punished her, and the Dutchman liked it because Pina liked it. She had often submitted to him this way when she lived with him. But after she left him to work for Mame, why did she go back and do it again? Well, he pursued her and promised her a major payday. Mame told her to go with him and find out what he'd told the troopers about Bindy's seven houses. Did he know how much, and who they paid off at the state level?

The Dutchman, Vernon Van Epps, age fifty-four, drinking more than usual, decided that only the rope trick would activate his engine, and Pina, because she had not yet gotten the information from him, said okey dokey. He sat her on the bed, put the gag in her mouth, tied her hands behind her, raised the skirt of her dress, and looped another rope around her ankles and up between her legs, leaving her exposed, pulling the rope tighter than usual over her shoulder. She shook her head no and he laughed and pulled it tighter still. She writhed in resistance but she was his bundle now, and he lifted her, fully wrapped, off the bed and carried her to a corner of the room near the bed and sat her on a wooden chair. He tied her to the chair, and the chair to a heating pipe that ran floor to ceiling, then he blindfolded her.

Pina, alone in her darkness, hears the Dutchman drinking, clinking glass and bottle. Time. He removes her blindfold and she sees him standing naked before her, toying with himself, drinking while he toys. He readjusts her skirt upward and goes to bed with himself and watches her. He gets up and blindfolds her again. Time. She smells the ganja. She cannot loosen her bonds, and serious pain is developing in her legs and thigh the way she is bent. A long darkness. A long silence, then voices. He removes the blindfold and she sees a naked woman in bed with him. Pina doesn't recognize her. The woman and the Dutchman use each other as they watch Pina. The Dutchman reapplies the blindfold. Pina does not know how long she has been here, but it is night and silent. When he removes the blindfold again it is daylight. She does not think she has slept. The Dutchman is alone, wearing a robe, and asks if she is ready. She nods and he undoes her legs but she cannot stand. The clock says four. He says he went on the nod and forgot her. She has been his prisoner for eighteen hours. She is very, very hungry. He has on his bed photographs of favorite starlets, tied up and not, from his pornographic lending library. He takes the gag from her mouth and loosens the rope between her legs. He carries her to the bed. She lies on it feeling wretched, stretching her legs to ease her pain. She asks him for whiskey to stop the pain and he pours her three fingers, which she drinks, and then she lies silent. Time. He watches her. The pain diminishes and she pulls herself into a sitting position by grasping the headboard of the bed. She stands, very wobbly. The Dutchman moves in front of her, unbuttons her dress, and takes it from her. He helps her step out of her panties and removes his own robe. He seems to be drunk again. She says she needs water and he nods once and falls back on the bed. She walks very slowly to the kitchen and fills a water bottle, takes a glass from the cupboard and drinks, puts the large steak knife inside the fold of a dish towel. She carries bottle, glass, and knife on a tray to the bedroom and sets it on a bedside table and puts herself between it and the Dutchman. She smiles at the Dutchman, who is now toying. She picks up one of his dildos and penetrates herself with it. He likes to watch this. He sits up in the bed, leans toward her, and watches. Balancing himself on one elbow, he takes the dildo in hand and works it in and out of Pina. He throws the dildo aside and puts his mouth on her. She takes the steak knife out from under the towel and pushes it into the left side of his throat, then into his chest. He rolls and she stabs him in the back, again and again. When he rolls over, she stabs his chest until she is sure she has hit his heart. While he gurgles his last, she washes the blood off herself in the bathroom, then washes the knife in the kitchen sink and puts it back in its drawer. She finds sliced Swiss cheese in the Frigidaire and puts it on saltine crackers from the pantry, dabs it with mustard, eats. She dresses herself and stands by the window watching a tugboat push a barge down the river. She thinks she will never see this sight again. It is five o'clock in the afternoon and the sun is shining. Pina does not have the information Mame wanted from the Dutchman, but some things did get done.

Roscoe chose Black Jack McCall's grill in North Albany as a meeting place because the Governor's investigators wouldn't be listening there. After Jack McCall died in 1937 at age seventy-nine, the grill was locked, and iron grids installed on its windows against intruders. But Roscoe chose it also because it was where the original McCall faction of the Party had taken root in Black Jack's day. Patsy perpetuated that tradition by opening it at election time for the annual meeting of ward leaders and candidates – a spread of roast beef, turkey, salads, and Stanwix – and Roscoe delivering Election Day street money to ward leaders, one by one, in the back room. Then it was locked till next year. O.B. was already inside with Patsy, the two of them leaning against the empty bar, when Roscoe, Mac, and Bindy arrived with Pina. The place was a cube of dead heat, punishing; but Roscoe closed the door.

'What's she doing here?' Patsy said. 'I don't want whores in here.'

'Hear me out, Pat,' Roscoe said. And he took three chairs off the tabletop and set them upright, put one in a far corner for Pina and gestured for Mac to keep her company, pushed one at Patsy, and sat backward on one himself. Then, in the rapidly spoken shorthand he had used all his life with Patsy, he told the story of Pina's bondage and retaliation and, in a whisper Pina could not hear, mentioned this was usable, which Patsy heard with reluctant clarity, frustrated that his own Notchery raid had not put his brother in jail. He stared with frigid eyes at Bindy, who, with O.B., moved closer as Roscoe talked softly of Dory Dixon and Dillenback. And we have to arrest Pina, Roscoe said. He would speak as her attorney.

'She'll have to go inside,' Patsy said. 'She know that?'

'Vaguely.'

'She won't be very friendly when that happens.'

'We're the only friends she's got. We'll go for justifiable homicide, and the grand jury may not even indict. You know those grand juries.'

'We'll give it back to those rat bastards,' Patsy said. 'We go public now with all we got.'

What Roscoe had heard from Patsy was evidence on an undercover state cop who was a wife beater, but his wife wouldn't talk against him – a weak case, but something. Also, an aide to the Governor had gotten drunk and punched a bartender; not much mileage there. But the best bit, and we'd find a way to use it, was the Spanish pimp held by his ankles out a tenth-floor State Office Building window by undercover state police trying to make him talk about Albany cops on the take. The pimp truly had been ankled out the window, but the anklers were two New York cops on their day off, doing Patsy a favor by impersonating sadistic state troopers.

'Bindy also has a movie, don't you, Bin?' Roscoe said.

Bindy shook his head. No deal, Roscoe.

'Whatta you got?' Patsy asked Bindy.

'Nothin' for you,' Bindy said.

Patsy came up out of his chair, a bear in a wild lunge, and flung a right hand to Bindy's chin. Bindy rammed him with a high elbow on the side of the head, and both brothers shook off their blows, Patsy gut-butting Bindy with his head, staggering but failing to topple the fat man, Patsy taking more head blows from Bindy's fists as the improbably nimble Bin bounced out of Patsy's range. O.B. and Roscoe moved between the brothers, brothers on brothers, and stopped the fight.

'Let's fight the Governor,' Roscoe said.

'Cheatin' sonofabitch,' Patsy said.

'You're a bad loser,' Bindy said.

'This isn't over,' Patsy said.

'You want your money back, welsher?' And Bindy took the cash from his pocket and tossed it at Patsy, who caught it, undid the rubber band, riffled the wad of thousand- and five-hundred-dollar bills.

'You get a rematch anytime you want it,' Bindy said.

Patsy pocketed the money and turned to Roscoe, trying seriously not to smile.

'Better get that little lady's story in writing,' he said.

Roscoe called Veronica and told her his news so she wouldn't discover it in the newspapers, the way she discovered the Gilby scandal-mongering.

'They're going to say I was consorting with whores,' Roscoe said. 'But I wasn't. This was political business, strictly. Do you believe me?'

'Do you ever go with whores?'

'No.'

'But you did.'

'Years ago. Years. I go with you, or I like to think I do. I want only that. You're the only woman in my life.'

'What makes a woman be a whore?'

'Need, money, bad luck, stupidity, a fondness for pimps, sometimes too much talent for sin.'

'Do I have that talent?'

'You have a bit of it. I like to think that you have a talent for love.'

'So do you,' she said.

The daily *Times-Union* and *Knickerbocker News* carried subdued front page reports on the raid on the Notchery and six other brothels operating cautiously, but not cautiously enough, and listed the names of those arrested. Both papers carried photos of Mame and Pina on inside pages, none of Roscoe, Bindy, or Mac. The *Sentinel*, printing its edition two days before its usual publication day, obviously with inside information, used banner headlines with photos of Roscoe, Bindy, and Mac on page one, and half a page of whore photos inside. The paper also had, exclusively, the addresses of every whorehouse in town, the number of whores working in each house, and names of madams and owners of each building in which a house operated. Hattie Wilson was listed as an owner. 'Upper-echelon members' of the McCall political machine were said to have masked financial interest in the real estate. Elisha was not mentioned. An unnamed Governor's spokesman called this a major crackdown on prostitution controlled by the Albany political machine. The Notchery, he said, was the collection point for money from all the brothels in the city. The *Sentinel* also carried an editorial calling the raids an overdue move to clean up the city, so sullied by wartime transients who used the city as a sewer. It argued for throwing out the Democratic scum in the upcoming election.

Patsy reacted by having the city fire commissioner condemn Roy Flinn's *Sentinel* building for multiple transgressions of fire and building ordinances that would keep Roy in court for years. He also had two dozen rats trapped at the city dump and then let loose into the *Sentinel*'s basement, with witnesses calling the infestation a neighborhood menace to children, and a photographer on hand to document the rats. Bindy gave Patsy his movie of the Governor's aide, in hose, bedded with three women, with a transcript of their conversation; and this was sent anonymously to the Governor, to newspapers, radio stations, and the Albany Catholic Diocese. By day's end the aide had resigned.

The dailies sought second-day comment from mayoral candidates, and Republican Jay Farley deplored the brothels and cheered their closure. Alex, who had returned to Fort Dix for discharge, issued a statement in absentia saying he favored a postwar renewal of moral purpose, and would pursue it upon his return. Cutie LaRue said the brothels should stay where they were. 'If you take away the opportunity to sin,' he said, 'you also take away the opportunity not to sin, which eliminates the opportunity for virtue. Those places should exist so we don't have to visit them.'

Albany County District Attorney Phil Donnelly announced he was empaneling a grand jury to investigate the Governor's police methods – hanging men out of windows, using degenerate dope fiends as informants against private citizens. O.B.

announced Pina's arrest for second-degree murder, and her confession to the crime.

People gathered as Roscoe's mid-morning press conference took shape in front of the Double Dutch bar: merchants from down the block, gamblers from the horse room next door, stray winos, passing soldiers, teenagers on the prowl, six policemen to monitor the crowd. The bar was padlocked, its shades were drawn, its neon tubes rat-gray in daylight. Roscoe had invited all local newspapers, radio stations, wire services, and out-of-town correspondents who covered the legislature; and two dozen reporters came to hear how Pina had killed a State Police informer to escape torture, rape, even death.

'The Dutchman had been after secrets,' said Roscoe, standing on two milk crates to be visible, his shirt so wet it was soaking through his coat, and drops of sweat from his chin spotting his tie. 'The Dutchman thought Pina knew secrets about prostitution and politics, which he planned to pass on to his partners, the state troopers, a cabal of pimps and prosecutors designed to persecute Albany Democrats. But Pina knew no such secrets. She made her living as a dancer and singer. She had worked in roadhouses like the Notchery ever since her flight from abuse, first by her father, then her husband, men who violated her beauty until all she could do in her rage was flee her native land for America. She made her way from Italy to Albany, using her beauty to find work, caught by the Dutchman, who hired her for this abominable place, this Double Dutch bar. It is sad that such places as this exist, but because of the low urges of the human being, they do. The Dutchman preyed upon these urges, hiring women to ply men with fake whiskey at inflated prices for the right to sit next to them at his bar. And that was Pina's profession, bar girl, B-girl, singer of songs for this vile man.'

Roscoe showed photos of the Dutchman's ropes, the chair he tied Pina to, the pipe he tied the chair to, the bed strewn with obscene photographs, the dildo he raped her with, '. . . and I do not expect you to photograph this or even mention the substance of these photos to your readers or listeners. I show them to reveal the obscene life of this man – and lower than he the lowlife of this city does not get – the opium and the dope he smoked, the books of pornography that agitated his warped mind, his sadistic quest for beautiful young women to enslave and torture. But Pina broke away from him and found the best friend she ever made in this city, Mary Catherine Ray, who gave Pina a job in her nightclub. There is no shame in expressing your God-given talent for song or dance in this world, and Pina had these talents. She sings like an angel, dances the way the clouds move. She had been at the Notchery singing with a violinist, a friend who recognized her ability. But suddenly she was arrested by State Police and put through ignominy and absurd rituals. This happened just as an Albany detective and myself were about to accept her surrender. For Pina's remorse over the death of the Dutchman had brought such an ache to her heart, and such disquiet to her soul, that she gave her confidence to Mary Catherine. And Mary, on hearing her story, sought advice from her friend Benjamin McCall, a figure of known stature in this community. Ben McCall then asked me to protect the rights of this young beauty when she surrendered, and I went to the Notchery to meet him and Pina, bringing with me one of the most respected detectives on the Albany police force, a man I trusted to move Pina through the legal process without prejudice. And as her surrender was about to take place, this detective and I were both arrested by the troopers and charged with a low misdemeanor.

'Why? Why did state troopers, working for the Governor's special investigators, do this? Publicity was their goal. Publicity to use against the popularly elected Albany Democratic organization they so irrationally hate and seek to destroy.

'And why do they want this publicity so badly that they stoop to such tactics as arresting a detective who is making a major arrest? I'll tell you why. I direct your attention to the great building at the top of State Street, the Capitol of New York State, where some of you work, but which is now the captive office of a gnarled and mustachioed little gnome who wants to be President of our nation – I refer to the power-maddened Governor, who will do anything to get elected. That's why we're here today, my friends, because of the lunacy of presidential ambition. May God deliver our city from it, and from that man so possessed by it.'

The *Knickerbocker News*, in its midday final, reported Roscoe's speech on page one, with his photo in front of the Double Dutch. The paper also carried an editorial wondering why a State Police inspector would make a politically motivated misdemeanor arrest of a detective lieutenant who was arresting a surrendering murderess. 'Have the State Police lost their brains?' the newspaper wondered.

In a sidebar, Cutie LaRue suggested that the Democrats nominate Roscoe as their next candidate for governor. When Roscoe read the paper, he sent a one-word telegram to Inspector Dory Dixon. 'Moo,' it said.

The heat was fierce after the press conference, and the pain was niggling at Roscoe's heart. He had never felt more vital or necessary, yet he knew he was not well. He should go home to Tivoli, let Veronica take care of him. But he could not go directly from the Double Dutch to Veronica's presence. He went to Hattie's, to comfort her in her time of public embarrassment.

'Gin and food is what I need,' Roscoe told Hattie, and she brought out her Canadian gin and phoned in an order to Joe's Delicatessen for pastrami sandwiches on rye (two for Roscoe) with coleslaw and dill pickles, which Joe sent down in a taxi. They ate in front of Hattie's parlor fans, and Roscoe apologized for not foreseeing the publication of her name in the paper. Roscoe opened his shirt to beat the heat and he thought of poor old Oke. Hattie waved the skirt of her housedress to air her thighs.

'They made a whore out of me, Rosky,' she said.

'They made me a consort of whores,' Roscoe said.

'I could've been a good whore.'

'Well, yes, but no. You've got too much heart.'

'Whores have heart.'

'Maybe at the beginning. Whoring eats your heart.'

'Everything eats your heart,' Hattie said.

'Nothing ate your heart, Hat. You're still the love queen of Lancaster Street. How can I make this thing up to you?'

'You could love me like a husband.'

'And you'd kill me like a husband. My heart couldn't handle it today.'

'You have to do something about that heart, Rosky, if it gets in the way of love.'

'I'll talk to it,' Roscoe said.

Roscoe and the Silent Music

Roscoe saw Jack Diamond waiting for a trolley, and told Mac to stop and pick him up. Jack wore a shoulder holster with no pistol, disarmed in death. He didn't say hello to Mac, but you can't blame him. Jack, moving through the timelessness of his disgraceful memories, had insight into Roscoe's destiny.

'Roscoe,' he said, 'there's chaos waiting for you. How will you cope?'

'I'm glad you asked that, Jack,' Roscoe said. 'I'll cope through virtue, and virtue I'll achieve through harmony. The musical scale, always a favorite of mine, is expressed in harmonious numbers: the octave, the fifth, and other fixed intervals, all reflecting an order inherited by this earth. An equivalently calibrated heavenly order guides our planets and stars in their harmonious trajectories, generating the music of the spheres, which, though silent, is mathematically chartable, and always a crowd pleaser. Do you agree, Jack?'

'I try to,' Jack said.

'Virtue,' said Roscoe, 'comes from heeding these unseen numbers, this silent music; also from the judicious exercise of power, contempt of wealth, and a prudent diet. The virtuous warrior who inherits the mantle must, with fire and sword, expel disharmony, amputate sickness from the body, ignorance from the soul, luxury from the belly, sedition from the city, and discord from the family, thereby ending all wars, and restoring music to God's cosmos. This is my plan of attack, Jack. What do you think of it?'

'Virtue was always one hell of an idea,' Jack said. 'Let me off at the corner.'

Some People Just Have To Go

At mid-afternoon Bart Merrigan came to Hattie's to find Roscoe and make sure he had not died of rhetoric and heat. He also brought news that Elisha's will had surfaced for probate in Surrogate Court, Elisha's siblings had seen it, and their lawyer wanted to talk. Roscoe was exhausted from the Notchery-Pina debacle and his worsening chest pain. He had napped at Hattie's for two hours, not enough, and now wanted only to retreat to the tranquillity of his Tivoli rooms until the world changed. But, as usual, he lost out to his rage for duty, and would have to forgo that elegant peace and go to his office to cope with Elisha's brother and sisters.

Elisha, on the night of his death, had shown Gladys the document naming Roscoe executor of his estate, and told her that if anything ever happened to him a family feud would erupt, but Roscoe would find 'the key' to solving it. Gladys assumed he meant Roscoe would be fair with all parties in settling control of the mill. But Roscoe decided 'the key' related not to fairness but to the protection of Veronica. How could Elisha assume Roscoe would be fair? Roscoe had never been fair, and who knew that better than Elisha?

Elisha's siblings – brother Gordon, the banker, and sisters

Antonia and Emily – even before Elisha's death, had aimed to control the mill and stop what they saw as its downward slide. Their plan was to replace the inattentive, dollar-a-year Elisha with Kyle Glockner, a bright man who had risen from the rolling mill to become a superior salesman, sales manager, eventually vice-president, a man the siblings believed they could control. When Elisha died, Glockner did move into the breach, and chaos did not erupt as Gladys had feared. After the funeral, the siblings pressed Veronica to agree to joint control, with Glockner as titular head.

Veronica, with Elisha's holdings, controlled the mill with 50 percent of common voting stock. The siblings had 45, but with Glockner's 5 percent, given to him when he became Elisha's vice-president, a standoff was possible. Glockner, however, a protégé of Elisha, was neither as malleable nor as friendly to the siblings as they expected, and as their dream of control faded and the mill's postwar slide continued, the siblings urged Veronica to sell it before *everybody* slid into bankruptcy.

Bart drove Roscoe to Party headquarters, which was also Roscoe's law office, one cabinet drawer holding his entire practice: the Elisha and Gilby files. The day was crisp and sunny, and a breeze had blown away the heavy heat. Roscoe, in wilted clothing, felt soiled in the shining afternoon.

'Everybody loved your speech on Pina the whore,' Bart said.

'I like to think of her as a singer,' Roscoe said.

'She gonna do any time?'

'Of course not. Have you no morality? The woman was a victim, not a murderess.'

'I hear the Dutchman's still dead.'

'Has anybody complained about that?'

At headquarters, Roscoe reviewed the files on Elisha's estate, then called in Mrs. Pringle, his secretary-on-call, and dictated a letter to the Fitzgibbon siblings' lawyer, setting out estate specifics: only half a million in Elisha's personal assets, plus Tivoli, worth another million or so, to be appraised; six hundred thousand to Veronica from Elisha's life insurance, none of these legacies involving the siblings. The mill's value, which did involve them, required detailed appraising. Roscoe advised them that monthly fees for himself as counsel and executor would be fifteen thousand, plus five thousand for Bart Merrigan as appraiser. Also, the mill's holdings in other states would necessitate hiring additional lawyers and appraisers. 'Sad to say,' concluded Roscoe, 'the Surrogate Courts of this nation are exceedingly dilatory, and we should not expect final resolution before three to five years. Some notorious cases have continued for twenty-eight, even thirty-five years.'

Roscoe sent Joey Manucci to hand-deliver the letter to the siblings' lawyer, Murray Fish, an old hand at probate who was well aware that Surrogate Harry Crowley was married to Patsy's niece. Bart then drove Roscoe to Tivoli. A taxi was at the front entrance as they pulled in, and Roscoe recognized the woman getting into it: Nadia, the spiritualist with only one name. Bart helped him out of the car and up the front steps and Roscoe then went in under his own waning power. He looked for Veronica in the front parlors, but she was elsewhere. One step at a time, so difficult to catch a breath, he climbed the staircase to his second-floor suite, then stripped and dropped his foul clothing into a hamper. He soaped and showered slowly, sat on the bed and painfully pulled on a clean pair of boxer shorts, and at five o'clock on this afternoon of sublime sanctuary, he eased his transient self between the sheets of his four-poster double bed. Alexander Hamilton had once owned this bed, so went the Fitzgibbon family legend. All his life Roscoe had been linked to this family, and because of it, because of Veronica, he'd remained in Albany and in politics. So was this new illness another fraud to keep him in the same house with her? He's equal to the idea, but no, Roscoe would not withhold breath from himself for any reason. But he loves being here. Even when he married Pamela and, as the groom, kissed bridesmaid Veronica, he told her she should've been the bride. What would it have been like not being near her all his life? Who would be his love? Could he have endured politics without her presence? He buried his face in the pillow and imagined Nadia at the séance in her darkened parlor saying she could see Rosemary, Veronica's five-year-old daughter, coming through the clouds, and that the child looked beautiful and happy in her pink dress and pink bow. This thrilled Veronica, who said, 'That's exactly what she was wearing the day before she died.' Nadia's snout came up the sewer drainpipe into the sink, but Roscoe ran the water and down she went. Up again she came, so Roscoe opened both faucets and let them run, and there went Nadia: down the pipe, into the river, and bobbing out to sea, no longer a threat to Veronica. And Roscoe could sleep.

He awoke in sunshine, the pain bearable only if he didn't move. Nine o'clock on the bedside table clock. He felt as if he'd slept a week, but it was only sixteen hours. Veronica was watching him from the heavy oak rocker by the fireplace. Beside her on a four-wheeled oak serving wagon lay mystery food under two silver-covered serving dishes. Veronica at morning: scoop-neck white blouse with pink roses on the bodice, tan riding britches and brown boots, a vague suggestion of lipstick, hair in a tie at the back of her neck, smiling.

'Somebody killed me and I went to heaven,' Roscoe said.

'You went someplace. I came to call you for dinner three times last night, but you were comatose.'

'You're looking out for me.'

'People know you're not entirely well, don't they?'

'Some people. Is that really nine o'clock?'

'What do you care what time it is?'

'I have to place myself in the cosmos. Time is important. So is food. I'm starving to death and you sit there quizzing me about time, hoarding mysterious food under silver covers.'

'I can't believe you're hungry. Not you.'

'I haven't eaten for weeks. People refuse to feed me.'

'Can you sit up?'

'I can try.' And, as he did, the pain stabbed him in the stomach, the chest, the heart. He fell back. 'It hurts,' he said.

'All right, I'll feed you.' She wheeled the tray to his bedside and uncovered lox and cream cheese and capers and onions and sour cream and applesauce. 'There's coffee in the thermos pitcher, and bagels and blintzes in the warmer, if you want any.'

'Of course. I want it all.'

She took a bagel and a blintz from the warmer in the bottom of the wagon, which was heated by two flaming cans of Sterno. She poured him a cup of coffee.

'You're serving me a Jewish breakfast.'

'It was my father's favorite.'

'I remind you of your father, is that your point?'

'You take care of me the way he did. Gordon's lawyer

called. He got your letter and they want to settle. Whatever did you say that made them so agreeable?'

'I don't want to talk about it. I want a bagel.'

She sat on the bed and ripped half a bagel, spread cream cheese on a fragment, piled it with capers, onions, a slice of lox, and put it to his mouth. He bit and chewed, stared at her, swallowed, sipped the coffee, waited for another bite, chewed it, stared.

'Press your breasts against my arm while you feed me,' he said.

'I can't do that.'

'Why not?'

'It's brazen.'

'It's not brazen. It's a friendly gesture.'

'It's more than friendly.'

'We're more than friends. I'm no stranger to your breasts. I remember them well.'

'Then you don't need them pressed against you.'

'Memory only goes so far. I need full-rounded reality.'

'You're very fresh.'

'Just like your bagels.'

She cut a blintz and dabbed it with sour cream and applesauce. She put it into his mouth, and a spot of applesauce stayed on his chin. She leaned close to him and licked it away. He pulled her close and kissed her, her arms over his shoulders, her breasts against him, and it was years gone, years since she had yielded her soft mouth so totally, everything unbelievably sharp to Roscoe. But are these real responses, Ros, or ritualized emotions you turn on like the radio? Is this even the same woman you fell in love with? Well, she still responds the same way in your arms, so the real question is, will she stay there? Don't ruin it. Don't go too far. If it's going to happen it could happen at Tristano, if we ever get there. Also, you couldn't do anything, anyway. You can barely move. He licked the top of her chest.

'Be careful there,' she said.

'You licked me. I'm getting even.'

'I'm in your debt again.'

Gratitude. Is that what this is about? Gratitude is cheap. True, but if that started it, don't knock it. And that worshipful-slave routine, so grateful for her handouts – get past it. No woman is that perfect. She's got the venal streak of the rich, money tunes in her music. Didn't the phone call on the mill settlement bring on this affection? And somewhere in that beautiful head she's still a bit of a nutcake, believing a con artist like Nadia has answers. Don't call her a nutcake.

He put both arms around her and squeezed her, his cheek on hers, and she squeezed him, hurting him, breathless pain he could love. They held this intimate clinch, the closest moment of their lives, at least since 1932, another year that made Roscoe crazy, and this would do it again, no doubt about that either, this embrace that was setting off alarm bells in both of them. You can feel that in her, can't you, Ros? She squeezed him again. He kissed her hair. He would kiss her soul if he could only find it.

'You are a wonderful man,' she whispered.

He was about to say something excessive and fatuous when he saw Alex in the doorway, a civilian in a gray suit, white shirt, blue necktie, his suit coat folded over his left arm. No smile.

'Alex,' Roscoe said. 'Where the hell did you come from?'

'I got in last night,' Alex said, coming into the room.

Veronica stood up and faced Alex. 'I was keeping him as

a surprise,' she said to Roscoe. 'That's why I kept coming up to get you.'

'How are you feeling?' Alex asked. 'Mother says you're not well.'

'I'm in trouble. I should see the doctor.'

'I'll call and have him come over. Can you walk?'

'I don't think so,' Roscoe said. 'I can hardly breathe, and the pain got worse overnight.'

'I'll get on it,' Alex said. He went out of the room and down the stairs.

'I think we may have shocked him,' Roscoe said.

'He knows we're close friends,' Veronica said.

'We looked like more than that.'

'We did absolutely nothing wrong. Nothing.'

'Unfortunately.'

'Quit it.'

'Why was that fortune-teller here?'

'Oh. Nadia?'

'Nadia.'

'Yes, she came by. We visit now and then.'

'You already spent a small fortune with that fraud. Are you paying her again?'

'Why would I pay her? We just talk.'

'You talk to your dead daughter?'

'I'm over that, Roscoe. You know that.'

'But something's going on. She's reading the future for you.'

'If you must know.'

'You want to find out how the hearing will go. You're afraid of losing Gilby after losing Rosemary.'

'You are clever.'

'Why didn't you ask *me* about the future? I'd have told you we're going to win.'

'How can you be so sure?'

'Because Yusupov wasn't Gilby's father. I have a blood test to prove it.'

'No. Where did you get a blood test on him?'

'I'm a resourceful citizen.'

'But what does it mean?'

'Everything points to Elisha as his father.'

'Shhhh.'

Then, in whispers, he said, 'Elisha had to have known it wasn't Yusupov, and why wouldn't he? Pamela was blackmailing *him.*'

'How could you possibly know that?'

'What else would she mean when she says, "It's a wise child that knows its father"?'

'You're really the cleverest man alive. That's exactly true. First she wanted money or she'd sue for custody. We offered her five thousand dollars, but it wasn't enough. And she said if we didn't pay she'd name him as the father and scandalize the family. He laughed at her, so she sued.'

'What she didn't foresee,' said Roscoe, 'was Elisha removing himself as her target. He aced her. It must have enraged her.'

'I can't believe he'd kill himself over that,' Veronica said.

'A sick man trying to protect you and Gilby, and looking at the short odds on himself? Those could be two very good reasons.'

Roscoe watched her trying to absorb the theory, offering no resistance at all to Elisha as father of Gilby. It had hovered for years with her as an idea, and now here it was as logic on the hoof from Roscoe, to explain the meaning of the Yusupov blood test. The blood-test part was genuine. The rest, well, Roscoe is a lawyer. He could believe his own theory, or he could believe some of it, or none at all. It was his theory. Whatever Roscoe decided, he would take direction from Elisha. Already he was decoding what seemed like an urgent message, one that Elisha could not write down or even speak about. Roscoe understood that Elisha, for good reason, could only point to the core of its mystery with this silent code, full of faith that Roscoe and Patsy would know what he meant; for weren't they the translators and keepers of all secrets?

'His death is still a mystery,' Roscoe said to her, 'but the mystery isn't quite as dense as it was a few weeks ago. Just do me a favor and stay away from that fortune-teller. If you want to know about things to come, ask me. And say nothing about the blood test. That's *my* surprise.'

She nodded and kissed him on the lips.

'I'll see what's going on with the doctor,' she said.

Roscoe and Alex

Roscoe heard the footsteps, and now would come Alex of the censorious eye. What are you doing with my mother? He would not say that, but he would watch Roscoe's every gesture. Well, so be it. He's a willful young man and always has been. Roscoe knew him as a bright and charming child, then as the seldom seen Alex-away-at-school: Groton first, then Yale, home on the holidays, off to Tristano for the summer, only twenty or so days a year spent totally with the family. But he was much loved, and reared in politics. When he was four, Elisha, Roscoe, and Patsy took the Democratic Party away from Packy McCabe. When he was six, they took the city away from the Republicans. His father sent him clippings of Party triumphs throughout his school days, and as he accumulated scholastic honors, he also lived a vicarious political life through Elisha, who told people: Alex is smarter than I'll ever be. In his last year at Groton, a wealthy classmate's uncle, a Democrat, was heavily favored for election to the State Senate. Alex heard Roscoe tell Elisha that the uncle would be sued for divorce and that this would sink him with the voters. Alex and his classmate took all their own best clothing, plus the classmate's sister's fox coat and his father's winter chesterfield, the lot worth thousands, from closets in the family's Fifth Avenue townhouse, carried it all in a taxi to an East Side pawnshop, hocked it for seven hundred dollars, found a bookmaker and bet the seven on the uncle's Republican opponent, saw the uncle sued and beaten as Roscoe had predicted, collected at four to one, redeemed the clothes from the pawnshop, had them back in their closets before anybody knew they were gone, and spent their fresh money roistering in Manhattan over the Christmas break.

Alex took time off from Yale in early October 1932 to come home for the Democratic convention in Albany when his father was on track to be nominated for governor. He sat with the Albany delegates, too young to be one, but learning how it was done. Patsy promised to, and did, make him a genuine delegate to the '36 convention, the year he finished Yale (history major, Phi Beta Kappa, *magna cum laude*), then Pat ran him for the Assembly in '37, and the Senate in '38.

In those early days Roscoe began advising Alex in the proper way to carouse, but he found he was also Phi Beta Kappa in carousing. In 1939, at age twenty-four, Alex married Marnie Herzog, daughter of a coal merchant of means, and moved into the mansion Elisha had built for him at Tivoli, the lower farm, where Marnie kept show horses, and Alex, in the family tradition, kept racehorses. He was elected

America's youngest mayor in '41, grew stellar as the GI mayor who refused a deferment, declined officers' candidate school, and volunteered for the infantry: the raw material for his myth.

He entered Roscoe's bedroom exuding a vigorous presence, every trace of youth gone from that face, in full manhood now, with the tailored good looks of a matinee idol and the self-assurance of a princely heir to power over the future. Roscoe remembered that condition. He'd once owned a bit of it.

'The doctor's on the way with an ambulance,' Alex said. 'He thinks you'll need one.'

'He's probably right,' Roscoe said.

'This means surgery, I gather.'

'I won't resist. I can't live this way.'

'How did you let it get so bad?'

'I got busy.'

'You surely did. What happens to Gilby's hearing? This week, isn't it?'

'We'll get a postponement.'

'Do you want another lawyer to step in for you?'

'Only if I'm dead and buried. If I'm just dead I'll be there.'

'Are there any developments? Any new bitchiness from slutty Aunt Pamela?'

'I don't expect much else from her.'

'And you? Anything new on the legal front?'

'I have plans. Nothing to talk about.'

'I hope you're making a strong case.'

'I like to think I am.'

'One thing I can't understand, Roscoe. How in the hell did you ever get sucked into the Notchery? I've heard the story, but why would you set foot in that place? This publicity is a disaster. It's made all the New York papers.'

'I think we avoided a civil war in the party. I'm glad I was there.'

'Glad? Arrested with whores? Your reputation is a shambles.'

'I haven't had a reputation since I was seven years old, Alex. And if Patsy had arrested Bindy, there's a very good chance one of them would now be dead.'

'Patsy wouldn't have ordered that raid. He told me last night he just wanted to make a point. Ask him yourself.'

Roscoe nodded, understanding Patsy's reversal of unbearable history. The man could not stand to be wrong. Situational truth. Roscoe understood also that Patsy's new version of his Bindy plan downgraded Roscoe's achievement. Nice going, Ros. What you did was miraculous, more or less, but not really necessary. Now get offstage and stop making me look stupid.

'Roscoe, I know turning the tables on the raiders the way you did was brilliant, and I congratulate you. But people just don't believe you were there only as a lawyer. You've got to reverse your image.'

'If they reverse my pain and fix my breathing, my image will take care of itself. Look, Alex, forget about me. I'm not important. Pay attention to your campaign.'

'I've got a rally and two radio speeches coming up.'

'Good. Take the limelight back from Cutie. The clown is stealing the show. Two days ago he turned up as Abe Lincoln. He read the Gettysburg Address and dedicated it to the Battle of the Bulge.'

Roscoe judged Alex's aggressive tone as probably a learned response to living among redneck sergeants; also, he doesn't want your arms around his mother. But what put an edge to this for Roscoe was Alex's misreading of Patsy's dissembling, and that virtuous worrying over Roscoe's reputation; which gave his discontent another dimension.

Veronica brought Dr. Toussaint to Roscoe's bedside, then she and Alex waited in the hallway during the examination. Roscoe's internal bleeding had obviously continued, its buildup of pressure worsening the pain, his blood pressure dangerously low. 'Into the hospital immediately, Roscoe,' Dr. Toussaint concluded.

'I'm not fighting it,' Roscoe said, 'but I'm beginning to feel like that fellow with the wound that never heals.'

'There's a lot of those fellows out there,' the doctor said.

'The brotherhood of the open wound,' Roscoe said.

The doctor sent Alex for the ambulance attendants, a burly pair who lifted Roscoe out of bed onto the stretcher, twisting his pain.

'I'll follow Roscoe to the hospital, get him settled in,' Veronica said, which did not thrill Alex.

Roscoe Muses on Politics and Death While Having His Heart Cut Out

It's true, Rozzie, we're going to slice you from hell to breakfast and then saw your chest, crank open your sternum like an oyster, go in and get at that heart of yours, and slit a corner of the sack it comes in to let loose all the dammed-up blood. We'll sew up any little nick to your heart where you hurt yourself, suck out the old clotty stuff, and let any fresh blood ooze out for a while. Can't sew up the sack or we'd just be damming it back up and have to go in again. So we leave it open and it'll either figure out how to fix itself or it won't. Then we sew up with catgut wherever we cut you going in, we wire that sternum back together, stitch up the chest and there you have it, another one of the old thoracotomies, another one of the old pericardiotomies. Your blood won't leak no more and you'll be good as new if you don't die, always a possibility, this is not easy what we do, stuff can go wrong and we just might slit the heart wrong and set off a little arrhythmia, or you could have a stroke or a heart attack or a blood clot with the last word. But just maybe it'll be sweet sailing, like on your favorite boat up at Tristano. Think about that boat.

Roscoe rarely dwelled on his own death: too many other things to think about. But now that he's staring it down, is he as ready for it as Elisha was? Doubtful. Roscoe wants to get away but not that far, wants to make a move but is still asking questions: What didn't he do that he should have? What did he do that he shouldn't have? No, never mind that last question, Ros, we don't have time. Keep in mind that if you die on the operating table you won't have to protect Veronica any more, won't have to figure out Gilby and Pamela, or get Alex re-elected in a tough year, or decide why Elisha killed himself. No matter what logic you summon, Elisha's suicide doesn't make sense simply as the end of something. Roscoe remembers Elisha saying in a black moment that everything eventually comes to nothing. 'That's the secret you don't tell the children,' he said, 'and even if you did, they wouldn't accept it.' But Roscoe now believes that Elisha, at the end, overruled his own conclusion on nothing. A suicidal getaway is usually flight from the unbearable, which wasn't Elisha's condition, was it? Or it's a form of cowardly escape, or maybe delusory innocence descending; and Elisha was neither coward nor innocent, and rarely deluded. He was a cunning and courageous man with multiple reasons for everything he did, and he would not design his death on the basis of fear or insubstantiality. Roscoe has almost convinced himself that Elisha, sliding into the inevitable, decided to do a bit of posthumous combat with the enemy, who was closing in. And who else would it be but Pamela and the hyenas she drags in her wake? And on whom could they close in? Not Elisha, who has slipped away on them; which leaves Veronica, Alex, Gilby.

The Candidate

The idea of Elisha's making a cowardly getaway was absurd. You should have seen him when he *really* had enemies: when we ran him for governor. When we all lined up behind Patsy in 1919, nobody knew that so much would come of it. We loved the game and we were in on change. Al Smith was a key player then. Everybody in Albany knew Al, east side, west side, for he'd lived here on and off since Tammany first elected him to the Assembly in 1904. He went on to serve six terms and become Assembly Speaker, then Governor. When he ran for governor in '22 and '24, we saw to it that he won Albany with fat pluralities. After his '26 victory, Al made Elisha Democratic State Committee chairman, and Eli roamed the state as advance man for Al's presidential bandwagon. While Al ogled the White House, we ogled his chair in the Capitol, and our Mayor Goddard was a fine fit.

Goddard, a Baptist banker with great public appeal, had run up such impressive totals as mayor in '21, '23, and '25 that people were saying he was unbeatable, a real candidate to succeed Al in '28. Upstaters are always a long shot, but the front-runner, FDR, was out of the race, down in Warm Springs trying to regain use of his legs after his polio attack. Tammany Hall, under Charlie Murphy and then George

Olvany, had always looked on us as upstate family, and so had John McCooey, the boss of Brooklyn Democrats. Their numbers dominated state Democratic conventions, and they were with us, so we truly had a chance to nominate Goddard for governor.

Mayor Goddard, Roscoe, and Elisha were always welcome at the Governor's Mansion when Al lived there, but Patsy, who didn't get along with Al, had never set foot in the place. As early as '23, Al frowned on Patsy's direct dealing in bootleg beer, and in '27, as pressure mounted on Al to close down the Albany baseball pool, he asked Patsy and Roscoe to come to the Eagle Street Mansion for a private talk. Al was waiting for them on the veranda as they came up the steps. He pointed them to a prearranged pair of rocking chairs and sat in a third rocker, facing them.

'The Republicans are making noise about this pool again,' Al said. He was in shirtsleeves with arm garters, and he also wore a cigar. 'And federal men are nosing around about the sale of plays across state lines.'

'What the hell am I supposed to do about that?' said Patsy.

'Shut down,' said Al.

'No,' said Pat. 'No. And also no.'

'Then why don't you let somebody win once in a while,' Al said.

'Where do you suppose the Party gets its money?' Patsy said. 'You think we carry the city and county for you by passing the hat on Pearl Street?'

'How much can you need? Why don't you share some of the wealth? Even the communists do that.'

'I always knew you were a red,' Patsy said.

Al stood up and walked into the Mansion, slamming and bolting the door against intruders.

'Well, you won that one,' Roscoe told Patsy.

In spite of Al, it still seemed that Patsy's dream of throwing a party for his own Governor in the Mansion might be taking shape. But then Goddard, on vacation in Havana early in '28, fell out of an open limo, injured his head, developed toxemic erysipelas, and there was death, sitting on the front porch of Patsy's Mansion dream. Hesitating not, Patsy picked Elisha as Goddard's replacement for the nomination.

'I don't want it,' Elisha said.

'You're a natural for it,' Patsy said.

'I'm state chairman. That's enough.'

'If we elect you we'll own the goddamn state.'

'Who says you can elect me?'

'I do,' said Patsy.

'I don't want it.'

'You'll take it.'

'I don't think so.'

'You're throwing us all in?'

'Why don't you run Roscoe?'

'And who'd run Albany if I did?'

'You.'

'I'm not smart enough,' Patsy said.

'Get somebody else to be Governor.'

'I got who I want.'

'I don't want it.'

'You'll get to like it.'

Al accepted Elisha as his successor, for a Protestant out of Yale would balance his major liability – his Roman Catholicism – in the presidential race. Also, Elisha had all the credentials. He was a prenatal Democrat, esteemed at all proper business and social levels, superb at running our Albany finances. As state chairman he was intimate with political leaders from Yonkers to Buffalo, heavily connected to old and new money everywhere. He and Al both had six million friends, both were known as honest men, Al with a somewhat saintly reputation despite his Tammany backing, Elisha considered too rich to be personally dishonest, and the two were pals even before the war: socialized with wives, sang in Mike Quinlan's saloon together. For months we believed that Elisha, backed by Al, could make it.

These were heady developments for Elisha: roving state chairman, potential Governor. At the same time, Fitzgibbon Steel, with a flood of orders, was becoming another bright horizon. In 1927, Elisha and the Krupp Works of Germany had agreed to pool their patents for making new case-hardened alloy steel, with Fitzgibbon Steel holding sole U.S. rights. Elisha put a triumvirate – a cost accountant, his chief metallurgist, and the hustling Kyle Glockner – in charge of the busy mill and kept in touch with the business by remote control.

Elisha was focused on politics and living with a recklessness that was not entirely new, but more expansive than ever; and Roscoe sensed that for the first time in his marriage he was dabbling, beyond flirtation, in other women. Elisha confessed nothing to Roscoe, but affectionate ladies dogged his trail, and Roscoe now thinks that if he *had* carried on with Pamela, this was when it began. His luck was running very fast in all directions during this era of fabulous prosperity, and Elisha then did what gamblers and people with too much money usually do: try to make more.

He became a partner in Burdett and Company, a group of bankers and industrial toffs like himself, who created an investment trust that owned nothing except stock in varied corporations (Fitzgibbon Steel among them) on the stock exchange. You could buy into Burdett for ten dollars a share, and when the trust's portfolio made money, so did you. In less than a year, Burdett's shares were worth three times the stocks on which they were based. It was the purest kind of speculation, and Roscoe likened it to watching the profits compound from Patsy's plugged baseball pool: another sure thing, blue-sky also, but with a difference; this was all legal, which is nice, and next year you'll be as safely rich as your friends. We're talking here about investing in the faith of people who believe that God, luck, and money go together. You can sell those folks anything.

Then, in the summer of 1928, Tammany and Al decided it was going to be a tough election year for Democrats, and they pressed FDR, the Party's best candidate, who'd been the vice-presidential candidate in 1920, to give up his polio therapy and go for the governorship. And there FDR came, galloping into the home stretch without a leg to walk on; and that was that for Elisha and the rest of us. Elisha shed no tears. He'd said yes only because he didn't know how to say no to Patsy, who was furious at Al. But it wasn't Al. It was the age defining itself at Elisha's and Al's expense. Al won the greatest popular vote in Democratic presidential history, but the anti-Catholic vote did him in. He lost New York State to Hoover by more than a hundred thousand votes, while FDR won it by twenty-five thousand.

That year the ill wind blew through Elisha's life. His five-year-old daughter, Rosemary, complained of a stomach ache and Veronica, as usual, gave her milk of magnesia. The child vomited for four hours, and when Dr. Deacy came to Tivoli he diagnosed appendicitis and said a laxative was a very wrong remedy. He arranged for immediate surgery at Albany Hospital. Six hours after the onset of her pain the child's burst appendix was removed, and Elisha and Veronica took up a vigil at her bedside and waited for her to be comforted by the ministrations of doctors and nurses. But they could give her no comfort. Veronica sat at her side and watched the nurse come with a bottle that dripped new medication into Rosemary's vein. On the next afternoon the child vomited blood, and her blood pressure plummeted. They put tubes in her stomach to wash out the blood, and gave her a transfusion. Her pressure returned to normal, her color came back, but her pain persisted.

Roscoe visited twice, but could find no function for himself beyond being here with a readiness to do anything. But there was nothing to be done. He went to Farnham's and bought everybody turkey sandwiches with the homemade mayonnaise Veronica loved; but nobody ate them.

Dr. Deacy examined Rosemary and confirmed the fear: she had peritonitis, a toxic invasion of her system by its own poisons. She was in constant pain, with effortless vomiting and distended stomach; and when Roscoe heard the doctor whisper to a nurse that the child was critical and asked him what medicines were used to fight peritonitis, the doctor said there were many but none of them worked.

On the early morning of the third day, when Veronica could no longer sustain wakefulness, she closed her eyes against her will. Elisha had been catnapping for ten- and twenty-minute stretches, but Veronica could nap only a few minutes and would then burst back into wakeful vigil. This time she slept two hours, during which her daughter was released from relentless pain into shock.

Roscoe arrived to find a nurse scurrying out and Elisha weeping at the foot of the bed, staring at the shallow breathing of his unconscious daughter. The nurse returned with an intern and prepared new injections. Veronica, curled on a leather sofa too small for her body, was wakened by the frenzy of the doctor and nurse, and then realized she'd slept through the fading of her child's consciousness. She threw herself down at the side of the bed, the crack of her knees on the floor a genuflection in hell, batted her head twice against the iron leg of the bed, raised her face and buried it in the bedsheet, and wailed and wept for her baby and cursed her husband.

'Goddamn you for letting me sleep.'

'You couldn't stay awake.'

'You tricked me.'

'You couldn't have done anything.'

'I could have. She's leaving me.'

'The doctors can't do anything. And she isn't gone.'

'She can't hear me.'

'She may rally.'

'She's dying and I can't even say goodbye. You cheated me.'

She stood and waved her arms in a sobbing frenzy and struck Elisha across the face, not an intentional blow, but she did not apologize. Roscoe saw in her face a bitterness he didn't recognize, a wildness beyond grief. She slumped again to her knees, and Elisha could not comfort her. Roscoe stood witness to the tableau of estrangement, and the changing yet again of intravenous medications that had no effect on the child. Elisha's sisters came to the waiting room, and Elisha's brother, Gordon, brought an Episcopal priest who came to deliver the last rites. Veronica refused to let him into the room. 'She's not dying,' she told the priest, 'and even if she were, she's too innocent to need any prayers.'

On the early morning that began the fourth day of the

vigil, Rosemary died without regaining consciousness. Veronica cursed Elisha anew: 'Bastard, you took her away from me, goddamn you for it.' She wailed and refused Elisha's touch. Only her howls assuaged her loss and her guilt over the laxative and the failure of her own body, how dare it demand sleep? She cried herself out and stared at the deathbed. Elisha knelt at the foot of the bed but later told Roscoe he could not remember one prayer. He could think of only one sensible thing to say to Veronica: 'All you see is loss. Does that wipe out all the joy she gave us while she was alive?'

After half an hour, two nurses came to take Rosemary, but Veronica sent them away. The vigil continued another hour, until two interns came back with the head nurse, who apologized but said she would have to restrain Veronica if necessary. Roscoe told her that if she did it would be her last act as an employee of this or any other hospital in Albany. He took hold of Veronica's arm and said to her, 'I'll take you both back to Tivoli, where your daughter will live forever.'

Roscoe then walked Mr. and Mrs. Fitzgibbon down to the hospital parking lot. They sat together in the back seat of Roscoe's new Studebaker, and he then drove them home to their very empty mansion.

Two days after the funeral, Veronica entered the Beth El Jacob synagogue on Herkimer Street as the cantor was singing with his four sons, three wearing hats. The sons had no worldliness in their faces, but much piety. Veronica stood by the door listening. The singing ended and Rabbi Horwitz began to speak to the congregation of bankruptcy, then equated it with moral bankruptcy. 'People spend out of control, but then comes the reckoning and we can't pay,' he said, and Veronica said aloud, 'You are absolutely correct,' and walked toward the rabbi and sat among the men of the congregation. Rabbi Horwitz stopped speaking, and a man arose from his seat and told Veronica that she must sit upstairs with the women.

'I can't do that,' she said. 'It's not my fault that I'm a mother.'

'I'm sorry, but you must move,' the man said.

Veronica stood up and left the synagogue. She drove to Sacred Heart Church in the North End, where her Catholic mother had worshipped. She lit all three hundred votive candles, then knelt at the rail and stared at the white marble altar. Will Logan, the sexton, sweeping the floor at the back of the church, saw her open the marble gates and go up the steps to the altar, take the tabernacle key from under the altar cloth, open the tabernacle door, take out a ciborium half full of the Eucharistic wafers, eat a handful, then begin to eat another. Will came on the run and took the ciborium from her. He put it back in the tabernacle and told her, 'You better leave, missus. You can't do this.'

Later that week, Veronica went to her first session with Nadia the mystic, who swiftly put her in conversation with her dead daughter.

Sale

Elisha left politics in late 1928, two weeks after Rosemary died. He retreated into solitude, refusing all condolences or conversation about the child, seeing no one socially; and Roscoe sensed that any carousing had run its course. Acting once again as the mill's true chief executive, Elisha moved through some months of prosperity. But the wind again blew from Black Thursday to Black Tuesday, the week the stock market betrayed everybody. Margin calls that Burdett and Company and its investors couldn't meet consumed Elisha's personal paper fortune, and also the considerable Fitzgibbon Steel money he had invested in his own sucker trap. Burdett not only blew away in the black wind of burned-out pipe dreams, it was also expelled from the New York Stock Exchange; and Fitzgibbon Steel stock fell from 21 to 4 to ⅛. Orders for steel were canceled and new orders stopped coming as the nation's business shut down out of fear. Layoffs followed, and the mill grew skeletal.

By the spring of 1930, Elisha was looking at debts the mill could not cover, and he confided this to Roscoe while they were in his library at Tivoli. They were sunken in sumptuous leather armchairs, drinking bootleg Scotch whisky, Eli, in tailored shirt and diamond pinky ring, saying that if he did not find money someplace he would lose the pinky ring, the Scotch, the furniture, the library, and maybe his shirt, the first Fitzgibbon in two centuries to be poor. 'The banks could, and might, take the mill away,' he said, 'and they'd come for Tivoli next. Bankers are bastards, and I say this because I'm on the board of three banks.'

'You seem to be saying you need money,' Roscoe said.

'Very acute.'

'Patsy already knows this. He has a hundred thousand for you in his safe.'

'That would pay a few creditors.'

'There's more when you need more,' Roscoe said.

'Patsy gives away money, but never this much.'

'Who said he's giving it away?'

'He wants it back, of course. And he'll get it.'

'Who said he wants it back?'

'What does he want?'

'FDR going for the White House makes him a lame-duck governor, and that gives Patsy another chance to put you in the Governor's Mansion.'

'I still don't want it.'

'It's so little to ask in return for saving the mill and Tivoli. All you have to do is sell Patsy your soul.'

'Didn't I do that a long time ago?'

'A soul as big as yours, you get to sell it more than once.'

In November 1930, during Artie Flinn's federal trial on charges of running the Albany baseball pool, Warren Skaggs, the man Patsy took the pool away from, testified that he heard Artie say pool profits were cut up among Patsy, Bindy, and Roscoe, and that 'we also figure Fitzgibbon into it.' Skaggs's volunteering, with great enthusiasm and without being asked, the Fitzgibbon name – could it be the ex-Democratic state chairman and the almost candidate of 1928 to succeed Al Smith as governor? – came as a public shocker. Elisha issued a statement stoutly denying involvement, and jurists and clergy rushed to his support. Roscoe and Bindy also made public denials, which nobody believed. The positive news was that Artie always distributed the profits in cash, either in Roscoe's Ten Eyck suite or at Patsy's garage, and there were never any witnesses. Roscoe always took Elisha's share and delivered it at a later moment. With only hearsay evidence (Artie testified he could not remember ever hearing the name Fitzgibbon mentioned), no gambling charges were brought against Elisha, Patsy, Roscoe, or Bindy. Patsy was convicted of contempt of court for his creative answers before the grand jury and was sentenced to federal prison for six months.

Elisha packed his trunks and sailed to Barcelona with Veronica and stayed two months in quiet isolation, even from the English language, identifying with hubristic martyrs and victims of too much opportunity. He returned only when the baseball pool had receded from the headlines, and a crisis of indolence had arisen at the mill: roofs leaking, machines rusting from nonuse, shops frequently broken into, and tools, supplies, even small machinery stolen. Also, there was one successful suicide, one unsuccessful suicide attempt among former mill employees, both of whom Elisha knew well, and whose financial sorrows he blamed on himself for having committed crimes for which there was no redemption.

Patsy was sent to the Federal House of Detention in Greenwich Village, in Manhattan, but not before Roscoe arranged, with Tammany's influence over the jailers, for Patsy to spend afternoons down the block at the home of Philly McQuaid, a bucket-shop operator and Patsy's close friend for years, and to return to his fourteen-bed dormitory for lights-out anytime before nine-thirty. On weekends when the weather was good, Mush Trainor, who also lost millions in the market crash, drove Patsy to his summer place in the Helderbergs in a Willys sedan Mush had stolen and repainted for Patsy's incognito travel. Patsy did five of his six months and earned a month off for good behavior. He came home in late April 1931, a notable year for crime and punishment in Albany.

Roscoe at the Apex

While Roscoe lay on the operating table having his heart invaded, the surgeon found, nestling near the heart's traveling bag, a sliver of one of the bullets that had pierced

Roscoe during his heroic desertion from the French battlefield in 1918. When told he'd been harboring a piece of the reality that had wounded him twenty-seven years earlier, Roscoe said the discovery proved some wounds never heal because they belong to primordial human trauma: the wrong choice. And he was thrust backward to early 1931, when Elisha was licking his wounds in Spain, Patsy was sleeping under a federal roof, and Roscoe alone was running the Albany Democracy. In those months, Democratic headquarters was never busier, visitors arriving without end – Party regulars bringing the temporary Caesar news, whispers, beseechings, money, and votive offerings, and also wondering: By the way, Roscoe, has the world changed? Is Patsy gone forever? Has Eli moved to Spain? You look good at the top, Ros.

Such obeisance Roscoe had been accepting for years, never on his own behalf, and now that the power was his alone, however temporarily, he didn't like it or want it. It did not improve the climate of his spirit. Serious meaning did not inhere in his power to transform the life of anybody who walked through his door. An entire society structured on extortion and subordination: what a way to live. Roscoe never coveted that, but never wanted to be subordinate, either; and yet knows he is (and isn't when you look in the opposite direction). So why, then, has he inhabited this place for so long? Not power? Then maybe the lush life, or access to love and beauty? A major side dish, said Roscoe, but how do you live on love alone? Only in the song. Going for the main chance is it? Possibly. But Roscoe is still trying to define that one. He had goals once: merchant-politician like Felix, no; scholar and teacher, historian perhaps, using your brain appeals, reading books for a living, but no; constitutional lawyer – now, there was an aspiration, but you had to practice law first – egad, no; maybe the theater, you're a great actor, Roscoe, with a hell of a voice, and everybody's known that about you since school days and the Elks Club minstrels; but no, no thanks.

The truth is that Roscoe would've had to take too many time risks, give up too much life-at-hand, to pursue such long-distance goals. So he gave up the goals: rational cowardice his basic survival tactic while he kept chasing that elusive main chance, where the hell was it? When would it turn up? Meantime, there was the communal motive: to live equal among revelers in conquest. Yes, that's what we were about, why we went into politics. Yes, indeed, conquest, yes, yes, that surely must be the motive. We'll work to elevate the people, our people, and any others out there who need a leg up into equality: generic Democrats who couldn't get jobs for twenty years. Right. The poor, the working class, that's us. Anybody with more than five thousand dollars should be a Republican. We don't want people starving because they're Democrats. Not nice to live and die in hungry silence. Patsy, Roscoe, Elisha couldn't bear such silence. Manic life, the gamble, game chickens, high action, the campaign, that's the stuff. Patsy, the redeemer, replaces every failure (a form of death) with success. Yesterday's defeat has got to become tomorrow's plurality, which is Patsy's formula as a relentless winner, and that's how he redeems. When Pat walks down the street a crowd follows, you'd think he was Jesus passing out the loaves and fishes, primitive patronage, but that's how it's still done.

Now, as Roscoe lies on the operating table with his heart sliced open, he ponders dying like Elisha, really dying this time, you can't live without a heart. He senses that he is being commanded to survive, so he makes a forcible point to himself – Don't die, Roscoe, survive – which some may say begs the question. But as the survival word sibilates on his tongue, Roscoe hears it as a eureka truth built into the fabric of the being, and he sees that it's the cause of all wars, of every argument for and against the Empire, the Nazis, the Fascists, the Japs, the reason we convert the infidels and save the pagans, the reason we subdue the aborigines, the barbarians, the Republicans; it's why kings have that divine right and why we absolutely must win the Ninth Ward; it's at the heart of Manifest Destiny and the lemming society, of the mad oligarchs, the killer hordes, the holy despots, and also Dracula, who certainly knows how to preserve his soul. How? You get the money. How do you get the money? Oh my Jesus. Money is blood. Get it any way you can. Money buys survival. Too bad about that stock market. Those fellows should've tried politics, which is the *real* stock market. Roscoe, with his heart wide open and susceptible to scalpel slashings and invasions of the blood by unholy elements, knows that Elisha and Patsy, and then he himself in his brief time at the apex, all stepped out of the crowd; and not only did they survive, they achieved pre-eminence, and forever after have been forced to live like lions among hares, arguing at the council of beasts that laws cannot be made for them both. 'Where are your claws and teeth?' the lions asked the hares. Demigods, mud gods, gods on a stick, but gods with the power of obliteration are what this triumvirate looks like from below. Shoot them in the chest, put them in jail, make them drink poison, they will refuse to die, even after they are dead. Equals in the revel, yes, and the revel will now continue if they can only put Roscoe's heart back the way they found it. And then he will continue with new clarity, for wisdom has descended and Roscoe has circled his malaise all the way back to first cause, which turns out to be just like that sliver in the heart: the consequence of the wrong choice. So very simple, Ros, but it raises another question. Which wrong choice are we talking about?

When Roscoe came back to Tivoli at Veronica's insistence, purged of dead blood, healed in invisible ways, Veronica kissed him sweetly, possibly a bit of the old passion there, but that's subject to interpretation. She coddled him with steamed clams, prime ribs with a mountain of mashed potatoes, and a dish he had once professed love for and forgotten he loved, chicken-liver-and-mushroom pie. Veronica had not forgotten. Alex offered restrained good wishes, with no hostility, and it seemed that heart trouble, for the moment, had liberated Roscoe from tension within this family, the only one to which he felt he belonged; for his only surviving sister, the sweet Cress, was as distant as a fifth cousin, and O.B. less a brother than a plenipotentiary of the Party, blood not necessarily thicker than politics.

Then Roscoe's fading tension flared anew when Gladys came to visit. He sat with her in the garden room with all the wicker and heard her say, with a tremolo in her voice, that O.B. had put Mac on departmental leave and told him to turn in his badge and pistol; and when Mac refused, O.B. punched him, breaking his partial denture and splintering his jaw. O.B. was still furious that Mac had gone to Roscoe and thwarted his Notchery raid, never mind Roscoe's quick-witted salvation of the harebrained disaster that didn't quite happen, that's irrelevant. The grave issue before us is O.B.'s authority affronted. Gladys also said O.B. asked her to go to New York with him for a weekend. When she refused him he retaliated, telling her the infamous Pina had been Mac's personal whore 'all the years he's been sleeping with you.'

'I beg your pardon,' Gladys said. 'I haven't been sleeping with him.'

'Having chocolates and port wine, listening to Claude Thornhill and Mozart,' O.B. said. 'Mac told me all about it. He said he slept with you twice a week.'

'Then he's not an honorable man,' Gladys said.

She telephoned and screamed at Mac, who went silent, then left the receiver off the hook. 'And it's still off,' Gladys told Roscoe. She had already gone twice to Mac's house on Walter Street, afternoon and evening, but no one answered his bell, the place was dark, and Mac's sister downstairs didn't know where he was.

'What do you want me to do?' Roscoe asked her.

'Find him and tell him I don't care what he said to O.B. or did with that woman.'

'That morning Elisha died, O.B. took you home from the mill.'

'Yes.'

'You were seeing them both.'

'I only visited with O.B.,' she said. 'He never stayed over.'

'Mac suspected.'

'Yes.'

'You're a *femme fatale,* Gladys. Two cops on the hook.'

'It wasn't like that.'

'It was something like that.'

'I never betrayed Mac. I was always true to him.'

'In your fashion.'

'What do you know about it? Did you listen to O.B.'s lies?'

'I'm just reading between your hesitations.'

'I never let O.B. touch me.'

'But he kept trying for a breakthrough.'

'I'm sorry I asked you anything,' Gladys said, and she stood up.

'I'll try to find him,' Roscoe said.

He sent Joey Manucci to all the bars and lunchrooms Mac frequented, checked Hattie to see if he'd sought sanctuary with her, no, then called O.B., feeling the rage he'd felt in childhood when O.B. tattled on him to Felix. O.B. knew intimately the power of the stool pigeon, indispensable ally in delivering justice to the miscreant. And justice for miscreant Mac was precisely what O.B. wanted.

'I hear you've gone crazy,' Roscoe said to him on the phone, 'persecuting the best cop you've got.'

'I'd expect you to stand up for him.'

'Your ego is ridiculous, O.B. You look like a self-serving sap.'

'Patsy doesn't think so. He likes people to obey his orders.'

'Patsy won't back you when he hears what you told Gladys.'

'She been talking to you?'

'You run down Mac to her, you think she'll say, Thanks a lot, honey, let's go to bed? She loves the man, O.B.'

'She oughta know the kind of guy she's screwing.'

'Thank you, Monsignor. Your moral stance is exemplary.'

'Keep out of this, Roscoe. This is my show.'

Discursive Critique, with Gin

Joey found Mac at the Elite Club, a onetime speakeasy on Hudson Avenue, drinking gin with Morty Besch, the ex-bootlegger who was one of the last people to see Jack Diamond alive. Until the war ended, Morty was bleaching dollar bills to print counterfeit gasoline-ration stamps on the paper, was also the Elite Club's silent partner with his brother, Herman; for Morty, a felon, could not legally own a bar. Herman, with a withered leg, was a slave to the place. Morty's function was to drag in customers and see that they kept drinking. Mac had known Morty for years, moonlighted with him during Prohibition, riding shotgun on his days off: pistol, rifle, and sawed-off at the ready on the Canadian booze run in Morty's seven-passenger, armor-plated Buick. The run was up to the border for the pickup, fill the Buick's undercarriage full of whiskey out of Montreal, then head back down to Chestertown, where the booze was offloaded into two other cars to be taken to sanctioned drops in Troy and Albany. Mac got off at Chestertown, drove home in his own car, and resumed being an Albany cop noted for collaring bootleggers operating without sanction.

Joey drove Roscoe to the Elite Club and waited for him in the car. The Elite was two rooms, modest bar, pendulum clock, a calendar with a naked woman bending over the engine of an automobile, and a wall menu noting the cheese and crackers and oxtail soup you might, on one of his good days, persuade Herman to serve you. When a customer passed on the cheese and crackers and insisted on the oxtail soup, Morty sold him the unopened can. Mac and Morty were at a table in the back, a bottle of gin between them. Mac never drank gin.

'How's your teeth?' Roscoe asked. Mac's jaw was still swollen, two days after the fact. He needed a shave, his shirt collar soiled, two or three days in the same clothes.

'No good,' Mac said. He barely moved his mouth when he spoke.

'You go to the dentist?'

'The city gets the bill. Jawbone's broken.'

'He can't chew,' Morty said, 'but he can drink,' and he poured gin into Mac's glass and topped it with a splash of Vichy water. 'Gin, Roscoe?'

'Make it a double. You talk to O.B. today?'

'What do you think?' Mac said.

'I think no.'

'Bong. Give the man a prize.'

Roscoe popped his gin. 'You been telling Morty your life story?'

'Morty knows it all.'

'No secrets at this table,' Roscoe said.

'None.'

'I was talking to Gladys.'

'O.B., the bastard, told her about me and Pina,' Mac said. 'She says she's all through with me.'

'That's not what I hear,' Roscoe said.

'O.B. is also hot for Pina, am I right?' said Morty. 'I don't ask this for any reason. Some things you just hear.'

'No question you could hear that,' Mac said.

'But that's all done with.'

'Isn't it,' Mac said.

'If you say it's all done, it's all done.'

'If I say it.'

'Why did he hit you?' Roscoe asked.

'His stupid Notchery plan. I told him if he'd only been a little bit smarter he coulda been a first-class moron.'

'I'll bet he liked that.'

'Bong. And there goes the jaw. The gin helps the pain, if you don't swallow it. Also if you do.'

'That Gladys,' Morty said. 'What's her name?'

'You should call Gladys,' Roscoe said to Mac. 'She wants to talk.'

'Meehan, Gladys Meehan,' Mac said.

'Right. Her boss is whatsisname Fitzgibbon, right?'

'Elisha Fitzgibbon,' Mac said. 'He's dead.'

'He bought my gin,' Morty said, 'and Gladys always told me when and where to deliver it. That was Jack Diamond's gin.'

'Another thing,' Mac said. 'He tells the Diamond story and it's all him.'

'Outside of his cab driver,' Morty said, 'I was the last one to see Diamond.'

'You weren't the last,' Mac said.

'You mean Dove Street. I didn't see any of that, none,' Morty said. 'They shot him right between the head. I heard it was coming.'

'Some people knew,' Mac said. 'The newspaper set the headline before it happened.'

'They say he was told to leave town,' Roscoe said.

'I heard that,' Morty said. 'Some cockamamie beer deal with the Thorpe brothers. Mush told me. The Thorpes tried to shoot Bindy, bring their beer into Albany over his dead body. They brought whatsisname in to do the job.'

'Scarpelli,' Roscoe said.

'Scarpelli, a mistake,' Mac said.

'The Thorpes weren't intelligent,' Morty said.

'They were born short,' Mac said.

'Mush comes in here,' Morty said. 'He don't have money any more. He ran outa luck. He had it all fixed to get Louie Lepke into the French Foreign Legion and then Lepke surrendered to the FBI through Winchell and they fried him. Mush woulda made a bundle on that Foreign Legion bit.'

'Diamond died broke,' Mac said.

'He shouldn'ta mixed up with the Thorpes,' Morty said.

'I liked Jack one way,' Mac said.

'He could make you laugh,' Morty said. 'He lived upstairs when you people were looking for him. Ate his meals here.'

'Cheese and crackers,' said Roscoe.

'He was afraid of cops,' Mac said.

'He took bad beatings from cops,' Morty said.

'He stood up for his rights, and a few lefts,' Mac said. 'He was a rat bastard, but I liked him. Almost nobody knows how to like.'

'You liked him?' Roscoe said.

'I saw him at the Parody Club singing with the piano, pretty good voice, skinny little runt, looked like my brother Joey fightin' lightweight.'

This made sense to Roscoe, the Mac-and-Jack affinity. They even look alike, now that he thinks about their faces: cheerful, crooked smile that goes away and here comes a dead-eyed chilblain of a grin. Two sides of the same coin would be stretching it, but consider that they both weighed, in good health, which Jack seldom was, about a hundred and thirty-five, stood five seven, knew how to dude up, loved women and supported several at a time, thrived on crime, shot people when necessary and sometimes when not, both of them notorious and feared – twinned, you might say, but as if separated at birth, and then found their separate ways to the same time, same place: Jack, the mythic ragamuffin of an evil calling, dead at thirty-four when Mac was twenty-five, and Mac, thirty-nine now, scourge of hoodlums, fearless assassin, a political secret, stable as quicksilver, likes Mozart and Claude Thornhill, now fuming at O.B.'s historical revisionism.

You Can Imagine How Mac Felt

Mac heard it from Jack McQuilty, the ex-sheriff who was talking to Patsy and O.B. at a clambake. When the subject of Legs Diamond came up, Patsy said, 'O.B. finished Legs,' and O.B. smiled a big one.

But, hey, what about Mac's contribution?

Does Patsy really know the crime and punishment that went on in the second-floor front at 67 Dove Street that very early morning in December 1931? Mac never talked to Patsy about it, never told anybody the details. Patsy couldn't begin to know what Jack looked like with two flashlights in his face, illuminating him and the asters, roses, and swirling tendrils of his wallpaper as he sat up in his double bed, not sure what was happening, then sure, but never figuring it would come to this: alone, no pistol, nobody to help him out; nor could he know how his image related vividly in Mac's mind to the van Gogh painting on Gladys's parlor wall, the postman in his hat and long, curly beard (Jack was clean-shaven, his hat on the floor) looking out from a floral design of blossoms and swirling tendrils on a field of green from which five hundred black-oval, white-dotted leaves stare like the eyes of the dangerous night. A floral postman is eccentric, but is he more so than Jack against a wall of roses and asters with tendrils, onto which he casts his large shadow, and into which three bullets are about to be fired?

'We told you not to come back,' Mac said.

'Gimme a break, fellas, I'll get out.'

'Lotta guys asked you for a break and didn't get it,' O.B. said.

Mac still remembers O.B. putting his pistol against Jack's

forehead. Deferential to O.B.'s senior pistol, Mac lowered his own.

'Five minutes I'm across the city line,' Jack said, turning his head away from O.B.'s barrel.

Nothing. No bang.

'Just five minutes, boys.'

Still no bang. He's not going to do it.

Mac shines the light on O.B. and sees those eyes, huge like the postman's white-dotted black ovals, and blank. Mac wonders if he's even looking where he's pointing.

He can't do it.

'Thanks, fellas,' Jack says and moves a leg to get out of bed.

No bang.

Mac raises his arm and fires three shots from the pearl-handled .38 that O.B. gave him after the Polka Dot Gang shootout, and Jack Diamond ceases to be. The papers will get it wrong at first, but the autopsy will show that all three shots entered the left side of the face (Mac's side of the bed), one into the left cheek, one in front of the left ear, a third forward of that, but upward, because Jack's head was falling back. After Mac's three shots, O.B. fires three, but they all go into the wall over fallen Jack. O.B. shoots to miss.

'You think that's enough?' O.B. says. 'I waited a long time for this.'

'Hell, that's enough for him,' Mac says.

In the front room of the first-floor flat directly below Jack's room, the landlady, Laura Woods, and the owner of the house, Hattie, who had come by on her predawn rounds of tending the furnaces in her rooming houses, sat in darkness listening to the voices, to the gunshots that sounded like cannons, and to the rapidly descending footsteps. By the light of the street lamp Hattie saw Mac and O.B. get into their red Packard. Mac drove.

Two .38-caliber pistols were found on nearby streets the next day, one with a wooden handle, neither of them Mac's or O.B.'s, which went into the river. Much was made of the pistols by police and press, and within a few days a Manhattan ballistics expert consulted by Albany Police Chief Dan Spurling would say unequivocally that the wooden-handled pistol was the death weapon. The chief believed the finding would lead to Jack's gangland assassins. Within six months, Mac would be promoted to detective sergeant, O.B. to captain. O.B. bought Mac a new pearl-handled .38, and they went back out into the night that they ruled, a legendary pair now, more feared than ever as the tale ran in whispers through the streets: Yeah, those two pulled off the killing of the century in this town, one bad bastard gone.

Hitch your .38 to a star. Mac didn't expect stardom, but began to think he just might live forever on the basis of being the man who put Legs away, solo. But Mac couldn't say that out loud. So he wrote it in the kid's composition book where he kept a record of his deeds. Only when the Governor began investigating Albany in 1943 did Mac burn the book, but until then, for twelve years, he and Jack were there on the page, to reconfirm the things that had happened, and that he had not hallucinated them after a binge: 'Followed Diamond two days. Execution at Dove Street. Solo. Dead meat.' Mac called it an execution, not a murder, for he had served the highest order of his society, the assignment awesome by itself, nothing like it in his life as a cop. Proud Mac basked in the enormity of the growing legend, until he learned his role in it had been stolen, that he'd been eliminated from a most significant moment in American history: he, the man without whom there wouldn't even *be* a moment, eliminated. You can imagine how Mac felt.

The Call

Herman Besch came to the table where Roscoe sat with Morty and Mac to say O.B. was on the line for Mac, the second time he'd called today.

'Tell him I went to Troy to get my laundry,' Mac said.

'He said he's got people in cars outside and he wants you to go to his office the easy way.'

'Tell him I went up on the roof for a suntan.'

'I'll talk to him,' Roscoe said. And he did. When he came back to the table he told Mac, 'I said I'd try to persuade you to come in.'

'Not going.'

'He said he's only kidding about turning in your badge.'

'Always a joker.'

'I think I calmed him down,' Roscoe said. 'And I'll fix it with Patsy. When O.B. sees he can't win, he won't fight it. I've seen this in him all his life.'

'I don't turn in the badge, I don't turn in the gun.'

'He wants to talk. I'll go in with you.'

Roscoe called Patsy from Herman's phone booth, and Patsy said O.B. was making too much of it and he'd cool him down. Roscoe told this to Mac. Joey Manucci drove Roscoe and Mac to police headquarters at Eagle and Beaver Streets, and Roscoe led the way into the chief's inner office, where, Roscoe decided, O.B. had truly arrived. This was the place O.B. had moved toward as soon as he knew it existed, a true believer in authority. Half their lives the Conway brothers worked the same territory, O.B. after the dominance, Roscoe not interested. O.B. called himself the Doctor: 'You had a problem? Why didn't you call the Doctor?' On his desk he kept a small sign: 'The Doctor is in.' The Doctor possesses the arcane knowledge that eludes you. The Doctor sees what ails you and can prescribe a cure. And Mac, walking beside Roscoe, is another of the arrived: quirky Mac, maker of dead meat. He had a calling, knew how it was done. O.B. didn't have that assassin's ease, but he and Mac both knew how to become, and they became; both knew how to be, and they are: final versions of themselves. It was a lesson to Roscoe.

O.B. was at his desk, sleeves rolled, red-and-ochre tie on a white shirt open at the collar, wearing his bifocals to read a complaint sheet. Roscoe and Mac stood in front of the desk. O.B. took off his glasses.

'So we're here,' Roscoe said.

'You goddamn ingrate,' O.B. said to Mac, 'after all I did for you.'

'Ingrate? You broke my jaw,' Mac said.

'Put your pistol on the desk,' O.B. said, his middle right knuckle a scab.

'Wait a minute,' Roscoe said.

But Mac took his pearl-handled pistol out of his back-pocket holster and, standing to the right of the desk as he had at Jack's bed, told O.B., 'I'm gonna break *your* jaw.'

When O.B. saw the way the pistol was rising in Mac's hand, he moved his head away from it, and so Mac's bullet did not enter the front of his jaw as Mac had intended, but his left temple, which sent O.B. to a new place. Mac then handed his pistol to Roscoe.

'Lunatic. You goddamn lunatic,' Roscoe said. 'You're as

dead as he is.' He stared at O.B.'s head on the desk. 'He's my brother.'

'He was the best friend I ever had,' Mac said.

The walls of O.B.'s office were the same pale blue as Elisha's final face.

Roscoe Among the Saints

When Elisha stepped off the train and stood alone on the platform, Roscoe called to him through the train window. But Elisha only tapped his right foot as the train pulled away. Now Roscoe entered the barn where the Communion of Saints was sponsoring its perennial flea market. Crowds moved from stall to stall, buying St. Teresa's eyelashes, chips off St. Peter's shinbone, St. Sebastian's arrowheads, and, new this year, the curly toenails of St. Anthony's demon temptress. Roscoe asked to see Elisha.

'We have no one by that name,' the Registrar said.

'He got off the train here.'

'Has he performed any posthumous miracles?'

'He's working on that.'

'Many are called, sir, but even the holiest of men rarely qualify, because of the severe demands of the moral law.'

'Elisha wasn't up on the moral law. He wasn't even a Catholic.'

'Ignorance of the moral law is no excuse.'

'No, but it's a living.'

Roscoe wanted to tell this fellow that not morality but fraudulence is the necessary modality for human existence. Nothing is, or ever was, what it seems. Thou shalt not commit honesty. Elisha died a martyr to this creed.

'Those thoughts,' the Registrar said, 'are unacceptable here.'

'I'm glad we agree on something,' Roscoe said.

The *Beau Geste* Revealed

There was Roscoe all over page one again: lofty pol, whorehouse lawyer, now intermediary for the killer-cop who killed his brother. What he must be going through. See Roscoe in mourning with his sister Cress, see widow Hattie in her weeds, see the police honor guard standing at the hero's grave.

'I never thought he'd die in bed,' said Hattie. 'But to have my little Mac do him. And I put them together.'

O.B.'s death put her in tears at first, weep, stop, weep again. Then she was over it. O.B. was an erratic, mediocre husband, not such a bad lover, a pal who made her feel like an insider, told her everything that wasn't an official secret, brought her fresh bread and cake from the Jewish bakeries, roasts and chops from the Armenian butcher, never came by empty-handed before or after they were married. And why did they ever marry? Well, he made her feel safe, and he chased her, as he chased so many, but probably he married her for more reasons than her enduring nubility: one, because it would – oh, sibling treachery – one-up Roscoe, whom, two, Hattie loved in her way – premarital blockade. But Hattie also had her reasons: one, Ros wasn't available to her, the way

Veronica wasn't available to Ros, who therefore married Pamela, as Hattie therefore married O.B.; and, two, Hattie, invincibly lonely, always has to marry somebody.

Mac immediately pleaded guilty when charged with first-degree murder. I did it, he said, give me the chair. Sorry, Mac, you can't plead to the capital crime. You need a lawyer, and don't ask Roscoe for any more favors. Mac stopped eating in jail, wanted to die; so many maniacs in this suicide roundelay: Jack and Elisha, and then O.B. deciding that stealing Mac's women and ending his career as a cop were mere amusements, and Mac assuming a jaw-shot would be judged as tit-for-tat, all of them lying to themselves as they designed their own finales. From his car on the curving road to O.B.'s new grave in St. Agnes Cemetery, Roscoe saw where Hattie's fourth husband, Benny (the) Behr, another one, was buried: Benny, who blew a hole in his head with a shotgun when he couldn't stand the pain in his spine. No hallowed ground for you, Ben, your place is with the suicidal trees. But Hattie wouldn't hear of that, and confessed to the chancellor of the Albany Catholic Diocese that she was the one who blew that hole in Benny's pain. Bless me, Father, I did murder. Punish me, not him, such a good man, how could I sit there and watch him suffer and do nothing to help him? The chancellor believed Hattie, and so Benny joined the hallowable dead in the St. Agnes underworld. The chancellor also said Hattie should tell the police what she did, but she told only Roscoe, and nobody prosecuted St. Hat – after all, she didn't do it. The chancellor kept Hattie's confession to himself, as did Roscoe, and it remained secret even to Benny.

O.B.'s fresh grave lay alongside Felix's obelisk, which rested on a pedestal into which the name Conway was engraved; and the pedestal was losing ground to the encroaching sod.

'You see that?' he said to Cress.

'Of course I see it,' she said. 'Mama's and Papa's graves.'

'I mean the sod. Look at the sod.'

'Yes, the sod. They're under it.'

'I mean we should come back up and cut away that sod. It's overgrowing the stone.'

'If you cut away the sod the grass dies, and then it comes back as clover and dandelions.'

Forget it. Roscoe would come alone. Cress had been a lovable sister, but grew into a dotty spinster with selectively skewed memories: all the celebratory minutiae of Felix's history as mayor, but not a whit of recollection of his removal from office, and no acknowledgment that he had lived half his later life in hotel exile from the family. It was not seemly to have such memories.

Mayor Alex, the fire chief, half the city government, police chiefs from other cities, and a hundred friends circled the grave for O.B.'s ceremonial descent to the eighth floor, no more worry about Albany's evildoers. No evil down there, either; only pain. Get ready for the boiling pitch, brother barrator, and I may be along presently. Look among the trees for Elisha when you get down there and tell him I'm on the verge of decoding his scheme. But he's probably elsewhere, you don't know where in hell to look for that man. And tell him I've decided the windshield head-bump injured his prefrontal cortex, which brought on all that anxiety and chloral hydrate, my fault. I hit the brakes, another oblique homicide. Send my regrets.

Monsignor Tooher from St. Joseph's gave O.B. a full Jesus sendoff, and Roscoe came close to weeping when he remembered the adolescent O.B., for, since Felix was usually on family leave, Roscoe half-raised his brother in those years, Rozzie and Ozzie inseparable: trapping yellow birds with George Quinn, running on top of freight cars; O.B., learning the hard way, fell and broke his arm. Roscoe taught him about Patsy's chickens and Eli's horses, took him to the burlesque at the Gayety to see Millie DeLeon shake herself and throw her garters to the audience; also introduced him to a community of reluctant virgins who tested their own limits with Roscoe and then with O.B., who became an apt student of their restraint. To civilize him, Roscoe took him regularly to Harmanus Bleecker Hall to see Chauncey Olcott, Lew Dockstеader's minstrels, Lillian Russell, the Barrymores, even a Shakespeare, was it *Twelfth Night*? But the theater never penetrated O.B.'s brain. He had no use for abstract or imposed pleasure, unless it was a woman sitting on his lap. He lived for women, God bless them every one. He also kept on rolling beer kegs for Felix until the brewery closed, then signed on as Patsy's beer protector. From the McCall brothers he learned truculence as a survival trait; learned so well that Roscoe talked Patsy into letting him exercise it on the force so he wouldn't turn into a hoodlum. And then O.B. rose, and fell. The newspapers thought they loved him: 'Farewell to the Doctor, Who Kept Gangsters out of Albany.' They know about Jack: the *sotto-voce* legacy that's now his epitaph. And there you go, O.B., never a bad brother, just a remote one: Roz and Oz, fraternal strangers after adolescence. But he was a blood presence, and now isn't. First Roscoe without Elisha, now without O.B., a pair without whom Roscoe would be somebody else. He looks into the grave as he gives O.B. the okay to move on, and he knows another small lobe of his soul is atrophying.

'We should talk,' Alex said to him as they walked away

from the grave. Roscoe saw Veronica in the moving crowd and returned her nod.

'Now?' he said to Alex.

'As soon as possible, privately.'

Roscoe gestured toward a slope with more illustrious obelisks and statues of angels. 'No eavesdroppers up there,' he said.

'Fine.' Alex gestured for Roscoe to lead the way up the grassy incline.

Roscoe and Alex (2)

'I worry about you,' Alex said, a marble cherub hovering behind him. He stood tall, sharp in his black tie on gray collar, getting his old weight back. 'This is almost too much to bear. Witnessing it, arranging it yourself. God, Roscoe, I'm so sorry. I wanted to say this at the wake.'

Weary Roscoe sat on the marble sarcophagus of Ebel Campion, the North End undertaker, a good fellow. Ebel would not consider the sitting an imposition. Probably glad for the visit. And Roscoe said to Alex, 'It's good of you, my boy. I'm in a bad place. O.B. was a decent brother, a foolish man. I'm trying to understand him.'

'I'm trying to understand *you*,' Alex said. 'You're central to every disaster – my father, the Patsy-Bindy thing, beating up editors, the Notchery scandal, the Dutchman and that murderous whore, now poor O.B. and mad Mac. What's next for you, Roscoe, wholesaling opium? White slavery? I wouldn't sell you an insurance policy. You're a bad risk.'

'I do seem to ride the lightning,' Roscoe said.

'I worry. I worry about Gilby's case. These are not good omens.'

Ah yes, Gilby's case.

'It's two days away. The judge may decide you're a villain yourself, to be such a friend to villainy.'

'Only a judicial villain could make such a ruling, and we have none so injudicious in Albany.'

'Are you ready for Marcus Gorman? He's a great trickster.'

'God and natural motherhood are on his side. We can't lose.'

'I don't think I follow.'

'Righteousness doesn't stand a chance against the imagination, Alex.'

'I'd like to believe that. But if Mother loses Gilby, she'll fall apart.'

'I won't let that happen.'

'That goddamned cunt.'

'The expressive word. I tell you, Alex, Roscoe is ready for whatever she offers, and you'll see that not only is he capable of change, Roscoe is capable of changing the world. I *am* a lonely man, but I am a crowd. I grow old. But ancient salt is the best packing.'

'You talk riddles.'

'The poetry of the giants, my boy. You see before you a transfiguration, a man so chastened by experience that he has shunted all his old faults into the brotherly grave. He is awash in mortification. He's bought several new hair shirts, and he may even go to church.'

'Don't go too far, old fellow. Lightning may light the church.'

'A new day is rising up from the fresh earth, and a new Roscoe stands astride it.'

'You sound like an old lush taking the pledge,' said Alex.

'Your tongue has a talent for brutish truth.'

'Isn't all truth brutish?'

'I wouldn't know,' said Roscoe. 'I rarely encounter any.'

Isn't It Romantic?

As Roscoe walked down the cemetery slope he decided that derision is not healthy behavior, a defense mechanism, really, and that he must get Alex beyond this attitude. A sour mouth is not becoming in a candidate. Also, Alex evoked Pamela, and, against Roscoe's will, there she is in memory at the Ten Eyck, why? And there's Elisha with her, and Veronica, ah, now he sees the day clearly, Patsy is at a peak, O.B. and Mac are ten months past Diamond, Alex the youth is spectating, and Jimmy Walker, Al Smith, and FDR are in crisis. Thirteen years gone, but it's yesterday, and Roscoe must have his reasons for this.

It's Tuesday afternoon, October 4, 1932, the day Elisha, the reluctant gladiator, is on the road to glory. Pamela is striding into Elisha's busy headquarters on the second floor of the Ten Eyck, just off the train, right out of *Vogue* in her maroon silk Schiaparelli dress with the emphatic bustline, complaining the front desk won't give her a room. Roscoe, no longer regretting he ever knew Pamela, now thinking of her as his principal mentor in lousy love, explains that all twenty-five hundred rooms in the town's ten main hotels have been overbooked for a month; the *Trojan*, the night boat that brought five hundred Tammanyites up from New York for the Democratic state convention, is a floating hotel this weekend; the New York Central is renting berths in Pullman cars on sidings; and even Al Smith had no room until Tammany boss John Curry dispossessed a delegate to give

Al a bed in the DeWitt Clinton Hotel, headquarters for both Tammany and John McCooey's Brooklyn organization, Tammany's Siamese twin.

'Right now the town has about ten thousand too many people,' Roscoe says to Pamela.

'My brother-in-law's going to be Governor,' she says. 'I want a room.'

'Why don't you stay out at Tivoli?'

'I want to be where things are happening.'

'Tivoli's a fifteen-minute ride, including stoplights.'

'Goddamn it, Roscoe, I want a goddamn room. Release one you're holding out for your goddamn thieving political celebrities.'

'How could I resist such a charming request?'

He sends her down the hall to see Hattie, who is in charge of spillover: placing people in her own rooming houses, or in one of the six hundred private homes that their owners have opened to visitors, sixteen hundred already placed. Ten minutes later, Hattie comes to see him.

'Don't send me any more like her,' she says.

'There are no more like her,' Roscoe says.

'What a bitch. She didn't want anybody's house, didn't want a room without a sitting room, didn't want a ground floor, and it couldn't be more than five blocks from here. I told her I had one house I wasn't going to rent but she could have it, a third-floor walkup on Jay Street, take it or leave it.'

'She took it?' asks Roscoe.

'Yes. I didn't tell her it used to be a whorehouse.'

The city has been ablaze with political firelight since Saturday, when Democrats began arriving to nominate a governor to succeed FDR, now the presidential candidate. They face two choices: incumbent Lieutenant Governor Herbert H. Lehman, FDR's choice, the heavy favorite; and Elisha, Patsy's choice, the underdog who doesn't even want the job. It will take 464 votes to win, and on Sunday Lehman claimed 480 and Elisha 469, both sides lying, even to themselves. Neither can win without New York City's vote, which isn't quite what it used to be since the death of Tammany leader Charlie Murphy in 1924 splintered the boroughs. The Bronx has been in FDR's pocket since he appointed its leader, Ed Flynn, his secretary of state, a ploy to make the Tammany splinter permanent. Queens and Richmond will still follow Tammany's lead, Tammany's own 154 votes are solid for Elisha, and Brooklyn's 159 are on the fence. Now it is Tuesday, and despite three days of argument and horse-trading future patronage among big and little city bosses, neither candidate has a majority; but the odds on Elisha are dropping. Johnny Mack, dean of Albany bookmakers, is offering even money pick one; and the FDR-Lehman camp is baffled by the Albany upstart's strength.

The Ten Eyck lobby is a crossroads for hundreds of delegates, for Elisha loyalists, visitors looking for convention passes, Party faithful showing their faces, plus the press and anybody who wants to hear the latest – 'It's over. Brooklyn went for Lehman . . . Forget it. Fourteen more votes and Elisha's in.' A table-full of Democratic women volunteers greet all comers with the gift of large Elisha Fitzgibbon buttons, flyers with his sterling credentials, and on the wall above the women, Elisha looks out from a poster half the size of a movie screen. The volunteers usher all delegates and alternates immediately to the Conway corner to meet Roscoe, who will vet them on Elisha: yes, no, maybe. Roscoe tends to count maybes as yeses, and Elisha's total is climbing.

During a lull Roscoe goes up to second-floor headquarters to compare numbers with Elisha, who is hiding in an inner office, exhausted from three days of selling himself to strangers and to all the upstate county leaders he had once courted for Al Smith, many of those upstaters now promising unshakable support for him.

'I added sixteen probables in the last two hours,' Elisha says. 'I'm beginning to worry I might get elected. What does Patsy say about McCooey?' Patsy, since Saturday, has been meeting with Tammany, Brooklyn, and key upstate bosses to break the impasse.

'McCooey's with us, but his people are afraid they'll lose the Jewish vote if they dump Lehman.'

'Do they know my wife is half Jewish?'

'Lehman is all Jewish. Al is coming in for the next session at four-thirty. I'll be there with Patsy for that one.'

'What is Al thinking?'

'Nobody knows.'

Elisha puts his head on the desk. 'I'm tired,' he says.

'That's not allowed,' Roscoe says.

'All right, I quit.'

'That's not allowed either.'

'Then I have only one thing to say. We're seeing a lot of stammecule when what we need is the real bing with some EP on it.'

'Noted,' says Roscoe.

Jim Farley, FDR's state chairman, convenes the delegates in the 10th Infantry Armory at 12:30 P.M., but not all delegates bother to attend. And at mid-afternoon, when five from Brooklyn come to the Conway corner wanting to meet Elisha, Roscoe can't find him. Not at headquarters, not in the restaurant, phone off the hook in his room. Roscoe stalls the delegates, says he'll be right back, and takes the elevator up. He knocks and says, 'Elisha,' and Veronica opens the door a crack and says, 'He's not here.'

'Where is he? Talk to me, open the door.'

'I'm not dressed.'

'Good. Let me in.'

'Behave yourself.'

She opens the door with her hair and lipstick ready for public viewing, but wearing only slippers and a pink satin slip.

'Where's Elisha? Five new Brooklyn delegates are downstairs waiting to pledge allegiance to him. They're important.'

'He's probably at the Armory. The last I saw him was his luncheon speech to the Democratic women. Pamela came over and wrapped herself around him.'

'She wraps herself around half the population. Don't take it personally.'

'I came up here to take a nap and get dressed for Eleanor's tea party.' The Governor's wife has invited all women delegates to high tea at the Mansion at four-thirty. 'Pardon my *déshabillé,*' Veronica says.

'You look the way you used to in my time. You never took it all off.'

In the most intense summer days of their romance, Roscoe would undress her in the Trophy House at Tristano, down to the chemise, which became her uniform of partial abandon. He could raise the chemise but not remove it. He felt he could live with that arrangement until their wedding.

'You can't stay here,' she says to him. She takes a robe from her closet and slips it on.

He stares as she ties her robe. 'I could love you right now,' he says.

'I know you could. I always know that.'

He moves close, strokes her throat with the back of his fingers.

'You can't do this,' she says.

'I used to.'

'That was years.'

'I have to love you, Vee. The pressure is impossible.'

'Not yet.'

'When?'

'I don't know. Someday, maybe.'

'I used to do this,' he says. He unties her robe.

'No, Roscoe, you can't.' She reties the robe.

'You used to do what you wanted to do when you wanted to do it.'

'I gave that up.'

'Maybe you didn't entirely.'

'How did you decide to come here now?'

'I thought Elisha was here. But I must have been listening to the planets. Maybe I saw something in your look this morning, or maybe you invited me with your silent music.'

'You think I still want to be that way. Just knock, and there she is.'

He opens her robe, but she turns away and stands by the bed.

'You can't do anything to me, Roscoe. We don't do this anymore.'

'It isn't my fault that we don't.'

'We can't go over all that again.'

'I go over it every day of my life,' he says.

'We can't. I made a decision about you.'

'You mean against me.'

'I have to live by it.'

'I regret that with every breath we both take, every breath of yours that might have been mine,' he says. 'Haven't you ever regretted it?'

'How can I talk about that?'

'I don't know. All I can think about is that this is the first time in eighteen years I've been alone with you like this. I can't believe you're standing there looking the way you do.'

'Neither can I.'

He opens her robe, raises her slip. 'I remember this,' he says.

'We can't do this to him on his day, Roscoe.'

'Love me,' says Roscoe. His hand is on her in the old way.

'I love that you love me, Roscoe. But we can't do this even if I want to, and I do seem to want to. But I won't.' She pushes his hand away but it returns. 'And I won't let myself be tempted, no, Roscoe, no more.' She pushes his hand away. It returns. 'Please, no more, Roscoe. Thank you, no more.' She pulls down her slip.

He sees strands of hair have fallen across one eye from her shaking her head no. He puts them in place with one finger, kisses her on the mouth. 'I own some of you again.'

'No. You can't own any of me. Nobody can own Veronica.'

'My memory can own anything.'

She reties her robe and says, 'I shouldn't have done this. You're a love, Roscoe, but please go away.'

'Will I be a love after I'm gone?'

'Yes, but we won't do anything about it. Once in a lifetime, Roscoe.'

Going down to the lobby in the elevator, Roscoe decides no devil in the eighth circle can punish him as exquisitely as

Veronica. It might be years before they are again so close, and he hears her portal clanging shut. When he gets to the lobby the Brooklyn delegates are gone.

He goes to the Armory, which is decked with flags, bunting, banners, and some seventy-five hundred people, the place loud with marching-band music. He wants to find Elisha and the lost delegates, also get the latest delegate poll from Bart Merrigan and his team of canvassers. But Elisha isn't here and the Brooklyn chairs are half empty. Bart says the latest figures look about the same, good, but it's impossible to poll this crowd – more than a thousand delegates and alternates, a herd in chaos. They've listened to Albany's Mayor Thacher welcoming them to town, and to a few warm-up speakers puffing the FDR-Garner ticket and the Democratic platform, especially their favorite wringing-wet plank: Bring back our beer. They've waited hours for their leaders to come up with a candidate to vote for and, still waiting, they're now clanging cow bells, shaking castanets, waving signs and banners, blowing whistles. And then, in a spontaneous decision, they join in a raucous sing-along as the 10th Infantry Band plays 'Sidewalks of New York,' Al's tune; 'Happy Days Are Here Again,' for Democrats everywhere who anticipate getting rid of Hoover; and 'Anchors Aweigh' for FDR, who was assistant secretary of the navy under Wilson. As they sing, Roscoe sees their heads fly back and forth through the lofty reaches of the Armory, a mob of ready-to-wear delegates, one size fits all. If they only knew Elisha they'd vote for him, but, of course, they don't vote, they dance headlessly to the tune being written this afternoon down at the DeWitt.

The Albany delegates – Mayor Thacher, a few aldermen and county supervisors, Party lawyers, a cadre of Democratic women – are, on Patsy's strict orders, staying close to their chairs, ready to rise up and march in an instant demonstration for Elisha if it comes to a floor fight. Roscoe sees Alex sitting in an Albany aisle.

'Are you learning how we elect a governor?' Roscoe asks him.

'Yes, you sit around and sing,' Alex says. 'I thought maybe somebody might argue about something.'

'They're arguing, but it doesn't show.'

'I love it anyway, Roscoe. It's true American democracy made visible.'

'I wouldn't go that far,' Roscoe says.

'What happens tonight, when the convention ends?'

'We celebrate. The town is waiting to party.'

'I'm ready to be the son of the new Governor.' And Alex shows Roscoe his hip flask.

'Precocious,' Roscoe says. 'But pace yourself, young fellow. It's going to be a long night.'

The band segues into 'Will You Love Me in December as You Do in May?' for the New York City delegates, the tin-pan theme song of their ex-Mayor Jimmy Walker, who wrote it. Ah, Jimmy, who isn't here and won't be, but is a key figure in this convention's impasse. Trouble has come to Jimmy this year after two years of investigations, begun by FDR and carried through by Judge Samuel Seabury, into Tammany corruption. And certain New York judges, the sheriff, and assorted flacks have fallen victim to the right-thinkers. But Seabury's charges also have led to Jimmy's being summoned to Albany for a hearing, at which FDR will sit as solitary judge of the evidence of Jim's 'gross improprieties' – secret bank accounts, evasive answers, an inexplicable million in a safe-deposit box, the usual. FDR could actually remove the Mayor from office, which would be a first in state history, and a truly grievous wound to Tammany's power.

On the August night in 1932 that Jimmy steps off the train at Albany's Union Station for his face-off with FDR, sky-rockets explode above the tracks, and the roar of ten thousand greets him – 'Jimmy, Jimmy, Jimmy' – from people on the platforms, people wall to wall in the concourse, people filling Broadway, people Patsy wanted and Roscoe summoned through ward leaders and city department heads, the largest political turnout since Albany welcomed home Al Smith in defeat in '28.

Patsy, Elisha, and Roscoe are closer to Jimmy than they are to anybody else from New York, including Al. Jimmy spent sixteen years in Albany as an assemblyman, a senator, then Senate leader until 1925, when Tammany tapped him for mayor of New York. He has dined often at Tivoli, pulled many an all-nighter with Patsy and Roscoe, supported Patsy's legislation; in short, a grand fellow who became the lovable, re-electable Gentleman Jimmy, the dapper political playboy with the showgirl mistress and the persona behind which Tammany could methodically loot the city, an arrangement dating back to Tweed. The persona elects, the money perpetuates.

Patsy, since his youth, has been an ardent student of the Tammany method and has evolved into Tammany's staunchest upstate ally. Why wouldn't he give Jim a royal welcome? Patsy will never forgive FDR for generating all this trouble. In 1945, the year FDR dies, and after supporting him for president for four terms, Patsy will still be saying, 'I didn't like him. He didn't like Tammany Hall, and they were the only thing in the world for me.'

There is a front-page *Times-Union* news photograph of Jimmy, Patsy, and Roscoe as they walk through Union Station on that August evening in '32. Jimmy the dude is in a double-breasted gray plaid with the one-button roll, his best vest and kerchief, his sailor straw stylishly tilted onto his right ear. Patsy is also wearing his sailor, but pulled down as if he fears it will blow away, and he bulges like a puffball out of his collar and suit – it's those mashed potatoes, Pat. And Roscoe, a bit to the right, appears almost thin beside Patsy, his fedora turned up like a diplomat's homburg, and though modesty will never let him say so, his presence is one of companionate intelligence and dignity beside Jimmy's dash and Patsy's dumplingscape.

This is a war photo: three warriors marching into combat against what Roscoe calls the Morality Plague, Seabury only its latest manifestation. The Plague comes out of oblivion every seven or so years and, like the locust, builds its white houses in public cemeteries, and propagates, with evil simplicity, 'truth' and 'honesty' as political virtues. This has the popular appeal of chocolate, the distorting capacity of gin. But Roscoe wonders: Since when has truth been a political virtue? Can you name one truth that is everywhere welcome? Certainly there are none in play in any quest for, or defense of, political power – Jimmy's, for instance – for power is based in the deep comprehension and perverse love of deception, especially self-deception, and any man who seeks power through truth is either a fool or a loser. Roscoe knows of no candidate's ever making a campaign pledge to reveal all his own self-inflation, all those covetous, envious, lascivious, venal, and violent motives that drive every move he ever makes in politics and will continue making if elected. Roscoe certainly did not invent the perverse forces that drive human beings, and he can't explain any of them. He believes they are a mystery of nature. He concedes that a morally pure society, with candidates unblemished by sin and vice, might possibly exist somewhere, though he has never seen or heard of one, and can't really imagine what one would be like. 'But I'll keep looking,' he concludes.

Mayor Jimmy comes to the railing of Union Station's elevated platform overlooking Broadway, and he salutes and quiets the cheering mob, then evokes new cheers when he tells them, 'I am here to fight.' Castellano's marching band parts the crowd and leads him down the stairs and through the concourse toward the limousine waiting to take him to the Ten Eyck.

'Where is Patsy?' Jimmy asks Roscoe as they walk.

'He's waiting for us outside.'

Bystanders hear the question and raise the cry, 'Patsy, Patsy, Patsy,' and out of the crowd comes Pat, his smile as big as his hat, and the two old friends shake hands with excessive affection.

'Grand turnout, Pat,' Jimmy says.

'They all love you, Jim. Are you ready for that sonofabitch in the morning?'

'If he cuts me, we cut him in the election and he'll lose the state.'

When they reach Broadway, Jimmy turns and tells the crowd, 'I'm confident Governor Roosevelt will not remove me,' and, to another roar of cheers, he clasps his hands in the air like a triumphant boxer and slides into the back seat of the Packard limo.

FDR sits in judgment on Jimmy for three weeks, and his anti-Tammany stance enhances his presidential campaign, just as

Al Smith's link to Tammany had wounded his presidential bid. Tammany Hall, history's tar baby. But FDR also knows the liability of removing a wildly popular New York City mayor, and he moves slowly toward such a decision. Then Jim, drowning in Seabury's negative evidence, solves the dilemma by abdicating before FDR can fire him, and flees to Spain to hide. Suddenly he deabdicates and heads home when Tammany decides to run him for re-election, and to hell with FDR. But the turbine of his ocean liner breaks down at Gibraltar.

Now, while the 10th Infantry Band plays his theme song at the convention, Jim is en route home on another ship, but maybe too late. You shouldn't have left, Jim. His renomination as mayor, though not a sure thing, remains the top priority for Tammany and Brooklyn, for his restoration is the key to the whole damn kingdom. Lehman, if elected governor, will, of course, echo FDR's hostility to Jimmy's comeback; but Patsy assures and reassures Curry and McCooey that as governor Elisha will never act against Jim, and that state patronage under Eli will open out like the petals of a great golden flower, and the Tammany-Brooklyn twins, along with Albany, will inherit the earth.

The Showdown

It is five o'clock in Tammany's eleventh-floor suite at the DeWitt, and Al Smith is late. Roscoe, in memory, sees Curry and McCooey, with kindred, drooping white mustaches, sitting on the same sofa, the divine duality without which there is no candidate. Patsy is in his usual armchair. Roscoe chooses to stand across the room, the keeper of the master list of delegates, all names alphabetical within each county, all maybes converted to yeses or nays, and Roscoe reports a surprising tally: Elisha six votes shy of the nomination, even without McCooey's Brooklyn. This is bizarre! Curry says Tammany is still solid for Elisha, and the upstate total is slowly rising. This rise is partly the work of Bart Merrigan and his crew, who have been polling upstate delegates all day; also, where tactfully feasible, promising a persuasive envelope after the vote, if there's a floor fight.

Money has come into play as Elisha closes on the brass ring. Some delegates wear 'For Sale' signs on their chests, but most delegate purchasing requires subtle skills, and Bart excels at those, for he's a likable fellow who makes friends instantly, he's a veteran, as are many delegates, and he's honest. Everything is based in trust, and money isn't for everybody. Bart knows which delegations are open to suggestion, and he can read the honest men who'll vote right. Albany cannot be passive in this battle after FDR's threat of last night: 'The enemies of Lehman will not only be defeated, they will be dead,' he said to the press. He means politically dead, but fortunately John Curry doesn't give a rat's tootie. He hates FDR for all his persecuting ways, is solid with Patsy and Elisha, and is waiting to put Jimmy back in City Hall. John McCooey, too, wants Jimmy back, and remains enduringly friendly to Elisha, still holding off his Brooklyn boys from tipping toward Lehman. But now Frank Roosevelt wants not just to overpower but to kill the enemy, and McCooey, not a suicidal fellow, has chosen restraint as his strategy, and by so doing holds the final balance of power.

It's hard to remember when John McCooey, or Brooklyn either, was so central to the future of New York State, New York City, Albany, and Christ knows where else, all rising and falling on what John says at these meetings. He leaves the room to pee and futures are bought and sold, fortunes are made and lost, such leverage! But he's an old man and this is killing him, maybe before the night is out. Jesus, this is difficult. Why does Lehman have to be a Jew, and why does Roosevelt hate us? He'd hate us even if Lehman wasn't a Jew. There's no need for that. John Curry and John McCooey are likable men; they take care of the money because there it is, as it always was. Somebody's got to take care of it. Just because you're born with money and don't need to accumulate any, don't mean you close out the less fortunate. Christ Almighty, Frank, it's only a few million, nobody'll miss it, don't drive your bowels into a stupor. The true question is jobs and families, the flower of our meaning, the source of our blessedness, we who have been chosen to raise up our people. These people can't make it on their own, Frank, but they're our future, those tots of ours in carriages, little boys on the altar, darling girls playing hopscotch, God bless them all, the world is not Irish, Frank, and it was never Dutch, if you'll pardon the expression. We're trying to do right, elect progressive people who want to promote the general welfare of our great city and great state, we need people in office who matter, people like Elisha, who'll do what is good for them, and for us. That's all we ask.

Then Roscoe remembers how McCooey, coming back from a phone call, yet another pee, and still buttoning the fly, finally puts it: 'I can't keep all my people in line. They want Lehman.'

'We don't need all your people,' Patsy says, and his flinty eyes are sparking as he looks over his little specs at McCooey. 'Give us the six we can make it, John. Six.'

'Six might as well be sixty. Frank means what he says. If

he gets in, and you know he will, he'll cut us dead on patronage, state and federal both.'

'He's already cut you dead. But Elisha won't.'

'Or Jimmy,' says Curry.

But the *Times* and *Daily News* this morning quoted Al as saying he couldn't support Jimmy for re-election. McCooey reminds everybody of this.

'Al won't back Jimmy,' McCooey says.

They all have seen the papers. Patsy grinds his molars.

'Al says that, but he'll go along with us,' says Curry.

'Where the hell is he?' Patsy asks.

McCooey shakes his head and sighs, so weary of this, and Roscoe remembers the door opening on Al just then. He enters in his rumpled tuxedo, back from an afternoon wedding, gravy on his shirt and satin lapel, and he's had a few pops, wants to change and rest awhile before the convention reconvenes.

'Hello, Governor,' says Curry.

'Christ, haven't you solved this yet?' Al says.

'Did you really tell the papers you won't back Walker?' Curry asks.

'Jim's all done,' says Al. 'The people don't want him in there any more. Tell him not to get off the boat.'

'We're running him,' says Curry, 'and we'll elect him.'

'If you run him, I'll run for mayor against him.'

'On what ticket?'

'I could run on a Chinese laundry ticket and beat you,' Al says.

'We're very close on Elisha,' Patsy says.

'You're not close,' says Al, 'you're finished.'

'Lehman's people are asking if Elisha will take lieutenant governor,' McCooey says.

'No,' says Patsy.

'What's the difference whether he takes it or not?' says Al. 'They don't need him. This argument's done and over. Lehman's through the roof.'

'You're with Lehman?' Patsy says.

For six weeks Al has been promising Patsy and Roscoe he won't endorse Lehman unless Curry does; won't do FDR any favors. Al brought FDR out of physical retirement to become Governor in '28, and FDR nominated Al for President, but this June, at Chicago, FDR took the presidential nomination away from Al, and the happy warrior went into a deep and angry sulk. But tonight he is back in the spotlight.

'Lehman,' says Al, 'supported me all-out in '28. He gave me half a million, and I'm with him till the cat comes back. I'm nominating him tonight.'

'You hook-nosed sonofabitch,' Patsy says, 'you did it again.' He stands up and Roscoe sees that curled fist. 'You threw us in.'

'You green baloney,' says Al, 'you don't even belong in this room. You're still a truck driver in my book.'

'Are you giving us those six?' Patsy asks McCooey.

'I'm tired, Patsy. We held it as long as we could. It was a good fight.'

Patsy turns to Curry. 'What do you say to this, John?' he asks.

'Tell Elisha we're solid with him for lieutenant governor,' Curry says.

Pluperfect Memory

Roscoe and Alex separated at the bottom of the cemetery slope. Joey Manucci opened the back door of the limousine for Roscoe as he slid in beside Hattie-with-no-more-tears.

'What was that all about?' she asked.

'He's worried about me,' Roscoe said. 'He thinks I attract disasters.'

'You attracted me.'

'You're not a disaster, you're a sexual force of nature.'

'Roscoe,' Joey said, 'you're not making a pass at the widow, are you?'

'She made a pass at me,' Roscoe said.

'I'm telling the priest,' Joey said.

'Good,' said Hattie. 'Tell Mother Superior too.'

'I myself find this shocking,' Roscoe said. 'I'm not used to sex in the cemetery. Tell me about 1932, the night Elisha lost to Lehman.'

'You mean did I have sex that night? No. And you were no help.'

'Don't blame me for your dry spells. Do you remember Pamela that night?'

'She stayed at one of my places. Obnoxious woman. Attractive. She climbed all over Elisha whenever she saw him.'

Roscoe can now see Pamela sitting with the Albany delegation during that last session of the Democratic convention. The night is growing wild as the politicized mob, almost as many thousands on the street outside the Armory as inside, rushes the police line to see the historic confrontation of Al Smith and FDR. Will they spit in each other's eye? Will Lehman and Elisha come to blows? Pamela sits in the first Albany aisle, two down from Veronica and Elisha, in Patsy's empty chair. Pat the loser won't sit, won't put himself on display. Elisha is in his chair when Farley mentions his name as the next speaker, and fevered applause breaks out for the almost-Governor, what a fight you put up. They love you now, Eli; but ten minutes from now? Who can say how long love lasts?

Roscoe, standing by the stairs to the speakers' platform, watches Elisha rise, then lean over and kiss Veronica. Pamela rises also, and as Elisha passes her on his way to the microphone she does her boa-constrictor number, big huggypoo, big kissypoo. Once past Pammypoo, Elisha makes a speech that has more sincerity and solidarity than is necessary from a betrayed man. It is an honest speech from a profoundly loyal Democrat. He truly wants FDR to be the new President, and Lehman the next Governor; never wanted that for himself, was repaying the Patsy debt, and will go on repaying it for two years as lieutenant governor, the job Patsy now calls the door prize: no authority, not much patronage goes with it, and your only hope of advancement is for the Governor to drop dead. But Elisha cannot wish anyone ill, or be false to himself, which is why Roscoe, try as he might with memory's eye, cannot see in Elisha's behavior the lie that would make all that flirty intertwining with Pamela anything more than family effusion. Did he actually go off with her to her Jay Street lair this afternoon when they both disappeared? Did he take her to some dark speakeasy for a backroom flip? He could have focused on her in any number of rooms at the Ten Eyck, but Roscoe doesn't believe these possibilities. Roscoe sees Elisha's face in memory and cannot find a trace of the necessary concupiscence, or intrigue.

'Stop at the grocery,' Roscoe said to Joey. 'Get me four Hershey bars. I won't have time for lunch.'

And when he was gone Roscoe asked Hattie, 'Do you think Elisha ever got it on with Pamela?'

'God knows she was ready,' Hattie said. 'And he did have a bit of a stable back then, didn't he?'

'I don't know how serious he ever was about that.'

'He was amused by women.'

'Many are. He was also at a low point, with the mill and the loss of his daughter. And he was drinking too much. He was in New York often, and she did live there.'

'Why are you bringing this up now?'

'I'm trying to imagine him as Gilby's father.'

Hattie went silent at that, and in her silence Roscoe again sees the finale of the convention, the thrill, the bathos really, of the reconciliation on that stage when FDR shakes hands with Al and says, before a hundred newsmen and the whirring newsreel cameras, 'I'm glad to see you, Al, and that comes from the heart.' And Al retorts, 'How are you, old potato?' Hats fly into the air, and roars erupt from the headless, hatless mob at the restoration of affection between its not-quite and next presidents. Even Roscoe feels, against his will, this ready-to-wear emotion in his throat as enmity is publicly buried and harmony rises from the grave. But Al really will not stay harmonious for very long after this night, for it will quickly become clear that he will never be a New Deal insider, that his days of power and influence are over. And he will then become FDR's vigorous enemy. Nor are Roscoe and Patsy destined to be New Deal wheelers. Their dream – the Patsy dream that Roscoe borrowed – of proximate power at a more exalted level, also died with Elisha's defeat. We came so close. But that's that and quit brooding, says Roscoe. Think of tonight as the festive prelude to FDR's presidential victory, which is only a month away: a Democrat in the White House at long last, a Democrat up at the Capitol.

Roscoe, Patsy, and their Albany legion will officially bury all rivalries, will deliver heavy pluralities for every Democrat on the ticket. They will awake on the election's morning-after and Roscoe will call Patsy to say for the first, but not last, time, 'Pat, we are Democrats, remember? And we are steeped in Democracy. We own the city, the county, the state, and the nation. Things could be worse.'

They also own the splendor of the night that follows the convention's end, the midnight streets as bright and crowded as Times Square at the theater hour, lines forming in front of the restaurants, dance bands carrying on with their hot and sweet duty at the hotels, speakeasies guarded by plainclothes Albany cops against untimely raids by dry agents who should mind their own business on a night like this. Lights will burn all night long in The Gut, a time to get well, girls, and, in the Ten Eyck's ballroom, Elisha's private party is throbbing for half the town. Roscoe in memory sees his allies and kindred strangers shoulder to shoulder in the social afterglow of all that political stardust. He sees Hattie being wooed by a state senator whose name has long been erased from Roscoe's memory. Bart Merrigan is ready to deck whoever pinched his wife on the elevator, but Bart can't decide which of three men did it. The Democratic women are in great demand by the randy Manhattan delegates, and when Roscoe brushes against Veronica he says, 'I remember you,' and she answers, 'And I you.' Waxey's beer is on tap, and Roscoe sees Mush monitoring the movement of two more kegs of it; but the Waxey–Mush axis will soon be redundant, the real goods coming back, and Roscoe's Stanwix will again become the label of choice at political gatherings, also at all saloons hoping to prosper in the city. Mike Pantone's six-piece jazz band is playing 'Walking My Baby Back Home,' and in a corner to the right of the band, partly hidden by a potted palm, Roscoe sees Alex offering his silver hip flask to his Aunt Pamela, precocious youthful reveler joining the party. They learn quickly.

Thirteen years later, alone with Hattie in the back seat of his car, Roscoe will ask her, 'Where did Alex stay that night? Did he have a room at the hotel, or did you get him one?'

'Wouldn't he have stayed out at Tivoli?'

'I doubt it. He was into the action. Do you remember seeing him at any point that night?'

'I remember him looking very young and very cute, and talking to women.'

'Which women?'

'Older women. That's who were there. There weren't many his age.'

'Which older women?'

'Damn it, Roscoe, how can I remember? Maddie Corrigan or Dodie Vance, maybe. I remember thinking they found a way to send their husbands home. And Pamela.'

'Alex with Pamela.'

'He was dancing with her, and I thought it was his social shyness, hanging out with the family, not quite ready to step out with a stranger. Does this surprise you?'

'Nothing surprises me, old Hat.'

And Roscoe mused on whether a one-night stand on Jay Street might have moved to Pamela's place in New York. Alex often went down to the city from New Haven on weekends. It would explain his anxiety over Gilby's custody case, and his fierce hostility to Pamela. And while Pamela's line, 'It's a wise child that knows its father,' means nothing to Elisha, who's beyond scandal, it could weigh as a genuine threat to Alex, who isn't. A theory. And Roscoe can tell no one.

Roscoe's Prayer to Elisha

Old father, who art in heaven,
Hallowed be thy name.
Thy bingdom come,
Thy will be done down here on earth.
Forgive us our trespasses, old boy,
And don't worry about a thing.

Beau Geste (1)

Judge Francis Finn in shirtsleeves, his robe on a hanger on the corner coatrack, sat at his desk in his chambers, a wall of law books behind him, and watched the two benefactors who put him in this chair, Roscoe and Marcus Gorman, as they settled into leather armchairs facing him.

'Are we going to find a way to resolve this suit amicably?' he asked them both.

'Amicably between mother and son,' Marcus said.

In Marcus's smile Roscoe saw the confidence of a man with encyclopedic precedents for the indisputable custody rights of mothers. We'll be here all morning.

'I'll want to talk with the young boy,' the judge said. 'Is he in the courtroom?'

'He is, Your Honor, with his mother,' Roscoe said.

'You refer to his adoptive mother,' said Marcus.

'His mother in fact if not biological fact,' said Roscoe.

'The petitioner is here, Mr. Gorman?'

'She is. We are ready.'

'I have information worth airing before anything goes on the record,' Roscoe said.

'I'll be pleased to hear it,' Marcus said.

'I'm not sure you'll be pleased,' said Roscoe. 'It's about money. Pamela Yusupov is seeking custody of her son as a means of gaining money from the estate of the father, Mr. Danilo Yusupov.'

'She wants her son. The money will support them,' said Marcus.

'So she now says. But I am prepared to prove that Pamela, seeking money, not custody, approached Elisha Fitzgibbon months before his death. Veronica will testify to the amount she asked and how much they might have given to help her out. Pamela not only insisted on more, she wanted a continuing income. When Elisha rejected the idea she threatened to accuse him of fathering Gilby during a forcible encounter.'

'Oh, for chrissake,' Marcus said, 'this is desperation strategy. This is melodrama.'

'In assorted ways, counselor,' Roscoe said. 'I presume you've both heard the slanderous rumor that Elisha died by his own hand. His autopsy fully proves otherwise, that he was terminally ill and died of a coronary occlusion. I could affirm this with abundant fact and fanatical vigor if necessary, or I could, for the sake of our argument, hypothesize that, if he did take his life, he did so to protect his wife and his son. Elisha had readily agreed to adopt Gilby at birth and raise him as his own, for he *was* his own. He did not tell this to Veronica when he agreed to the adoption. She was still grieving to distraction over the loss of their five-year-old daughter and eager for another child. And he was not ready to admit that, in a bout of heavy drinking and debauched wildness, he had raped her sister. I can personally verify that Pamela is a supreme seductress, even when she isn't trying, and that uncountable men have acted upon this obvious truth,

Elisha being one of them. I don't blame Pamela for their carnal encounter, nor did Elisha. He took the blame and lived with the shame, and in time did what he felt was necessary – he adopted his own sin and lived with it lovingly, giving the boy the fullest and richest life a father can give a son. He thought he'd lived the sin down, but then here it came back to plague him. Pamela, poor soul, fallen on hard times, sought financial relief through Elisha, and the man became unhinged. He was dying and he knew it, but when he tallied up the credits and debits he saw a way out. Pamela was determined to destroy his reputation to gain a bloodsucking income, but Elisha could not let that happen, nor could he chance the possibility that, in vengeance, she'd destroy not only him but his son Alex, and his beloved wife. And so he revealed to Veronica his shame and her sister's threat. Pamela had no qualms about destroying her sister's family. She had envied Veronica all their years growing up – Veronica the greater beauty and the fortunate wife; Pamela, the inferior little strawberry tart, always viewing herself as the sister in the cinders.'

'Jesus, Roscoe,' said Marcus. 'Sister in the cinders?'

'I know you enjoy language, counselor,' Roscoe said. 'And so Elisha, as a way of putting himself and the family beyond Pamela's reach, designed his own death. You can't blackmail a corpse. He knew that, for those aware of the blackmail, his death would be judged as the act of a shamed man who could not face public disclosure. But he also knew Veronica would understand why he was really doing this, and she did. He even told his secretary, just before his suicide, that the enemy was closing in and that Roscoe would understand who that was. And I certainly do. But Elisha misread his enemy's perseverance. In the courtroom outside the door of these chambers on the first day of this hearing, Pamela whispered to Veronica, "It's a wise child that knows its father." We all knew what she meant. Her blackmailing would continue. I wonder, counselor, did your client mention any of this to you?'

'Roscoe,' said Marcus, 'you are a maestro. Your inventions are as entertaining as your rhetoric. But I fail to see your point. The father of the boy is Danilo Yusupov, and this is not disputed, not even by my client.'

'Perhaps she'll change her mind,' Roscoe said, and he opened his briefcase, took out copies of Yusupov's and Gilby's blood tests, and gave them to the judge and Marcus.

'Mr. Yusupov's blood group, which is O, doesn't match Gilby's, which is AB,' Roscoe said. 'As you well know, Your Honor, such disparity is a legally sound basis of nonpaternity.'

'That's correct,' said the judge.

'This is a fraud,' said Marcus. 'You politicians can fabricate any document and you often do.'

Roscoe opened his briefcase and handed his listeners more papers. 'A letter from Yusupov's lawyer,' he said, 'with verification of his blood test. Call the man in Los Angeles if you like. He resents Pamela's lawsuit as much as we do. And finally,' he added, finding more papers, 'Elisha's and Pamela's blood tests.'

'How did you get my client's blood test?' Marcus asked.

'I married her,' Roscoe said. 'We took blood tests together and I kept them. Call me sentimental. The blood groups of Elisha and Gilby are both type AB, and are compatible with Pamela's blood group, which is A. This is not positive evidence that Elisha was the father, but it means he could have been.'

'We need time to investigate this, Your Honor,' Marcus said. 'The paternity of Yusupov has never been in question before today.'

'Very true,' Roscoe said. 'Yusupov rejected the child and behaved as if he never existed, and we now know he had good reason. And that's how it remained until Pamela became a blackmailer. Her story of rape, however true, will be just another lie when her blackmail and perjury go public, and you should convey to your client, Marcus, that we stand ready to prosecute her for both blackmail and for perjury in representing Mr. Yusupov as Gilby's father when she knew he was not. Let's face it, counselor, your client is a scheming and perpetually lubricious woman, and I will celebrate that fact with exuberant fanfare if we go forward. I also admit the possibility that she was truly confused and believed she had diddled Yusupov when it was actually Elisha, or Elisha when it was actually Yusupov. Or maybe it was John Gilbert, for whom Gilby was named. Perhaps she could track down Mr. Gilbert's blood type and seek relief from *his* estate. I don't want to seem too severe with Pamela for losing track of her multitudes, and for the sake of Elisha, we will not bring any charges at all if she desists from this charade.'

Roscoe closed his briefcase.

'I trust, gentlemen, that these hypothetical facts will be kept confidential. Elisha's death, which is not provable in this context unless we decide to prove it, stands as a heroic act of redemption – a *beau geste*, if you will – a noble gesture, a self-martyrdom by a saintly man, and his good name must not be despoiled. I have no intention whatever of prolonging this hearing any further, and if opposing counsel has no objection, Judge Finn, I move that you quash the custody petition, considering perhaps J. Hogan, "In the Matter of

Gustow," that, "while the parent ordinarily is entitled to the custody of a child, the welfare of the child may be superior to the claim of the parent." I hope we can now have a speedy conclusion.'

The judge looked to Marcus, who said, 'I'll speak to my client.'

In the Courtroom

Veronica's and Gilby's smiles radiated sunbeams as they heard the judge say, '. . . the home life of the child for his entire life has been so fortunate that it certainly should not be changed in favor of a technical mother's care, and all parties now agree the boy should stay where he is, with the relator having the right to visit at reasonable times. The habeas corpus writ is quashed and dismissed.'

Roscoe recognized fury in Marcus's look, deceived by his client, a perjurer who didn't even tell her lawyer the truth. Losing your touch, Marcus? Can't tell the real ones from the fakers any more? Roscoe felt warm palpitations in his pericardium imagining Pamela baffled by Marcus's attack on her. Rape? Elisha? What has rape got to do with anything? I never said Elisha raped me. But Marcus can't quite believe her. Even if there was no rape, there was action, and Gilby is over there to prove it. But Daddy Yusupov was no daddy, and that's a fact. He was just an ex-Georgian prince, professional Russian exile, who had three million once, so they said. Pamela tried to tap into what was left of it and, another fact, she failed. Fashionable in black chalk-striped jacket and burgundy dress, her cubist bee-stung lips so out of fashion they are back, Pamela sat beside Marcus in stunned condition, hit by a brick she wouldn't be quieter, eyes glazing as she wonders how the world could have changed so suddenly. She was yesterday's darling and the world was still possible, with money on the table. But this is today, sweetheart.

Roscoe insisted that Gilby speak to his mother before they left the courtroom. He was wearing his blue suit and a new red-and-blue necktie Veronica had bought him for this event. The necktie aged him five years, Roscoe decided.

'I don't want to talk to her,' Gilby told Roscoe.

'Just say goodbye, that's enough.'

'The judge said she could visit me.'

'She probably won't.'

Gilby went across the courtroom to where Pamela was hiding under her picture hat. 'I came to say goodbye,' he said to her.

'I'm so very sad to be losing you,' Pamela said.

'I'm not. Goodbye.'

Roscoe saw the sag of Pamela's shoulders, her collapsed expression. She seemed to be shrinking as he watched. He stayed at a distance from her but walked to Marcus to offer a collegial handshake.

'I'm glad we didn't get into hand-to-hand combat,' Roscoe said.

'I underestimated you, Roscoe. You are utterly without scruples. I congratulate you.'

Roscoe spoke a few sentences of gratification to several news reporters in the hallway and then walked down the corridor with Veronica and Gilby on either side of him, the three arm in arm, so cooing, so happy they couldn't, didn't have to, wouldn't talk about this thing, it was such a fat, happy, obvious fact of life. They giggled as they waited for the elevator, and when it came they all stepped on together, single file, arms still locked, and Roscoe said to the elevator man, 'I greet you in a state of bliss, Webster.'

'Win one, did you, Mr. Conway?' Webster asked.

'I think I did.'

'You're not sure?'

'I'm being modest.'

'He won,' said Veronica. 'He *so* won. We all won.'

Webster closed the accordion gate of the elevator but saw another passenger coming and reopened it. Pamela. Roscoe saw Marcus walking alone in the opposite direction, toward the far stairway. Pamela stepped toward the elevator, unaware of the enemy within. She stopped as Webster opened the accordion.

'Going down,' Webster said.

'You goddamn lying bastard,' Pamela said, seeing Roscoe.

Roscoe stepped off the elevator into her words, moved into her face to block her eye contact with Veronica or Gilby. 'What was that, my dear? Were you speaking to me?' And without turning he added, 'Webster, take my friends down. I'll only be a minute.' And Webster shut the elevator door.

'Rape?' Pamela said. 'Rape?'

'Why not rape?' Roscoe said. 'It's as popular as blackmail.'

'Liar, liar, liar!' Pamela shrieked.

'Ah me, the perjurer offended by a falsehood,' Roscoe said.

There was no rape by Elisha. Roscoe invented that. But truth is in the details, even when you invent the details. It was sweet the way true and fraudulent facts wrapped themselves around each other so sleekly. The next sentence is a lie. The preceding sentence is true. Which means the first sentence is a lie, and the second sentence is true, which means the first sentence is true and the second is a lie, which means the first was a lie again, or does it? A pair of impregnable truths. True-and-false equality, we call that.

'It wasn't rape,' said Roscoe, 'and it wasn't even Elisha, was it?'

'You think you've won,' Pamela said.

'Elisha won. He prepared us for you. Nobody will believe anything you say from now on, my dear.'

'There are many ways of letting the truth be known.'

'Yes, and if anything is said anywhere, *anywhere,* we will prosecute you, in this city. Give scandal, you'll get jail time, and that's a guaranteed fact of your future. Don't bring your venal jealousy back to this town, Pamela. Leave the family alone.'

The elevator arrived and Webster opened the doors. Roscoe gestured to Pamela and they stepped into it.

'Do you have any money?' he asked.

'Millions,' she said.

He took a roll of cash from his pocket and peeled off two one-hundred-dollar bills. He offered them to her. She stared at them.

'Take a train somewhere. Shuffle off to Buffalo.'

'You're a lousy bastard,' she said, taking the money.

'Thank you, Webster,' Roscoe said when they reached street level. He gestured to Pamela to step out first and held the street door for her. 'What's your phone number in New York?' he asked her. 'We should stay in touch.'

Pamela thought that was a riot.

Beau Geste (2)

Veronica sat in the back of the car and told Gilby to sit in front as Roscoe drove from the courthouse back to Tivoli.

She had not yet thanked Roscoe for the victory. Gilby had thanked him with his facial expression of joy, but that had now turned quizzical as the mystery hit him.

'Why did we win?' Gilby asked.

'I convinced the judge your father made a life for you that was better than any other you could have,' Roscoe said.

'What about her? Will she try again?'

'No chance. She's gone.'

'What about the Yusupov man?'

'He's gone too.'

'Gone where?'

'Out of your life.'

'Yusupov isn't my father?'

'Never was.'

'Why did they say my name was Yusupov?'

'She said it was. She was married to him.'

'Is my name still Yusupov?'

'Never was. Rivera is the name on your birth certificate, but that's wrong too and we'll change it.'

'Who's Rivera? Was he my father?'

'A woman named Rivera was Pamela's housekeeper in Puerto Rico when you were born.'

'She named me after a housekeeper? Why?'

'Same reason she threw hard-boiled eggs at her poodle.'

'What's my real name?'

'Gilbert David Fitzgibbon, same as always.'

'Who's my father?'

'Your father is still your father. Still the main man in this family.'

'Is Alex my cousin?'

'He's your brother.'

'My father is his father?'

'That's how it used to be, that's how it should be, that's how it will be.'

'My father wasn't married to Pamela when I was born.'

'No, thank God.'

'That means I'm a bastard, doesn't it?'

'Who said that?'

'People.'

'Your father would die if he heard you say that.'

'He already died.'

'Maybe, but don't let him hear you say it again. Even if he's up at Tristano he can hear that kind of stuff.'

'Are we going to Tristano?'

'I certainly hope so.'

'When?'

'Talk to your mother about it.'

'If we see my father up there we can ask him who my real father is.'

'I doubt he knows,' Roscoe said. 'I doubt anybody knows.'

'People say I look like my father.'

'So does your bulldog.'

'I don't have a bulldog.'

'No, but if you had one he'd look like your father. That's how it goes.'

'How did my father die?'

'His heart left him. I think he gave it away.'

'To who?'

'To you.'

'I don't understand, Roscoe.'

'That's because you look like a bulldog.'

Beau Geste (3)

At Tivoli, Roscoe called Alex and gave him the news. Alex said that was fantastic and asked Roscoe to come to City Hall to talk.

'Your mother is preparing lunch,' Roscoe said. 'I'll be there in an hour.'

Gilby went elsewhere, and Roscoe sat in his usual chair in the east parlor and watched two of Veronica's servants, Joseph the butler and Jennifer, a kitchen maid, set trays of food on the buffet in the dining room. Then Joseph came toward Roscoe with two glasses and a bottle of Mumms in a bucket of ice. Veronica came back with a box of Barracini chocolate creams, which she opened and set in front of Roscoe.

'Shall I open the champagne, Mrs. Fitzgibbon?'

'Please do, Joseph.' And the butler popped the cork and poured for two. Veronica closed the sliding doors to the dining room and sat across from Roscoe on the sofa.

'I got these chocolates for you in New York last week,' she said, putting a cream in his mouth and kissing him as he began to chew. She picked up her champagne.

'To your genius,' she said.

'I had great incentive,' he said.

They clinked and drank. She kicked off her shoes and tucked her legs under her, which put her knees on view like twin works of art. 'Now tell me how you did it,' she said.

'I told them she was blackmailing you because Elisha raped her and fathered the boy, and that it was all true.'

'Roscoe, you didn't say that. That's horrible. You didn't.'

'I did. I said he committed suicide to remove himself as

the target of her blackmail, and that you understood why he did it.'

'God, Roscoe, what have you done? How could you say such awful things about us?'

'I also said it was all hypothetical and nobody would believe her rape story anyway, when and if her perjury and blackmail went public. I told Marcus we'd prosecute for blackmail if she didn't end the custody fight.'

'Everybody will believe the rape story. It'll be all over town.'

'I'm sure Marcus realizes by now I invented it.'

'But how could you say such a thing about Elisha?'

'He asked me to.'

'How did he ask you?'

'Little by little he's been revealing what he did to protect you and Gilby. All our lives I could read what he was and wasn't saying. Now I keep discovering what he did and didn't do. Didn't this story work? Isn't she gone? Aren't you and Gilby safe? And Alex?'

'I think we are. The family's closer than ever. Alex is like a second father to Gilby since he came home from service. They go riding. He's taking him to Army's opening football game at West Point.'

'There you are. Elisha knew what he was doing.'

'You knew what *you* were doing. *You're* the one who made it work.'

'I only did what he told me to do.'

'But rape, Roscoe, why rape? It's the last thing Elisha would ever do. She never said he raped her.'

'I know that. Did she even say they'd been lovers?'

'That was her blackmail.'

'Was it?'

'What are you saying?'

'I'm not sure. I'm waiting for further word from Elisha.'

Beau Geste (4)

In the Mayor's corner office at City Hall, seated in his high-backed leather armchair at his hand-carved oak desk, framed by the American and Albany flags, with the portrait of Pieter Schuyler, Albany's first Mayor, looking down at him, Alex, in his tailor-made, pale-gray herringbone and repp tie, had become new, had traded his lowly infantryman's status for that of commander of the city. He was on the telephone as Roscoe sat down across from him. He winked at Roscoe as he talked, and when he hung up he leaned across the desk to shake Roscoe's hand.

'Congratulations, old fellow,' he said. 'You did good.'

'I told you not to worry.'

'You certainly did. What was your argument?'

Art Foley, Alex's secretary, came into the office with the afternoon mail and set it in front of the Mayor.

'This isn't the place to talk,' Roscoe said when Foley went out.

'All right,' said Alex. 'We'll go for a walk. But I have news. The Supreme Court just ruled that state troopers can't be present at the polling places. Too much intimidation of the voters.'

'Another battle won,' said Roscoe. 'What's next in the campaign?'

'A radio speech tomorrow night,' said Alex, 'right after Jay Farley. He's harping on whores and immorality.'

'That's last week's news.'

'His new line is, let's clean up the city for the returning

soldier boys, give them a pure town to come home to.'

'It really is an excellent idea,' Roscoe said.

'What?'

'Cleaning up the town. Give the whores a vacation till after election, and padlock the whorehouses.'

'Didn't the whorehouses close after the raid?'

'Does a whore ever really close her legs?'

'What about the Governor padlocking the Notchery? It looks like we're taking dictation from him and Jay Farley.'

'Politically motivated is our line on the Notchery and on Farley's view of it. We can't let the Republicans take the moral high ground. We must protect our soldier boys and young people against goatish lust and illicit smut. We raid the after-hours strip clubs, Mother's, the Blue Jay Bar, we nail Broadway Books for pushing pornographers like Henry Miller, Baudelaire, Rimbaud, and those dirty Cuban comic books, then we sweep the newsstands and confiscate every girlie magazine that shows more titty than is absolutely necessary in a virtuous society.'

'That's a freedom-of-speech issue. How do we get away with it?'

'We don't indict anybody, and after the election things go back to normal. Meantime, it takes people's minds off Jay Farley.'

'I saw Patsy this morning and he didn't mention you had this in mind,' Alex said.

'He hasn't heard it yet. I just invented the idea.'

'Well, then, fine, fine,' Alex said with a smile, 'very fine. How will Bindy take it?'

'Bindy can't object. He's got a consorting charge hanging over him. We'll organize it all with Burkey and Donnelly.' Melvin Burke had been named acting police chief after O.B.'s death, and District Attorney Phil Donnelly would prosecute.

'We'll make the raids tomorrow afternoon, in time for you to talk about it on the radio.'

'Sex on the radio?'

'It's an idea whose time has come. We'll call it something else.'

'Shouldn't we let Patsy know the plan?'

'He'll be thrilled. We'll tell him after we take our walk.'

They left City Hall and walked along Eagle Street, past the Court of Appeals and the County Courthouse and up Elk Street with its old townhouses, once the city's elite Quality Row, sometimes compared in elegance to Gramercy Park. The Governor's Mansion had been at number 13 Elk in the last century. Now the whole street was aging with scant grace, two nightclubs on the block and one handsome building defaced with a kitschy black-and-white Art Deco façade. What would Henry James say?

On the street Alex revealed Patsy's news. The state Party leaders were thinking Alex might make a good run for governor in 1946: a decorated combat veteran with a Yale degree, an upstater who could speak well and think on his feet, a good-looking young fellow with a million-dollar smile. What else do you want in a governor? Well, will he get any votes? Oh, he will. And now Patsy has another reason to escalate this year's totals: shove *these* numbers up your nose, Governor, and look how they love our boy Alex.

'I know Patsy would like a landslide,' Roscoe said. 'I have it on our agenda. How do you feel about a run for governor?'

'I think I like it. Shouldn't I?'

'Don't get used to it. They don't nominate upstaters. But we can try again to be the exception. You remember 1932?'

'I've been thinking about it all morning.'

'Six more delegates, your father might've been governor.'

'Maybe history will repeat.'

'And maybe they'd offer you lieutenant governor.'

'I wouldn't take it.'

'Don't say that. You can't know where it might lead. Your father took it out of duty. He never even wanted to be governor. If he'd really fought for it in his heart, he might've got it. And he'd have been a memorable governor. He did as well with the number-two job as anybody ever does.'

Roscoe was feeling something new in his throat, a rising gorge that might choke him, resistance to doing this thing again. He couldn't put Alex through it, couldn't watch it; the incumbent would be very tough to unseat next year. Food for powder, Alex, food for powder. They walked across the park behind the old Albany Academy toward the Capitol, and Roscoe felt the long line of governors hovering over their lives: Cleveland at the top of the Capitol steps watching the torchlight parade (Lyman his grand marshal) coming up State Street, lighting his road to the White House in triumph over a paternity scandal: 'Ma, Ma, where's Pa?'; and Teddy Roosevelt racing a newspaperman up the Capitol's seventy-seven front steps, ready to give an exclusive interview if he loses, which he won't, for the press is the enemy; and our old pal Al Smith in wing collar and cutaway, standing for his 1928 portrait of a presidential loser; and FDR entering the Executive Chamber, held at the armpit by an aide, rotating his dead legs in braces in a simulated walk to the desk where he will sit in judgment on Jimmy Walker, the trial that will destroy Tammany; our delightful incumbent Governor trying now to do the same to the Albany Democrats; and, of course, Governor Elisha Fitzgibbon delivering his State of the State message to a joint session of the legislature: 'My fellow New Yorkers – I wonder do you kitty? Do you cut pips?'

These images were neither nostalgic nor cautionary, but Roscoe thought they might be trying to reveal that everything familiar was illusory and to be avoided, and that only the mysteries in Eli's double-talk and ambiguous death were worth pursuing: Eli feeding Roscoe ammunition for the battle against oblivion. This is not the end, Eli was saying. An imaginative man will find a way around the impossible. After all, Roscoe, you are now the courtroom hero, the inventor of yesterday and tomorrow, the Prophet of Fraudulence, and what obstruction could possibly stand in your way?

They stood in the shadow of the Capitol, the fortress of the enemy. Roscoe could not foresee when the Party would again have an ally in the Executive Chamber. It depressed him to think of waging futile battles to win it back. When should an old soldier call it a day? Shouldn't you quit a winner, Ros? And so he told Alex about Gilby's court case.

'You actually used the word "rape"?'

'Better than "incest,"' Roscoe said. 'This way it's an instant of sexual wildness, not a family vice.'

Alex tightened his face, his eyes narrowed, his lips flattened. His resemblance to Gilby was as obvious as his anger.

'You had no right to talk of rape,' Alex said. 'You should've checked with me. Goddamn it, Roscoe, this disgraces my father, makes him an animal. And it humiliates me. God knows what it might do to Gilby.'

'It was a distraction for Pamela's lawyer. The blood test destroyed their case, and our threat of prosecution guarantees she won't come back.'

'It was lousy. It stinks.'

'Try to remember why your father killed himself.'

'I've never understood it.'

'He did it for the family.'

'You say that, but I never bought it.'

'He did it for the Party, for you.'

'For me?'

'The scandal could've erupted in the middle of your campaign. But he eliminated that possibility by eliminating himself.'

'You're reading too much into it.'

'I think not. He not only got rid of her blackmail, he proclaimed himself Gilby's father. He knew his blood was the same as Gilby's – type AB. We found his blood test with papers he left on his desk before he killed himself. Why leave a blood test there that night? His last chance to let us know about the paternity, to admit it to anybody who could read. He knew what the church and the public would say about it and he didn't want anyone else blamed.'

Alex said nothing. He had probably not known his father's blood type. Why would he? Roscoe hadn't known it either. Elisha hadn't left any blood test with his papers. Roscoe created the test for the court hearing, also created AB as Elisha's type because of its compatibility with Gilby. And Alex.

At the mention of the blood type, anger instantly left Alex's eyes, replaced with a new vigilance. He stared at Roscoe with uneasy respect, with awareness, perhaps, that this new fact had a future, and that Roscoe had found a way to say to him what had never been said, never could be said.

'Bringing in rape just sealed the bargain,' Roscoe said, 'and turned it into classic melodrama. One shot and the poor soul fattens. Wouldn't you prefer a drunken family member forcing himself on a female rather than an incestuous intrigue that carries on for months, as Pamela said it had?'

'Pamela said that?'

'She did.'

'The woman is evil.'

'It's pitiful she has such a need for it.'

'She doesn't deserve any of your compassion,' Alex said.

'She's not getting much. We defeated her with Elisha's help. She's no longer a factor, but the war goes on.'

'What war?'

'The war between love and death.'

'Whose love and death?'

'Good question,' Roscoe said.

Roscoe and the Sounds

Roscoe sat up when the balloon burst, but of course there was no balloon. He had been visiting the Museum of Forgotten Sounds and on the wall he found a sign: 'Call me and I will come to free you.' He did not know who might be the 'I' of the statement. He went on to listen to the triangle the junkman jangled, the pumper's bells when the horses came out the firehouse door, the sound of Owen Ward's ice pick when Owen stuck it into a cake of ice, the Jewish peddler's voice chanting pineapples for sale, 'Pineys, pineys, the things with the shtickies on them.' Roscoe heard the women in black dresses and black head-kerchiefs speaking a foreign tongue as they cut dandelions from the field and dropped them into a cloth sack. He heard the bolt action of an '03, the bell of the horse car entering the Lumber District, St. Joseph's church bell on the morning of his father's funeral, the bell on Judge Brady's cow, the scissors sharpener's emery wheel grinding the butcher knife. The sounds seemed to imply trauma. A voice from the gramophone asked, 'In what year did compassion win the election?' As he left the museum, the female usher told him, 'Call me and I will come to free you.'

The Genie in the Vase

Cal Kendrick, second-generation caretaker at Tristano, piled up three tiers of logs to start a major fire burning in the great fireplace of the Trophy House after he heard from Veronica that visitors would be coming for a short stay. The house was Tristano's original building, built in 1873 by Lyman Fitzgibbon.

Cal's father, Zachary, an Adirondack guide, had been hired by Lyman as Tristano's first resident outdoorsman. The main lodge and the Swiss Cottage, where the family stayed, had both been closed since late September, and Cal and his wife, Belle, were shuttering all secondary buildings when Veronica called and said to keep the Trophy House open. So Cal started the fire at dawn to banish the deep chill and bake heat into the fieldstone walls, which would hold the heat long after the fire faded. Belle dressed all six beds in the three bedrooms with extra blankets, flannel sheets, and hot-water jars for cold feet. More than thirty years ago Roscoe and Veronica discovered, in all of those beds, varying intensities of what they considered love, as well as the thrilling dimensions of most of each other's bodies – discovery that went just so far and no farther. Roscoe did not expect any of the beds to be put to comparable use tonight, yet it was Veronica's decision to stay here, and not in the lodge, so there was no reason to abandon all hope, ye who enter.

'I want to see the mink family and I want to see the ghosts,' Gilby said.

They were in Veronica's 1942 Buick station wagon, Roscoe driving, the back of the wagon piled with suitcases, an ice chest with sandwiches and Tru-Ade for Gilby, plus four bottles of Margaux from the Tivoli wine cellar. When they stopped at Chestertown for coffee, Roscoe said he'd have to call Alex in the morning to find out how the press received his ungodly sex speech; but Veronica said, No, don't call. No? No. And Roscoe: All right, why? And she: Don't change the subject, we're supposed to have a good time without politics, this is a family visit, this is Tristano time, isn't it? It certainly is, said Roscoe.

And Gilby asked, 'Will we see the ghosts tonight?'

'My definitive and absolutely final answer to your question,' Roscoe said, 'is maybe.'

'You said we would.'

'I said it and I stand by it. But you don't think I know exactly when ghosts come and go, do you, Gil? There's nothing to stop them from ramming around the house at sunset, or dawn, or high noon, or not at all. Nobody knows the timetables of ghosts.'

'Ghosts aren't real, anyway. You're just playing a game. Ghosts are dead. People don't come back as ghosts when they die.'

'Well, it's true ghosts are dead, but you're one hundred percent wrong, Gilbino, and you're also one hundred percent right. I'd say you're probably more right than wrong and probably we won't see any ghosts because, as you say, there aren't any ghosts. But if there are ghosts, and we see them, then you'll be a hundred percent more wrong than right. And if we sit in the Trophy House and ghosts come out of wherever ghosts come out of and sit and talk to each other, then you'll be wrong in spades, and I'll go to my grave saying I've never known anybody to be more wrong than Gilby was about Tristano's ghosts.'

'I'd like to see the ghosts, too,' Veronica said.

'Don't tell me you've never seen them,' Roscoe said.

'I saw something once but Elisha didn't believe me. Another night we were supposed to see them but I fell asleep in the chair. When I woke up they said the ghosts had come and gone. Like Santa Claus. You remember Santa Claus, Gilby?'

'He was a fake,' Gilby said.

'In spades,' said Roscoe. 'I believed in him till I was forty-two years old.'

'You did not,' Gilby said.

'The *Times-Union* wrote a story about me. Oldest living believer in Santa Claus. Nothing could shake my belief. I saw those scrawny Salvation Army Santas ringing their bells and I knew their whiskers were phony, but I believed they were all Santa. What a sap. On the other hand, you can't legally say that imitations are all there is. I could prove the existence of Santa Claus in any court in this country if somebody hired me. Of course, I wouldn't take the case, because I no longer believe in him.'

'Why did you stop?'

'I found something else to believe in. I fell in love again. You got a girlfriend, Gilbo?'

'I've got five or six.'

'Whoa. Playing the field.'

'People say you have lots of girlfriends, Roscoe.'

'People are wrong,' Roscoe said.

'How many do you have?'

'You mean legally?'

'Any way.'

'Just one.'

'Who is she?'

'I'd only reveal that on the witness stand under oath.'

'You never tell the truth, Roscoe, do you?'

'Always never,' Roscoe said. 'Or is it never always?'

When the ferry stopped running on the lake in 1938, Elisha built two bridges, at the east and west ends of Lyman's Island, and made Tristano accessible by car on the gated macadam road, until snow closed the road for the season. When they parked and unloaded the wagon at the house, Belle told them dinner was roasted wild turkey and woodcock that Cal had shot. Veronica unpacked in a hurry, and Gilby asked would they go hunting for birds. Roscoe said, No, Cal got enough; we won't kill anything more today. Will we go fishing? No. Cal put all the boats in the boathouse for the winter, and it's too cold to fish today. The fish will all be keeping warm at the bottom of the lake. We'll fish off the dock in the morning, when the sun is up, all right? All right, but what are we going to do today? We'll walk the land, said Roscoe, and we'll look at stuff, and try to see things nobody wants us to see. And so the three of them dressed for the chill weather and went first to the boulder near the house to visit the mink family that Gilby had seen living under it.

'They're gone,' Gilby said.

'When did you last see them?'

'In the summer. They were brown, four of them.'

'What were they doing?'

'Nothing.'

'That explains it,' Roscoe said. 'They got bored and went looking for action.'

They walked to Seneca Rock, where Veronica said she found the large deer horns that were now mounted in the Trophy House, Veronica's deer that got away. They walked north along the shore of the lake and along the dead sumac with the carmine fruit, still on some branches, that the game birds would eat in the winter. Ferns surrounded the small, clear pool coming up from the well that served the Trophy House, and overflowed into the lake. The forest they walked through came almost to the shore of the lake, tall white pines whose needles had created a carpet through which nothing grew, and the only green was the moss on the rocks and the fallen trees. Gilby said, We're not seeing anything. And Roscoe said, You're not looking. You can see everything there is, the secret life of blue jays and pheasant and owls and petrels if you're careful and don't intrude. They sat awhile in silence and watched and listened. They heard a bird, a few high and squeaky musical notes, and then heard it again, and Roscoe said, That sounds like a starling, one of those little black devils. They travel in huge flocks, like Albany Democrats. Just keep watching and maybe we'll see some ducks that haven't gone to Cuba for the winter. They stared across at the vast mountain range that rose up beyond the far side of the lake.

'I don't see anything,' Gilby said.

Roscoe led the way up an incline to a plateau of rock that gave a view into the forest, and to a swampy area bordered by elms and maples and birch, and a vagrant pattern of dead trees that had fallen, or tried to fall, in the directions of greatest rot or strongest wind. A few frogs found reason to utter a few croaks, and you could find silken webs intact in the standing trees, signs of life. So many rotting stumps and fallen trees: bark gone, branches gone, their punky selves good for nothing. You could suffocate here in decay and death. What dry ground they could see was solid with dead brown leaves. At the edge of the plateau they could look down at the dark, quiet water of the lake.

'Keep watching the shore,' Roscoe said. 'We sat like this one day and saw a fox and her four cubs come out and fool around for ten minutes. It was like being at the movies. Another time we saw a doe, and two fawns on the beach cavorting like puppies, and the mother very watchful, wasn't she, Vee?'

'Mothers are usually watchful,' Veronica said. 'But I don't think I was with you.'

'Of course you weren't. I admit sometimes you can't find the hidden life, but you keep looking. You know where you find monster largemouth bass in this lake?'

'Where?'

'Anyplace you're not. Once we saw a school of perch swimming right off this rock, out there, as far as we could see. You wouldn't believe there were that many perch in the universe. But we saw them. Didn't we, Vee?'

'I don't think I was with you.'

'Of course you weren't. It was Elisha. He said to me, "What do we do with all these perch?" And I said we should invite them to dinner. We always invited the fish to dinner. But you were definitely there the day you caught that famous bass, nobody could believe how big it was.'

'Especially me,' Veronica said.

'You put up a great fight.'

'How big?' Gilby asked.

'So big it's still a world record for Tristano. The previous record was three pounds twelve ounces. But your mother's was four eight. We put it on the scales and showed everybody. We had it mounted with the names of all the witnesses. You can see it at the Trophy House, on the wall near the big table. You remember that day, Vee?'

'Oh yes. A special day.'

'Fantastic day. That was a trophy and a half. I caught a silver trout on a fly that afternoon. We both had a good day.'

'You have a good memory,' she said.

'I never forget anything,' Roscoe said. 'Do you remember the day you met the beaver on the mill stream?'

'Yes, and I remember the partridge with her chicks that we found at a fork in the road,' Veronica said. 'One chick was the size of your thumb.'

'Elisha found a loon egg in a nest on Adler's Island,' Roscoe said. 'We kept looking and we found a loon. Elisha talked to it for ten minutes to find out who owned the egg.'

'What did the loon say?' Gilby asked.

'Nothing. It just laughed at Elisha for trying to talk to a bird.'

They walked on and passed what Roscoe called the deer highway and sat awhile to wait for traffic, but none came. Then two birds soared into view over the edge of the lake, and Roscoe said, Don't move, don't talk, and they watched the larger bird fly low and dive into shallow water and come up with a dead eel. Both birds flew to an outcropping of flat shale, where the bird dropped the eel and held it with a talon while the smaller bird ate into the eel carcass, and then the big bird also ate.

'They're eagles,' Veronica said. 'You ever see an eagle, Gilby?'

'I saw a duck hawk, but not an eagle.'

'They're bald eagles, father and son, probably,' Roscoe said. 'The national emblems of our democracy, having a late lunch. Anybody hungry?'

After dinner Roscoe tried to tune in WGY on the shortwave radio to hear Alex's speech, but all he could get was Canadians speaking French and a station somewhere in Scandinavia. 'We are outside civilization,' Roscoe said. 'We could be in the nineteenth century. I wouldn't be surprised if Lyman walked through the door.'

Veronica and Gilby had exhausted checkers, and the 1903 books on planting trees and perennials, and Audubon on hawks and eagles. Veronica read Gilby from a 1908 volume of *Arabian Nights*, the story of the fisherman who finds a vase in the sea and when he opens its cover he releases a genie. The genie, not at all grateful for being freed, is so angry at having been a prisoner he says he must kill the fisherman. But he grants him one wish: he may choose the manner of his death. Since he cannot escape death, the fisherman conjures the genie, in the name of Allah, to answer one question truly: Were you really inside that vase? The genie, compelled to speak the truth, says he was. The fisherman doesn't believe him and says, That vase wouldn't even hold your foot. So, to prove the truth, the genie changes into smoke, and re-enters the vase. The fisherman claps the cover on, throws the vase into the sea; so long, genie.

'That fisherman was smart,' Gilby said.

'I'm glad you think so,' Roscoe said.

'Let's play cards, Roscoe,' said Gilby, and Roscoe then lost eighteen thousand dollars to Gilby playing blackjack with five-hundred-dollar chips. Veronica found the notebook in which records were kept of the great catches and sightings of birds, fish, and game. '"Tried to shoot giant turtle near dock,"' she read. '"Fired at one deer but no luck. Killed two hundred pound black bear, female, behind Swiss Cottage." That's her there on the floor, Gil.' The bear, twenty-two years dead and now a rug, black, tan, mottled gray, lay in front of the fireplace, nose, teeth, and nails intact, but her hide cracked, frazzled, balding, a sad case.

'Who shot her?' Gilby asked.

'Roscoe,' Veronica said.

'You're making that up,' Gilby said.

'Roscoe is a great shot, aren't you, Ros?'

'I used to be. Don't shoot much any more. I don't want to kill anything. Killed the bear because she was dangerous. She came out of the woods behind the lodge and attacked Wilbur, an Irish wolfhound your father owned, Gilby. I shot her before she did more damage.'

'What happened to Wilbur?' Gilby asked.

'He died. Bear mauled him pretty bad.'

Gilby kicked the bear rug in the head.

At the back of the old notebook Veronica found a list of Christmas presents she and Elisha gave to friends in 1928. 'We gave Patsy a set of steak knives in 1928,' she said. 'We gave you a pocket watch, Roscoe.'

'I carried it until you gave me a wristwatch,' he said, raising his wrist with the Elgin he'd worn since 1936. 'And it's nine o'clock on my watch, big fella. Bedtime.'

Veronica stood up. 'That's right, and also we have to go up to the lodge for a short while,' she said. 'I want to pack some of your father's belongings.'

'I can carry them for you,' Gilby said.

'If you want to be ready when the ghosts arrive, you better

get to sleep,' Veronica said. Roscoe told him Cal had fishing rods and bait ready for the morning, and instead of fishing off the dock he'd talk to Cal about getting one of the small boats on the water. Gilby approved of that, and Veronica heated water for his hot-water jar, put him to bed, and piled on the blankets.

The Phantom of Love

Roscoe opened one of the bottles of Margaux '29 he had brought from the Tivoli wine cellar, and poured for himself and Veronica. They sat in the two wicker armchairs facing the fireplace, seats favored by visiting ghosts, according to a Tristano tradition dating to the age when spiritualists flew in and out windows; Veronica thinks they still do. Friends of Ariel are how the ghosts were first identified, specifics long lost; but some things recurred in stories: they were gray-haired men, dressed rustically and well, and they sipped brandy.

The ghosts lost vogue when the lodge was completed and Tristano's nightlife moved onto a higher social scale up the hill. But it regained venue in the early 1930s, when, at a late hour, one of the Boston Peabodys, a financial friend of Elisha, swore that two gentlemen sat across from him for fifteen minutes, ignoring his efforts to enter their conversation, content to be spectrally aloof, but not inaudible. They made sounds, said Peabody, nothing you could repeat in words, more like whooshings and wheeings, and yet their demeanor and syntax seemed quite in keeping with proper behavior and chat you might observe at any Boston club. The elder ghost, Peabody said, drank more brandy than the other. When they vanished, so did Peabody's bottle of brandy.

A rash of sightings followed, some vivid, one or two terrifying to the witnesses, but during the rest of the decade the vogue faded. In 1940, Pamela said she saw a ghost in the Swiss Cottage, a muscular man without a shirt, but it was adjudged to be her gin-fizzed fantasy of the young French Canadian who worked in Tristano's kitchen. That same year, Veronica awoke from a nap in a reclining chair in the Trophy House to see a spectral young woman standing by the fireplace. Veronica asked who she was, the woman gestured vaguely to the hearth, and Veronica said, Is this your home? The woman seemed to say yes, though Veronica could not say how she did that. Veronica went to the bathroom and threw water on her face and came back to find the woman standing where she'd been, but fading, and then she was gone. Veronica told Elisha, who said, Don't tell anybody, they'll think you're as crazy as Pamela. But she told Roscoe, who remembered the story and now asked, 'Who do you think she really was?'

'Somebody who'd lived here and was upset by strangers in her home.'

'You didn't invent her.'

'I did not.'

'She wasn't an extension of your desire to believe in ghosts.'

'Positively not.'

'She had nothing to do with Rosemary.'

'Nothing whatever. Stop giving me the third degree.'

'I'm just preparing for ghosts in case we see any.'

'You think we will?'

'No, but, then again, yes, or even possibly. Let's move to more serious matters.' He raised his glass. 'To Tristano. We're actually here.'

'I told you we would be,' she said, and sipped her wine.

'I never trust anybody who tells me the truth.'

'I have to celebrate what you did.'

She had taken off her bulky knit sweater and now wore a fashionable fawn cardigan. She had pinned her hair into a lovely upswept yellow bun, and her smile gave Roscoe reason to believe he was not only in his right mind, but gaining access to an important truth, always dangerous.

'I'll go over to Belle's cottage and get a key to the lodge,' he said.

'I have my key,' Veronica said.

'And I thought the lodge would be my idea.'

'I know you thought that. That's why I brought my key.'

Veronica looked in at Gilby until she was certain he was asleep, and then they walked up the long hill to the lodge, Roscoe creating a path with his flashlight. They went up the steps of the now empty porch, past where Estelle Warner had tried to seduce Roscoe while her doctor husband was excavating Pamela. So many subsequent times Roscoe had come up these steps, and yet that wretched memory still drove out all others. Veronica unlocked the front door to the main parlor and switched on the sixty-bulb chandelier, an electrified version of the original sixty candles. The room had been exquisitely furnished by money: wall and ceiling studs made of polished logs, rustically sleek; the stained-glass unicorn window Veronica saw in a Venetian home and coveted, and Elisha bought it and shipped it here for a midsummer night's surprise in 1936; Oriental carpeting now rolled and covered, draperies packed away, the leather sofa and large tapestried armchairs, all in their winter covers, opulence in hiding.

Veronica turned on the butterfly standing lamp, one of several Tiffanys in the lodge, and switched off the harsh light of the chandelier. The house held a damp chill, as cold as outside; but they could light no fire, for the chimneys were capped for the winter to discourage squirrel residencies. Roscoe stood by the walk-in fireplace and stared down at Pamela half naked on the raccoon rugs, come into my parlor, darling, the parlor of false love, get out of here, Ros.

'Where do you want to start?' he asked Veronica.

'Start what?'

'Don't get specific. I don't want to ruin it with the wrong words.'

'So we'll silently figure out each other's wishes.'

'You'll never be able to figure out mine,' Roscoe said.

'We'll start upstairs,' she said. They went up to the main bedroom, and as she lit the bedside lamps Roscoe pulled down the shades on the room's four windows. She took a suitcase from the back of a closet and opened it on the bed, then rifled the drawers for Elisha's favored things and packed them: a pair of English suspenders, the binoculars he used at the track and for birdwatching, two of his abandoned wallets, a jewelry case with tiepins, stickpins, and rings, a handful of bow ties, souvenir programs from Broadway shows and the Saratoga racetrack, half a dozen handsomely tailored shirts Gilby might grow into next year.

'That's enough,' she said, and closed the suitcase and set it by the door. She pulled the dust cover off the bed and threw it into a corner, then turned to Roscoe, who was standing by the bed watching her. 'I feel young,' she said.

'We were young in this house, but never in this room.'

Young lovers of a sort, lovers as children, strangers in middle age grown back into children. But she did not want those children's games, the touch in the half-dark, just so far, no farther. And Roscoe's poet: What did we do, I wonder, before we loved, unweaned we sucked on country pleasures, childishly. She took off her jacket and unbuttoned her sweater for him, sleight of hand behind her back and, woman as magician, breasts appear in the light, the full, bright light, aging, falling but not quite fallen, Roscoe never weaned from these, and he: I suck thee, thou, you, these, each, both, and she let her jacket fall and took off her sweater and let the bra fall into her hand, and to the floor. Roscoe crouched before her and raised her skirt, found nylons, the belt holding them tight on her thighs, silk knickers, he slid them down her hips, her bush appearing in the full, bright light, the color of fall's last foliage, and I kiss thee, thou, you, this, it, we've done this before in our moderate way. And she: Yes, you have, somewhat, but we no longer need to be moderate. And she unbuttoned her skirt and let it fall, stepped out of it, picked up her jacket and put it on, naked as possible under the circumstances, but I'm freezing. Roscoe took off his jacket and shirt, put his jacket back on in solidarity with her, rid himself of clothes, shoes, socks, you can't make love with your socks on, as Veronica sat on the bed and waited for him to be ready, was he ever, put her mouth around him, full mouth in the full, bright light, and felt him with both her hands, nothing childish about these moves, and said, That's only hello, and stood then and put her mouth on his mouth and said, There is more. She smiled with a certainty of purpose Roscoe had never seen in these circumstances, and she sat again on the bed, still holding him, then let him go and lay back and spread her legs, thinking, This is why they punish you, this is why my mother was punished when she did this, and of course she did do it, more difficult for her, wasn't it, in her repressive day, Catholic Jew, subordinate woman who could not be willful by law or moral ordination, we will punish any aggression, madame; yet she was wanton for my father and said as much to us, and for whom else was she so? None else, not she, and what of you, my dear? The good husband Elisha, now the good soldier Roscoe, and who else? Roscoe moved toward her and saw her face changing yet again, head flat and mouth now curved with the pressure of oncoming love, is this love, Veronica? She watches him to see what he looks like when he sees her this way and to imagine what she becomes in his eyes, and he in hers, and what those images do to them – singular instant – and the poet again: My face in thine eye, thine in mine appears, as with both hands she opens herself, rare gesture, never so open, so aggressive with this man, and modesty can go to hell, this I give Roscoe, who gave me back my life. For you, she said. He has readied himself for this for thirty-one years, make no mistakes now, Roscoe, easy is the avenue to the divine places. Roscoe is a man of too much girth, too much need, too old for so much life, isn't he? No, and don't go around telling lies about Roscoe in the midst of his young man's realized dream, even his own uninhibited imagination trumped by what he is feeling now, nothing abstract, no words, and of course he thinks this time it must truly be love, always was with her even when this was off limits and you could only imagine, deceive yourself that it would ever be otherwise, but here it is, isn't it? Open love? And as he moves into the breach he says, I do think this is love, and she says, I believe it is, and Roscoe is ready to say that this is a consecration of two shopworn lives, yet he wonders, as usual, what is *really* going on here, love equaling love, another lying equation, is it? Which leaves out the hidden element beneath the familiar, the invisible bustle and hubbub under the carpet of foliage, what a frenzy there must be down under. Veronica sees herself emerging from the cocoon as a blue butterfly, new to her, though she has always known love with Roscoe, he always wanting her, she always pulled toward him, demonic, really, in its endurance, but she had to resist it, you can't live on deceit and humiliation, one long-ago lapse at the hotel is all, and none with others, oh, brushings, maybe, a kiss of sorts, who were they, she doesn't remember, yes, she does, one or two, but they don't matter, Roscoe always saw that sort of thing, Elisha never. Roscoe feels achieved in her arms, illustrious man of privilege who believes no other except Elisha has been here, which is probably your self-deceit again, Ros, aggrandizing you-you-you and canonizing her, this adventurous woman, woman on a horse, she always did have the bold public image. You think you're the only one who's been here, then? Lived only on her fantasies, did she? Really? Yes, that's all there was, don't run her down. And they move, but inseparably, her golden hair fallen loose from its pins, visions of her now like the positionings of other women in Roscoe's erotic museum, but she is not like others, these visions are new, because Veronica needs no coaxing, turning, or urging to be new to all that they've ever been, nothing like her in the museum, for this is love, my love, love, my love, it is all all all all love, my love, and we should accept that term as true for now, seek the reality that tried to kill you, and Roscoe certainly has learned to do that, but avoid truth, Roscoe, it's the enemy. Isn't it true that she accepts Roscoe? It is. She does. She knows how she has intimidated him, not through years of denial, he can handle that, but through rejection, which he didn't handle well at all. But, oh, these pressures of love, and Roscoe owns them tonight, yes, he does, sweetest of pressures, less sweet than manic, swelling her senses as they come, and she holds back nothing now, once, then she is twice, and again, and oh my God again. Don't tell Roscoe this is fraudulence, he knows fraudulence, this is love, my love, this is love, let it come. This is where we begin.

Does Roscoe really Believe in Ghosts?

He has lived with the ghosts of Hamlet and Banquo, with post-Easter Jesus on the road, with Lourdes, Fatima, Padre Pio's stigmata, with Marley, Dracula, the Topper gang, the depressed dead of Grover's Corners, the Holy Ghost guised as a bird. He has listened to reasonable people, including Veronica, who believe they've seen ghosts. He has seen fabricated ghosts deceiving the gullible, including Veronica, seen his own dead father calling his name, and dead Elisha shaving with an electric razor. He knows ghosts are hallucinations, optical fantasies, formulations by visionaries, hypnotic suggestions, imaginative impositions, wishful resurrections with no more substance than a political promise. But promises sometimes materialize and so do ghosts, who can change life for the quick, as Elisha changed us all with his postmortal fiddlings. And so Roscoe allows for all realities, including those that do not exist.

The dominant reality for Roscoe tonight is passionate love, which has risen, fallen, risen, and then some, and is now in seemly quiescence. They have been back in the Trophy House for an hour, Gilby still in profound slumber, Veronica napping on the sofa, ready to rise up for ectoplasmic visitors, and Roscoe rocking in a rocking chair by the reinvigorated fire, watching Veronica breathe. He is what is sometimes called lovesick. He cannot stop thinking about making love with her: how they stood, sat, moved, lay, how they spoke to each other in the language of love, how they stood, sat, moved, etc., repeat all, then rerepeat, then do it again, and then one more time, etc. This condition will prevail for days with diminishing intensity. Beyond the love words that he did speak, Roscoe now thinks he should have spoken to her about the future, his intention to leave politics and start a new life with her – How are you with that, my oh-so-sensual love? They could find a new great house, money not a problem for either of them. Alas, he cannot move too fast on such things, usurping. But when she awakens, he will point out that today is the second time he, she, and Gilby have been alone together away from home, the first in Puerto Rico in 1933, when they flew down for his birth, baptized him there, godfather Roscoe, surrogate adopting father. As the boy grew, Roscoe became father on call, father by desire, and after Elisha's death, caretaker father, juridical father, preludes, were they, to becoming stepfather of the holy Roscoe family? But he cannot move too fast, usurping.

He set out the Salignac and the brandy snifters he had brought down from the lodge. He placed one snifter by sleeping Veronica, the others on the table for himself, Elisha, and the two traditional ectos. He left the old wicker chairs ready for the two, and he brought a third chair for Elisha. He poured the Salignac, varying the pours, one of them drinks more than the other, gave a bit to Veronica, left Elisha's snifter empty, then poured his own, sat, and tasted it, *magnifique*, and considered how to summon ghosts. Sit here till Christmas, Ros, no rustically well-dressed gentlemen will turn up speaking wind sounds and ectosipping your splendid brandy. Blood tests, elections, judges, juries are easy, but a habeas corpus for the dead? You don't know their names or faces; they don't speak any known language. Perhaps they're generic ghosts, perpetuating a bygone Tristano life-style: brandy, tweeds, soft handmade Italian leather boots, you made up the boots, Ros, and they're not generic ghosts, they were friends of Ariel, came here often, before your time, had money, one a Scotch-Irish insurance man name of Amos Ford who liked duck hunting, the other a fly fisherman, Seth Cooper, department-store owner from Albany. They found common ground at Tristano, discovered they could talk fish and birds forever, at which point their lives achieved lucid but brief symmetries, for a great wind blew up, capsizing Seth's boat, and blowing a tree down onto Amos's duck blind.

'The same wind did you both,' Roscoe said. 'Imagine that.'

In the afterlife they were apotheosized as ideals of their pursuits, and were allowed to meet each other at Tristano on select days to remember the stillness of the water just before the great wind blew them into death, to remember the precise size, weight, color, and markings of every bird, every fish that ever died by their hand, to consider whether fish or birds were more intelligent, or equally gifted with reason, for each does know the enemy and does know to flee destruction at his hand; and, considering that nature is based in injustice and suffering, Seth and Amos were also mandated to dwell on how the subtraction of all those creatures' lives changed the natural world.

'You now know each duck and fish you killed?' Roscoe asked. 'Have you named them? . . . A few . . . But you really do recognize every one? . . . Amazing memory . . . Ah, everybody has that over there.'

'Who are you talking to?' Veronica asked, one eye open.

'Amos and Seth,' Roscoe said. 'They used to come here.'

'Who? Where are they?'

'Here in their chairs, can't you see them? Say hello.'

'Hello, Amos; hello, Seth.'

'This is Veronica,' Roscoe said. 'Yes, she's a beauty . . . sleeping beauty . . . No, we're not married, but that's not a bad idea.'

'Are they worried that we're not married?'

'No,' said Roscoe, 'but I am. They were friends of Ariel, and they died in a big wind in 1906. Seth is the older one with the white mustache and the tan leather vest. You shopped in his store, Cooper's, on North Pearl Street, when you were a child. Seth remembers you and your mother . . . Uh-huh . . . Seth says he also saw you at Saratoga.'

'Roscoe,' Veronica said.

'Just let them talk,' Roscoe said.

'Are you talking to the ghosts?' Gilby asked. He stood in the doorway of his room, in pajamas, robe, and sweat socks, his cowlick standing tall from sleeping on it.

'Come and sit down,' Roscoe said. 'Meet Seth and Amos. They both knew your father when he was a boy. This is Gilbert Fitzgibbon, gentlemen, my godson.' Gilby walked slowly across the room and sat on the sofa beside his mother, never taking his eyes off the empty chairs. Roscoe refilled Seth's and Amos's brandies.

'There's nobody sitting there. Nobody'll drink that,' Gilby said.

'No? You should've seen what was in those glasses five minutes ago. We were talking hunting and fishing, and which one is smarter, a duck or a trout . . . Oh? . . . They say your father's coming.'

'I don't see him,' Gilby said. 'I don't see anybody.'

'Just watch that chair,' Roscoe said pointing to Elisha's place at the table. 'I mean seriously watch it. Pay attention. Listen. Quiet. The loudest noise you hear is the fire, listen, then you hear your own breathing, listen, then you hear mine, listen and you'll see everything that's there, and then you'll start to see everything that isn't, keep listening and you'll find sympathy with all things, you'll hear the moon shine and the grass grow. Do you remember what your father looked like the last time you saw him? He looks like that now, except he got rid of most of the gray in his hair, and he looks younger. Close your eyes and look at him. Hair combed same as always, they didn't make him change it. . . . Oh yes? . . . Seth says you get to pick your favorite age when you come back. Your father picked forty-six, eight years ago, 1937, the year the Yankees took the Series from the Giants in five games and Pleasure Power won the Travers at Saratoga. A good year for us. The lines in your father's cheeks aren't quite as deep as they became, and his energy level is up. You were four years old that year, and your parents bought you a blue tricycle for Christmas. John Thacher was re-elected our Mayor, FDR was a year into his second term, and the second war hadn't started yet. The Nazis hadn't taken over Vienna, so your mother's Jewish uncles and aunts were still alive. See what your father's wearing? His gray houndstooth jacket with the suede elbow patches, much like our visitors' jackets . . . What's that, Elisha? . . . He says he likes what we've been doing for him, especially the way the trial came out . . . He predicts Alex will be re-elected . . . I know that, Elisha, and I'm not even dead . . . Ah . . . He says, yes, he's trying to say . . . "I died too quickly, too soon, and I left a vacuum. I'm sorry about that,"' and Roscoe's voice deepened, picked up the Elisha timbre and cadence he'd been mimicking for forty years. He poured the Salignac into Elisha's snifter. '"I wish I'd had a chance to talk to somebody, tell you all what was on my mind, but I didn't have time."'

'You killed yourself,' Gilby said.

'Gilby, what are you saying?' Veronica said.

'Everybody knows it,' said Gilby. 'I'm always the one who never gets told. You took poison,' he said to the empty chair, with a glance at Roscoe. And Roscoe saw in Veronica's face the terror that truth brings; and he feared it more than she.

'"You know what they did in the Middle Ages?"' Elisha asked. '"They drove a stake through the heart of any man who killed himself. They still do that with Dracula, but not with suicides any more. Because now everybody knows there's no such thing as suicide. There's only death. Some people die years before they bury them. People get sick. People go crazy. I met a fella over here, his wife insured him against going crazy and then he went crazy. They put him in the asylum and she went every week and brought him bananas, he hated bananas. Then he died. You think she killed him, or was it the bananas? You don't know what makes people crazy. Just a little too much of the old EP and then – bingity bing! – there goes the whole kitty bosso. My trouble was I couldn't say what was on my mind, it was so complicated. I tried, but it wouldn't come out. A secret, even from me. Some kind of code, I suppose it was, but I never could solve it. Breedy ale wouldn't kitty, wouldn't cut pips. I was sick and got sicker and then I died. You say I killed myself, but I was dead before the poison. That poison was there for years, just waiting. So many times we don't know we're drinking poison. Could be just like sipping this great brandy,"' and Roscoe lifted Elisha's snifter and sipped from it, put it back where it was. '"We try to do something, but before we can finish it, everything changes and there's no point doing it any more. That's a disease, when you don't do the only thing you ever wanted to do. Probably you made the wrong choice, lived in the wrong town, did the wrong work for the wrong reasons, married the wrong woman, I didn't do that. Poison in your system but it doesn't seem like poison. You're dead but you keep living. You're a corpse but you can't get to the cemetery. You talk, eat, smile but you don't know you're doing any of it, how could you? You're dead. But, Gilly my boy, *you're* not dead, and neither are your mother and Roscoe. You all had quite a day today, seeing those eagles. Seth can probably call them by name, right, Seth? No. Seth says he only knows ducks. But a good day like today, that's worth a lot. It's gone, and you'll go home tomorrow, no more Tristano, no more eagles. But just because a good day slips into history doesn't mean it's gone. You had it once and you'll have it forever in memory. You came up here looking for me because I'm in your memory, and here I am talking about death. I don't mean to be gloomy when you all have so much life. You'll be all right, all of you. Just keep asking that question, the one you don't know how to answer and hardly know how to ask. I miss you all terribly, and I hope I'll see you later."'

In the silence that followed, Roscoe took a long swallow of his own brandy and started rocking again. Gilby stared at the chair, then at Roscoe, anticipating more. 'Is he gone?'

'He is.'

'Are Seth and Amos gone?'

'They are.'

'They weren't really here.'

'No?'

'Were they?'

'I think they were,' Veronica said. 'I heard them.'

'Where did they go?'

'Back in the vase, maybe, like that genie,' she said.

'They were all Roscoe,' Gilby said.

'One of them was your father,' she said. 'I'd know his voice anywhere.'

'You were my father, weren't you, Roscoe?'

'No, but I'd like to be, in case anybody asks.'

'He did sound like my father,' Gilby said to his mother.

'I hope you remember his words,' she said. 'It was so sad to hear him. But wasn't it a lovely visit?'

Elective Affinities

The newspapers trumpeted Alex's sex speech and the police raids: 'Mayor Cracks Down on Sin and Smut,' 'Our GI Mayor Wants Sinless Town for Returning GIs.' Twelve pimps and assorted whores were arrested, but, folks, you pay dues to do business in Albany. The raids outraged bookstores and newsstands, but Night Squad detectives assured them they'd get their merchandise back after election.

The next day, still courting page one, George Scully, the Governor's special prosecutor, personally led a State Police raid on three Albany betting parlors, including the central office, from where racing information was sent by phone lines to horse rooms throughout the city. Forty workers and horseplayers were arrested, including Johnny Mack, Patsy's pal, whose famous White House was padlocked. And Johnny faced a judge for the first time in forty years. Candidate Jay Farley called a press conference to say such open gambling was proof of political collusion with gamblers in this corrupt city.

In an election-eve rally at Knights of Columbus Hall on Clinton Square, Alex told the Party faithful and the press that 'the Governor spent half a million dollars investigating this city, harassed our citizens, pried into our private lives, put fear into the hearts of people who had no connection to politics, and what has he got to show for it? He disturbed the peace of a few gamblers, but he solidified Albany more solidly than ever behind our Democratic Party. I feel sad that our former Lieutenant Governor, my father, Elisha Fitzgibbon, who founded this Party with Patsy McCall and Roscoe Conway, isn't here to see what's about to happen in our city. But I spoke to Patsy a minute ago and asked him to make a prediction for us tonight. Will you come up, Patsy?'

Patsy, who rarely spoke in public but this year saw himself in close combat with the enemy, rose from his front-row chair and stepped onto the small stage. Alex made room at the microphone, then asked, 'How do you think we'll do tomorrow, Pat?' Patsy put his hands in his pants pockets, looked out at the crowd of five hundred that thought he was Jesus Christ in those baggy pants and that wide-brimmed fedora, and told them, 'The Governor made our campaign for us. Mayor Fitzgibbon will be re-elected by upward of thirty-five thousand plurality.' And as the cheers, huzzahs, and whistling exploded, Alex ended the meeting by saying into the mike, 'You heard the man, now let's go out and do it!'

Patsy had wanted to say forty thousand, but Roscoe was dubious. Forty was a nice Biblical number to humiliate the Governor with, but our registration this year is down eight thousand from when Alex won in 1941. That year a single taxi driver registered one hundred and eighty times and voted two hundred and three times. Nobody was looking. This year many servicemen haven't been home to register, and with the goddamn State Police on our backs, taxi drivers are no longer so intrepid. Roscoe felt the need to pump up the numbers another way, so he decided to put Cutie's votes into Alex's column. Cutie might get a few thousand protest votes, and the switch would be done in the courthouse by the six-man presumably bipartisan Election Commission, who were all Democrats. Roscoe would tell Cutie not to protest the election: We'll let him have a few hundred and a no-show job for his mother. Roscoe also ordered the ward leaders to have all four hundred committeemen do a second canvassing count – No half-assed guesswork this year, we want to shove firm numbers down the Governor's throat. After the second canvass, Roscoe showed Patsy that forty was too high, he should go with thirty-five.

Extra desks came into Party headquarters for the election count, half a dozen city accountants manned adding machines, and women volunteers handled the six special phone lines. Joey Manucci went to Keeler's twice for sandwiches and coffee, and Charlie Foy and Tony Mirabile from the Night Squad sat outside the door to keep out visitors and press. When the polls closed at nine o'clock, the phones jangled and final numbers flowed in from every district. The only real surprise was one district of the Ninth Ward where Republicans got no votes at all; but Bart Merrigan explained to Roscoe that on that voting machine the Republican line was soldered. By nine-fifteen, Jay Farley was conceding at his headquarters and Alex was promising a victory interview at ten in City Hall. At nine-twenty, Bart found a phone message for Patsy that Joey had taken at five-thirty, long before Patsy arrived. The caller asked for Patsy's home phone, but Joey wouldn't give it. The caller said he was from the White House, but that didn't cut Joey's mustard. Bart chided Joey. 'You fucking moron, it was the President. You wouldn't give

Patsy's number to the President?' Bart called the White House back and connected Patsy to President Truman, whom Patsy first knew through Tom Pendergast. Patsy had been solid with Truman for vice-president at the '44 convention, when half the New York delegation still backed Henry Wallace. Mr. Truman asked Patsy how Albany Democrats were faring under all that pressure from New York's Governor. 'That fella's probably gonna run against me on the boss issue in '48.' And Patsy told him, 'We beat him bad, Mr. President. He never laid a glove on us.' And Mr. Truman said, 'Nice work, Patsy. You boys know what you're doing up there.'

By nine-forty, the absentee ballots were counted, Cutie's votes were switched, and the official count was Jay Farley 14,747, Cutie LaRue 320, and Alex, as Patsy had called it, upward of 35,000, specifically 35,716.

After Patsy talked to the President he went into Roscoe's office and closed the door. 'I want you to go see the President,' Patsy said. 'I want to send him a Civil War book, let him know how strong we are for him up here.'

Roscoe made no reply and Patsy looked at him with a cocked eye.

'Send Alex,' Roscoe said. 'Or anybody. I'm all done, Pat. I told you that in August and now I say it again. The returns are in and I'm through.'

'Goddamn it, Roscoe, don't start this.'

'It's done, Pat. I'm out as of tonight. Bart can handle this office.'

'You can't quit politics. That's like a dog who says he don't want to be a dog any more.'

'Even if I'm a dog, I quit.'

'Does this have to do with Veronica?'

'It might. Why do you ask?'

'Eh,' Patsy said.

'Eh what?'

'You living at Tivoli and all that.'

'All that what?'

'I talked to Alex. You're not keeping any secrets.'

'I haven't been trying. But, all right, being around her changed my life. But I was ready to change. I doubt I'll ever have a better life than I've had here for twenty-six years. But twenty-six is a long time. You're my best friend, Patsy, the only best friend I've got left. I wouldn't con you. I can't handle it any more.'

'You really mean it.'

'Now you got it.'

'I don't like it.'

'We won the election, you still own the town, we control all fifty-two cards in the deck. Let's go celebrate. The party's at Quinlan's.'

When they wrapped up the final count and left Bart to close the office, Patsy said he wasn't up for Quinlan's. Alex said he wouldn't get there right away, had to do those City Hall interviews.

'But I'll walk you up the hill, Roscoe,' Alex said, and they rode the elevator down from the eleventh floor in silence. Only when they were walking up State Street did Alex speak. He looked once at Roscoe, then spoke while staring up the hill at the Capitol.

'I know you and my mother went to Tristano with Gilby,' he said, 'and I know something's going on,' he said. 'Roscoe, you may own the best political mind of anybody who ever drew breath in this town. You know how to manipulate power, you know how to win, and politically I'm immensely grateful. You were also a great friend of my father, a guardian to my mother after he died, and wonderful to me when I was growing up. Those were memorable days, and I hung on every word out of your mouth on how to play and gamble and drink and appreciate women. I no longer value that kind of life. But you've sunken back into it, worse than ever – punching out a cheap editor in his own office, caught with naked prostitutes, personally championing that vicious whore, watching your psychopathic friend murder your own brother, and then your insane hypothesis that my father raped Pamela. You won the case, but what a price you paid – a scurrilous false rumor that profanes his memory forever. It's always the lowest common denominator that you cozy to, Roscoe, and I include your friend Hattie Wilson, landlady for the whorehouses. We're a big city and we have to deal politically with all kinds, but you've brought the lowlife home to my family once too often. I say this with very mixed feelings, but I consider you a negative influence on Gilby, and an unfit suitor for my mother. So here's the line, Roscoe. From now on, my family's off limits to you. Do you understand me?'

They were in front of the Ten Eyck, and as two couples came out of the hotel one of the men called to Alex, 'Congratulations, Mr. Mayor. Well deserved.' Alex waved and walked alone up the hill toward City Hall. Roscoe turned his back to the hill and looked down State Street, the street of celebrations. A bonfire burned in front of the Delaware and Hudson Railroad building, kids feeding it, a fire engine on the way with siren wailing. Buzzy Lewis came up from Pearl Street with two dozen first editions of the *Times-Union* under his arm, just off the truck.

'Hey, Roscoe, big night. Want a paper? It's got a picture of the Mayor.'

'Sure, Buzz,' Roscoe said, and he gave Buzzy a deuce and put the paper in his coat pocket without looking at it. He had made no retort to what Alex said. None was possible. He imagined Alex delivering a similar harangue to Veronica, who would have expected it. Driving up to Tristano, Roscoe concluded she hadn't told Alex where or for how long they were going, because he might have said don't go. Roscoe felt the sudden reflux of a dreadful time long gone, negative luck running. What happened at Tristano wasn't luck. It's luck only when it's bad. Roscoe quit luck at a young age. Power, not luck, transforms possibility. You don't trust things simply to work out, are you serious? You fix them and then they work out. Elisha's *beau geste,* his glory march to self-destruction, was now a reality for everyone, even though Roscoe had invented it. Logic so fine it becomes history. Create what doesn't exist, and the false becomes true through existence alone. Roscoe even invented Elisha's epitaph: 'Stay alive, even if you have to kill yourself.' Everything Roscoe did was to ensure continuity of the Party, of Alex, of the family, of love. Roscoe decided Elisha had intended to restore the lost brotherhood. And, hey, didn't the man's will prevail tonight at the polls? Now you know, Governor: cakey action don't kibble at the Café Newfay.

Mike Quinlan's Capitol Grill was imploding with hilarity and the vest-busting effusions of Democrats, who effuse more effectively in victory than Republicans. Roscoe became their target when he walked in – handshook, clapped, kissed, hugged, winked at. He tried to respond to the congrats but could barely make out any words over Tommy Ippolito's six-piece band playing 'Paper Doll' with a beat that made Roscoe's bones dance. But nobody could dance, the bar and back room both chockablock with bodies. Roscoe waved to Tommy and smiled as he waded through the mob. He knew every second face, could put a name to so many, knew how the ancients here had looked in childhood, how the young people would look at eighty. Phil Fagan, Kenny Pew, Ocky Wolf, all from St. Joseph's, here they were, parading wrinkled necks, absent hair, crooked backs; and Roscoe corrected their flaws with visionary recall of their adolescent integrity. Not only could he reconstitute them backward into the past, Roscoe controlled their future, which is why they were here. You don't know this, Ocky, but this is my final night of power over your life. Tomorrow, Roscoe will be powerless in a new life that will owe nothing to coercion. He threaded himself (some thread) toward Hattie, who was at a table for two near the band.

'Hello, love,' she said. 'You did it again, didn't you?'

'We did.'

'Say hello to Ted Pulaski, who lives in my building.'

'Hey, Ted, that's a hell of a building to live in,' Roscoe said.

'Got a great landlady,' Ted said.

'He loves dogs,' Hattie said.

'Good for him.'

'I told him I buried my dog in Washington Park so I could visit his grave, and Ted wants to go see it.'

'You'll enjoy the grave, Ted,' Roscoe said.

'I look forward to it.'

'That's convenient. You like Ted, do you, Hat?' Roscoe asked her.

'I do, Rosky, I do.'

'You getting into that famous mood again?'

'Could be,' and she nibbled on the left Pulaski earlobe.

Roscoe moved toward the bar fielding questions: Is the Mayor coming? Where's Patsy? At the bar, Cutie LaRue was explaining to several female admirers why he and Jay Farley lost to the McCall machine: '. . . they know how you vote by how you shift your feet in the voting booth, by the sound of the lever when you pull it. They go in the booth with you, or leave the curtain open, or cut a hole in it, or sandpaper it. "How come you split your ticket, my dear? I hope nobody else in the family does that." I tell you, they make those machines dance. Some machines got fifty votes in 'em before the polls open, and somebody'll pull that lever forty times after they close. Jay Farley's a nice fella for a Republican, and he looks honest, but honesty is no substitute for experience.'

Adam Whalen, an assistant DA, cut through the crowd to whisper, 'A friend of yours wants to see you, Roscoe. Trish Cooney. She was giving a guy a blowjob through her car window when somebody shot him in the back. They think she set him up. We're charging her with conspiracy and lewd behavior.'

'Just go for the lewd,' Roscoe said. 'She's not smart enough for conspiracy. Tell Freddie Gold to bail her out and send me the bill.'

Roscoe found Mike Quinlan being third man behind the bar this frantic night. 'Great election, Roscoe. Where's the Mayor?'

'City Hall, where he's supposed to be. Listen, Mike, I'm just passing through. Got some business uptown that won't wait. But keep an open bar for an hour tonight on me, and don't bill the Party. Bill me at the hotel.'

'Hey, you're a live one, Roscoe.'

'That's one possibility,' Roscoe said.

He threaded himself back out the door, stood in the cold night looking down State Street, full of parked cars but nobody on the street. He truly believed Elisha killed himself for a purpose. Just because you invent it doesn't mean it didn't happen. Roscoe reflected often on his own suicide, but he wasn't worth killing. No point to it. That, of course, was Roscoe's old fallacy that everything has a point, when it could have forty points, thirty-five. A man is never single-mindedly wrong or right in such heavy matters. What was said about the Celt applied to Elisha, who certainly was a Celt somewhere in his soul, by osmosis from Patsy and Roscoe if nothing else. The man said that the Celt was melancholy not out of a definite motive but through something unaccountable, defiant, and titanic. An Englishman said that. Roscoe walked down State Street until he found a cab.

At Tivoli, Roscoe found Veronica sitting alone in the breakfast room, the servants all in bed. Roscoe had to call her name aloud to find her. She was dressed for the victory party, clinging new black sheath, hair that parted in the middle and fell into a large, single yellow curl that surrounded her neck like a lush collar. Her cheekbones seemed more emphatic tonight, nose more aquiline, eyelids the color of rose of Sharon; Christ, what beauty. She sat at the same table, same chair, as on the morning Roscoe brought her Elisha's final news.

'You're back early,' she said. 'Didn't you go to the party?'

'I left when I figured out you weren't coming. I saw Cutie LaRue. He thinks Jay Farley lost because honesty is no substitute for experience.'

'It may be true.'

'There's no way to be honest. I've always said that.'

'But *we* try to be honest, don't we?'

'Do we?'

'I do.'

'Good. I had a talk with Alex.'

'I know. He called me.'

'He thought he was being honest, but of course he wasn't.'

'How wasn't he?'

'You don't know?'

'Did he lie? What did he say?'

'Didn't he tell you what he said?'

'I hated what he told me, but it made perfect sense to him.'

'Perfect sense but not the truth.'

'What's the truth, Roscoe?'

'I never tell the truth.'

'Tell me, damn it.'

'I can't talk about it. Don't you have things you can't talk about?'

'I suppose I do.'

'There you are. You look glorious. Anything to say to me about tomorrow? Or the next day? Or the next?'

What Veronica said then was supremely logical. How could she abandon Alex and sacred Gilby, her children? Consider her god-awful loss of Rosemary. You, Roscoe, have been responsible for every beautiful thing that happened to us in these past months. You're so selfless. You love Gilby, Gilby adores you, you are adorable. But what will happen when Alex sees Gilby adoring you, or you moving in with us, or us with you? It would explode the family. Alex believes you'll be a negative influence on the boy. I know he's very wrong. It's perverse to exile you from us after all the wonderful things you've done. But if you'd done them differently, would we now have such a hostile climate for love? As it is, Veronica has only one choice. Perhaps it's the wrong one, but she can't evade it. Oh, how much she loves who Roscoe is, her longtime love, and she knows his love for her is as great as Elisha's was. She loves Roscoe every way possible. Didn't she make total love to him? She withheld nothing from this man she truly wants. Veronica and Roscoe now desire each other so much that it seems they were destined to be together. But one rarely sorts out desire and destiny satisfactorily. And then Alex rises up and says the unthinkable. And nothing to be done. But you and I don't know what will happen, my dearest Roscoe. And you do have my heart, my only love. I won't give it to another.

She cried. Her tears would melt steel. She kissed him so many, many times. He cried with her. His tears stained the floor tiles. They kissed and kissed. They fumbled each other. She could not stop crying as they kissed. He raised her clothing to touch her everywhere. She did the same with him. Then they put everything back in its proper place. She leaned against the door and slapped it softly as she cried. He blew his nose and went upstairs for his brown valise with the fifty thousand in cash in the false bottom, quiet wages. Everything else he left in the room. Goodbye, room. He asked her to call a cab and it came, and when she saw him coming down the stairs she sent it away. They continued to kiss by the door. Love. Oh, love. Such love as this. God help our love. You have my heart, Roscoe. I won't give it to another. We don't know how life will change. We never know the future. You take my heart with you. Our hearts, our hearts, oh, our hearts. We never know what will happen to our hearts.

William Kennedy

On the Night Boat

From where he stood on the promenade deck, Roscoe could hear the first strains of music from the boat's orchestra: cellos, then oboes, a Wagner overture, with desire implicit in the music. Just what Roscoe needs. He moved up the deck until he could no longer hear it. As the boat's motor began to thrum he noticed two lone men on the quay, one prone with eyes closed, arms outstretched, unmoving. Dead? The other standing at the downed man's feet looking toward the boat, a *tableau vivant*. The downed man had done something unspeakable; this Roscoe sensed through his kinship with the fallen. Roscoe called out to him to get up and explain himself, but the man was beyond words, as was Roscoe, who can never utter the words that would trigger Alex instantly, and forever, into fear and trembling.

He walked the deck, assessing time by the intensity of the flickering shore lights and contemplating the myriad forms deceit takes, how they intersect and magnify, or cancel each other out. Veronica, the sleeping beauty, will awake to find she is forever wed to a dead man and can never explain why. Does she know why? She may always have known. So much comes down to self-deceit, such as Roscoe shooting that bear. How could he have convinced himself, or anybody, that he shot that bear? Yet Roscoe believes in his creations: his *beau geste* saved the Party, and won him Veronica's love. A lie, after all, is only another way of affirming the desirable. A live lie is better than a dead truth, and there is no ultimate wall that the creative individual cannot breach through deceit. To repossess Veronica's love, Roscoe would lie until he forgot how. Any time he chooses, he can see her stunning in her black sheath, naked in her jacket on the bed, smart in her riding britches and boots, contoured in her black bathing suit, fetching in her slip at the hotel, new at morning in her Chinese dressing gown. He will not lose these visions.

Two chubby nuns walked past him on their way to becoming cherubim and went into one of the boat's private parlors. Roscoe followed and looked through the parlor window to see nuns and priests sitting at several card tables, silently exchanging holy pictures and tarot cards. This looked new. He entered to find a luxurious gambling establishment: carpets obviously from Brussels, an explosion of finely wrought brass railings, brass light fixtures and cuspidors, mahogany chairs, velvet wallpaper, unique décor for a Night Boat. He moved among the gaming tables, stopped at a corner where five well-dressed gentlemen were playing a dice-and-card game Roscoe could not identify. He studied the blackboards which listed stock prices and odds on ball games, fights, marriages. He moved to the board with the racing entries, noted a familiar name: Cabala 2, and then coming toward him he saw Johnny Mack, Patsy's bookie, and the elegance here made sense. Owner of racehorses, man of taste and fashion, premier gambler, why wouldn't John furnish this parlor as handsomely as his White House, Albany's premier chamber of games?

Johnny wore a stylish black-and-gray-checked suit with black piping, his *pince-nez* anchored to his waistcoat by a broad black ribbon.

'I didn't know you were on the river, Johnny,' Roscoe said to him.

'After the Governor arrested me, I lost faith in cities,' Johnny said.

'I've had a similar epiphany,' Roscoe said.

'Epiphanies come when you least expect them.'

'What's that game in the corner?'

'What would you like it to be?'

'What a question,' Roscoe said. 'Who are those players?'

'Who would you like to play against?'

And then Roscoe realized that the world as he knew it had been overthrown while he was in cloister. He would have to move from scratch, like a novice. The very thought of new game strategies depressed him. Who cares what you bet on now, Roscoe? Do you? What exactly is your legacy, even if you win? Ten years from now, will anybody know you ever gambled on anything, or ever drew breath?

'I'll pass on the game, but I'll bet that filly, Cabala 2,' Roscoe said.

'Again?' Johnny asked.

'I'm a sucker for it,' Roscoe said.

It was August 1937, he in the Fitzgibbon box in the Club House at Saratoga, next to Veronica. The horse he owned with Elisha and Veronica, Pleasure Power, would run in and win the Travers, two races hence. Perhaps through unconscious symmetry, Roscoe and Veronica had both bet Johnny Mack's two-year-old filly, Cabala. But the horse entered the starting gate in fear, reared wildly, threw her jockey, flipped herself onto her back under the gate between two stalls, and, in her insane flailing to stand upright, fractured a pelvic bone that severed an artery. When they pulled her out from under the gate she tried to stand but fell on top of her useless leg. She bled so rapidly into the turf she was dead before they came to quiet her with the pistol. Veronica hid her eyes. Roscoe watched through binoculars. The turf below, the sky above, are true. It's true only if you can't fix it. Everybody in the cemetery is true.

'Your bet is accepted,' Johnny said, marking his notepad.

Roscoe decided long ago that only a bet on the impossible makes sense. It is an act of faith and courage requiring an irrational leap over reason. A man wins simply by making such a bet.

He went back out onto the deck and could hear the heavy churning of the paddle wheel and the th-th-*thump* of its crankshaft as the boat moved out into the center of the darkening river. Perhaps a thousand passengers were in their berths making love. That's why the Night Boat was born. When Roscoe circled back to the entrance of the main saloon, the orchestra was still doing Wagner, but was now into the love theme; or was it the death theme? One of those.

Ah well, he thought, going in, either way I could use a little music.

Author's Note

This is a novel, not history. There was a political machine in Albany comparable to the one in this book, and some of the events here correspond to historical reality, and some characters here may seem to be real people. But I don't do that sort of thing. These are all invented characters, the McCalls, the Fitzgibbonses, even Al Smith and Jack Diamond; and their private lives are fictional. They might be better than their prototypes (if they have any), they might be worse; but I hope they and their book are true. As Roscoe points out, truth is in the details, even if you invent the details.

For some of the details I owe abundant thanks: to my assiduous researcher of so many years, Suzanne Roberson, who finds whatever I need, including things I don't yet know I need; to Bettina Corning Dudley, who gave me access to her-father-the-Mayor's cabin and certain of his papers; to Dr. Juan Vilaró and Kiki Brignoni, who introduced me to fighting chickens; to Dr. Alan Spira, who gave me pericardial counsel; to Judge David Duncan, my legal counselor; to Joe Brennan, who twenty or more years ago gave me his World War One diary in hopes I would find a way to use it, and so I have – but Joe should not be held responsible for what Roscoe did with his war; to Bettie Reddish, who told me some exceedingly rare stories; to Detective Lieutenant Ted Flint, who has talked to me for fifty years about being an Albany cop; to Rikke Borge and her fellow trainer, Richard (Pinky) Edmonds, MOL, who counseled me on horses; to Paul Grondahl for his illuminating biography of Mayor Erastus

Corning; and to S. K. Heninger Jr. from whom Roscoe learned about Pythagorean order and virtue.

I owe thanks to people who told me great stories: John and Tony Treffiletti, Ira Mendelsohn, Betty Blatner, Mae Carlsen, Peggy O'Connell Jensen, Marge and Andy Rooney, Ruth Glavin, Johnny Camp, Fortune Macri, and I revisit endlessly the marathon conversations I had with leaders and insiders, early and late, major and minor, and certain effective enemies of the Albany political organization; enemies first: Victor Lord, a Liberal, Congressman/editor Dan Button, State Senator Walter Langley, and Assemblyman Jack Tabner, all Republicans; and the Democratic players: Mayor Corning, the unbeatable, Mayor Tom Whalen, the first reformer, Mayor Gerry Jennings, the incumbent from North Albany, Charley Ryan, Frank Schreck, Bob Fabbricatore, Swifty Mead, Johnny Corscadden, Joe Zimmer, Sheriff Jack McNulty, Assemblymen Dick Conners and Jack McEneny, Congressman/newsman Leo O'Brien, the Judges John Holt-Harris, James T. Foley, Edward Conway, Martin Schenck, and Francis Bergan, and the boss himself, Daniel Peter O'Connell.

Countless others, including unnamable Democrats, bemused Republicans, hostile reformers, a felon or two, and news reporters and editors back to pre-Prohibition days, enhanced my knowledge of the machine.

But don't blame any of the people above for what's in this novel. Blame Roscoe.